EIGHTEENPENCE, COMPLETE,

RUTH, THE MURDERED CHILD;

OR,

THE STORY OF THE ROAD SIDE HOUSE.

WITH ILLUSTRATIONS BY PHIZ.

MARK CHARGES KEPPEL WITH BEING THE MURDERER OF HIS CHILD.

LONDON: GEORGE VICKERS, ANGEL COURT, STRAND.

RUTH, THE MURDERED CHILD;

OR,

THE MYSTERY OF THE ROADSIDE HOUSE.

SOPHY'S SCREAM OF DISTRESS IN THE GARDEN ALARMS THE HOUSEHOLD.

CHAPTER I.

GRIEVOUS.

THE trees down in the little valley were already lost in the evening shadows, out of which, however, the delicate blue smoke that curled from the cottages embowered there rose more distinctly. The day was done, and the labour of the day quite over. The Sabbath-like quiet, which in the country reigns every day and all day long, had deepened: so that as the watch-dog at Keppel Lodge barked at the sound of some belated footstep, the echo came over the little valley, and up the hill, and was heard plainly in Widow Howlet's cottage, a good half a mile distant. Sheep-bells tinkled with a clear sweet sound. The little brook, which, after pursuing a demure and stately course through the grounds of Keppel Lodge, came tumbling out, fresh and free, into the village, gurgled and plashed most musically: it was so glad to be no longer on its best behaviour. Then, beyond the great beeches, a rook, the lateness of whose hours admitted of the worst constructions, soared gravely home with a melancholy caw. Dame Crumford's poultry had all gone to roost— their favourite legs comfortably tucked in; but Dame Crumford's cow was as wide awake as cows ever are, and was expressing her enjoyment of clean straw and solitude in melodious lowing; which further served to mark, if it did not actually

deepen, the stillness of the evening. Moreover, a great star had arisen; and though, as we are all aware, stars neither bark like a watch-dog, watchful as they seem—nor babble like a brook, though they do appear to brim over with liquid light—nor tinkle like a sheep-bell, though twinkling to the eye is what tinkling is to the ear—still it really would appear that this star had some important meaning in it, judging from the manner in which Lucy Howlet gazed upon it through the diamond window-panes of her mother's cottage.

The girl's eyes (they were like the star, very large, and of a grave pale blue), seemed not so much to look as to listen; and she herself was quiet as the night. Also her lips were parted; and though it was clear that her heart was strongly beating, for her bosom heaved like the deep sea before a storm, yet she seemed not to breathe. But Lucy's eyes had something else in them besides this rapt attention; they were also full of weariness and longing. The weariness seemed to be the weariness of hope deferred—the longing like that of some poor solitary, looking from the sea where all his hopes are wrecked, to the heavens, where, perhaps, no new ones remain. Lucy, in other respects, wore the aspect of a shipwrecked solitary. The mariner who shivers on the desert shore alone was not more pale, though the colour had been washed from her cheeks by salt tears, and not by salt waves. The mariner lies listless, casting pebbles into the turbulent waters; Lucy stood nerveless, unconsciously stripping the leaves from a withered geranium, and casting them after her happiness: that is to say, under foot. The seaman would care little if the next wave swept him back into the great grave in which his companions all lie buffeted to and fro; and in Lucy's eyes you could see the wish that the same grief which had drowned her joys, hopes, affections, would break her heart at a blow, and sweep her up and away beyond the big star.

"Lucy," said a hard voice, which had something of affection in it too, "it is time for prayers, child."

The girl used to reply, "I am ready, mother." Now, however, the summons startled her; and, a painful gray shadow passing over her face, she turned silently from the window, and took her place opposite to her mother, at the little table in the centre of the room.

When the star had come round the sky, and looked in at these two women, it saw as great a contrast as anywhere else in the world. The one kneeling figure fair, fragile, like a flower brought too suddenly into bloom; the other tall, strong, with fierce gray eyes, a stony forehead, a mouth which, in its hard severe lines, was only to be matched among the mouths which our Puritan fathers kissed more than two hundred years ago. The close-fitting black silk cap which she wore favoured this resemblance; as did also her erect carriage, her straight thin limbs, and the proud air of self-possession which deserted her at no time. Now, when she prayed, denouncing more the sins of the world in general than beseeching forgiveness for her own—beginning coldly, but raising higher and higher her iron voice as she proceeded, it was easier to imagine her the mother of some new Balfour of Burley than of the pale child trembling near her.

Lucy's knees smote together when she kneeled down; indeed, if she had not rested her forehead on the table, she must have fallen. As her mother proceeded, however, Lucy trembled less; but that was because she was awed. The judgments which the stern woman called down upon the wicked, the vain, the idle, and backsliders, were imagined by our poor girl too distinctly; but when Widow Howlet, her voice sharpening, her accents trembling with religious enthusiasm, inveighed against hypocrites and sinners in secret, her daughter lifted her face, and gazed at her mother's bent head with a look so full of awe and terror, that her secrets were revealed, every one of them. The good widow, however, did not meet the look conjured up by the unusual vehemence of her devotions. Before she rose Lucy had relapsed into the sad stupor that had encompassed her too often, and which to-night was especially apparent. Coming events cast their shadows before.

Pretending to continue her devotions, Lucy remained kneeling, her face hid in her hands. Her mother, the widow, looked at her, first with a tenderness almost like that with which our cousin Fanny gilds her baby's cradle, but afterwards with glances kindled at the redder fires of her own religious enthusiasm. She placed her hands on her daughter's shoulders, and said—

"You are weak, child."

"Alas!" said Lucy, not more than half aloud.

"Weak in health and in faith too."

"In faith! Oh, mother!" answered the poor girl, sinking still deeper on her knees.

"Yes, Lucy, in faith. I leave you to struggle with heaven for more strength; which you shall have, my child. You are born of the elect, Lucy. You, weak as you are, are sealed and chosen!"

With that she left the room, which looked all the cheerfuller for the absence of her dark face.

An hour after, when the night had fairly fallen, the two women were in their several bed-chambers. One slept in the calm and fixed assurance of one whose future is secure, the other sat upon her bed, in a tremor of hope and fear, very insecure. The house was still, and all around it silent. Only now and then the dog barked; and though the brook more noisily babbled, that only showed how deep the stillness was.

Lucy went to her window and looked out. It was time now, she said, and throwing her old cloak about her went downstairs.

Mrs. Howlet believed that when the faithful slept, an angel stood with watch and warning on the threshold. Lucy, then, was not faithful; for no hand held her back, except, perhaps, for the single moment when she passed her mother's door. Then that darker blush that belongs to shame purpled her cheeks; and then she made a strange impatient movement with her hands, motioning away all thought, which, indeed, was simply impertinent, since it came so late. Recovering herself, she went down into the lane, the quietness trying in vain to catch her footfalls.

A summer wind went by just then, and kissed her forehead with its innocent cool lips. The leaves rustled as this little breeze passed, and then were quite still again, listening for its return. When Lucy got to the end of the lane, there was a bye-road to the right and a meadow to the left. She chose the narrower path this time, and then going along by an old wall, very mossy, and then round a thick plantation, she came at length to an open place—a hollow—where was a pool. Here she stopped.

An ugly piece of water this was, and generally avoided, though why, nobody could tell. It was broad, and deep, and deliciously cool, but it never tempted the bather in summer time; and when winter made ice of it, no skater ventured to cut even his solemnest figure upon its surface. Consequently, perhaps, it was a sulky pool, and seemed rather to delight in the gloom which the overgrowing alders threw upon its bosom. And what beggarly trees those five alders were!—standing apart, uncompanionable, barren, tired of their lives, to all appearance, and brooding over the pond as if they had suicide in their sapless hearts. The pool itself was capable of putting even worse ideas than suicide into your head. It appeared to you that a half-resolved murderer might complete his resolution here, when he saw how abrupt were the banks, without a weed to catch at; when he observed how deep it was, deep as if a mass of earth had sunk fathoms suddenly, leaving the springs to fill its place; and when he beheld how faithfully the alders stretched their shadows over its surface.

There was not for five miles round a stranger place for lovers to meet at; but gloomy scenes consort with gloomy thoughts; this pool here is not darker than Lucy's misgivings, and her heart is not nearly so quiet. It is full of rebellious grief, which her hopes and her faith have to do battle with every two minutes, invariably getting the worst of it. And it is observable that whenever she mistakes the rustling of a bough for the expected footstep (a mistake she often makes), she passes her hand quickly over her eyes, as if she knew that any tears that happened to have collected there would be unpleasant to him whom she awaits. Now we are all agreed that that is a bad sign.

Every time she found she had mistaken the sound of the rustling, Lucy turned her back peevishly in the direction whence it came, and said: "But he'll come! I'm sure he'll come!" repeating it so often that there seemed to be some doubt about it after all; and that these words were in the nature of a charm, to keep her heart up. At length the formula took an ominous change; that was when the village clock apprised her that she had waited nearly an hour. The misguided young woman sat upon a fallen tree trunk, and said: "Surely he will not break *all* his promises!"

She did not know, poor child, that all this weary hour Mr. Horace Keppel had been quite undecided as to whether he should keep the appointment or not. Nor was she aware that several times in this same period, her name had been coupled with the words "nuisance," and "bore." Ignorance *is* bliss sometimes. However, Keppel throws on his hat, and as he thrusts his good-looking fingers into his gentlemanly gloves, he exclaims, "Well, this *shall* be the last time, by Jove!"

At length, by the grace of Horace, Lucy was not mistaken. That was the noise of dear Horace's feet among the leaves—there was the luminous end of his cigar, glowing calmly! How glad was Lucy, in her blissful ignorance of the conversation which dear Horace had been holding with his angels!

"My dear," said she, "I am so glad you have come. But it's very late, isn't it?"

"Late! that's a matter of comparison, Lucy. If you'd seen the bright eyes and jolly faces I have left behind me [this was a little lover-like falsehood], you'd think it early enough yet. It is late here, though," continued he, looking round with a shiver, "at least two hours later than up yonder—and what's more, it is particularly cold and wretched."

"You have found bright eyes and a merry face here, Horace; though you did not expect them to-night, perhaps."

"Why, no; I confess I did not, to be frank. But it's hardly fair to expect *me* to be always in sackcloth and ashes, because—well, what I mean is this: it appears to me that you do moping enough for both of us."

Lucy had nothing to reply to that; and if she had, could not have uttered it, on account of that choking in the throat which the reader may have heard of. Horace pulled away at his cigar, and tried to pin a glow-worm in the grass with his walking-stick. He had a very pretty graceful way of accomplishing such trifles; now, however, his heart thumped so nervously, that he buttoned his coat down over it, to fortify himself.

"Well," said he, by and by, "what's the news?"

"Why, what news can I have to tell *you*?" answered the girl, plucking up heart a little, and placing her hand on Horace's arm.

"What do you mean?" he sharply said.

"I meant that, as you read all sorts of books and newspapers, and talk with so many people, there can be nothing left for me to tell you."

"Oh, that's what you meant," rejoined Horace, lunging at a frog, which, alighting on his foot, hopped off again. "I thought it wasn't."

"And then I live such a lonely life."

"You always did, my dear, didn't you?"

"Ah! dear Horace, but it is lonelier now."

"Oh! how's that?" asked the young man, in a northerly voice—keen and cold.

"How? You ought to know the difference, Horace, between contented loneliness and the loneliness of——"

"Out with it, my dear."

"Shame!" she said.

"Of course. I thought we were coming to that. But is that all? You have not got me out on a night like this, merely to listen to the same old tale! I know it by heart!"

(He came resolved to quarrel with her, and this is the way he began.)

"And so do I. By heart? Ay, well by heart. All day long I think of it—all night long I dream of it!" cried Lucy, in a voice so new that she herself was surprised at it.

"Well?"

"Horace, you should not speak like that. It's cruel!"

"Cruel, is it? Come, we are getting on."

The young man affected to pay great attention to his cigar, which was supposed to be going out. What of her mother there was in Lucy gathered together in her eyes; and it was light enough for Horace to see how they flashed; his heart began to quake, his lips quivered, but he raised such a cloud of smoke that these symptoms were unseen. Lucy's anger passed away with the cloud; but, as her tenderness returned, his courage revived. Mr. Keppel was a man again.

"Dear Horace," she said, placing her hand on his shoulder, "you used to have a kind heart; what have you done with it?"

"I a kind heart!—a heart of any kind? My dear child, who put that into your head? You've been reading novels in your loneliness." Lucy's hand fell from his shoulder.

"Do I read *you* right, Horace?" she said, flashing with anger again in spite of herself—only a melancholy sort of anger, though.

"I suppose so. You have turned over a new leaf, perhaps."

"Horace Keppel——!"

"Well—don't be angry."

"It is *not* well!" cried she. "It is cruel—it is treacherous!"

Horace blew another great cloud of smoke before his face, and then replied, with affected calmness: "Upon my word, you plead your case very energetically; forgive me if I cannot add—and ably. Energetic women are not to my taste; an energetic wife I should detest; and if you proceed in this style, any idea of that kind—— By Jove, you know!" he continued, trying hard to puff his cold soul into a flame, "it's abusive! I begin to think these meetings may be too dangerous to indulge!"

"Go on, Horace," said Lucy, as she rose from the tree-trunk where she had again seated herself after her last passionate outbreak. "You have left half that speech unsaid—out of respect to my feelings, perhaps. There are my feelings, Horace," she cried, with suppressed vehemence, and with a gesture as if she

threw them down and placed her foot on them; "there they lie; now speak out. You are tired of me!"

"Why should I talk preposterous nonsense? I'll leave that to you, Lucy, if you please." The young man stammered. This abrupt dragging forth of his little secret, naked as it was born, embarrassed him.

But Lucy did not hear the re-assuring reply. When she ceased speaking, she turned her face towards the pool, and remained gazing at it with fixed abstracted eyes. Horace was not a dunce, and he read a meaning in her vacant breathless air, than which nothing short of an actual leap into the water could have been more explicit. The man was afraid; and changed his note accordingly.

"Come, Lucy, we have carried this nonsense far enough. Stupid fits of ill-humour will not mend matters, you know—and we don't mean what we say, my love. Look here, now," said he, taking her hand. "Just look cheerful for five minutes, and listen to a little plan I have concocted for the future. Perhaps you will find that a fellow has a heart after all—that I am not quite the monster you give me credit for being."

She passively turned her eyes from the water, and rested them on the grass near Keppel's feet. That was not a cheerful beginning. The young man passed his arm through hers, and walked up and down with her as he talked. He said something about not being free, in the most amiable and persuasive voice. He said something, in a despairing tone, of his sorrow because he *was not* free. He said something about women being governed always by feeling, and judging by their hearts, while men were obliged to keep themselves bridled by reason, and persuaded by their heads: this in a philosophic manner. And then he went on to say, lightly, cheerfully, what here follows; which, if the good reader will forgive us for printing, we promise never to touch upon such shameful ground again. Said he—

"Now, my dear, suppose I happen to have an old aunt (down in Devon, say) who would be glad of your services for a few months. Very well. That excuse would readily satisfy your mother, and your brother too; though he is a little boy, and of no consequence whatever. Eh?"

"Oh, no!"

"Very well. Meanwhile, off you go to some good old woman in an out-of-the-way nook for the time, and then you come back to me, as brisk as a bee, and as beautiful as ever. Understand, Lucy?"

Of course she did. But she faltered out, with an absent air, "I don't hardly."

"You are thinking of the expense. Oh, I'll find money, of course; and as for the rest, why, dear me! it occurs twenty times a day, all round the world."

A little pause. They stop at the pool; and their arms are disengaged.

"Is that—have you nothing more to propose?" asks she.

"Nothing more? Why, my dear child, if that—unless, indeed, you will accept my purse to begin with."

Lucy makes no answer to that proposition; and in another moment Mr. Keppel finds himself alone. With a look of stupid surprise, he watches her dark figure flitting homeward, like a black ghost.

"By Jove!" says the young man, half-audibly, when Lucy is out of sight and he is recovered from his amazement, "she's got more pluck than I gave her credit for. There's no knowing women, that's clear. I'm glad she's gone, though, on the whole," continued he, as he cast a scared and meaning glance over the black, still surface of the pool. "By gad, you know, that would have been awful for a fellow!"

CHAPTER II.

SENTIMENTAL.

"A FELLOW's weed gone out, too!" said Keppel, as he walked away. "*Another* bore!"

And in fact, all that was left to him, under the circumstances, was to chaw the end of it, which he accordingly proceeded to do, like a philosopher and a gentleman. With a slow, easy swing, he sauntered along; but he was by no means easy in mind. He had two miles of a dreary road to travel; his reflections were unpleasant ; and it was night : whereas it is well known that evil-doers see their wickedness best in the dark.

Not but that Keppel's first thoughts were rather pleasant than otherwise. He congratulated himself on the escape he had had from the disagreeable reflections which would certainly have haunted him if the girl had ran into the water, instead of away from it ; he argued that the first impulse over, she was not likely to do anything rash when she got home ; besides, she was too delicate a creature to make a disagreeable corpse of herself by cutting her throat, or hanging ; and, pleased at his good fortune, he struck into the highway with the last new tune on his lips. The further he plunged into the darkness, however, the more he did not feel inclined to sing. When he attempted it, Echo cut him dead, and the night reproved him. It was wonderful how lifeless the notes seemed to drop to the ground, like so many birds brought down by ghostly sportsmen with ghostly guns. Before Keppel had gone much further, therefore, he entered into a new series of reflections. He began to feel spooney.

"She used to be a nice girl, though," said he—"pretty little figure—hands, by George ! fit for a duchess. Foot good. Throat ! —why, it was the back of her neck, as she stooped to draw water with that infernal great pitcher, that first engaged my attention. Then what a pretty, calm face ! With her hair shining round it, like a regular Salvator di Carracci. Young, too—seventeen. Ah, that was the deuce of it ! Dear me ! Never wore a regular bonnet, you know, till she knew me ; and I'd wager ten to one, from the feel of them, that her lips were never kissed by man nor woman till *I* kissed 'em. Do I remember when ? Well I do. It was in Springfield Lane. Said I, as she stopped to look up at the sky, 'Do you know the stars, my child ?' ' I know they shine,' said she— (Heavens ! how innocent !) ' But their names ? Now, what do you think that star's name is ?' 'Tell me !' 'That's —a—that's Calliope.' Calliope ! how pretty. That ought to be the name of a tall, bountiful lady,' said she. Rum crotchets she always had—never *could* altogether make her out. ' There, that one's Mars—that red one !' ' Mars is a red name,' says she, as if nothing could be more natural. ' Oh, well, you know how that bright one's called ?' No, she didn't. ' Venus. ' Ah ! all women are alike, young and old : she took that directly. She turned her blushing head aside, as the song says, as we stood there by that jolly old wall, and then she turned it round again ; and then she looked at me so, so— by Jove, you know !—so much like a baby with a woman's jealous eyes, that I kissed her, in fact. Georgy-porgy ! how like a youngster she used to make me feel ! At that very moment, I remember, I saw myself once more, a kid in a green skeleton suit, hugging Polly Sylvester in her father's bakehouse. How was it she first kissed *me* ! That was *too* bad. I *did* feel ashamed of myself then, and I ain't done being ashamed of myself yet. I'd been drinking. My eyes were dull. I was feverish—seedy. ' How hot your hand is,' said she, 'and, oh dear, how heavy your eyes are !' ' My dear child, study, study !' said I. Then she said, 'Oh, you mustn't ! Stoop !' So I stooped ; she put her hands on each side my face, and kissed both my eyes. ' There,' says she, 'I've refreshed them !' And so she had ! I saw sparks flying from my eyes as her lips left them. By George ! that was a shameful do—bad business that was. Why, I don't feel worse now, after all, than—— "

Here Keppel's reflections came to a dead stop. It almost seemed for a time that he *did* feel worse now ; and even when no very remarkable or melancholy episode was uppermost in his thoughts, he continued to repeat " Bad business—bad business !" without being aware of it ; though that there was somebody or something about him that was aware is evident. Presently he repeated the words with such emphasis that they frightened him, judging from the way in which he looked round. Then he walked quicker. Then he took to whistling, bravely beating time with his walking-stick—but also *not* as if he were beating time, but as though he were warding off the awful reflections that assaulted him from all sides. Remorse is the last sting of conscience—if you are proof to that—farewell.

Here goes another aphorism equally new : Love and money rule the world. They ruled Horace Keppel. Love had had its turn—now the pecuniary element stepped in for a share of the young man's meditations. For he was as poor as a church mouse ; as a beggar's dog ; as a cobbler's widow ; to use some of his own phrases, and to avoid others less elegant if equally em-

phatic. That is to say, he was a born gentleman with two hundred and twenty pounds a-year, which is a great misfortune. It has been said, or it should have been said, that his path lay *past* the gates of Keppel Lodge, and that exactly represents the state of the case. He will be asked his business if he rings at those gates. Should he enter without ringing, and be caught in the fact, he will be shown the way out again, ignominiously. True, many generations of his family had owned Keppel Lodge—it was built by a direct ancestor of his in 1557, as a stone in the wide porch testified. But the direct ancestor, and all the generations of his line, whose boast it was that they came in with the Conqueror, had gone out with the *other* Conqueror ; and there was Horace, with no more of the soil than stuck to his boots, and that, strictly speaking, wasn't his. A fact which rankled sorely in the young man's heart.

A low wall surrounded the Lodge, which stood in a little park, much curtailed of its original proportions ; but thereto appertained several good fat farms, all the neighbouring village, and a little of the land whereon stood the town of Shorewell, three miles away—a small but sound property, worth three thousand a-year perhaps. Horace ceased whistling, ceased beating the air, and paused to look over this wall. Every window in the house was alive with light ; which, as he looked, kindled within the young man a burning discontent. When the sound of his footsteps ceased, the watch-dog broke out afresh, baying vociferously.

"Confound you, you cur !" growled Keppel ; "you know me, I suppose. But you are not unreasonable ; for if I had you within reach of my heels, my four-footed friend, I'd serve you as—as I'd serve that grandfather of mine, who gave you, like a fool, the right to treat me like a thief."

(There came an aggravating sound of music over the wall.)

" *You'll* keep me out of my grounds, will you ? By Jove ! if you don't close your jaws" (for the dog was a persevering dog), " I'll step over and pay off on your bones both his account and your own. It'll be a great satisfaction, too," he added, after a moment's hesitation ; " and with that he leapt over.

It happened, however, that at this moment the dog's attention was called off by an unwonted rabbit, to which he immediately gave such hot chase that he was speedily at the other end of the park.

" Cur you are, then !" cried Horace ; "you turn tail upon the true owner and the true blood—an example which your low-bred dog of a master would probably follow, under the same circumstances. I've half a mind to beard him in his kennel !"

And so, not with this intention—Keppel had neither the pluck nor the folly for that—but with a new and increasing curiosity, he approached the house.

In a few minutes, he stood just without the shrubs and flower-beds that immediately surrounded it.

Some unusual festivity was going on within, that was plain. Floods of lights poured out upon the garden, tinging the flowers with strange hues. Floods of music poured out upon the air ; and though Keppel could not hear the feet of the dancers, he could see their shadows as they gaily passed the windows. It was not a grave dance, it was a merry dance—merry, that is to say, to those engaged in it. To Horace it was quite another thing ; and when some beautiful young woman, bounding down the hall with an *abandon* not at all ungraceful in country houses, laughed as she went, he savagely ground the gravel under his feet, and his teeth grated audibly.

"If that riotous old spendthrift, my grandfather, had not ruined himself (to which I should have had not the least objection, if he had not beggared me too), I should have been the first man in that company. The prettiest girl there, with an eye to be Mrs. K., would be dancing with *me* ; and she would take in her arms this good house, and these good acres at the same time. But now !" he cried, seizing a rose-bloom, and tearing it with his hot fingers, "if the gardener were to catch me at this, he'd take me to the pump !" concluded he, with an indistinct perception of his deserts.

He opened his hand—the bruised petals fluttered to the ground.

At this moment a door opened ; two female figures passed out, and "the true owner and the true blood" ducked behind a clump of shrubs.

4

"Dear me, Miss Butler," exclaimed by far the stoutest figure of the two, as they approached the spot where Horace was kneeling, "what a happy creature you ought to be!"

"Don't you think I am, Mrs. Popples?" Mrs. P. was the curate's wife.

"Well, on that point I'm not quite convinced, my dear. You are *so* sedentary; you are reading eternally; now, if that doesn't arise from melancholy, it leads to it; at least, that's *my* belief."

"But I could hardly be unhappy without being ungrateful."

"Indeed, I think so! Why, here you are, young, pretty (many people think fair women handsomer than dark ones), the only daughter of a father who dotes on you, sole heiress to one of the nicest properties of the county, and surrounded with lovers and all sorts of luxuries."

"Are lovers luxuries, Mrs. Popples?" asked Sophy, in the most innocent of voices.

"To well-regulated minds, my dear. My Popples always said——"

"Then I haven't a well-regulated mind. I have never seen the lover who was worth this flower."

"Now, that's a symptom. Old maids begin to love cats, or something of that sort, when they have given up the expectation of a sweetheart; and young maids grow ridiculous about flowers just as they begin to think they would like one. And the moon again! Excuse me, my dear child, but this is only your seventeenth birthday, which accounts for you talking so romantically. Now, listen to me. I've seen the world, you know, and I'm a prophetess into the bargain : or, at least, I ought to be, after all I've had to go through in copying that dreadful Commentary on the Apocalypse which Mr. Popples is writing. Oh, my dear child, never marry a man who studies old things of that sort. I'm sure with such a number of children as we have, it's wonderful——"

"But you were about to prophesy. What is going to happen?"

Mrs. Popples smoothed the plaits of her skirts, expanded her already broad bosom, and folded one hand over the other in a drooping manner.

"Well, my dear, *this* is going to happen : Before a year is out, you will be married. Perhaps it will be young Meadows. Not young Meadows? Too curly and conceited? Say Arthur Campion, then. Arthur, not tall enough? Well, he *is* a little fellow, but he has got a beautiful set of teeth, I'm sure. Well, Mr. Woodford; he's big enough, in all conscience. However, we need not settle the particulars at this moment—the great fact being that you'll be married. Very well. Now, my dear Sophy, everybody knows what will follow that event; there's nothing so easy as to prophesy a baby under those circumstances; though really if, like Popples—well, well! Good heavens, how delighted your father will be to find his hopes realized at last—to take in his arms the sweet, darling, precious boy-baby, that shall continue his name to posterity! Ah, I know what man feels on that subject. When I was born, what did *my* father do? He was rolling the lawn—at fifty years of age, that was—and he'd all girls. I was the last. Our maid Jane flew out to him. 'Oh, master!' said she, 'it's all right, and it's a sweet girl!' 'Is it, my dear?' said he, dropping on to the roller so suddenly that Jane was quite afraid he had hurt himself, 'then give my compliments to your mistress, and tell her I shan't be in to dinner. I won't enter the house for a month!' He took his hat from the ground, put it on the back of his head, and walked straight out of the village. And, I assure you, he kept his word."

"Never!"

"But he did. He came back next day, but he slept in the hay-loft till the month was over."

Sophy burst into a fit of laughter, as much as possible moderated. "Why the same thing might happen to my father, too, Mrs. Popples; and how dreadful that would be!"

"Oh, it would not occur to your father. He'd only swear a little, perhaps (he does swear now, doesn't he, Sophy?) and have I not prophesied otherwise? No, there shall be a little boy—named after his grandfather; and he will be the proudest man and you the happiest woman in the county."

Said Sophy more seriously—

"What a charming fortune you have marked out for me! First, I am to have the choice of three or four indifferent nice

young men, and then I am forthwith to found a family. *La vie d'une femme c'est toujours un roman.*"

"Oh, not too much romance, if you please. And we must manage it so that no spendthrift blood creeps in. As the property came, so it must not go. Be sure there is no gaming, cockfighting Butler, my dear, whatever you do; no Butler to leave a legacy of pride, poverty, and vagabondage to *his* descendants."

("What does the old baggage mean by that?" said Horace to himself, reddening with indignation.)

"Because," added the curate's wife, "that's a kind of legacy which people generally put out to interest; and we see what becomes of them."

"You are severe, Mrs. Popples," returned Sophy, whose answer Keppel eagerly listened for. "After all the Commentary, too, it's quite uncharitable."

("Bravo!" cried Keppel, under his breath. "A better answer than was expected of you, Miss Butler.")

"Severe, Sophy! Uncharitable! You surely have no sympathy with people of that description."

"I am not sure but I have, though!"

"For gamesters, spendthrifts, sponging-house people?"

"For the poor, proud descendants of a ruined family."

("By gad!" whispered Horace—to whom a new idea was wafted with this little speech—"if you go on like that, Sophy, I shall be obliged to alter my opinion of you.")

"Oh, come! really you are joking. Presently you will tell me, I suppose, that in your sympathy for *roués* in general, you include the young man Keppel in particular. Whom you have never seen," added the injudicious Mrs. Popples.

"Don't be surprised if I go that length, one of these days. Indeed, I have often thought that Mr. Keppel's position must be very painful. There is something even touching in the way in which, as I have heard, he haunts the spot where so many generations of his family were born, and which has been ennobled by the presence of many brave men, many fair women of his name. His ancestors ruffled with King Charles and fought with Marlborough, and came home to a whole territory here. He hasn't a rood. There's romance in that, Mrs. Popples, and I am sorry for him."

Horace lifted his head and looked at the girl, whose face, beaming with enthusiasm, was revealed in the light that streamed from the windows.

"*Romance*, indeed!" echoed Mrs. P., in a most matter-of-fact tone. "My dear child, you are excited. You have danced too much, which reminds me that you'll be wanted to dance again. Come, we'll return into the house, if you are sufficiently refreshed."

"Leave me for a few moments, then. Perhaps I am a little excited, and a quiet talk with my flowers will do me good."

"And they may understand you, perhaps. Certainly, my dear, *I* don't. In three minutes, then." And so, waving her hand, Mrs. Popples retired.

"Mother of men!" Horace exclaimed in a whisper: "the situation's becoming serious. It *is* serious, by Jove!"

"And yet, you poor little red geranium," muttered Sophy, taking up the thread of her thoughts, and speaking distinctly enough for Horace's ears, "and yet, you poor little red geranium—for I suppose you have been listening, and it is true that I may as well talk to you as to Mrs. Popples—the poor proud gentleman would scorn my pity. If he—I don't mean Mr. Keppel, you know, but *any* poor gentleman—has no golden guineas in his pockets, he has priceless traditions in his memory—traditions of honour, and chivalry, and power, and love. The wives and sisters of his people buckled swords to their sides, kissing the blade as a benison, when the wives and sisters of mine carded wool, or bruised peas to make porridge with. The gentleman would despise me and my pity, you poor little red geranium!"

Whatever of generosity there was in Keppel's nature was now on fire. His vanity was inflamed, too; and there was no more prudence in him. Bending over the narrow flower-bed which divided him from Sophy Butler, he extended his hand towards her, and was about to declare that the poor proud gentleman would do no such thing, when he was suddenly brought to his senses by the most natural circumstance in the world:

Sophy screamed. She took him, we fear, for a thief; and she thought she saw a pistol in his outstretched hand. He stood for a moment, therefore, dumbfoundered, while the girl was petrified with alarm. But those within had heard Sophy's signal of distress—a door was flung open, and light poured out upon the path. With sudden self-possession, Horace took a letter from his pocket, tore off the envelope, which he flung at Sophy's feet, and was off and over the wall again in a twinkling.

The injurious gods! They will interfere even in the most romantic moments of our existence, to remind us that we are but flesh. Mortified to the last degree at not having caught the rabbit, Tiger was wandering home, when he caught sight of Keppel's flying form. With a joyous howl, the dog bounded forward, and so hotly chased the young man that he barely escaped with whole garments.

When once Keppel had gained the road, however, he was himself again. He dropped into a walk, chewing his cigar, and meditating many things. So pleased was he with this adventure, that poor Lucy never occurred to his mind again, till in the night he awoke.

"Where is she?" said a voice in his ear, at the moment of waking.

"Oh, she's all right!" said he; and not finding any comfort in thinking further of the matter, he concluded that it would be as well to go to sleep again: which he accordingly did, after two or three unsuccessful efforts.

As for Sophy Butler, she, too, observed that her friends had heard her cry, and were hurrying to her assistance. The little time she had to lose, therefore, she devoted to a second glance at the intruder, when she came to the conclusion, frightened as she was, that the young man was not a thief. Then how mysteriously he threw the paper at her feet! Suddenly stooping, she picked it up and thrust it into her bosom, just as her father and a half-dozen of his guests hurried out.

What was the matter?

Only her folly. She thought, she fancied—oh, it must have been Tiger.

"Tiger, no doubt," said her father.

"No doubt it was the dog," said his guests, especially Mrs. Popples, who made the remark with uncommon spirit. The young girl looked keenly round at the curate's wife, but the countenance of that lady betrayed more curiosity than information, and Sophy was satisfied.

Satisfied, that is to say, so far as Mrs. Popples was concerned: but for the rest of the evening there was an alternate restlessness and absence in the young girl's demeanour, which can only be accounted for by—the paper in her bosom. With what longing curiosity she awaited the moment when she should be alone—quite alone—to read it! She was sure there was writing on the paper. What could it be about?

At length she was alone, in her own room. She locked the door carefully, and, going back to the light with an almost stealthy air, she took the paper from her bosom and placed it on the table, blank side up. Sophy regarded this as rather a lucky accident than otherwise; and now she seemed to be in no hurry to read the paper, but quietly set about the business of unrobing herself. Only now and then she gave a glance at the dirty little document that engrossed all her thoughts.

At length her toilette was completed. Now for the *bonne bouche*, to be digested in visions of the night. Sophy's fingers hovered for a few moments over the envelope, then quickly turned it over, and read the single line—"Mr. Horace Keppel."

Sophy jumped into bed, and dreamed accordingly.

CHAPTER III.

FLIGHT.

LUCY, when she left Keppel to his reflections—not very brilliant company—glided home rather than ran. Out of such a figure, with fixed pale face and dishevelled hair, rustics make ghosts.

Lucy said to herself through her clinched teeth, clinching her hands at the same time, "I will go home, and tell all, and make an end of it! *He*, with his tender speeches, his fond words and looks, forsakes me in this extremity. My mother is hard, but she is a woman, and will understand me; she *is* my

mother, and will forgive me." And so she hurried on till she came to the little gate, and placed her hand upon the latch. Then she wavered, and that one moment of hesitation was time enough for the stillness, the peace of all around, to appeal to her heart. They reproached her. They seemed to know all about her affairs, and to say, "We, Peace and Quiet, have lived here years and years. We dwelt in this house, and round about this little garden, before you were born; we have never been disturbed. Why do you now come, therefore, to banish us altogether? Take your secrets away!" Then a gust of wind buffeted Lucy on the cheek, and the rustling of the old apple-tree reminded her of her mother's prayer of that evening. The very words in which she had denounced hypocrites and sinners in secret recurred to the poor girl's mind, and her hand fell from the latch. She could not, she would not, go into the house any more. What she *was* to do was a question that never crossed her mind, though she still lingered, going shyly round to the back of the cottage, and looking wistfully up at her mother's window. It was dark; it was shuttered and barred, like the old woman's heart. Lucy felt the comparison, and without more ado laid her head on the sill of the window below, and cried aloud.

"Mother, mother, you are to blame too," she cried; "love you never showed me. When I was a little child, I saw other mothers kiss their children, but you never kissed me. Sometimes a hard cold kiss on my forehead, but many and many a night I missed even that, and cried about it before I fell asleep. And as I grew, worse and worse; not a caress, not an endearing word—never! Was I altogether to blame, then, when Horace came, to listen to the only—only——" and then, suddenly remembering how these "only" drops of affection had turned to gall and wormwood and all imaginable bitterness, she burst anew into a passion of tears.

The reflection that her mother had in some degree wronged her abided in Lucy's mind; it lingered there after the passion of tears had subsided, and, indeed, fixed her determination not to enter the house. For all that, just as Lucy turned away, she started suddenly, and kissed the senseless shutters; they were the nearest things to her mother's lips, and her mother's hand would touch the place.

So she closed the little gate behind her, and set off in the darkness.

Where she thought she was going to, how far she imagined she could travel before it was time to lie down in a ditch to die, or whether she had any ideas in the matter, nobody knows. At a guess, I should say she had no idea at all, except that she was carrying her shame and her sorrows to some place where they might be hidden. Wait a bit. Upon reflection, I remember that she *had* a dim sort of notion about this place; the notion being that it had a church with a spire just like that of her own village, there was a pool in it like this other pool, only not so wide nor so black; and that it was about fifty miles off. She did not *think* this about the place; she only saw it now and then as in a picture.

Excited and feverish, Lucy got over the first four miles bravely; but—man proposes, heaven disposes. She was not in good training to walk fifty miles straight off; in fact, her condition for performing that feat was singularly bad, as she herself too plainly saw when, in much tribulation, she sat down upon the roadside bank, and thereupon fainted.

She looked very like a dead woman as she lay there under the big star, which still stared down so coldly, so cruelly, that it might have been "Lucifer, Son of the Morning," gone up to heaven again from the place into which he had fallen. But Lucy was not dead, and the star was only a planet, minding its own business in the universe. Nor will the poor girl die just yet, if Mrs. Joliffe knows it; and taking the following circumstances into account, it is likely that she will.

Mrs. Joliffe sells poultry, eggs, and butter. Every Tuesday and Friday she takes her wares to the nearest market, driving an old, blind, gray mare, which, in turn, drew an old tumble-down cart, which appeared to be blind too, judging from its tendency to run into ruts and hedges, to the provocation of the mare. Now, this happens to be a Tuesday; and if Judy (that's the mare) is commonly successful in keeping the cart *out* of the hedges, Mrs. Joliffe will pass the spot where Lucy lies in ten

MRS. JOLIFFE DISCOVERS LUCY.

minutes at most. True, it is dark; but then Nettle—the most good-humoured cur that ever trotted before a horse, black, white, or gray—is on the look-out; and Mrs. Joliffe would undertake to eat him alive if he passed any creature, living or dead, without due notice of the fact.

Accordingly, five minutes after Lucy had sunk upon the bank, Nettle's shabby, lanky, most disreputable figure comes forging along the very middle of the road, a hundred yards in advance of the cart. Presently he stops, returns a few feet, puts himself broadside on across the road, and delivers his signals: 1, a bark, with a whine, which means, "Look out, old woman!" 2, a bark, in a shriller key, followed by a growl, which signifies, "I'm here, stranger! what's your game?" And then off he goes to see.

Mrs. Joliffe's tactics, under these circumstances, are simple. She catches up her umbrella, claps her finger on the spring, and prepares to let fly in the face of any robber who ventures to intrude near her cart. She has heard of the young lady who scared a tiger in that manner, and relies upon a similar effect in the case of a footpad. The precaution is unnecessary, for, with her huge bonnet tied down with a shawl, and her large proportions enveloped in a coat of many capes, she cuts such a tough and formidable figure, that few thieves would face it.

The next signals which Nettle throws out, as he trots round and round the prostrate figure, are signals of distress. Mrs. Joliffe recognizes them, drops her umbrella, and peers keenly over the collar of her coachman's coat. "Whoa! you brute! Whoa, I tell 'ee, this minnut!" and, pulling hard at the reins,

she startles the gray mare out of a comfortable doze. Nettle jumps into the cart, and, tugging at the capes in a "look-alive!" sort of way, jumps out again.

"Lor' sakes alive!" cries the dame, as, catching a lantern which swung at Judy's tail, she approached the prostrate Lucy, "what be 'ee arter? Deary me, a poor creetur of a woman, if there's one above ground! What!" Mrs. Joliffe dropped the lantern, drew herself upright, with her hands upon her comprehensive hips, looked straight before her, and—whistled!

"Wh-e-e-w!"

"Now, none o' that!" said Nettle, running at Mrs. Joliffe's legs to emphasize the remark. "What's the use o' whistling? Look here!"

"Heavens, Lucy! Come to this, has it?" cried the dame. Bustling back to the cart, she seized her unsold ducks, stacked them upon her equally unsold chickens, and finally punched them into a corner. "There you be!" said she. Then she bustled back to Lucy, took off the capes, rolled the girl into them, and, with an alarming exhibition of strength, lifted her into the crazy vehicle.

The gray mare dozed no longer on *that* journey. She could not sleep while going at more than four miles an hour, and, finding that at least seven were expected of her, she abandoned the attempt. Only once was she permitted to stop, and that was when, on passing the house of Doctor Poot, the dame stepped out to leave him a message.

In twenty minutes Mrs. Joliffe reached home—in half-an-hour, Lucy, still insensible, was in bed—in two hours Doctor

Poot had come, and gone. He might have gone half-an-hour earlier; but before he was allowed to depart, he was detained at the door in earnest conversation with Mrs. Joliffe. A timid little man was the doctor, and a wary; and yet such was that old girl's eloquence that in thirty minutes she had persuaded him to undertake the task of breaking the news to Widow Howlet—the news being that Lucy had a baby.

The doctor knew well the danger of the undertaking. Years ago, before Mrs. Howlet was known in the village, he had called upon her, in company with the curate, to solicit a subscription towards repairing the church steeple, and on that occasion had witnessed such a display of fiery intolerance (to say nothing of the indignity of being pushed out of the door) that he had never forgotten it. Nevertheless, true to his promise, he arose after a few hours' slumber, and abandoning an ineffectual attempt at breakfast, set off to break the news.

Mrs. Howlet had discovered her daughter's absence at the break of morning; she saw, too, that the girl's bed had not been slept in that night. Petrified with fear and astonishment, she went out into the garden. Lucy was not there, but her foot-marks were legible in the rear of the cottage; and under the window, where she had "had her cry out," was a bit of ribbon she had worn in her bosom. The woman prevailed over the enthusiast for a moment, when Mrs. Howlet took up this mute little ribbon knot, and concluded (what was near the truth) that Lucy had gone off with a lover. The enthusiast prevailed over the woman, as, with a sudden gesture, she threw the knot into some currant-bushes, and went into the house solemnly, and took down her Bible, and began to read.

It was not very long after when Dr. Poot rapped at the door, and his nervous fingers rattled at the latch.

"Come in," said the widow, hoarsely.

In sidled Dr. Poot, with his hat in his hand, and his cane advanced before his body. The doctor's countenance half betrayed his errand; with affectation of coolness, of which he was certainly not in the enjoyment, he proceeded to explain the other half.

"You probably guess, Mrs. Howlet, what brings me here. When you turned your—when your daughter left you yesterday, you knew, of course?"

"Where is she?" bluntly interrupted her mother.

"This is her present address, my dear madam," cried the doctor, delighted that the old woman had come to the point so readily—and he took from his waistcoat-pocket a card, on which was written "Mrs. Joliffe's, Peartree Lane." "That is her present address, and," continued he, "she is doing quite as well as can be expected—considering the fright, and a—so a—*quite* as well as can be expected, ma'am!" and Dr. Poot caressed one hand with the other, pleased that he had got so far well.

"What do you mean, sir?" cried Mrs. Howlet, closing the book with a bang which scattered the doctor's wits like a covey of partridges. "Who is with her?"

"At this moment, you know, I cannot say; but when I left her she was alone. When I say alone, of course her little boy (it's a boy, Mrs. Howlet) was with her; and as fine a child he is as it was ever my good fortune——" Keeping his eye on the widow, and watching the black wrath and the red shame darkening upon her hawk-like face, the doctor suddenly broke off at this point, and backed towards the door.

"Stay, sir!" cried she, gliding up and shooting the bolt. "Now, repeat that. What child are you talking of?"

"Your daughter's little son that was born——"

"My daughter's little son that was born," repeated she with a calmness like that which intervenes between the shocks of an earthquake.

"At Mrs. Joliffe's——"

"At Mrs. Joliffe's——"

"At a quarter past two precisely."

"At a quarter past two precisely!" whispered she, regarding Dr. Poot with a most embarrassing eye. Then came the after-clap. "*My* daughter! you said; *my* daughter! No! If the woman has this sin to bear, then the devil has one child the more—I one the less. Never call her my daughter again."

"Very good, ma'am," said Dr. Poot, putting on his hat, and unbolting the door. "I'll deliver that message the next time I visit the young person. Meanwhile, you know where to

find her." And throwing the card upon a side table, the doctor escaped.

"Very fierce woman!" said Dr. Poot, hurrying down the hill; and when he came to the foot of it, and was about to turn the corner, he faced about, levelled his cane at the cottage, and said again: "A very fierce woman that! Respectable sort of fierceness, though—and a truly pious person. There are angels, doctor, and destroying angels; and Mrs. Howlet likes the latter. Very well. I don't; but it's clearly a matter of opinion." And having thus harangued himself, the doctor buttoned up the reflection, and renewed his walk.

For a long time Mrs. Howlet stood as Dr. Poot left her, at the door of the cottage, looking vaguely over into the little valley. So tenderly was the sunshine creeping down there, upon the just and the unjust—so sweetly breathed the breath of the morning upon the just and the unjust—so beautiful was the beauty, so bountiful was the bounty of the earth, given by the Lord God for us all—that she might well have been softened. Perhaps she was; but she presently closed the door upon the scene, drew her window-curtains, and again sat down to the perusal of the Book written by the very hand of Mercy, in the very spirit of Love. But however easy she found it to crook the blessed promises of mercy to her own stern, fiery, right-line ideas, nothing that she found there made Lucy anything else than her own daughter. The fact that she had laid in her bosom, and grown up in her home, and was a part of herself, and bore the features of him whom she had loved in old time, and who died in the service of heaven; the fact that Lucy had been her only companion ever since that time, and that, perhaps, she had not dealt so tenderly with her as a child so sensitive and affectionate should have been dealt with—these were not to be smothered altogether; and little is it to be wondered at that at length Widow Howlet allowed her head to fall upon the book, and groaned and cried. It was the first time she had exhibited such weakness since the news of her husband's death arrived: it was the last time she betrayed it in this world.

Dr. Poot explained the result of his visit, in a conference with Dame Joliffe, when it was decided that no notice of the interview should be taken to Lucy. They found no difficulty in keeping silence, for Lucy asked no questions, nor even mentioned her mother's name in their presence, however often it was in her thoughts or in her prayers. Dame Joliffe was not quite easy on this account. 'Twas unnatural, she said. Drat the old ooman, said she, it wasn't in nature that the poor creature should lie there, day arter day, with her only kith and kin not much more 'an an hour's walk off, and never dare to sen, for her, if the old ooman worn't the unforgivinest thing about. And if she worn't the unforgivinest old thing, why didn't she come without any arksin? She (Mrs. J.) hadn't no patience with that there sart of religion. It were wus 'an lookwarmness; at any rate, it made *her* sick vaarty times more. Flesh an' blood was her motter, please God!

Still, sometimes, Mrs. Joliffe doubted whether the daughter's indifference was not as great as the mother's; and one evening, some three or four weeks after the baby was born, this suspicion made her so hot and angry, that she determined to "try the rights of it."

On the walls of Mrs. Howlet's cottage grew a pretty climber, called "canary creeper," from its blossoms, which were like little yellow birds; there was then not another plant of the kind in the village, though they are common enough there now. Armed with a pair of scissors, Mrs. Joliffe set off with a design upon this creeper; and creeping in at the gate (at much risk of detection, for the dusk had hardly fallen), she slipped off a branch, delicately green, on which were perched twenty bird-blossoms at least.

"Lar' forgive me for thievin'" muttered the good dame, when she had got out of ear-shot; adding, as she shook the stolen spray at the widow's chimney-pots with one hand, while she defiantly rammed her bonnet on from behind with the other, "but 'taint so bad as cruelty to your own flesh, it ain't."

As Mrs. Joliffe passed through her own garden, she plucked a handful of flowers (for it was now June), mingled with them the sprig of canary creeper, which was divided into three or four pieces for the purpose, placed them in a mug, and carried them to Lucy's room.

MR. TWEAKLE SURPRISED WITH THE LITTLE STRANGER.

Lucy was sitting by the window, pale, careworn, and with an air of stillness about her as if she had been born dumb. The window looked down the road that led into the village.

"Here, Lucy, dear, I've brought you a few flowers to smell," and setting down the homely vase, Dame Joliffe left the room as abruptly as she entered it.

It was almost dark, but not so dark that Lucy, casting a careless look upon the flowers, failed to distinguish the old familiar golden blossoms. Her eyes became instantly riveted upon them, her lips parted, and the pallor of sickness was succeeded by the very pallor of death. She stretched forth her hand to touch them, evidently thinking that her senses deceived her. No; they were real! and oh, blessed hope! they could come from no one but her mother. It was a token of love, of forgiveness—of remembrance, at least.

The thought sent a crimson flood into Lucy's cheeks, and kindled a light in her eyes, that would have made Dr. Poot look grave, had he seen it. Her heart was filled to suffocation, and suffocated she would have been if she had not walked the room—up and down, up and down, with her hands clenched and held tightly over her bosom. Indeed, I doubt whether this would have saved her; if, as she turned to pass down the room once more, her baby had not tossed his fat arms up in her sight. Then she gave a cry, full at once of joy and grief, and, throwing herself upon the bed, caught the child to her bosom, and wept away the great load which had lain there so long. "Oh, my dear baby!" cried she, "there is hope for us at last. We are not altogether abandoned and alone in the world; we are saved!"

Now, Mrs. Joliffe, good soul! had been all this time awaiting, outside the door, the success of her scheme. The door was not quite closed, and therefore she saw as well as heard the result. It astonished the good woman; it turned her completely over, as she afterwards confessed; for, small as was her discernment generally, she perceived that she had committed a fatal error.

As soon as Lucy had become more calm, the dame went stealthily down stairs, threw her apron over her head, and then proceeded to heap reproaches upon it. The abuse she gave herself was dreadful.

"Now, then," said she, "you are a gumptious old ooman, you are! Tarrible smart! Ho! 'Stead o' looking arter your donks an chickuns, you go waddlun' an pufflun' arter they 'funnal canaries, and that is what that theere cums too! Oh! poor lass! poor thing! Smoothun of her up, and cockering of her sperrits in this here way, you wicked old, foolish old, fat old woman! Ho! Sakes alive!"

At this moment, in came Nettle with that air of steady, straddling gravity peculiar to grooms at all times, but especially when they have top-boots on.

"Hallo!" suggested he, cocking one eye at Mrs. Joliffe, "what's up now?"

"Who's taalkun' to you?" screamed the dame, catching the expression of Nettle's eye. "What do you know about un? Come—out of ut!" and, seizing the "Pilgrim's Progress" that lay in the window-seat, she made a furious gesture of throwing the good book at his head.

"Well, just as you please, old girl," intimated the brute, turning an imperturbable tail on his mistress. A few minutes after he was seen strolling down Peartree Lane, not only with top-boots on (apparently), but with a straw in his mouth.

"What's to be done?" asked Dame Joliffe. "*Now* what's to be done?" It clearly would not do to let Lucy dwell too long in the sweet, terrible delusion into which she had been betrayed, and yet to disabuse her mind might be to overthrow it altogether. It was a sad dilemma; and, finding herself perfectly incapable of thinking her way out of it, and equally incapable of resting under the circumstances, Mrs. Joliffe determined to act—that is to say, to go up to Lucy, and see "how she took it."

She was in a sound sleep. Coleridge says—

"Oh, sleep, it is a blessed thing,
    Beloved from pole to pole;
To Mary Queen the praise be given;
    She sent the gentle sleep from heaven
That slid into my soul."

Whether to Mary Queen the praise was to be given, or to any other of the Maries, I cannot tell; but surely it was a blessed sleep that "slid" into Lucy's soul, and crept into her limbs, and quieted her heart. Many a night had she lately passed with unclosed eyes; and, when she slept, her slumber was weariness and her dreams tribulation. A great care brooded over her night and day, like Edgar Poe's Raven, croaking an unceasing song of "Never more!" Now, however, how all that was altered! When the creeper came in, the croaker went out; at sight of the golden bird-blossoms, the great care vanished—the Raven took "its beak from out her heart"—took to its black wings, and soared back "into the darkness and the bleak Plutonian shore." She and her baby were not altogether cut adrift into vagabondage, and there went despair. And then came down the gentle sleep from heaven—balm to the wound whence the thorn had been withdrawn.

Alas! poor little woman!—the thorn has only gone to be sharpened; and despair is whetting his beak on the window sill, at this very moment, when you smile, and wake.

Her baby woke her, of course. Nothing else short of the crack of doom could have broken that deep, sweet slumber. As it was, the crack of doom came afterwards.

"Oh, Dame Joliffe," cried Lucy, as that lady stood at the bed-side, ruefully nibbling the corner of her apron, "stoop down, you good soul, and let me kiss you a thousand times!"

"Me! Kiss me a thousan' times! What fur? what fur?"

"What for? You saved us once, and you have saved us again; haven't you? Oh, I know who'll repay you for it, and when, and where!"

"Haven't I?" echoed the good dame, aloud. "No, I have not! I done nothin' o' the saart! I'm a brute! I'm a fool! I ought to be whipped at cart-tail!" bellowed she, with a burst of uncontrollable emotion.

"Oh, Mrs. Joliffe!" exclaimed Lucy, just a shade paler. "Didn't you save me from dying in the road?"

"Oh, ah! a pooty saver, I am! You wait till you knows all about ut."

Lucy made no reply. She fancied she heard the sound of the wings of that same Raven returning. This silence was more painful to Mrs. Joliffe than a thousand reproaches. Looking sharply up (she had covered her head with her apron again), she demanded as sharply:

"Well, why doan't you arks about t'other savun? You says nothin' about that, now. Coorse not? You knows I'm a lyin' old baggidge, and your mother didn't send they yuller flowers, and never meant to, and never would! I picked un myself to try you! There!"

So saying, she plunged into a pillow and roared again. So said, despair came in with a swoop, and buried its beak to the root in the old wound. Lucy was literally stunned. She looked at her baby—such a look it was! Where's the painter that will paint it for us?

What followed then I cannot describe—at least, not what immediately followed. It will be enough to relate what happened two hours after, at midnight. Twenty words will do it.

Lucy rose, and put on her bonnet, and wrapped up her baby (who couldn't help crowing, for the life of him), and stole out of Dame Joliffe's cottage as she had stolen out of her mother's. She did this with a degree of clever stealth only common to thieves, ghosts, and mad people.

Somebody was watching her. Somebody had been rambling round the place—keeping off and on, as sailors say—for the last hour. This somebody saw the light which had been extinguished rekindled, saw Lucy's shadow pass and repass the window-curtains; saw her open the door, stand a moment on the threshold, and then fly away like a frightened bird, but with a degree of swift stealth common, as I said before, to thieves, ghosts, and mad people only. The somebody who saw this started forward the instant that Lucy appeared on the threshold; but the moon broke out, and revealed the infant borne in her arms. Then again the somebody started back, and in another moment the fugitive was gone. Somebody was Lucy's mother.

CHAPTER IV.

THE AFFECTIONS.

IT was to be observed that Horace Keppel smoked a great many cigars in the weeks marked by these events, took solitary rambles, ate salads, and otherwise behaved like a contemplative man unused to contemplation. His companions missed him; his landlady marvelled at him; while he went about softly, musing, meditating, castle-building, chewing the cud of bitter-sweet reflection.

His companions thought he was in debt; his landlady (who had no doubt about that) thought him in love. Perhaps that was Keppel's own idea. His cogitations certainly took some such direction—touching, however, at the same time, on the Keppel estate, hovering over a certain share in a colliery, and dwelling round some ten thousand pounds otherwise invested by Mr. Butler. In other words, he cogitated Sophy.

If the estate, the share, the investments occupied a more prominent place in his mind than Sophy herself, there were reasons for it. In the first place, the property was an ascertained unmistakeable thing—Sophy wasn't; he had seen her only once, and of her heart, intellect, manners, he was almost ignorant. Again, for this particular property, or for that part of it which bore his name, he cherished a strong hereditary affection; for this particular young lady, he lately entertained a deep dislike—not, perhaps, personally—but was she not the daughter and sole heiress of the coal dealer, whose meanly-gotten gains had bought the roof from his head, whose ignorance and purse-proud vulgarity desecrated his ancestral home? Sophy had clearly to be reconciled with these facts. But, then, those very kind and sensible remarks about poor gentlemen!—her meek, pretty face! There was something in that.

This, we must presume, was the conclusion that Horace at length came to; for after a month spent in rumination and tobacco, he was again and again seen within the bounds of Keppel Park. When I say seen there, I mean he *was* there—unless, indeed, Sophy saw him.

He was lounging a short distance within the walls one evening, apparently careless, but carefully shrinking into the shady places nevertheless, when he was surprised by the old gardener, who stepped suddenly out of a greenhouse.

"Why," cried Samuel Tittypee, "that ain't you, Mr. Horace, surely! Lor, sir! how d'ye do, if you'll excuse such a liberty?"

"Old Sam, is it? Glad to see you, Sam," rejoined Horace, blushing to the eyes at being discovered by an old servant of the family poaching like the fox in the vineyard when the grapes were sour. A dismal fox, to go prowling round the high trellises, licking his lips so. In order to cover his confusion the young man added quickly: "But what keeps you at work till this late hour, Sam?"

"Forcin' sir! forcin'," answered the party addressed, with a groan of resignation. "Nothin' but it here, sir, now, from the French guvness as is tryin' to force her forrin' lingo on missus's English sile, down to me as forces gooseberries in December. What money can do, money shall do, is the motto here, sir, now."

Now, Mr. Tittypee—originally a Cockney, which is to be always a Cockney—had been gardening in those grounds for forty years, and was one of the few servants who had been retained when the "new people," as Sam still contemptuously called them, took possession. When he first came upon the estate, he had the hay-coloured hair peculiar to rustic young men, and now stood on it (the estate, not the hair) with only a few white locks dividing his mellow countenance from his shining bald head. Indeed, had not Time, with the whitest of chalk, scored his account so unmistakeably upon Sam's head, his fresh, ruddy face would have passed him off for forty. He *was* fat, and the blue apron which encircled his waist hung at a respectful distance from his knees. Nature had repaid his care of her; for, whereas many of his fruit-trees, bountiful mothers of the orchard, had borne their autumn progeny so long that their limbs now failed them, and Sam had consequently to provide them with props and crutches, he yet stood as firmly on his short, plump, knee-breeched legs, as any gardener of sixty-four could wish.

"Ah!" said Keppel, "you fellows find a difference, I daresay."

"Difference? You may say that, sir! Look here! All between these walls, the missus she has full swing; and it's awful, it is!"

"Snobs, Tittypee," said Horace, sententiously. "Cads, Sam."

"Iggerant!" added the gardener. "Why, it was on'y the other day—just step behind the greenhouse, Mr. Horace; my ears is good, though my eyes ain't. It was on'y the other day she sends for me. 'Mr. Tittypee,' ses she, 'we want some strawberries.' 'Do you?' ses I (to myself, o' course). 'Want some strawberries,' ses she. Ses I, 'My lady, I ain't got none.' 'Got none, Tittypee! what does that mean, sir? we saw some lovely ones yesterday in town, we did.' 'Oh, I dessay, my lady,' I ses; 'forced things, without any sort o' flavour, 'cept steam.' Ses she, 'Now don't talk to me, Mr. Tittypee. It's very evident they *can* be grown, and I shall expect a basket of strawberries from you to-morrow afternoon.'"

"And her ladyship was disappointed," said Horace.

"No, she wasn't. Mrs. B.'s a prancer, and that wouldn't do. I ses, 'You'll find 'em very expensive, mum,' 'And suppose they cost a guinea each, if I choose to have them?' 'Very well, mum,' ses I; so I just sends up to London, and by next day there they was."

"Come, come, Sam, that was too bad."

"Wait a bit, Mr. Horace, you ain't heard the end o' the story, yet. Mrs. Butler then come into the hot-house, just as the boy brought in the basket, and I had scarcely time to throw a mat over 'em, when she ses to me, all smiling, 'Well, how do the strawberries come on, Mr. Tittypee? Can I see them?' 'No, mum,' ses I, 'I'm afeard not; I'm just gettin' the colour into 'em, and the light might spile 'em.' 'Ah, well, never mind; but how red and flurried you look, Tittypee,' she ses (she's werry suspicious). 'Well, mum,' ses I, 'raisin' strawberries at this rate *is* worritin'!' 'No doubt, Tittypee; no doubt,' she ses; 'here's a shilling for the trouble I've given you!'"

And the worthy gardener went off into a chuckle which at one time threatened fatal consequences.

"But," said he, pulling up gradually, while a significant and curious expression crept over his countenance, "that ain't the best joke from that quarter."

"Nothing better, surely, Sam?"

"Oh lor yes!" replied Tittypee. "But no offence, Mr. Horace; you'll never let it be mentioned again."

"Don't make conditions, Tittypee; and don't imagine that I have the smallest interest in these people's affairs."

"Beg your pardon, sir, 'm sure; but as it was about you——"

"About me!" exclaimed Horace, in a less dignified tone; "what do you mean, Sam?"

"Well, I had no business to tell it, because I promised my little Martha to keep it a secret. But, hows'ever—little Martha's my niece, you know, sir; and, since she has been at the house with Miss Butler, she hears things and sees things; and gals will be gals, you know, Mr. Horace; they snuffs sweetheartin' like Mr. Popples says horses snuffs the battle, a far off; and so——"

"Well?" cried Horace, impatiently; for Tittypee paused, rubbing his head.

"Well, the long and short of it is, Mr. Horace, Miss Sophy's got your porkrate, sir!"

"Got my——? Beg your pardon, Tittypee."

"Your porkrate; your likeness—you know, sir—done in black-lead pencil, in her sketch-book. And from a few little things as I've heard drop from our Martha, I really think she's sweet on you, Mr. Horace. That's tidy, ain't it? The impudence of some people's wonderful!" And Sam commenced a contemptuous chuckle, nothing doubting that he would be accompanied by Mr. Horace. He had not laughed long, however, before he was checked by the embarrassed and serious expression of the young man's face.

"Come, Tittypee, don't be absurd; there's nothing to laugh at in that, I'm sure: and nothing very marvellous either."

"Oh no, Mr. Horace: not at all surprisin'; but I looks at it as a liberty. That's how I looks at it."

"My dear Tittypee, it is not necessary for you to look at it at all; and in fact you'll oblige me by not looking at it any longer;" remarked Horace. "And let me remind you that a bad stock sometimes sports a good bloom!"

"Oh, as far as that there goes, sir, that's all right. Miss Sophy's as nice a young lady as anybody could wish to see; it's her family, put alongside your family, as makes me speak."

"Very kind of you, Sam; but now, to please me, drop it."

"I'm willin'," said Sam sulkily.

"Tittypee!"

"What is it, sir?"

"You are sure that black-lead affair *is* a portrait of me?"

"No mistake about it, Mr. Horace. My little Patty have seen the likeness of your grandfather, as old Weaver, at the Goat and Boots, bought in from the what-ye-call-it—sale, you know—and she ses there's not a pin to choose betwixt 'em, only the old gentleman's porkrate is more robuster, she ses."

Keppel bit the handle of his cane. "Sam," said he, after a pause, "do you think I might trust you?"

"What with?" inquired Sam, cautiously.

"Do you think I might take you into my confidence in a certain little affair I have at heart?"

"Well, I daresay you might if you liked, Mr. Horace!" replied the gardener, more sulkily than ever.

"Oh, if I have hurt your feelings, I beg your pardon, Mr. Tittypee. Well the fact—the long and short of it, as you would say—is, I have come here to meet Miss Butler."

"Oh—h—h!" ejaculated the old man, slowly scanning the young one's face with his little grey eyes.

"And you can enable me to do so comfortably—not only now, perhaps, but at other times. You understand."

"Don't see how, Mr. Horace."

"You know when and where Miss Butler usually walks."

"I do: early in the mornin' 'fore the park gates is open, and late in the evenin' arter they're shut; that's when, don't you know. Well, down away among them bushes, near over to the meadows: that's where."

"Ah! Thank you. Very well. Then lend me a gate key: opening a gate is much easier than climbing a wall."

"*Is* it?" said Sam, with another keen glance.

Replying to this glance, Keppel said: "My dear old Strephon, I've tried it! but that is not the greatest inconvenience. Tittypee, you were once a little boy, I suppose!"

"Thank God!" cried the old man, clapping his hands suddenly together, and looking over Keppel's shoulder, with a half-melancholy, half-pleased, wholly abstracted gaze.

"And consequently you used to steal the preserves?"

"Thank God!" said the other in a low tone to himself. "That is—beg your pardon, sir, but I was thinking of when I was a boy; and the moment as you mentioned it, I see myself sittin' in our school, eatin' of a sour apple of a werry hot day. Lor' bless us all! No, sir, preserves may be good poachin' for gentlemen's sons, but poor people's little uns crib for wittles. *We* used to fish dainty bits out of the pickle tub (which we made our own pork), and cook 'em on the sly in the bed-room when we went to bed, with a few 'taters. Ah, what suppers they was!"

"Rather spoiled at the time by the fear of being caught in the fact, though?"

"Right again, sir. How we used to bolt 'em, to be sure!"

"Well, that's precisely my case now, Sam. I introduce myself into the pickle-tub—that's this park, you know—and I have an interview with Miss Butler, who's the—you understand,

Tittypee? But the risk is considerable; and, once discovered, you perceive——"

"All up!" said Sam. "No more pork."

"Very well. Now, you must assist me. Fortune threw you in my way with that view. What's the name of that confounded dog of yours?"

"Tiger."

"Chain Tiger up: for I shall walk here for an hour longer to-night, and re-appear in the morning. You, of course, keep somewhere between the beeches and the house (hovering like a guardian angel; you would cut up into three); and should any one not Miss Butler approach, do you whistle, or something in that way. I shall know the signal, and a disagreeable surprise will be avoided, perhaps."

Having thus comfortably settled the matter, Keppel did not care to wait for a reply; so, slipping a half-sovereign into the old man's hand, he strayed off coolly, but in a roundabout way, toward the beeches.

"My eye!" cried Sam, looking now at the half-sovereign, and now at Horace's retreating figure, "here's a stroke of business! Suppose now—let's see! Nothin' succeeds, whether it be plants, or whether it be plans, wirrout it's wetted. I'll step over to the Goat and Boots—'taint two minutes' walk outside the gates—and think o' that over a little drop. I can be back plenty o' time to do Mr. Horace's business. Besides, master, he never stirs out arter dinner, and nobody else ain't got no time to; so there's no fear about the young gentleman's being interrupted." And off he trotted.

Having got his little drop, the old man carried it into the parlour, and carefully shutting the door, planted himself exactly opposite the portrait of that Keppel with whom died the respectability of the family.

Tittypee winked. "I say, old cock," said he, nodding familiarly at the picture, "it's all right—that's my opinion, mind ye!" As if the portrait, naturally having no opinion of its own, might possibly lay claim to the idea at some after period. "The property's coming back to us, and more too! What do you think of that? I say, look here! Your grandson's arter the gal, and the gal's arter him: and the old coal-seller ain't got no more relations than her. Werry well. Then he'll get the property—won't he, eh? Werry well, then; and I shall have my salary rose for assistin' on 'em to do the coortin'; and that's more. Here's toward yer! Here's towards a jolly good master, what never sent the overpludge of my fruit-trees and cowcumber-frames to market, and took the dirty money! Mr. Hugh Keppel, you was a master as was a master, and a gentleman as was a gentleman: and here's to you!" and Samuel Tittypee, having previously imbibed at the bar, stood up, and drank to the portrait in solemn silence.

Meanwhile, Horace strolled among the beeches, which were pretty close, and offered sufficient seclusion, especially as not a few clumps of thorns were dotted amongst them. From this end of the park he got a view of the house at a point which had been strange to him for many years, and he started with surprise and disgust at finding the ivy which had graced the north side all stripped off, and a half-dozen tin cowls veering over as many chimneys. "By George! I'll make an alteration here," cried Horace, "if you prove amiable enough to give me a chance, Miss Sophy."

Many other "improvements," internal as well as external, had been made in the hall since its occupation by the "new people." In the skull of Daniel Butler the bump of veneration was extremely small. He was fond of saying that there was no mistake about him, and no humbug about him. He went in for the practical and useful; the poetical and ornamental were not in his line; and besides, they did not pay. With those ideas, ten pounds ten, and only eighteen years of experience, he had started as a retail coal dealer in Ratcliffe, and now what was he? Now where was he?

Accordingly, when he took possession of the place, he went in company with a surveyor over the whole mansion, in search of poetical, sentimental, or ornamental nooks and corners, to be converted into practical uses. "This," said he, pointing to a magnificent stained-glass window, "I will have altered." "Please yourself," answered the surveyor; "but I doubt if you'll get anything handsomer." "Know nothing about that; what's the use of having paint on glass?" "As a work of art, that window is unmatched in the county, and never will be matched now; and as to the use," added the surveyor, hoping to save it on the score of utility, "the glare of light through so large a surface of plain glass would be unpleasant, if not at times unbearable." "Oh, well, there is sense in that. Now I'll tell you what we'll do, then. We'll have that casement bricked up to a handy size: and then filled in with decent clean glass, with nice narrow sashes. Besides, you see, that will give us a good bit of wall each side to hang up a looking-glass or something." It was accordingly done; the architect buying the "old painted glass" for five pounds, and afterwards selling it in Belgium for almost as many hundreds. And in this way Mr. Butler proceeded, turning the house out of window, or rather the windows out of the house, till he had brought it up to his idea of perfection.

If it was true, as Tittypee remarked, that Mr. Daniel Butler never moved out after dinner, it was unfortunate for Horace that he selected this evening to make an exception to the rule. It was singular, too (though I do believe Mrs. Popples could account for it), that Butler was slightly disguised, and made straight towards the spot where Horace was "pacing sadly up and down," like the Lord of Burleigh. Horace saw the brisk, keen, razor-edged Daniel approaching; and, seeing that he could not possibly either remain where he stood or walk away without being recognized, glided behind a clump of thorn, and began a botanical investigation at the roots. For the second time, he hid from the face of the house of Butler.

He did not escape the searching eyes bent towards the spot. Butler walked straight to the young man's lurking-place, stopped, and poked toward him with his stick.

"Halloa! Who are you?" he cried.

Horace rose to his feet, crimson with confusion; and after stammering in an unintelligible manner for several moments, drew out his card and tendered it to the razor-edged person, who stood still poking his stick at him.

"Oh, *you* are Horace Keppel, are you? Well what do you want here?"

"Well, really," answered Horace, evading the question. "I beg ten thousand pardons for the trespass, since you seem to regard it as such; but between gentlemen, and all things considered——"

"What things?" interrupted Butler, sharply.

"Why, of course, you are aware," said Keppel, with a sort of forlorn hope that the father might be touched by a little of the daughter's sentiment; "you are aware that every foot of ground in this neighbourhood has a peculiar interest for me. It is surely not extraordinary that I, the last of the old stock, should once, and ardently, feel a yearning to visit a spot made sacred by the presence of the ancient gentlemen of my family." And Keppel waved his hand with graceful deprecation.

"Really now!—a pretty little speech, upon my word, a neat little speech! And such a violent and gentlemanly hankering to come and squat yourself behind that bush! Perhaps you will inform me what the ancient gentlemen of your family did there to make it so particularly sacred."

"I am in the wrong; and therefore I'll patiently explain. You may observe, Mr. Butler," said Horace, with a waggish twinkle in his downcast eyes, "that we have here a noble specimen of the *Leontodon taraxacum*, and I was stooping to observe it, as you yourself would have done, when you accidentally came by."

Butler had been sufficiently irritated by Keppel's allusion to the "old stock," "ancient gentlemen," etc.; he was doubly aggravated at this satire against his ignorance; but he could not help peering round the bush to see what Horace alluded to. Conceive his disgust at finding it to be a dandelion. Jerking his hat to the back of his head, rattling his watch-seals with his left hand, and shifting rapidly on either leg, as was his habit when in a passion, he cried shrilly—

"Lying toad an' practisin'! You yourself are a lying toad! and as for practisin' 'em—by George, you shan't practise 'em in my grounds! Now!"

Horace handled his stick threateningly; Daniel Butler detected the movement, and shifting so rapidly from one leg to the other that it almost amounted to a war-dance, he sharply struck the head of his own staff upon his hard palm, when out leapt a bayonet, thin and glittering."

"Not so fast, young man," he exclaimed. "I expected to meet a poacher, sir, and came armed accordingly."

"Poacher? You low-bred dog, what do you mean?" the other cried.

"Yes, poacher—poaching after an honest man's daughter, for what she weighs in guineas. I know what you came here for, sir, with your precious ancient gentlemen. A nice lot, judging from the sample. I tell you what, young fellow" (forcing himself to be calm, and thrusting the bayonet back through the head of his stick), "take a word of advice that won't be offered a second time. Don't you come here again! For the present, I am going as far as the great gates, and will see you out with pleasure."

It does not seem so singular now that old Butler did choose this evening for a stroll. Ah, that Mrs. Popples!

When the old man turned upon his heel, Horace, who had grace enough to see that he was in the wrong, and who was rather overawed by the other's determination, followed, or rather he went a pace or two in advance.

Daniel Butler walked along moodily, his eyes bent to the ground. That is the reason why he did not perceive a female figure glide hurriedly from the house, and pass quickly towards an opposite gate. Horace did see it, and exulted accordingly. So good-humoured did he become, indeed, that on gaining the gates, he said to his moody companion:

"Mr. Butler, I forgive you!"

"Just as you like!"

"You bear me no malice?"

"Not if you keep out of my way, and remember my advice. Wait! I'll give you another piece in. Look here! You might do a great deal better if you cut the company you now keep. Two hundred a year, you know, is about ten shillings a day: and that won't stretch over horse betting and wine suppers. If you're not very careful, you'll soon find yourself at the bottom of the till. Why don't you look about you?"

"Come, sir, that is my business."

"Exactly what I say. And being the only one you've got, it's a pity you don't look to it better; though, for that matter, you needn't be ashamed of any business. It makes money, sir; and see what money does!" And Mr. Butler looked proudly around him.

"I do see!" muttered Horace, bitterly.

"Why don't you go into business?" asked the old man, turning squarely round upon the young one. "You'd have a better chance than me; I started with a ten-pound note, sir, and no education!"

"Do you advise me to go into your own line?" sneered Keppel.

"Why, no," rejoined Daniel, quietly: "you'd find that too rough. But since you are good enough to ask my opinion, I should say something in the hair-dressing way would suit you! George, open the gate for this young gentleman; and look it after him. And if ever you find him here again, take him. He's a poacher." And Daniel Butler walked steadily away.

"By Jove, sir!" fiercely muttered Horace, as the bolt was shot upon him: then remembering the figure that glided so carefully from the house, he hurried round to meet Sophy.

Sophy it was, timidly awaiting the arrival of some one, whom we must conclude to be Keppel. For she came a few paces to meet him as he drew near, saying—

"This is rather cruel, Mr. Keppel. You know the last time you were there I only came and spoke with you, to warn you of the difficulty you were exposing us both to. It was rash: and—and—it's so unpleasant." Sophy blushed all the while, her romantic little heart beating loudly.

"My dear Miss Butler, if I have offended you too, my rashness is very sufficiently punished."

"I don't say that, but you see the awkward position into which you have thrown me; and then, as to yourself, I am sure I'm extremely sorry that, on my account——. I hope my father was not very angry, Mr. Keppel?"

"I must say he was," replied Horace, looking down with an affected air of anxiety.

"Dear, dear! what a pity."

Horace looked up, and their eyes met.

"You really should not have done so," she added, again blushing deeply, while her eyes glowed with that confused, embarrassed fire, which Love lights only in the eyes of Innocence. And so she offered him her hand, to bid good-bye.

Keppel took the hand, laid it gently between his own palms and said—

"Dear Miss Butler——"

But as that was the substance of his speech—the beginning, middle, and end of it—no more need be said. Enough that, as Sophy listened, she forgot that every moment added to the probability that her absence from home would be discovered; that, when he concluded, she did not withdraw her hand from his hands, but rather placed the other over them, saying nothing: and that again and again, after this time, Horace Keppel and Sophy Butler met, and no one was the wiser. Sophy certainly was not.

CHAPTER V.

DROWNED.

"ALL things considered, he is one of the very finest infants it was ever my good fortune to introduce into this world."

Although the impetuosity of Mrs. Howlett did not allow Dr. Poot to finish this remark (which, in a mutilated state, will be found in Chapter III.), the reader lost little. On such occasions, Dr. Poot always made this remark, to the delight of mothers, and to the great satisfaction of fathers: and he did so with more truth and consistency than at first appears. "All things considered," invariably prefaced the remark; and though in poor Lucy's case it meant much, in the majority of instances it referred to some obliquity of eye peculiar to mamma, some weakness in the head, or legs, appertaining to papa: malgre which, as naturally reproduced in the baby, it was as fine an infant as ever, etc.

In the case of Lucy's baby, however, the doctor's opinion may be fully indorsed, without reference to any considerations save those which his tender corpus itself suggested. Lucy's boy really was a fine baby. He was pudgy, he was mottled; he had an indescribable little bump between his eyes and his mouth, which at some future period was to take the form of a nose, however improbable that seemed at present. He sometimes bleated like a lamb gone melancholy—sometimes like a lamb gone mad: he had the regular number of fingers, his feet presented a properly corresponding variety of toes: and he was altogether a straight-backed, likely little fellow. That, of course, is as much as a man can say of any baby; and I feel especially bound to say it, because he is likely to take a prominent part in this history.

All men are equal when heaven calls them from the world, and they die: all men are equal, too, when heaven sends them into the world. As a dead man, I don't care a jot whether I am worth ten thousand pounds or ten pence; and, as a baby, whether you feed me with a horn spoon or a silver one, I am so indifferent, that I positively cannot apprehend the difference. One thing only I stipulate for, and get, whatever the quality of the spoon—bread, water, and milk. Lay me, as a healthy English baby, on straw, and see if I don't sleep sound: throw me, a dead Englishman, on velvet and eider, send my lady the duchess, and see if she can wake me! You might as well send the bellman. Give me, infant that I am, an airing in a carriage, and I may possibly take it quietly: but let me be borne in my mother's arms—that is the ne plus ultra of the thing.

What a blessed dispensation this is for indigent babies! Poor, indeed, must be the mother who has not enough bread, not enough water, for the little mouth that has to be fed first: as for the other article, it is the poor mother that gets the most, in my humble and, perhaps, indelicate opinion. At any rate, she has arms to carry her baby in; and she has no objection to carry it to the ends of the earth, should that be necessary.

How Lucy's boy would have got on had it been otherwise, I don't know. As it was, however, he prospered and crowed defiance to the world; he waxed fat, and kicked; and had you wasted your sympathies upon him, he would have smiled in your face, merely. With his mother, alas! it was quite another thing. How many days she tramped it, listlessly rather than despairingly;

how many times she slept between the farmer's ricks, when he would not let her sleep in the barn; how often she took a little bread from her pocket and dipped it in the brook, and so sat down to dine before she had broken her fast; how a great gipsy woman robbed her of her shoes, exchanging them for her own worn and clumsy ones; how Lucy was immediately after detained two days in the roundhouse, because the soles of those clumsy boots were found to correspond with footmarks left in a poultry-yard, whence some ducks had been stolen; all this we will pass over, especially as it failed to cause Lucy any new sorrow, or to rouse her out of the old one. It may be as well to remark, however, that the ricks of the farmer who would not let her sleep in the barn, did not thrash out a bit the better for it; the gipsy woman, whose motive in stealing Lucy's shoes were chiefly to adorn her feet for the surer ensnarement of a gipsy lover, got married, and was miserable ever after; while the parish functionary who could not distinguish an honest woman from a thief, afterwards discovered in himself an uncommon aptitude for appropriating the deposits of a savings' bank. So the world wags, and what a wag the world is.

Passing over these events, then, we overtake Lucy in a stranger's house, and her boy in another child's cradle. There he lies sucking his thumb as vigorously as if it comprised the whole duty of babyhood, and as if he were not born to be a hero. In a well-worn, matronly-looking chair by the fireside sits his mother. Footsore, pale, and meagre, shattered, sick, and a beggar, she does not look as if she had ever been healthful or beautiful, or that she once won the heart of a fashionable young gentleman.

A night or two ago, sleeping at a most comfortable hay-stack, which had been cut low down upon one side, so as to form a sort of couch about one truss high, and where there was loose hay enough to form a counterpane, warm and fragrant, she dreamed that Horace was in London. Now, her waking hours and sleeping hours were so confused and dreamy alike, that, to her mind, the one was scarcely distinguishable from the other. Therefore, after turning, or rather tumbling, over the matter for awhile, she arrived at an indistinct idea that he *was* in London; and as indistinctly resolved to go there too. She travelled very slowly, to be sure (for she was but weak), and with many restings on stile seats and wayside banks; till at length breaking down, and having a notion that no hay-stack, however comfortable, would serve her turn, she begged a few hours' rest in the little cottage where we now find her. How strange was the feeling which came over her when she sat within four walls again!

"How far did you say it was to the City, ma'am?" asked Lucy, of her cottage hostess, who had concocted a hasty meal for the baby, and was busy stirring it in a little pipkin over the fire —"how many miles did you say?"

"Let me see: the milestone stands outside the village, down the road, and it's just twenty-three mile from that."

"Twenty-three miles!" echoed Lucy, faintly as the faintest echo.

"Ay," answered the dame, taking up the strange baby (her own was busy with the cat on the floor), and handling it in a style which would have filled the inexperienced Lucy with astonishment and admiration, under other circumstances—"leaving out the length of the village, it's just twenty-three."

"I thought I was much nearer than that."

"*You* thought! Surely you bean't goin' to London?"

"Oh yes, I must. Mustn't I?"

"Lor' save the ooman! You don't look fit to go as far as the milestone as I was speakin' on. Nor you shan't, neither, yet awhile, if I knows it."

"Oh, don't say that!" said Lucy, with a strange trepidation, and rising hastily. "I *must* go. You don't know what I'm going for, do you?"

"Should be uncommon smart if I did," said the woman, laughing, and whipping a full spoon into the child's mouth with wonderful sleight of hand.

"Well, I am going there to meet—to meet my husband," said Lucy, cunningly.

"Oh! you can't have a lighter journey then. But it's all nonsense. You can't start till you've had bite and sup. Sit down, will 'ee?"

Lucy obeyed like an unwilling child.

"How old's the little un, missus?"

"Five weeks and a day," answered Lucy. "Why do you ask?" It was plain that she was full of strange suspicions.

"What for do I ask? Reason enough, I should think, arter that. This little un on'y five weeks old, and you thinking of tramping straight off to London! Arter walking the shoes off your feet, and your bones a'most out of your body a'ready? Why there bean't two stone of yer altogether! Tom, now, would no more let me ——"

Here the good woman gave a glance at Lucy's hands, and saw no ring on any finger of them. So she just looked gravely at the baby, and began feeding him faster than ever. "Sold it, p'raps, to get bread," said she to herself. "How do I know? 'Tain't no business o' mine." Then aloud she said, after a while—

"Do you know any one in London besides your husband, 'ma'am!'" ("ma'am" was spoken quite distinctly.)

Lucy answered that she did not, and that she had never been there in her life. But what did that matter?

"Oh, nothin', if you're sure to find him. You *are* sure to find him, I s'pose? Got the address, and all that?"

"Yes, I shall meet him again. Sure—certain!" cried Lucy, with more vehemence than seemed natural, and staring at the fire as if she saw him there already. Rather an ominous place to behold him in, under the circumstances.

"Because if there should be any mistake, you know, and you *shouldn't* find him ——"

"What then?"

"Why, you'll wish as you'd stopped here, and been buried in the churchyard. That's all."

"You are only trying to frighten me—you want to keep me here!"

"God bless the ooman!" exclaimed the other, with a little burst of impatience; "what should I be doin' that for? I got troubles enough of my own—you mought take bail of it. Johnny gone for a soger and bread eighteenpence a gallon! No! I speaks for your good; and I speaks what I knows. Why, with this poor little creetur 'cumbrancin' of you, you'd starve in London—if you didn't do wuss!"

"Oh!" softly exclaimed Lucy, still looking into the fire.

"Countryfolk haven't no idea of London—they haven't," continued the woman, pummelling baby's back, after having half choked him. "I've tried it. Ses Tom to me, when we was married, 'Come to London, lass; there's fortins scrambled for there every day.' And so there is; and every hour and every minnit, too. But how many gets trod to death in the scramble? And how many people's bread goes to them fortins? And, then, talk of loneliness and solitude in the country! A forest's a forest—whether it be of trees, or whether it be of bricks and mortar—and I prefers trees; and I tell you what—it's better to starve on a bank, a-seeing of squirrels blowing their bags out wi' nuts, than to starve on a door-step, with people starin' at you with gold chains on their breasts and never a heart inside. One's natural—t'other ain't. None o' them gold-chained people 'll give you or your baby a crust, if you don't find your husband, ma'am—that's all I've got to say. And you'd better think on it."

"Don't tell me any more. He's there, and there we must go."

"At all events, you'll stay till morning. It's wearing on now, and you'll have to put-up a spell further on if you don't."

Without waiting for an answer, the good woman plumped Lucy's boy into the cradle, and busily set to work to "get Tom's supper under way." A little time after Tom came home. He was a gruff, good-natured fellow, and Lucy found it easier to answer his questions than his wife's.

Presently there was a whispered consultation between the husband and wife at the door of the cottage; and then they prepared to go out, begging Lucy to keep house till they returned. Simple enough was the subject of their conference, and simple the errand they went upon; but in Lucy's imagination it concerned her; they were plotting to prevent the continuance of her journey. So, taking heed of their road, she quickly attired herself, caught up her child, and, after leaving upon the mantelpiece the last coin she possessed—sixpence—she hurried away.

Now, as the cottagers had themselves taken the road which led to London, Lucy of course was obliged to turn in another direction. The cottage was almost at the upper end of the village, so that in a few moments she was again tramping alone on the dusty highway. A few paces further, and she came to a stile abruptly leading into a narrow lane. To escape out of the highway was exactly what Lucy desired: so, clambering the stile with nervous haste, she hugged her baby still closer to her bosom, and sped rapidly along.

Like a lazy lane as it was, it wound its way in a loose zigzag sort of manner, now running over to the right, now straggling off to the left—with this advantage to the wayfarer, that it gave him several distinct views of the surrounding country. Lucy, plodding along in considerable excitement, rejoiced in the windings of the lane; for at every turn she felt as if some new difficulty were placed between herself and pursuit. When she came to a little hill, she rejoiced especially; once over that, she should be securely hidden from the road on which stood the village from which she was hurrying. She redoubled her speed, therefore; eyeing the brow of the hill with a strange degree of impatience. At length she reached it, and as singular was the change which passed over and through her when she looked down below. She paused; the excitement which the moment before was so plainly marked upon her features began to subside—softer and softer—till at length it was superseded by a look of awe and surprise almost childish. Then, like one who goes through a valley famous in ghostly story, she timidly went on.

For on crossing the eminence, she looked down upon the church that was like the church in her own village, upon a clump of trees bordering a pool like Dedman's Pool, the place that was faintly pictured on her mind when she fled from home, and that was fifty miles off! Holy mother, it was the same!

The effect of this vision upon Lucy's mind was not remarkable, under the circumstances. It has been remarked that when she stood upon Mrs. Joliffe's threshold, and then, like a poor bruised and broken-winged bird, flew away, she did so with a stealth peculiar to thieves, ghosts, and mad people alone. A thief she was not; a ghost she was not—as yet; then a mad woman she must have been; and so, to a certain degree, she was. Still she was only mad nor'-nor'-east, like Hamlet; with method in her madness, and memory, and will. But now, alas! when she saw this church and this pool, memory, with too sudden and vivid a light, showed her that this was the place that had been prophesied in her dreams as the end of her wanderings: and then came gradual darkness, pitch dark. She had memory no longer—nothing but the childish awe and surprise, in which she went groping.

I think I had better come to the end of this chapter without further preamble.

Now, if you please, Lucy was like a ghost. A gamekeeper, who looked over a hedge, and saw her gliding down the hill with a pale light upon her face, and eyes filled with the solemn abstraction of the stars, turned away half frightened; and further on, a bird, flying over the lane past Lucy's head, suddenly wheeled about, and returned, with a shrill chirp. Lucy saw neither the man nor the bird, but glided steadily on.

The longest lane has a turning: so had that which Lucy travelled. It turned off into a meadow, and at the end of the meadow was the pool like Dedman's Pool. Lucy, walking at the same pace, went straight over to the pool, and sat down on its banks. She was not actually conscious that it was like that at which she had last parted with Horace Keppel: she was only conscious of some shadow of it lying darkly over her heart, and of some subtle fascination sweet and deep. Meanwhile the dusk fell, and a cool breeze blew, and the moon glimmered through the branches of the trees on the further side. When the moon rose above the tops of these trees, then rose Lucy. She placed her boy upon the ground. She went hither and thither plucking dry grass and gathering fallen leaves, placing them from time to time at the child's side. When enough was collected, then she made a little couch carefully, laid her baby upon it (asleep he was), and covered his feet snugly. Then she went to the water's edge, and, covering her face, fell forward into it, as a statue might fall. A drop of water sprang upon the face of the child, who woke, and looked innocently at the moon.

CHAPTER VI.

PAROCHIAL AFFAIRS.

A CONSIDERABLE parish is Latherwell. It possesses the quaint old church, which was so significant to Lucy, a rectory, a regular market-place, a roundhouse, and a vestry. A beadle, likewise, does Latherwell possess, so far as a cocked hat, a brass-tipped staff, and a coat with large cuffs, and much covered with gold lace, constitute that functionary; but as for an actual living beadle, that Latherwell will never rejoice in, till Mr. Tweakle dies, or, exhausting the patience of the authorities, gets himself turned out. The real beadle everybody knows; his portrait has been often painted, and is to be found in a dozen books more or less dull. The real beadle is the most official personage under the sun, not excepting the bimbashee or the drum-major. He is clothed with dignity, and perspires with authority; he is the terror of fruit-women, the Nemesis of vagrants, a scourge to the charity boy, a thing of fear to the pauper. He is a prowler round corners, a cutter up of "slides," an impounder of hoops, a devouring dragon for marbles. None of these characteristics belonged to Mr. Tweakle, and therefore he merely flattered himself when he called himself beadle. He was a tall man, on the whole—I say on the whole, because his legs were intolerably short, having a shy, uncertain air about them, as if they were ashamed of the imposture of trying to pass off for legs. Then Tweakle was fat, not with the fatness of a fat man, but of a fat boy; and a boy he also was as regarded his nose, which gave up the attempt to prove equal to the general proportions of his face at a very early period; likewise, he was boyish as respected his hair, which always looked as if his mother had just combed it out, preparatory to his going to school, or to visit a respectable relation. Mr. Tweakle possessed another peculiarity, almost unpardonable in a man of his station—his voice was much too small for his body. When he spoke he startled you with the piping of a tin whistle, when you rather expected to hear the tones of "the loud bassoon;" and involuntarily your eyes wandered to the middle button of his parochial waistcoat, that being the natural height from which such a voice should emanate. Moreover, he was a man with a heart one half jolly, and the other half soft. Again, partly perhaps on account of his juvenile voice and nose, he had an astonishing partiality for boys of all sorts and sizes. He was known to have made seasonable tip-cats for them; he corded the handles of their cricket-bats in private; and on one unhappy occasion, when he thought nobody was looking, was actually surprised by Mr. Gorelam, on his knees, in the act of drawing the peg of a top from between the chinks of the pavement! The reader naturally asks, How did he become a beadle? Alas! How did General What's-his-Name come to command a British army?

Tweakle's case, however, is to be explained; the general's isn't.

Mrs. Winch was a widow, and the matron of Latherwell workhouse (by a pleasant refinement it was called the "House of Industry"), when Mr. Tweakle kept a little tripe shop in the High Street. The rest is clear to the meanest capacity. Mr. T. was a widower: he was a nice domestic man. Mrs. W. had a little money, too much solitude, an amiable face, and the tact to disguise an unamiable temper. She visited Mr. T.'s shop for calves' feet, whenever they were ordered by the humane doctor for some poor pauper patient; and it naturally struck her that a man who could sell such deliciously white tripe would make a tidy, comfortable, homely husband. This idea was succeeded by another. How noble, how majestic he would look robed in the robes of beadledom! And how nice it would be to have a large beadle to support her through the vale of years, when rheumatism, which already threatened to make a permanent settlement in her back, would render necessary her retirement from public life! It had long been settled in the matron's mind, that if she married again her husband should fill the post which now in her imagination was occupied by Tweakle; and as that post was at the time vacant, and might be filled by "another," it became necessary to bestir herself at once. She did bestir herself; and the end of it was that, first, she engaged herself to Mr. Tweakle, and then, in consideration of her long and faithful services at the

15

poorhouse, obtained the vacant beadledom for the man of her choice. In a moment of weakness (it was during the honeymoon) the man of her choice accepted it.

Lest the Latherwell board should be accused of favouritism, I ought to say that motives of economy and Mr. Tweakle's great size largely influenced his election. The salary was fixed; the livery (made by an upholsterer—no tailor in the place was equal to it) was furnished by contract: and the board wisely thought they might as well have as much beadle and broadcloth for their money as they could get.

It is not too much to say that for a time Mr. and Mrs. Tweakle were uncommonly happy; but then appeared two great facts, and ever after they were only as happy as married people usually are. The fact which first came to the surface was, that Mrs. T. was a shrew; the second, that Mr. T. was no beadle. Mr. Tweakle pondered much over the one discovery; Mrs. Tweakle—who was of the parish, parochial—lamented over the other: and there was no more happiness for them in future. Nor did the matron alone discover the weakness with which her husband wielded the official cane: the board became aware of it to a painful degree; and it was only because of Mrs. Tweakle's super-excellence as a matron that her husband was tolerated at all.

In vain they expostulated, in vain they threatened; the *pseudo* beadle kept the even tenor of his way—the mild reprover of vagrants, the tacit encourager of street-games. True, the onerous duties of his office in vestry, at inquest, at christening, marrying, and burying, kept him pretty well employed; still, whatever leisure fell to the lot of the soft-hearted beadle was quite at the service of anybody who needed it. He would fetch medicine for the sick, run with messages from the dying, and carry home the loaves granted to some poor widow at the workhouse door. It happens this morning that he has risen very early to pluck nettles with the dew on them, having being told that a decoction of that herb was good for a little girl down with scarlatina, or something of that sort.

Beadle Tweakle wasn't satisfied with the nettles in the wood, so he proceeded into the meadows. "Why, dearie me," exclaimed he, as a child's crying reached his ears, "it's gipsies! It's those gipsies come again. What a fortunate thing it is that I have not my cocked hat on! Then they'd be tumbling up their children and their poor bits of traps, and scampering off for fear of me! I don't see any smoke, though, and yet the crying seems very near." And Mr. Tweakle, advancing in wonder a few paces further, and still looking upwards for the smoke, stumbled over the little couch that Lucy had so carefully made, and fairly kicked out its occupant.

"God bless my soul!" exclaimed he, clutching up the baby, who cried most lustily at his scarlet preserver; "wonder I ain't killed you! Dessey I *have* broke a whole lot of your ribs, like a stupid! But who'd ha' expected to find a hinfant all alone out here? And how *did* you get here?"

Tweakle looked round him for an explanation, and found none. Therefore, folding the child in the long lappels of his coat, he was about to move off, when his eyes encountered the little bed of grass and leaves, which his foot had only partially disarranged.

"Well, now, this is a most extraordinary thing!" said he, looking from the bed to the baby with an air of great perplexity. "You surely don't live here, little un?" And Mr. Tweakle's eyes wandered to the water, as he thought of mermaids and water spirits; but these speculations were brought to a conclusion when he reflected that neither mermaids nor water spirits were ever known to dress their infants in calico; besides, there was a woman's shawl about the child! So Mr. Tweakle concluded to think no more about it, but to turn his face homeward without delay.

Not to the workhouse, but to 22, Pump Street, where he lodged, and where Mrs. T. visited him, when all was right at "the house." And it was such a quiet workhouse—it had been snubbed down to so meek a spirit, that the matron sometimes left it to its own devices and an under-matron for a whole twenty-four hours; but being, of course, within hail at any moment, like the fire-engine. Not but that Tweakle well knew that to the workhouse the child must ultimately go; but then it was now only five o'clock, the board did not meet till eleven, and

the beadle well knew that paupers, great and small, had to undergo a great deal of examination, and not a little sarcastic pleasantry, before they were admitted to dip their spoons into the parochial gruel. But of course this was not all. The fact is, Tweakle liked babies, immoderately and bashfully, as some little boys love dolls. Never was he more happy than when he could get one within his long awkward arms, unobserved; and strange were the noises he would make over it. Mrs. Tweakle the First had never blessed her husband's home with an olive-branch; a misfortune which they mutually deplored for many years. When he was again married, he took an early opportunity of apprising Mrs. Tweakle the Second (in a round-about way) of his sentiments as regarded children generally; on which occasion he was instantly snubbed, and that in a manner which completely overthrew his rising hopes. Upon the whole, then, Tweakle rather chuckled over the prospect of having a baby all to himself for five good hours.

Behold him at home with the little stranger, accordingly. Behold him in his shirt sleeves, his face beaming with satisfaction, and the little stranger extended across his knees. The beadle has taken off baby's boots, and rubbed baby's cold feet with his great hands, before the fire; while the unconscious object of all this solicitude stretches out its limbs, and prues and crows. Tweakle is pleased to observe this, but still it is evident that he is not satisfied. The reason of his disquiet is, that he can't persuade the little fellow to eat anything. Tweakle has done his best, and has behaved most hospitably, as appears from the various viands with which the table is strewn, and all of which he has recommended in turn to baby's attention. There's a nice piece of cold pickled pork, some biscuits, a slice of beefsteak (hot), some cheese, the remains of an apple-pudding, and some toast; yet none of these good things will the infant stranger swallow. Tweakle is at a loss. From time to time he exclaims—"Can't be hungry, he can't;" but when he regards the eagerness with which the innocent creature endeavours to suck his thumbs off, the beadle cannot help being painfully oppressed with the suspicion that he has not tried the right thing. Happening to reflect, however, upon what would be the foundling's diet when it fell into the hands of a poorhouse nurse, suddenly a kindred idea beamed upon him—bread and milk. It was enough. Gently he placed the baby on a pillow which he had brought from his own bed, and at once proceeded to realize the happy idea.

A large loaf takes Mr. Tweakle, and strips it of its crust, which he places in a saucepan with a jug of milk and the whole of his sugar. All this he stirs together as anxiously and cautiously as a young witch over her first broth, while baby looks up complacently, as if he knew that the right thing had been hit upon at last.

By the time that half the milk has boiled over, Mr. Tweakle begins to think that the mess is ready; and accordingly tilts it into a basin with a turn of the wrist which he rather imagines is the thing under those circumstances. Then the beadle takes his little protégé again upon his knees, and conveys the food to the hungry little mouth with all the forms and ceremonies that usually attend the operation. Very picturesque they looked, the functionary and the child—the one so tender and careful, the other so contented and hungry; for, in fact, he seized the spoon with a voracity which rather frightened Mr. Tweakle, until he got used to it. This he did, however, after a few moments, and then all went swimmingly.

Behold them.

Behold the door open, and Mrs. Tweakle standing aghast, one step within the threshold.

"Good morning, my dear," stammered Mr. Tweakle, making an attempt to cover his confusion with a smile, and the baby with the table-cloth. "I hope you passed a good night—a very good night, Henrietta?"

"Mr. Tweakle!" exclaimed his spouse in a hollow voice, "what do I see? Heavens! what do I see?"

"See, my dear!" explained he, heartlessly pretending to suppose that she must refer to the victuals on the table. "One's cheese! one's puddin'! That's a nice little spare-rib, that is, as ever I eat."

"Monster!" shrieked the awful matron, rushing forward and flinging up the side of the table-cloth with which the boy was

THE LAST HOURS OF WIDOW HOWLET.

covered. "Is that cheese? Do you call that puddin'? Does this resemble pork?"

"No, my love," quietly answered the beadle. "That's a little baby."

"Merciful powers, he owns it! He admits to my very face that it's a child! And whose brat may it be, sir, if I may make so bold to ask?" continued she, with overwhelming irony.

"Henrietta, I found it!"

"Ho! ho! ho! Ha! ha! ha! He! he! he!" screamed the matron, with the voice and complexion of a green parrot, and the grin of an exasperated she-cat. "That's good! That's beautiful, Mr. Tweakle! You won't beat that, sir, if you try for a month. You can't tell me, I s'pose, in what baggage's premises you chanced to pick it up, can you, sir? or whether there happens to be another or two anywhere? Oh, Tweakle! was it for this I raised you from obscurity? Was it for this I allowed myself to be cudgelled (she meant cajoled) into becoming your wife? Tweakle, you're a wretch!" and with this the afflicted soul threw herself into a chair.

Not that she believed her husband unfaithful any more than you do. She would have staked her life, and, what is more, her savings, on his domestic rectitude; and she enjoyed her sufferings accordingly. Sweet are the pangs of jealousy when you know there is no foundation for it. Mrs. Tweakle would not have lost this chance of becoming an injured and indignant wife for five pounds sterling; and she had serious thoughts of putting a climax to an occasion which might never occur again by going into hysterics, when Tweakle placed the child on the floor,

and came over to soothe her. This being the case, she burst into tears instead. Thrice did the poor beadle recapitulate all the circumstances attending the child's discovery, before Henrietta would be comforted, and then she only shook her head and stared miserably at the tea-kettle.

At length she said, faintly—

"Tweakle, don't ask me whether I can forget or forgive, but take it immediately to the House. You may deceive me, you may insult me, you may break the vows that you made at the altar, but all I ask is, Take it to the House immejate!"

"Well, well, missus, of course," replied her crest-fallen husband, who really began to feel as if he had trampled on the feelings of her whom he had sworn to cherish; "but there's time enough yet: let me give him the rest of this bread and milk."

"William!" ejaculated she, in slow and agonised accents, "do you wish to break my heart?"

That settled it. Even Tweakle's humanity could not withstand such an appeal. He sighed, and put on his coat, while Lucy's boy returned to his thumbs.

At eleven o'clock, borne by the beadle, he appeared at the board and, not being able to stand before it, was laid upon it: said board being a large oblong green-baized table, whereabout sat twelve gentlemen, with Mr. Gorelam, the chairman, at its head.

"What the deuce does that brat do here?" said Mr. Gorelam, as his eye rested on the child. "Take it away, Tweakle."

"Please, sir, it ain't settled yet. It's a desertion, gentlemen."

"Got the deserter?" asked Mr. Gorelam, looking fiercely round the room.

"No, sir. I found it, sir," explained the beadle, a sickly smile glimmering over his large face, like the light of a farthing candle expiring on a window-blind.

"*You* found it, sir? What do you mean by you found it?"

The distressed beadle then detailed all the facts of the case, during the recital of which Mr. Gorelam leaned back in his arm-chair, placing his thumbs in the arm-holes of his waistcoat, and from time to time dealt out an "ah!" in various tones. Mr. Gorelam was great in the use of that exclamation—no man more so. There was nothing in the way of incredulity, or sarcasm, or abuse, that he could not express by it. Its dexterous use had made many an honest man stammer and blush, and many an honest woman cry; on one occasion it was so successful, that a poor fellow whom it insulted, having no more logical or appropriate rejoinder, threw an inkstand at Mr. Gorelam's head, and was sent to jail accordingly. In Mr. Tweakle's case, it only meant, "You confounded ass!" and now, "You call yourself a beadle, do you?" And every time Mr. Gorelam vented the exclamation, all the other gentlemen smiled, and looked as if they had said so too.

"Ah! Found it and brought it here—did you?" ejaculated the chairman, when the story was finished. "Do you know what you have been probably doing, Mr. Tweakle?"

"A Christian act, I hope, I'm sure, sir," answered he, meekly.

"Well, if it's Christianity in robbing a mother of her child, sir, I entirely agree with you. What proof have you that the infant is deserted? Come now!"

"Ah," said the board; "come now, Mr. Tweakle!"

"Because I found it at half-past four, gentlemen; and because there ain't a house within a mile from the spot where it was laying, and nobody about; and it was on private grounds, where no labourers ever have to go; and," added Tweakle, coming to a climax with enthusiasm, "because it was so gallows hungry!"

Mr. Gorelam roared, not with indignation, but with laughter. "By George, Tweakle, that isn't bad! Gallows hungry, eh? Gallows hungry is the word, sir! Gallows hungry they all are that come here!"

And the board laughed too, and dug their elbows in each other's ribs. Great men are said to be known by the influence they exercise on those around them. What a great man, then, was Gorelam! Even Tweakle laughed—a little.

"That'll do, sir!" cried the guardian, again becoming severe, as he heard the beadle's feeble laugh. "I'll take your view of the case, and suppose this child purposely deserted. Now, Tweakle, you call yourself a Christian"—(Mr. Gorelam had noticed the beadle's remark about Christian charity, and felt bound to controvert it, as a dangerous dogma to introduce before a parochial board), "of course, then, you believe in Providence. Very well. Now, how do you know that Providence did not cause that child to be abandoned for a special purpose, to be worked out in some inscrutable manner, which you have marred? Have marred, sir!" and the chairman looked about him with pious severity. The board, who did not pretend to be equal to the chairman's indignation, only looked pious, and shook their heads at the beadle. "Now, I tell you what I call that: presumption, Tweakle; flying in the face of your Maker, sir!"

"But, if you please, Mr. Gorelam, if I had not have taken up the child, it would very likely have rolled in the water."

"Well, sir! What's that got to do with it? It's pretty clear to me that you don't read your Bible, Tweakle. The same Providence which hung Soloman up by his hair, sir, and carried the Jews to eat locusts and wild honey for forty years in the wilderness, may have designed that child to roll into the water. And you go and interfere!"

The beadle looked down and shuffled uneasily with his feet. That view of the case was too much for him. There was a brief pause, during which the board settled themselves in their seats, and coughed, as people do in church after prayers. Then Mr. Gorelam, having exhausted the moral and religious views of the subject, turned to the practical.

"It's a fortunate thing for this parish, Tweakle, that its officers are none of them so weak as you. Two such officers as you, in

fact, would bring us to insolvency. Now, I assure you that in my walk from Gorelam House to this place, I met scores of children, some on doorsteps, others in gutters, looking nine times as lean and hungry as this creature here (for I suppose it *is* a creature); but what do I do? Was I ever known so far to forget the laws of political economy as to relieve them in an indiscriminate and irregular way? Did any one here ever know *me* to go prowling round byeways, and hedges, and ponds, looking for paupers to burden the parish with? No, sir! No, Tweakle! I know my duty better; I know the laws of political economy better; I know that when you give a destitute man a shilling in an irregular way, you pauperise him; and when you pauperise him, he's done for. He loses his independence; he gets idle, he gets indifferent, he gets drunk: in fact, you pauperise him, and he's done for."

Who would have thought that a shilling could do so much injury to a hungry labourer? And yet, according to the political economists, Mr. Gorelam was right!

The board looked at once learned and angry at their beadle, as Mr. Gorelam finished his little speech. Tweakle, though he did not at all see that Lucy's baby was in danger of getting idle, or indifferent, or drunk, at present, was overawed by the chairman's arguments, and felt miserable, ignorant, guilty.

"Well, gentlemen," said he, with a meek voice, "suppose I take it back again. I'm sure I don't want to run agin the ways of Providence, neither of this parish; but still——"

"Oh yes! you can take it back, of course, and lay us open to a charge of fiendish inhumanity in the next number of the 'Latherwell Lynx.' Very thoughtful of you, Tweakle, and worthy of the judgment with which your functions are generally performed. No, sir! The child is here, and here it must remain. It only rests with us now, gentlemen, to give it a name."

"Gin and bitters!" drawled Mr. Rudd, opening his eyes like a tortoise.

Mr. Rudd (a butcher and one of the board), who had lapsed into a doze, caught Mr. Gorelam's last remark, and thought it referred to something to drink.

"Ha! ha! Not bad in its way, Rudd; but that name will hardly do. Godfrey's Cordial would be more in his line. Our friend Tweakle, however, will probably suggest Julius, or Hannibal, or Adolphus: won't you, Tweakle?" said Mr. Gorelam, turning the tap of his small-beer sarcasm upon the already crushed beadle. Adolphus we may remark, was the name of Mr. Gorelam's own first-born; and a beauty Adolphus was.

"No, sir; not at all, sir. None o' them heathen and pagan names," responded Tweakle, who thought this might have something to do with Providence too. "But since I'm asked, gentlemen—Moses, now."

The board having made up its mind to laugh at Mr. Tweakle's suggestion, whatever it might be, were at once convulsed, of course. Consequently, Tweakle's feeble explanation about "bulrushes," and "Pharaoh's Daughter," was drowned in the cachinnatory flood that flowed all round the table.

"Well," said that portion of the board which was formed by a haberdasher, "the child must have a name you know. What do you think of 'Thursday.' It's uncommon, but still we have a precedent."

The haberdasher uttered the word precedent proudly, as if it were worth fifty reasons.

"Where, I'd be glad to be informed?" asked the chairman.

"Oh! Robinson Crusoe, of course," replied the little haberdasher. "When Robinson was cast on the desolate island, don't you know, and the savage hooked it away from the cannibals, don't you recollect, he called him Friday; and then, don't you know ——"

"Of course, I know all about it, and I won't say that, in Crusoe's case, the notion was a bad one; because, you see, it wasn't likely that he was going to adopt more savages then there are days in the week. Our case is slightly different, Mr. Jones: we may have twenty children thrown upon our hands in the course of the year; and if we adopt the Crusoe style of christening, we shall have to add to the day, the date of the month on which the children are found. This, for instance, would have to be Thursday, October seventeen, which would be awkward, Jones."

"Altogether too elaborate a handle for a workhouse mug," said the wit of the board.

There was another laugh, which had the effect of waking the innocent subject of all this discussion, as he lay on the table; and who, lunging out his legs, discharged Mr. Gorelam's inkstand into his waistcoat.

"Here! hi!" shouted the chairman to the matron, who entered the room at that moment, "take the little wretch away, Mrs. Tweakle. Here's the ink running all down my legs, inside!" And the chairman, rising, shook his legs like a ballet master.

"But," said the matron, taking the baby in her arms, and kissing it (she was always amiable before the board), "what, gentlemen, are we to call the little poppets?"

"Poppets!" snarled the inky Gorelam. "Woppits, if you like!"

"Thank you, gentlemen," the matron said, taking Gorelam's bad joke in good earnest; and "Woppits" was accordingly borne off to be "raised" in the customary manner.

CHAPTER VII.

A SKIP INTO THE FUTURE.

TIME flies—there's nothing to prevent it.

Near the place where Horace Keppel now lodged was a grand old house, the seat of a grand old Catholic family. To the house was attached a little chapel, in which early every morning rang a bell calling the domestics to prayers. At one time it called the people of the neighbourhood to prayers also, and therefore it was a loud bell; and it roused Horace Keppel in a morning of May with its sweet solemn tolling.

"By Jove!" he exclaimed, springing up into a sitting posture in his bed, "I've slept too long! There go the bells!" He eagerly looked at his watch, but though his eyes were wide open, his senses were still half asleep, and it was several moments before he ascertained that it was only five minutes past seven o'clock. Then he gave a glance round the room, remembered where he was, remembered what bell it was that had broken his fitful, fevered slumber, and threw himself back with a sigh of relief.

"Slightly turned, I suppose," said he, alluding to his head, which he propped up with his arms. "Slightly turned by the imminent consummation of my good fortune; and so mistook the droning of that papistical kettle for the chime of my marriage bells. Not surprised, though (what a way little Sophy would have been in!), for it still seems a piece of luck too good to be substantial; and though I've thought of it for years, and calculated on it, and though this is the very day—by George, who knows? Miracles are uncommon in these days; and if this affair *does* conclude at ten o'clock a.m., as easily and as beautifully as it has gone up to this point, that'll be a miracle of good fortune.

"But I tell you what," continued he, supporting himself upon one arm, and addressing himself to his reflection in an opposite looking-glass, "I wish everything had *not* fallen out so luckily in this business; it has been too even—too easy—and looks suspicious. When a woman's all smiles, she's probably a 'do!' When Fortune never frowns, she's probably a humbug. She intends to demolish the castle of your imagination just while you roof it with your last card!"

Horace Keppel in the bed nodded impressively to Horace Keppel in the looking-glass, who returned the salutation with great gravity.

"Look at the facts," continued the more substantial Horace. "Old Butler might as well have had ten children as one. In fact, considering that he began life in poverty, it was most natural that he should have a considerable number; but no—he had one only; and so his property remains undivided. Smile of fortune number one! Then there were equal chances that that one child would prove a male, especially as Mrs. Butler was a woman of a very manly constitution herself, it seems; however, the child was female. Smile of fortune two! Now, I might very easily have got married eleven years ago to Diana, daughter of Major Rack, and the succeeding year to Alicia, relict of Captain Manger; but the first was taken off by a rash, and the latter,

being in liquor, was drowned at a water-party. These circumstances (which were fortunate, anyhow considered) we will take conjointly as smile three. For at the time when poor Alicia was lost, the daughter of the house of Butler was fast becoming marriageable, and (smile four) went deep into romance instead of applying herself to book-keeping, as might naturally have been expected of her. In process of time, she of course began to construct a romance for herself; and a hero being necessary, she selects *me*, whom she had never seen, and had never heard of, save in disparagement. Smile five, by Jove! Then, quite fortuitously, as it seemed, and contrary to all possible calculation, I make discovery of the young lady's sentiments. I obtain an interview; I stand the test of actual inspection; I am the lover of the lady who's the heiress of the father that hasn't got any more children! There's a series of caresses which defy computation. But what follows? The father discovers the intimacy, and decidedly forbids it, with insult to me. At first that seems like a reverse; on the contrary, it only fixes the daughter's inclinations; she nails her colours to the mast—she resolves to die fighting, with the true blue in her bonnet. Fortune again. Now, Butler sees his danger; he says to himself, 'The young man is a gay and reckless young man; get him into a barrack at a distance.' Accordingly, he presents me, in a round-about way, with a commission; and henceforward I make love to his daughter on every opportunity as a soldier of the King's; and I've so much more money to spend. Another smile of fortune. Meanwhile, time flies. Sophy comes of age! she offers to sacrifice everything for me; to fly with me. 'Patience, my dear,' say I. 'Little do you know the misery of respectable poverty. But promotion must soon follow, and then——.' For I had a strange sort of a confident idea that something would turn up. And how did it prove? Why old Butler *did* die! just as I had got tired of the mess-room! just as dear Sophy had begun to fret and get troublesome! just in the nick of time, in fact, and without leaving an impediment to our marriage! Now that's a course and a degree of fortune to be afraid of, almost, eh?"

The two Keppels again nodded at each other significantly.

"But if it's the will of Providence to restore the fortunes of the family——"

"Of course, then——!" responded the Keppel in the looking-glass, with a pious and philosophic glance. On which the former threw himself back upon his pillow, and the latter disappeared altogether.

There was another piece of good luck which Horace had not forgotten, perhaps, but shut the eyes of his memory upon. How fortunate it was that Lucy had taken herself out of the way so completely! How likely it was that by this time she was dead, and the youngster too! Not that he wished her dead, that would be merely monstrous; but if, in the regular course of nature, such a thing had happened, so that she could never turn up again, it would be an absurd delicacy to deny that it was so much the better for him. This train of thought led the young man to imagine the manner of her death—if she *were* dead—which her long absence, and the silence of all the world respecting her, rendered probable. And when he remembered what had passed at their last meeting, when he considered how she had been found by Mrs. Joliffe that night, and how suddenly she had fled the house of that good woman at an after time, he came very naturally to a correct conclusion; he was afraid that it was likely that she had committed suicide, or had died of exhaustion, sorrow, and all weariness, in some friendly cottage, or under some friendly hedge. That was not a pleasant reflection for a young gentleman about to marry, and he didn't like it. But what could he do? He couldn't help it.

"Tell you what I can do," he cried, starting up upon his elbow again, and looking the other Keppel full in the face, who instantly came forward. "When this affair is over, I shall be able to do something for her people. There's her brother Mark, who was scarcely in his teens when that affair happened. Now I shall want a man: I'll take him."

This generous resolve released him from all further reflection on the subject; and his more sanguine spirit returning, he leapt out of bed, and arrayed himself as a bridegroom should; by which time, a neat carriage, drawn by a handsome horse, was at the door, which carriage Keppel entering, he was driven away. It will surprise the reader to learn that it was his own private equipage; but that is easily explained. As soon as Mr. Butler died, Horace sold the commission which that gentleman had bought him. This gave the young man a sum of money sufficient to enable him to live handsomely for a year or so, at the expiration of which time he would be master of Keppel Lodge. The carriage, however, he hardly dared to venture on, and he had no credit. But his friend, Captain Doo, had a horse which he did not quite want, and this offered a suggestion to Keppel. He at once bought a carriage admirably suited to the proportions of Doo's horse; the animal was harnessed, and then Keppel threw up a shilling. "Tails!" said the captain, faintly. "Heads it is!" exclaimed the other, with equal nonchalance; and accordingly drove off, the owner of the entire "turn out."

"It was not more than two miles to Keppel Lodge, where Horace alighted. Five minutes after came his friend Captain Doo, accompanied by young Snaffle, of the same regiment. Another and another carriage arrived, and then the bells of the old church burst out with a peal as if they had gone mad. That seemed to be the opinion of the rooks, who retired to their haunts, and listened in grave silence. Ding-dong-a-dong-a-dong-a-boom! Boom! boom! ding-dong-adong-adong! with a rattle and a clangour that flowed out upon the air, like ripples in the water when a stone is thrown. At length, in an unhappy moment, the sound flowed in at the lattice window where Widow Howlet lay, at her last extremity.

CHAPTER VIII.

DARKNESS AND LIGHT.

WHEN Keppel's marriage bells—swinging, plunging, rattling—made themselves heard in Widow Howlet's bedroom, she raised herself in her bed, listening. Dong-dong!—and then a look that was incredulous, and yet too credulous—a look, ironical, bitter, and altogether strange, passed into her face. Her eyes, that were now the dim eyes of age, gleamed with a slow-gathering and wicked smile; her lips, thinned of all their youth, parted and curved in sardonic anger; broad deep lines, legible with evil writing, came out upon her forehead, over which her gray locks came creeping down. Boom! boom! ding-a-dong-a-dong! —the bells hurtled it at her all the same, while the air hummed louder and louder, well pleased: even the dull air in her own sick-chamber purred about the window with quiet satisfaction. The woman noticed it: dying people have eyes and ears for many things which health is too stupid and animal to observe.

"I hear that!" said the woman, her listening face turned to the window, and speaking with a voice more emphatic than thunder, though it was as low as the sharpening of a knife in oil. "I hear that! I am alive to hear it, and the Lord lives. Oh! the Lord lives—defending the innocent, strengthening the hands of his servants—their rod and their avenger—the scourge of the unjust—the upholder of his people! Faithfully I have served him, day by day: he has let me live to see my reward!"

The poor, infatuated, mortal woman shook her thin old hand towards the window, with a scorn that was terrible, and a defiance that heaven put mercifully aside.

"I have waited," she went on, with an eloquence borrowed from the blessed Book whose teaching she had so often misinterpreted: "I have waited with an abiding trust. I said when I was strong, and full of my righteous vengeance, 'He is stronger than I; he will avenge me! My child's blood cries from the ground, and it is heard. I am his servant—faithful from infancy upward; he will put my enemy under my feet. He will destroy him, and I shall see his destruction: righteousness shall be glorified. So I waited day by day. So I withheld my hand, so I kept my peace, so I saw my child's murderer flourish, without anger; nay, I rejoiced at it! The greater should be his fall—the longer should he be in falling—the more terrible his example to the sinful world—the greater the glory of his saints. Deceived! deceived!" screamed she, banning the fair heavens with uplifted hands: "cheated of my service! robbed of my just vengeance! Who strikes for the vassal of the Lord? Who put the sword from my hand when I could hold it? Who gives it into the hands of that child of the devil to pierce me through to my death-bed, as he sent the soul of my daughter to infamy and her body to an infamous grave? Who? who?" again she cried, while her gray hair strayed upon her shoulders affrighted, and her eyes glowed with a madness—that was to pass away.

Who? who? The room echoed with it. Who? who? The echoes escaped out into the little valley, so that Mrs. Howlet was compelled to listen as they sadly seemed to return the question upon her. For a moment it awed her—she was still as the pool in which her daughter was drowned. No matter. In the midst of the silence which followed, before the dumb air could recommence its humming, she threw up her arms and again shrieked—"Who? who?" defiant.

The echoes repeated it more pitifully than before. When they fell, the crazed woman also fell back upon her pillow.

Mrs. Howlet was for the moment alone. A neighbour there was who waited upon her pretty constantly, though Mrs. Dadd's own household affairs required attention from time to time. Mrs. Dadd, who lived not many rods off, heard the old woman's cries; and though she was at that moment in the act of once more washing little Billy Dadd, and had just reached the point at which the soap always entered his eyes, she nevertheless abandoned him, and ran to Mrs. Howlet's assistance.

"Dear hairt, Mrs Howlet! dear hairt, what's mattur?" said this good woman, all the way upstairs. "What!" she cried, aghast at finding the old woman as still as if she had never known how to speak or move, "ralee asleep! Can't be dead!" and Mrs. Dadd was at her bedside in a moment, the image of terror. "No, that she bean't! But dear, what a yowlin'! Well, then, it warn't she—it warn't no human voice that yowled. Mercy on us, it's a warnin'. 'Who! who! who!' three times, as I'm a sinful ooman. Who gave you that neame?" said Mrs. Dadd, crossing herself, and spitting three times over her left shoulder. "My godfeathers and godmothurs in their battisum! Oh, dear! there's Billy a yowlin' too."

And Mrs. Dadd softly descended the stairs, audibly renouncing the devil and all his works, and proposing to call in the neighbours.

But before she had reached the door, the old woman had opened her eyes, and taking a stick which stood at her bedside, she struck it on the floor loudly and repeatedly. Mrs. Dadd was arrested by the signal, but not daring to go up again, she cried, "What is it?" The old woman only thumped upon the floor all the harder; but this being in the nature of a natural and reasonable response, Mrs. Dadd mustered courage, and went half-way up the stairs.

"Yes, ma'am," said Mrs. Dadd, when she had got so far.

"Come up," replied the old woman.

Mrs. Dadd went up.

"Close that window, and fasten it."

Mrs. Dadd, little re-assured by the concentred excitement which the old woman exhibited, did as she was bidden with an alacrity almost wonderful.

"Draw the curtains—close! Shut out those abominable sounds!"

The large cap of Mrs. Dadd flew back from her head, so hurriedly did she obey the command. But it was scarcely obeyed when the sick woman cried out—

"No—no! open them again! Open all—doors, windows, everything! It stifles my vengeance, which shall not be stifled! It shall be fanned into fire by the winds that bring these sounds in. Fanned into fire—fanned into fire!" gasped she, as the curtains were drawn, and the lattice swung back, and the sound of the marriage-bells came pouring in again, like a freshet.

"Now fetch my son—run!"

Mrs. Dadd ran.

"Now, Edith's son, Mark, was employed in the neighbouring town, at the house of a tailor and haberdasher, to whom he had been apprenticed. It was, therefore, too much of a run for Mrs. Dadd herself, especially considering her situation, so she went home, completed Billy's toilette, and despatched that quick little boy on the errand.

Billy Dadd had scarcely come in sight of the Barlow's Arms —an artful alehouse, which waylaid the traveller at about a quarter of a mile from the town—ere Edith Howlet began to look anxiously for her son's return. By the time Mark had received the message, she had grown impatient; and he had scarcely set out before the old woman had risen in her bed, and was watching the door.

At length he came in, not without having spoken rather loudly below, that his mother might know he had arrived; for he disliked anything sudden. There was nothing remarkable in this young man's appearance, except that he was like neither Lucy nor his mother, that he had a look of shy determination, and appeared like a man who kept his friends, as he fought his enemies, at a distance. Such a man as he was, he awkwardly entered his mother's room.

The old woman, whose eyes lit up anew when she heard Mark's voice, held out her hands to him the moment he appeared.

"Mark!" said she.

"Well, mother—how are you?"

"Did you come through the village?" she asked, taking one of Mark's hands, and stroking it in a caressing manner, though little to his delight.

"Yes."

"Past the church, Mark?"

"Yes, past the church. What for?" said he, afraid that his mother was about to broach the disagreeable subject of burying.

"Was anything going on, my boy?"

"Going on, no! Mr. Keppel's married to-day, I believe."

"Oh! Mr. Keppel married to-day—Mrs. Howlet dying to-day. Ah!"

"What are you talking about, mother?" Mark asked, as the old woman, looking now into his face, and now at the hand she was stroking, poured out this remark, with that voice of hers like the sharpening of a knife in oil.

"Don't you think *that's* something to be going on, Mark?"

"I really don't see what you mean, mother."

"Mr. Keppel married to day—Mrs. Howlet dying to-day, you know."

"What has he to do with you? He don't owe you anything, does he?"

"Not owe me anything, eh?" cried she, through her set teeth. "Not owe——! You have heard of Lucy, I suppose?"

"Went away and died," said Mark, epitomising all he had ever heard on the subject.

"Lured away, spurned away, hounded, driven, dragged away, and died. That's it, Mark; and Mr. Keppel owes us *her!* My son!" murmured the old woman, stroking his hand faster and softer, caressing it, purring over it, her tongue trembling, her head nodding a ghastly emphasis, "Make him pay! make him pay!"

As his mother spoke, Mark's mind woke slowly out of its customary torpor, and made as if it would open its astonished eyes. Many years had his mother lived in a dark, angry silence, like the bronze statue of a Fate, her life simmering within like the uncooled metal of the mass. Now it appeared as if her impassive, exterior nature was itself becoming plastic again in the fierce heats of passion. Mark could but wonder at, and fear the change. Erect, stern, stately, she had been; now she was supple enough, and menaced, and wheedled, and screamed, and whispered, all in a breadth. There must be some profound reason for all this, or else, like a poor old dying woman as she was, she wandered. That was a natural solution, and it gave Mark less trouble than any other possibly could, if it gave him some grief. But he was prepared for grief, totally unprepared for anything like mental exertion; and therefore he rather hastily embraced this explanation of his mother's strange words and equally strange manner. It allowed his mind to close its astonished eyes, and go to sleep again.

"Mother," said he, "take some of this barley-water and lie down; you are wandering." At the same time he released his hand from between hers, and insensibly drew it down the skirt of his coat, wiping it of those witch-like caresses.

With the molten metal glowing in her old eyes, she regarded him. "Is this," she said, "another of those providences which attend the steps of the righteous? a son that mocks me—a man blind to dishonour, crawling in a stupid cowardice, dead to the flesh of which he is alone? A thing barren of good, and destitute even of wholesome evil? Am I defrauded of the world too? Mark, I'll show you what it is to be a man—all that you ever pretended to be. Lift me up. No, stand away! Adam is born again in me, and in his strength I rise!"

Accordingly, she rose, standing in her tall white gown upon the floor.

"Now I go, in half an hour, to Keppel Lodge—to the wedding! Go down-stairs, Mark!" With one hand she pointed to the door, with the other she snatched her gown from the wall.

This was such a methodical sort of madness that Mark opened his eyes to the full, and then dawned upon him a complete comprehension of the case. Nevertheless, his attention was, of course, immediately riveted to the ghostly figure which, by the grace of the devil, was made to stand there, strong in life, even upon the very brink and verge of death. He was awed; and his awe consolidated him. "Mother," he said, with a firmness thus derived, as well as from some other feelings newly awakened within him, "don't be foolish. Come—I begin to understand you. Just get into bed again, and say what it all means." At the same time he placed his hand upon her arm. The clothes which she had taken from the wall fell to the floor; she cast there, also, a grim, satisfied smile, and obeyed her son.

"Now, then," said he, taking a chair which stood by the bedside, "what's it all about?"

"Take this key. Open that little drawer there, at the bottom."

Mark did so. In the drawer he found a knot of ribbon, and a baby's cap—very little, and yellow, and soiled with much handling.

"That's it," said she, as Mark took this innocent little article between his finger and thumb. "That's what it's all about."

"Keppel?" he asked, a dark stain gathering round his lips.

"Keppel!" and she cursed him.

"And Lucy?"

"Died in a ditch," nodded the old woman.

Upon which Mark uttered a curse also.

"Ah, that's all very well," ejaculated she, with a short, low, bitter laugh; "but it's not to the purpose. I've tried it, my son."

"I'll try it another way. I'll go and cry him publicly in the village. I'll tell the story in at his very windows, and that to-day!"

"And get put in the stocks."

"What! I'd kill him! I'd kick him to death in the streets!"

"His own horse could do it better."

"Then by heaven here's something that'll settle the score to your satisfaction." And lashing himself into a sort of fury, which, at the best, awkwardly became him, he took down an old birding-gun.

His mother, who knew him well, smiled again, muttering—

"If you dared—and then they'd hang you! Ha! ha! You brave, wise, terrible men! hunting and slaying from immemorial time, and swaggering for ever with a knife! Foolishness! Did it never occur to you, my son, that of all things that can be taken from a man, his life is exactly that which he least misses?"

Mark stared. This was a new view of the subject.

"Shoot his dog," pursued the old woman, "if you must spend your wrath in powder, but don't be guilty of the folly of shooting *him!*"

Mark from looking philosophical, looked moody. "What *is* to be done?" he said; "I suppose that's the question."

"Kill his dog," she repeated derisively. "That's a life he *would* miss. His wife would probably be a smaller loss. Had he a child now——! Ah, Mark, as he may have! Do you hear? That and the money he has married for! That and to bring home to him the pangs that a murderer *should* feel! Mark! Mark, come closer, my son! I see it! I'll show you the way to vengeance."

Mark approached her. She took his hand again, and stroking it as before, talked and talked softly, while he listened with constrained attention. "Suppose," she began, and "suppose" was the basis and the burden of her charge; but then she supposed with so much detail and precision that Mark could not but stand astonished. When she had finished, she said, "Now you have observed, and you'll remember."

"I will," he replied.

"Say that again, my son."

"I will!"

"Or any other opportunities, any other chances that lead to a like result, you'll take advantage of?"

"I will, mother."

"That'll do, then. It is not fit, it is not right, that villany should go high-handed through the world. It must be plucked down, and laid in the dust as a warning to all future villany, and for the safety of the innocent. Now there's an end of it." Releasing his hand, she sank down upon her pillows. Mark, glad to close the interview, went away.

He had scarcely left the room, however, when Mrs. Howlet, thumping the floor with her stick, recalled him. "Mark," she said, "I have a fancy. Give me a lock of your hair."

"What for?"

"You shall see."

The old woman handed him a pair of scissors from a work-basket that lay upon the bed, with which Mark reluctantly cut off a lock from the back of his head. What did she want of it? Mark was curious to see, and a thrill passed through his never hot veins as he beheld her painfully weaving it into her own gray locks. Significance flashed from her eyes as again she said: "That'll do!" It was a strange pledge to carry to the grave, an imperishable pledge, that would remain when she herself was resolved into dust.

But who thinks that it was to remain there—that brown lock amidst her gray locks? Who dreams that this woman, who had toiled so painfully along a mistaken path of righteousness, was thus to be abandoned to evil at the end of it? The hard, stern, merciless creed in which she lived could only end in darkness and confusion; but she had been *earnest and faithful* in her creed—she had sacrificed her own flesh, she had consumed her own human heart in it—and a way was made out of the darkness and confusion, and at length there was Light.

How, we cannot describe. This only can we say, that presently the night fell, and when it was quite dark, then this poor soul, who had been tossing in dreams that seemed years long, woke—opened her eyes wide as the eyes of youth, and wept the tears of youth.

"O mistaken, mistaken!" she said in the dark. "O blind, O deaf, O dull as a stone! Mercy and love, you wicked heart—mercy and love are the laws of heaven. There are none other, and how easy are they! Lucy, my love—little child that was Lucy's, oh forgive me! Heaven forgive me!"

Why, this *is* forgiveness, thou poor soul! Earnestness and faithfulness go for much; and as for this late madness of yours, this darkness and confusion, it is a sort of light, too, by which you see that ALL is not godliness that glitters in this swaggering world. But——

"Mark, Mark!" she cried.

No Mark in the house.

"Mark!"

Here comes the half-witted Mrs. Dadd, if you please, saying the rest of the Catechism. But as for any son of yours, poor soul! he's far out of earshot. Now, what will you do?

Trust, and question the providences no longer. And take out his hair from hers, leaving it as a token for him; and take forth from its careful wrappings a little silver curl, that had been Lucy's when she was a child, and which (ah! who knows himself?) had been all this while near her lips when she slept, and fast braid that in her gray hair instead—carrying it to the grave as a token, too.

Which she did, no man nor woman knowing it.

CHAPTER IX.

AN INTRODUCTION.

So the mother of Lucy is also dead, and Mark Howlet is in due time promoted to be the valet of Keppel, according to the resolution which that young man made on his marriage morning. He thought it a good, virtuous resolution; we shall see how it ended. Mark himself had a dim superstitious forecast of what would come of it when the post was offered to him. For the rest, time still flies, and still there's nothing to prevent it. Among other things, it presently flew over the grave of Sophy Keppel, *née* Butler, died young; and not, on the whole, sorry to die, except for the sake of an infant daughter. The manner of her death we pass over for the present: it was what will happen to tender-minded, susceptible women, when they find the romantic dreams of their youth dispersed with coarse language, and discover the idol of their youth to be a log, floating at the mercy of strong waters.

But although years a round dozen have now passed away since, in the parlour of the Goat and Boots, Samuel Tittypee imparted to the Keppel portrait his idea of the future fortunes of the family, that snug, brown, home-cured, and rambling old hostel has undergone little change. It does, indeed, seem to have grown smaller, from that mysterious cause which narrows and vulgarises every house, and street, and village, and town that was dear to us of old. But whatever that agency may be, it has little present influence over old Weaver. He increases in dignity and in bulk day by day, and is at this date at least three stone heavier than when he was first heard of in connection with this story. Consequently, he is more plainly than ever to be seen in his cosy seat between the bar fireplace and the little keg of "particular," on which he still keeps a favouring eye, and across which still strides the vine-crowned Bacchus, in his customary state of intoxication. Farm labourers still roar pastoral songs in the tap-room of an evening; and as the evenings are many, and the songs few, there is a certain monotony about them, which serves to keep up a conservative spirit. The parlour company, too, seems to be the same. True, the barber, that book-learned man, who knew more of the state of the nation than any man in Old Sleaford, who, though he was sometimes beaten at bowls, never succumbed in politics, who used to nail his colours to the malt, and who would at any time die (*i.e.* get dead drunk) rather than give in, is at last finally deceased. But he has a promising successor. A younger man he is, and, perhaps, not so learned; but he is certainly as Radical, and is even thought to be the superior of his predecessor on the subject of Bishops. Indeed, he ought to be a clever man, who night after night has to tackle the saddler, and bold must he be to attack the Church in presence of that ferocious Tory.

There is another remarkable addition to the parlour company of the Goat and Boots. On looking about you modestly, you particularly observe a young man, who takes no conspicuous part in the assembly, but rather sits apart, in a corner which custom has made his own. If you were to see him from behind, you would be first impressed with the difficulty of fitting him with a coat; observing him, as you do, from the front—and, face to face, you are still more struck with the difficulty of fitting him with a character. It is worth while, however, to describe this young man's features, as, should you happen to know any one like him, it may throw some light upon a material part of this narrative.

His head is small, elongated, and evenly turned, like a cocoa-nut. His hair, which is thick, and red, comes much nearer his eyes than it ought, considering the height of the head; and it lies there—the hair upon the forehead—in a straight, unparted line. His eyes, of a warm brown, are overhung by sandy eyebrows, which, partly from their hanging so low, and partly from a certain air of their own, quite indescribable, seem to keep his vision constantly at half-cock. He also appears to be short-sighted; and he blinks and winks in a manner which leads you to suppose that light affects his eyes, and that he might see best in the dark. The young man's nose is peculiar too; and, judging from the fact that the young man's head is always thrown back, as if to accommodate that member, it is also an important one. It starts from between the eyes in an abrupt, keen angle, like the index in a sun-dial, and joins his lip as abruptly and as keenly. It is here, evidently, that all his character lies; and if his nose only changed its expression, as his eyes and mouth naturally do, that index would pretty clearly tell you what o'clock it was. The nose is ably seconded by the chin, which strikes you at once as painfully sleek and bald, fringed at its extreme edge with red hair, so as to have the appearance of a little forehead. It seems strange that the hair, which grows so thickly on his brows, should vegetate so scantily on this portion of the rich fat soil; but you remark that he has a habit, whether speaking or listening, of kneading his chin with his finger and thumb, which probably accounts for the baldness. As for his mouth, it is a little mouth—like a kitten's.

The young man lived with his mother (his father had been

dead for many years), at the further end of Old Sleaford; and over his door is a board with this inscription: "Joel Hatcher, Broker and Miscellaneous Dealer." And there he sits smoking his pipe, not as if he had any acquaintances, but rather as if he were looking out for one or two.

Mark Howlet enters, and Joel, slowly waking out of his torpidity (which, after all, may be merely assumed), greets him with some show of interest.

"Good evenin', Mr. Howlet," says he, extending a huge pale hand. "Hope I see you well, sir."

"Ah, Hatcher! how goes it? How do, gentlemen all?" observes Mark, as a sort of introduction, and so seats himself comfortably.

Mark's master was landlord of almost every man present; and Mark was treated with a great degree of respect consequently.

"See you out this afternoon, sir, with the little lady," said Joel, interrupting the silence which Mark's entry had occasioned. "Beautiful she looks, sir; beautiful, I'm sure."

"Oh, yes, Miss Ruth's very well," answered Howlet, in a manner which seemed to betray some repugnance to the subject. "So she ought to be."

"Of course she ought! That's what I was going to say."

"Very well, then."

"Quite took to you she seemed, too; pretty little soul!" persisted Joel. "Bending down over that there saddle, and a talking to you as innocent and affable!"

"Why shouldn't she talk to me innocent and affable!" Mark struck in, abruptly.

"Ah! why shouldn't she?" echoed Joel, caressing his chin, and looking at the other with his dull, half-cocked expression. You'll be about the best friend she's got, now her mother's dead. I suppose you *are* the best friend she's got—eh, Mr. Mark?"

"Ain't she got her father?" asked the barber demonstratively.

"Got her father! Yes, she's got her father; but I've observed that somehow since Mrs. Keppel died, Mr. Horace he seems too moody like to take notice of the young lady much. What's more, I've heard so. Seems as if the missis's death preyed on his mind. Don't you notice it, Mr. Howlet?"

"Death's a dreadful thing anywhere and anyhow," answered Mark shortly.

"Ah!" said some of the company, wagging their philosophic heads. "'Tis so!" exclaimed others in a more practical tone of voice, while the rest, lifting their mugs, drank, and sighed.

"Especially when it comes as it came to her—so young and that. I wonder what she did die of, after all the talk?"

"Broken hearted; that's about it, eh, Mr. Howlet?" said one, who knew, as all the company did, that Mark entertained no very cordial feelings for his master.

Mark looked as if he had nodded.

"Fudge!" cried Joel; "she didn't die o' that. There's no such thing."

The parlour took its pipe out of its mouth, and looked at the speaker in astonishment.

"How do you know?" said the saddler, fiercely, for this was an attack on a very ancient institution indeed.

"Because it's impossible. I've read a good bit about these things, and I know it's no more possible to break your heart with grief than to break your leg with it. What the lady did die of, of course I don't know; dessay it was one of these new complaints with Latin names, as comes from London. What I say is, her heart wasn't broke."

"Do you know better than the papers? and ain't you read over and over again in crowner's 'quests and that, 'Died of a broken heart?'" The barber said this: Mark looked on and said nothing.

"Well, if I was a crowner——!"

("*You* a crowner!" growled the saddler.)

"And one of them cases was to be called before me, I should say, 'heart be blowed,' and I should dive lower down."

"And what would you dive for?" asked the Tory, contemptuously.

"Poison," answered Joel, quietly, "whether I found it or not."

"Ah! you're wrong, young man," broke in the thin mild voice of the parish clerk. "According to you, the many broken hearts we hear of are murders! No, no! It's my opinion that murder always has and always will come out, some day or another."

Everybody looked grave.

"Look at the queer things that turn up to convict murderers," continued the clerk. "Look at the fine hairs and clues that God Almighty takes care to let out for justice to get hold of, and how patiently justice pulls in and weaves them together, till it makes a rope to hang the villains."

"That's all very well," Joel remarked, "but it ain't all. As we see how near the thing is to go undetected, oftentimes, it's pretty certain that some cases never get detected at all. The murderer, the murdered, and the secret all get buried together, and no mortal's the wiser. Not but what threads and clues will hang round the finest and cunningest plots it is possible to weave, do all we can to hinder. Talking of murders, and how they are discovered, reminds me of a story which, if you're agreeable, I'll tell you."

Hatcher had told some extraordinary stories already, in that parlour, on occasions when, as on this evening, he had exceeded a second pint of ale. Therefore everybody was agreeable. Joel looked round him. He saw the tailor's wife come in for the tailor, and dexterously starting the story, the tailor's wife allowed peace to her lord, for she was constrained to listen too.

Let the reader follow her example, nor imagine that this episode has nothing to do with the story.

CHAPTER X.

JOEL HATCHER'S STORY.

"To the best of my recollection, where happened what I am going to narrate was called Ashford, or Ashfield; at any rate, it was somewhere on the Sussex coast. Like most places, Ashfield had its Beauty, who, according to all account, was about as vain and wilful as they all are that I ever met, both man and woman. Her father was a coast-guardsman; and, as he had lost his wife many years before, and this was his only child, you may depend he was proud enough of her. She did pretty much as she liked with him, as she did with the rest of the men-folk. When she said 'shall not,' old Gathercole said no more; when she said 'shall,' he said 'Ay, lass!' Among other whims, she found it disagreeable to live in the towers, as some coast-guard families did; she chose to live in a house like other Christians, she said. So the old man hired the upper part of Widow Valpy's house in the village. And there she was.

"As I've told you that Kate Gathercole was very pretty and very wilful, you expect to hear, I daresay, that she flirted and jilted all around. To settle that point at once, I'll tell you that she did nothing of the kind. Not but what she had offers enough; but the stupid ones she laughed at, the bold ones she frowned at, and kept from making promises and vows, as if she was waiting for some one that she knew would come at last.

"That, at least, was the impression; for, although John Valpy, the widow's son, carried her books to church, and accompanied her here and there, it was never supposed that he was the accepted. Nor was it easy to be supposed, either. John, besides being younger than Kate, was stunted and ill-featured; he had a slight hump, a club-foot, and his dwarfish figure and shuffling gait contrasted painfully with the tall, light-footed Kate Gathercole. At first, indeed, her father was afraid of the intimacy, till Kate assured him, in strict confidence, how things stood; when old Gathercole assured a crony on the same terms, and he assured some one else, till at length all the village was told in strict confidence, that Kate had chosen John Valpy to perform the small services of a gallant at his own earnest entreaty, it being understood that love was altogether out of the question.

"Although Kate Gathercole might have felt sure she had not yet seen the man whom she was destined to honour and obey, she must have possessed a very lively fancy if she imagined at all truly when, how, and where she should first behold him. She must, in fact, have imagined the good ship *Bunyalore* drifting on the rocks one stormy night, and seen it broken up in such a sea as no boat could live in. She must have pictured two score of perishing wretches, drifting on spars and planks, most of them to death, and all of them towards the shore. She must have seen, in her mind, a brave man loosening his life-belt from about him, and fastening it about a perishing woman, while he trusted his own precious life to a piece of ragged plank, and the Lord above that saw the Christian act. But, of course, she could not have imagined any of these things. I can only tell you, though, that they did happen in sight of old Gathercole himself, and that his heart so warmed towards the brave seaman, that he had him carried to his own house to be cared for, for he was half-drowned and terribly bruised.

"William Ray was the name of the seaman—mate he was of the good ship that went to pieces. He was a fine, clean-built, handsome fellow, quite handsome enough to win a woman's heart, setting aside his brave repute. His hurts were not serious, so that a few weeks' careful nursing saw him as well as ever. But gradually as young Ray had been coming round again, so gradually had John Valpy grown lean and pale, and his piercing black eyes more feverishly brilliant. The clever old women of Ashfield said he was in a decline; others, that his trade was telling on him (he was a distiller of vegetable poisons); but none guessed the true cause of his altered looks. Who could? Who could guess that John Valpy was over head and ears in love with the Beauty, in spite of his humped back and his club-foot? True, he knew his passion was ridiculous, and he knew what made it so; but he did not love Kate the less, he only hated and cursed his crooked figure the more. Nevertheless, he still spoke of her and to her in the same old tone of obedient respect, though the knowledge that the sailor man was walking over his head went far to gnaw out of his heart what little goodness he ever had in it. There were times, too, when John's self-possession failed him; but that was never while any one was looking.

"Meanwhile, as I said, Ray got well, and was, to all intents and purposes, Kate Gathercole's lover; and a mighty source of delight that was to the old gentleman, who relished the idea of having such a right-hearted fellow for a son-in-law amazingly.

"For three years did this go on—not continually, of course, for young Ray had his duties to perform and his bread to earn, and he was absent the greater part of the time. Judging from the number of letters he sent her, however, it was plain he never forgot his Beauty, on land or sea; and whenever he came back, he brought with him such a wonderful store of strange stuffs and outlandish curiosities, as kept all the village in gossip for a week after. On one occasion, he brought her a tiny crystal bottle, filled with such a pungent rose-scent, that (as everybody believed) if it had been emptied into the mill-stream, the miller might have ground his corn by rose-water for no end of time.

"Well, there was a voyage longer than any previous one, and then Ray came home, and then he married Kate Gathercole. The young people still occupied part of Mrs. Valpy's house, the old man went back to the Towers, and John Valpy pounded and simmered his herbs below. Although he knew it was foolish, and had a faint idea that it was wicked too, he had up to this time nursed a faint glimmer of something that could scarcely be called hope—but rather a vague 'perhaps,' which would not be altogether unpleasant if verified. Who knew? Ray might be wrecked; he might be starved or burnt at sea—things that did occur to mariners; or he might find on some foreign shore a woman he fancied better, and never come back—a thing which also happened to mariners, sometimes. When, however, Valpy found that no such casualty happened to his hand—when, as Kate and William came from the church where they were married, he watched them through the grating of his cellar, then the hope, or whatever it was, went out, and a much worse thing came in.

"It must have been a terrible sight—John Valpy in his laboratory that morning, tearing his face, striking at and cursing his humped back, and trampling upon his deformed foot with the other. No one did see him, however; more's the pity—it might have been a warning and a saving of life. His mother was nearly blind, and altogether deaf, and the happiness of the company above was too engrossing to be disturbed by what, if they had heard, they would have paid no attention to. No noise was thought strange in John's work-room.

"I can't describe John's feelings, as he sat there on a bench

after the first burst was over; but I can tell you what he looked like—as if he was having a snug conversation with the Devil. Presently he was startled by the strong, manly voice of the seaman calling him from above.

"'Come up! Come up, John! Since you wouldn't go to church with us, perhaps you'll come up and drink our healths, now we've come back.'

"Valpy, as he ascended the stairs, replied, 'Certainly, Mr. William, I'll drink your health. I felt too unwell to go to church, but now I'm much better!'

"Judging from the ease with which John now changed the expression of his countenance, as, in the sweetest of voices, he replied to Ray's invitation, it was clear the snug conversation had not been unprofitable to John, one way or the other. You'll see presently it was the other.

"'Come on, John, my boy,' cried old Gathercole, extending his hand, 'come and sit aside of me. Neither I nor Kate could think of your pounding away all alone in that smutty cellar to-day! You must know, Bill,' said he to Ray, with a proud familiarity, 'John was Kate's sweetheart before ever she saw you, and you put his nose out of joint, you dog!'

"'And suppose I was to be her sweetheart after that!' mumbled the devil within Mr. Valpy. If his heart had been bare at that moment, you would have seen a grin on it.

"'Ay, but we never thought of such nonsense as love-making; did we, John?' exclaimed Kate, looking at the same time happy and anxious.

"'No, we never thought of such nonsense as love-making,' echoed Valpy.

"'Never? Then you're not made like the rest of us, John!' laughed the triumphant husband, giving Kate a kiss with a smack that sounded like a pistol-shot in Valpy's ears. 'However, it's too late now, my boy, and you must make the best of it.'

"'That's what I intend to do,' cried Valpy, laughing, to conceal his rage. 'Not made like the rest of you, arn't I,' thought he, distorting the young man's innocent remark in his ill humour. 'No, my handsome jackanapes, I know I'm not. I've just found it out to the full. But as for its being too late, that's another thing!'

"'Too late, is it?' he muttered again, as he returned to his work-shop, that afternoon: which showed that he had not a bad memory for injuries, real or supposed. He stopped on the stairs as he muttered this, and for a moment he seemed to grow twice as big, and ten times as strong.

"By all accounts, Valpy was very clever at his trade—uncommon clever. He took such a pride in it, that he was known to get up in the night and practice it. He loved the company of those little squat bottles, with the heavy stoppers, better than any mortal thing, except Kate; far better than if they had been all silver and gold, and filled with good wine. Mind, I don't say he valued them because they held poisons and things that might take away men's lives. If this bottle contained a tasteless stuff, one drop of which would kill you—or that one a stronger still, so that if its stopper were taken out, and the snaky neck placed at the keyhole of your door, a vapour would steal away your senses and leave you dead before you knew it—I don't say that was the reason why he prized them, but because he himself had found them out. He loved them because for all his ignorance and his ugly despised form, he had found secrets which the tallest and the cleverest only dreamed about. Well, it was natural, too!

"Now, it had been arranged previous to this marriage, that Ray should give up his seafaring life—having saved a little money, which brought him in a little more—and turn coast-guard. So he did: and happy enough he was at it for months. But then the old yearning for the sea came back, and told on him. He grew restless; and, at last, when a letter came from his old captain offering handsome terms for a rather ticklish voyage, Ray coaxed his wife out of her consent that she should go just for one last trip. He left Kate well provided for, as in duty bound; and old Gathercole and Valpy saw him to his ship at Southampton.

"'Mind you, John, you little villain,' said Ray, cordially, as he shook hands with Valpy at the final leave-taking, 'take as much care of my wife as you did before I had her; and on the same terms, you know—no love-making and nonsense; and I'll

MR. HATCHER TELLS A LITTLE STORY,

bring you back one of those queer serpents that you talk of, if I can get aboard of one.'

"Now," said Joel Hatcher, pulling a long breath, and leaning forward to address the whole company, "I put it to you. They're all dead, and no mortal being is ever likely to know the exact truth. At the same time, I can't have any object in romancing; and, what's more, it's a thing I'm not given to, nor am I fond of it. So I just put it to you, to make out how you can, recollecting that women never *was* fathomed, and never will be. And then, again—these dwarfs. It arn't so much because they're ugly and deformed, that people feel fear of them, but because they seem to have a power in them which you're not quite up to, or aware of. Well, then, here you have the young wife on the one hand, full of admiration for her handsome husband; just known him long enough to make her love him ten times more while he was away; and knowing right well that he would have kissed the shoes she walked in, loving her though he did like a man. On the other hand, you have an ugly, and savage, and contemptible-looking rascal, fussing for ever among the queer bottles. Now, then, you don't think it likely, perhaps, that Kate Ray had a baby near two years after her husband went away, and that John Valpy was the father of it! Well, she did!

"No one knew it but themselves and Valpy's mother, for old Gathercole died not six months after his son-in-law went to sea —broke his neck down a cliff, he did; and Mrs. Ray had the habit of confining herself to the house so much that nobody got a suspicion out of that.

"The child was a miserable, puny little thing, and its mother's constant hope was that it would die. John Valpy hoped that it might not die—at least, not naturally; but that it might either live or be murdered: he did not much care which. For in the first case, you see, he had no doubt that her husband, when he returned, would cast her off; and then she would be glad to remain with him (John, that is) entirely. On the contrary (supposing, of course, that its mother put the child out of the away), he would then have a secret which would give him a constant hold upon her. It certainly did sometimes strike him that Mrs. Ray might confess to her husband, and that then he might not cast her off, but twist his, John Valpy's, neck instead; and then his thoughts would take another channel, and he would speculate on the chances of both mother and child dying before the return of William Ray.

"Well, the child was about two months old when news came that Ray's ship (which had been long detained) was homeward bound, and might be expected in port in about three weeks. That news came in just such a letter as a man *would* send to a young wife whom he had not seen for two years, and whom he had longed to see every day of that time. It wound up with the intelligence that the little venture he had made in the ship had proved wonderfully successful, and that he never meant to leave his wife again.

"Just you guess what she thought when she read that letter! and when, as she came to the end, the child cried from the cradle, and she went and looked at it! There it was—one day dying, the next day looking as if it had years of life in it. This day it lay very weak, and very little and thin. Perhaps it might die after all before he came! But then it might not, and something must be done. In two minutes she had made up her mind. The little villain down-stairs had hinted over and over again at the consequences of her husband's return, with a view to make her to go away with him to some place far off. That she would not do, for she hated him more than death, or even than disgrace; and so Valpy hinted at some other safe and easy means of avoiding exposure. It was time, she thought, to take this hint. So she sat down, wrote an account of the whole affair, sealed it, locked it up in a drawer where her husband kept his papers, and called John Valpy.

"'I want you to give me the stuff you spoke of—for the child,' she said calmly.

"'That *I* spoke of?' says he, quite surprised.

"'Yes, that *you* spoke of.'

"'Oh, ah,' said John, his black eyes glittering. 'I recollect now, but you must use it very carefully; for, you see, it's poison! Put one drop in a gill of water, and give the child a spoonful once a day, and it'll do him good. But not more than one drop to a gill, mind, for it's very powerful. Why, do you know that five drops would kill a grown woman.' And keenly he looked at her.

"'What of that? Let me have it!'

"'Have you a small bottle?' says he, meekly.

"'You have plenty below.'

"'Ah, but they are of a peculiar shape; and—well I'd rather not give you the medicine in one of my bottles.'

"Mrs. Ray, who saw the motive, and shuddered at and hated him all the more, went to her work-box—straight to her work-box—and took out, yes, the very little crystal phial all covered with gold threads, in which her husband brought her home the essence of roses. 'As well as another,' said she, in a bitter and a weary way, and so handed it to the distiller of poisons.

"Valpy took it, and a few minutes after was pondering with it in his hand before the squat bottles on the shelves. Now," cried Mr. Hatcher, striking the table, and startling the entranced company to a sense of the hot, eager, vivid interest that glowed in his face, "I've seen those bottles! Just as they stood there then—all of a row! White some, and some black-green, and all looking awfully quiet and still. Never mind, I handled them too; and being alone, I felt that if I did not get out of the cursed place without any more thought about it, I should soon be tasting of them! Well, then," he went on, wiping his forehead, and looking round at the company, at length fixing his eye on Mark, as the most deeply attentive—"Whichever of those bottles Valpy then took down, I don't know; but I've seen it, and touched it. He took it down, and let one drop of what it contained fall into the phial. 'How many?' mused he, staying his hand. 'Five drops for a grown woman—she quite understood. Shall I? If I do, she'll take it for certain;' and he balanced the bottle in his hand. 'I'll do it, and there'll be an end to the whole concern! If she's fool enough to kill herself, it's no business of mine—I've warned her.' And nine more drops plashed into the phial with the golden threads. He then replaced the big bottle on the shelf, and taking the little one up to Mrs. Ray's room, he placed it in her hands without a word.

"As Valpy hobbled down-stairs again, he heard the key of her door grate in the lock, and then he looked upon the death of mother and child as certain. Nor would he have been disappointed, but for an event which was scarcely expected. The child, who had been once more sinking these few days past, became suddenly worse. So sudden and decided was this change, that the mother was perfectly startled, when, on turning towards the cradle, she saw its dark and suffering face. Throwing aside the phial, she caught up her baby, and clasped it and rocked it at her bosom; and when she was tired of that, and the evening came on, she stretched it on her lap; and there it lay, till presently the light faded off it, and the life faded out of it.

"In such silence had she watched her baby, that when John Valpy crept up to listen, he heard not a sound to break the death stillness, and went down with a different feeling about him than ever he had known before. He hurried into his den, as if there he might escape from this feeling; but it was a dodge that did not succeed; on the contrary, he felt rather worse. Many

a night he had spent hours and hours in his cellar, with no other light save the glow of the little furnace; but now that was not enough. He must have light—a great light; for the furnace-glow cast such curious shadows about, and the shadows hovered and flickered, and went and came so strangely, starting up here, leaping at him there, crouching in corners like wild beasts ready to spring at him—that he could not stand it. So he lit a lamp, looking around with a sort of grin at the shadows, as they flitted away before the slow flame, as if they were really devils or wild beasts, and he had scared them.

"But though there was now a strong, great glare of light all round him, John Valpy's case was very little improved. The lighter it was without, the darker it was within. He felt stifled, as if he breathed only smoke and darkness, and was full of them. He loosened his cravat, kicked off his boots, and went shambling up and down, and round about, like a drowning mouse in a pail, to get air. Nothing would do. He must send his mother up to make discovery of the murder and suicide, and then he might go and rouse the neighbours with the news. He longed for the bustle and uproar which would follow; he longed to bustle and bellow himself, as the only way to be relieved of the smoke and darkness that were choking him.

"First, however, would it not be well to go up to Mrs. Ray's room, softly, and make *sure* that it was all right there? Obviously. So, taking his lamp for company, he crept stealthily up-stairs. But the light was thrown through the chinks of the door before he reached it, and at the moment when his hand was raised to knock, the door opened; and there, upright on the threshold, was the woman whom he thought dead. Pale was her face—she might have been a spirit: fear and horror burned red in her eyes—she might have been a spirit escaped out of the pit for a season. Valpy clutched the lamp with both hands, holding it before his face, and dropped on his knees.

"'Saints in heaven!' he groaned, 'what are you looking like that for? What do you mean? I thought—I supposed——' But John Valpy's lips had stiffened with the fright, and now they began to work so convulsively by way of coming to, that he could say no more.

"'You thought I was dead, you coward! You supposed I had made some unfortunate mistake with the medicine, and killed both myself and the child. No, here I am, alive, John Valpy!' She said this between her teeth, looking dangerous. Then she turned on her heel, and went back into the room.

"Valpy, who was too pleased to hear her speak to notice her manner, gathered himself up, and followed her. Peering round, he saw that the baby's cradle was covered close with a white scarf, which Kate Ray used to wear when she was an innocent girl, and the beauty of the village. Placing the lamp on the table, he tiptoed cautiously across the room, lifted the white veil, stooped, and looked into the cradle.

"'Hallo!' he exclaimed, starting upright as suddenly as if he had a spring in his back, which had just been released. 'Hallo—dead!' says he, looking at the woman. Now she had watched him tiptoeing to the cradle, with a terrible, fierce, and scornful smile.

"'Of course,' she said, smiling more and more, and worse and worse. 'According to your directions!'

"Valpy looked again at the child, and saw that it had *not* died of the poison. This perplexed him; but the part he had to play was quite the same, in any case. So, turning to Mrs. Ray, he said, 'Me! my directions! Your mind's unsettled, evidently. There! give me the remains of that stuff; you can have no further use for it.'

"'*Remains* of that stuff!' cried she, quiet, but looking dangerous again. 'Do you pretend then, villain! to suppose that in reality——'

"'Certainly I do,' responded he. 'You said so. What does "according to my directions" mean, except that you took advantage of my telling you of the dangerous nature of the stuff to poison the child?'

"Mrs. Ray gazed towards him in a vacant manner, and then, closing her eyes, turned away as if she was tired. 'Go!' she said.

"'Not without the bottle.'

"'You cannot and shall not have it. I may want it.'

"'Oh nonsense! Now, you know, dear woman, there's no

need of anything of the sort. Of course this is a terrible affair ; but still, everything considered, it is not to be wondered at ; and perhaps it was the best thing you could do. Heaven knows ! However, you can rely on me. What's to be done ? No one but ourselves and my mother know that it was born, you know. What do you say ?'

" Valpy had to wait some time for a reply. At last she said, huskily—

" ' Bury it.'

" ' And the poison ?'

" ' John Valpy,' she replied, facing him, ' if you say another word about it, I'll call in all the village, and take it in your presence and at your cost.'

" And so she went into the ante-room, and the child was buried.

" From that time till the return of her husband, Mrs. Ray kept herself, if possible, still more secluded. As for John Valpy, he found himself regularly baffled. He thought to have her under his thumb, as the sharer of her secret ; but her conduct by no means showed a disposition to be dictated to. On the contrary, she treated him with contempt and horror ; on some occasions so undisguisedly, that it almost seemed as if she wished to provoke his hostility. That she did not fear it, that she was perfectly indifferent to it, was certain ; and thus John Valpy found the tables turned on him. It was he who was constantly haunted with doubts and apprehensions. Could it be that rather than make terms with him, she had determined to let things take their course ? Did she mean, after all, to tell her husband the whole story, and abide the consequences ? When Valpy took this view of it, he resolved to quit the neighbourhood ; but the resolution was destroyed the moment after by his impish passion ; besides, he thought, if the worst came to the worst, it was safer to fight it out than to fly.

" In the midst of the dwarf's perplexity, and a week before he was expected, Ray returned—the same frank, handsome fellow. To be sure he was much shocked at the altered appearance of his wife, but he had already heard that she had been lonely and pining in his absence, and attributing the change to that, felt quite ashamed of his own healthy, cheerful face.

" ' You're a nice sort of a chap to take care of a man's wife,' said he to Valpy. ' Why, she's as white as a sheet, and not much stouter ! I've half a mind not to give you those snakes, after all.'

" It was shortly after he came in, and before he had an opportunity to speak in private with his wife (which, indeed, she rather avoided), that Ray said this. However, he at the same moment produced a perforated box, containing the reptiles Valpy had such a superstitious longing to see and experimentalize upon. He took it with the best grace he could muster, and went down to his den forthwith. There he locked himself in, awaiting whatever might result from the first interview between man and wife.

" An hour after, Ray strolled out of the house, whistling as merrily as a thrush ; so it was clear that, whatever his wife had planned or intended, she had revealed nothing as yet. Furthermore, in the course of the evening, Ray, who had all a sailor's tastes, and who felt that his wife was duller than she might have been, insisted on Valpy's company for a little carouse. Then John Valpy saw that with the return of the husband his own position was mending. The sailor was so frank, so unsuspecting, so happy, his wife dared not let him know the truth for fifty lives ; and she betrayed that feeling over and over again in the course of the evening, as, with a face now pale, now red, she glanced from the bead-eyed wicked-mouthed manikin, to the hale, ruddy, star-eyed man.

" This discovery elated the manikin a little too much. He felt superior. He took another tumbler, and began to look down upon Ray himself as a poor fellow after all—a poor blinded and deceived wretch, innocent, without guile ! The woman, soon detecting this sentiment, turned paler and paler as Valpy's beady eyes sparkled the more with grog and triumph, and as a free-and-easy insolence of air succeeded to the awkwardness that naturally belonged to him. For his part, he saw the effect of his recklessness ; and, finding in it an opportunity of punishing her for the contempt with which she had treated him of late, was encouraged all the more to make her feel his power

He grew jocular ; he told double-edged stories, of which, while the company only saw one edge, the other went into her flesh, as it were ; and whenever he said a thing more piercing than another, he fixed his black eyes on the woman all the while, with a sparkle and a grin that made her cold. At other times, however, she tried to be as cheerful as she could, for she knew that Ray had more than once caught her looking not quite like a wife who's glad to have her husband back.

" Valpy, who was by this time far gone in drink, and at the height of his hilarity, saw Ray watching one of these grave sad looks. ' Ah, Bill !' said he, clapping the sailor on the shoulder as familiar as if he'd been his father, ' she looks as melancholy as if she'd just come home from your funeral, don't she ?'

" ' Never you mind, John,' said the other ; ' you fill your glass again, old boy, and leave the women to me. We understand all about it ; don't we, Kate ?'

" ' Yes, William,' says she, trying to smile, and feeling herself to be the wickedest creature in the world.

" ' That's right, my dear. Valpy, you villain, sing us a sentimental song !'

" ' Perhaps Mrs. Ray will be so obliging !' said the dwarf, politely, perking his chin at her.

" ' Ah, come, Kate !' exclaimed Ray, affectionately.

" Now she had just got into that dull and weary state—feeling stupid-like—when people will do anything without knowing what. So she says—

" ' Very well, William. What shall it be ?'

" ' What shall it be, John ?' echoed Ray, turning to Valpy.

" ' Wapping Old Stairs !' says John, grinning at the bowl of his tobacco-pipe.

" That was a new song then ; but new or old, it was all the same to her. She was too far gone thinking of other things. So she struck up as mechanical as a musical-box :—

" ' Your Molly has never proved——'

and then, like as if a knife had stabbed her, she recollected what she was singing. She started up, looking at Valpy as if she could have burnt him up with her eyes. That was only for a second ; then she burst out crying : ' I can't ! I can't ! You know I can't, William ! You should not have asked me to sing !' and so rushed out of the room.

" Ray bit his lip, and looked at Valpy as if for an explanation. Valpy, for his part, had got all the triumph and the grog taken out of him by this scene, and sat stupid and sober. The more Ray regarded him, the less he himself seemed pleased, and a few minutes after broke up the meeting. Two coastguard friends of Ray's were there, and with one of these he said he would walk a little way. Valpy, conscious that he was not half so good a man sober as drunk, caught up a bottle of rum, and by way of a glass at parting, tossed three down his lean throat. And then they separated—the manikin going valiantly to bed.

" I have not told you that the sailor was a jealous man, but you can see he was a man of strong affections, and jealousy follows. He did go with his friend a little way, but only a little way. He then returned, and hung about the house, watching and listening, and ashamed of himself. At one time, indeed, he could have heard voices ; and opening the door with a key softly, he placed his ears just within. Now, however, all was silent. Yet he could have sworn to the voices—his wife's and Valpy's. Whether he was right or not, I don't know. Whether John, having gone valiantly to bed, valiantly got up again, and so some altercation happened, I don't know—very likely not. Ray, however, was very much disturbed and ashamed ; and feeling that the cool night air did him good, and that a look at the sea might do him more good still, he strolled down to the beach.

" Now half an hour passed. Valpy was drunk and asleep ; the Beauty trembling and awake. She said something at last, between her teeth, about putting the cup to his own lips. Then she rose, and presently crept, pale, and stealthily, to John Valpy's room. The banisters shook under her hand, but she did not heed it ; the stairs creaked under her feet, but she did not hear it ; and to look at her, you would have thought she was a sleep-

27

walker, only for her eyes, that blazed in her dead white face with the light of fifty eyes. She opened Valpy's door without a moment's hesitation, and went straight up to the bed, having first pulled the window curtain aside, to let the moonlight in. There lay the little monster, his head buried in a red night-cap and thrown backward hideously, while he gasped and snorted in his drunken sleep. The woman, stooping, carried her hand with a swift, determined movement to his open mouth. On the very instant Valpy started up, throwing out his arms, and grasping at her convulsively: the next instant he was a dead man, huddled up like the drunken man was.

"When Ray returned, refreshed and quieted, all was still enough. His wife was fast asleep, or seemed to be; so kissing her gently, and taking her in his arms tenderly, so as not to wake her, he went to sleep too.

"It was Valpy's old mother who first discovered his death. She made a great outcry, of course, though perhaps we don't think it was worth while. 'Come down! come down to my poor boy!' she screamed, rushing into Ray's room. Mrs. Ray, who was not up, only turned uneasily in her bed, like a person disturbed in her sleep, though, in truth, she had been expecting the summons for an hour before. Her husband was down-stairs in a twinkling. There he saw John Valpy without a sign of violence upon him, not a spot of blood, not the faintest scent of poison, looking like a man who had died with the fright of a bad dream.

"So Ray said to himself, for he was in a curious and suspicious frame of mind; and looked about him keenly; as, indeed, anybody would, considering the suddenness of John's death. There was, indeed, a mark or streak in the clenched palm, like a bruise, or more, perhaps, like a pinch; but this had plainly nothing to do with the man's death.

"Ray was little inclined to talk of the affair, but he told his wife how they had found Valpy, and that there was to be an inquest. She made few observations, and though it was clear she was more absent and paler than before, she seemed to take little interest in a matter which had thrown the whole village in confusion. Her husband noticed this, and did not know whether to like it or not. He was very fidgety, passing in and out of the house a dozen times in the course of the day.

"In the evening, however, when they sat down together, Mrs. Ray's manner changed. She looked as if she had been crying; and Ray, irritated, and determined to know the reason of this strange conduct, was about to tax her with it rather roughly, when she placed one hand upon his arm, and softly called him by his name. It appeared by the sound of her voice that she was about to tell him something; and he felt that that something would not be agreeable; and instead of answering, or looking into her face, he said nothing, letting his eyes glance down upon her hand. 'By heavens!' he muttered, 'there it is again!' and sure enough, upon her wrist was a mark more like a pinch than a bruise. She allowed her hand to fall from her husband's arm the instant he looked on it, and when he looked up her lips were as white as her teeth. Whatever she had meant to say, now she said nothing; but after a few moments of awkward silence, she rose from the table as if on some errand, while he dug into the fire with the poker.

"Ray had now something to think of that he could fix his thoughts on; and he sat there and turned it over and over in his mind, till ten o'clock came, and his wife retired to bed once more. She had not been long in the room when Ray quietly turned the key upon her, took a hammer, and went to the room where Valpy's body lay. The woman heard the key turned upon her, heard her husband leave the room, and crouched down on the threshold with her ear pressed hard to the door in a sweat of agony.

"The door of the room where the corpse lay had not only been locked, but nailed up, to await the coroner. The sailor, who had strength enough at that time to draw the bricks out of the house, one by one, took the nail-heads in the pronged end of the hammer, and pulled them out neat and clean, without leaving a trace on the woodwork. Then, with a button-hook or probe which formed part of his clasp-knife, he picked the lock, and so got admission to the dead man. You guess what he wanted there: he wanted to look again at the mark on Valpy's hand. There it was, and, sure enough, exactly like the stain on

his wife's wrist—a mark as if the blood had been strangled in the veins. He saw, however, that it was on—not in—the skin, and he then saw that it was broader where the fingers clinched than at the wrist, where it ended; and, also, that it came from between the middle fingers, as if it trickled out of the fist. In the fist, then, would he look. With great difficulty did he wrench it open—but he was rewarded. In Valpy's closed hand he found the stopper of the rose-scent bottle, all covered with gold threads and surrounded with a broad, deep stain.

"Now William Ray had got something else that he could fix his thoughts on. The only difficulty was, that at first it was rather too much for him. However, he was a man of uncommon resolution, and he had been preparing himself for something terrible all the evening. In a few minutes, therefore, he recovered his senses, put the stopper in his waistcoat-pocket, and left the room—shooting the lock again, and pushing the nails into their places, so as to make no noise. His wife, therefore, listening at the door, heard nothing except his footsteps as he came up-stairs.

"Ray's business now was to find the bottle itself. There were not many places to seek it in; and, after about a quarter of an hour's silent search, he found it in the drawer where his papers were kept. There was a drop of white liquid in it—and there was a tame squirrel asleep in a cage. He cut a quill pen clear of ink, dipped it into this drop, and placed the pen carefully on the table. He then dropped the rest of the liquid upon a crumb of bread, and went to the cage, and whistled to the squirrel, calling him so cheerfully that his wife's heart jumped with joy to hear it. Nothing dreadful could have happened; for his was playing with the squirrel.

"She knew nothing about it. The little animal popped his head out, with a squeak and a burr, took the piece of bread the sailor offered him, and died half a minute after, with a very small squeak and no burr at all.

"Things were looking bad, and so was William Ray.

"Now for the other test. Ray took up the quill, and tried to drop the moisture at its end upon his palm: it was quite as well it did not drop—it might have left an accidental-looking stain, suspicious against himself. So, as the liquid would not run—as fate had it—Ray made a cross, in writing as it were: and, in ten minutes after, the cross became of the same colour as the marks on the hand of Valpy, and on the wrist of his own wife. That settled it; and a settler it was.

"However, after putting the bottle back in the drawer, Ray went to bed, apparently as usual; and his wife, opening her eyes in the darkness, again thanked heaven that her secret was not yet discovered. To-morrow, perhaps, she would tell him: that would be a million times better than his finding it out. Thinking that, she went to sleep too.

"In the morning, Ray did not wait to be told anything, nor could he wait till after breakfast; but while the kettle was singing as comfortable as if nothing had happened, he went to the drawer in a careless way, took out the bottle, and said, turning round to his wife—

"'Missis, this bottle used to have a stopper in it. What's become of the stopper?'

"'I can't tell, William,' says she, stooping to pick up a pin, which, of course, made the blood come into her face.

"'Are you sure?'

"She looked at him with an awful look, twisting her fingers together, and shaking her head.

"'Oh, well, don't be alarmed! I've found it!'

"She knew it was all over, though she did not know where her husband had found the stopper, or that the dead man, when he started up, had clutched it out of the phial. Straightway she fell on her knees; and, without a break or a stop, screamed out the whole story as I've told it to you!

"That was a scene, as you can guess. Not that Ray said anything, or did anything, except turn blacker and blacker as the story went on. He knew very well, when she writhed upon the floor, despairing of making him understand that she always abhorred John Valpy, and that she hated his black, unblinking eyes at the same time that she could not escape from them—he knew, I say, that she was only telling the truth. He knew that she was suffering agonies of remorse; but he was a hard man, bred up to think duty everything; and it all made no difference.

As soon as she had said all that she had got to say, he left her on the floor, went straight to a magistrate's, and gave such information that in two months from that time the Beauty was hanged! I don't say what he thought about it afterwards, but he did it. And that's the end of the story."

The parlour of the Goat and Boots gasped, and the tailor's wife went home with the tailor as meek as a lamb.

"And what became of the sailor?" asked Mark.

"Went a whaling voyage, and got drowned," Joel answered.

"Served him right!" said the saddler.

"God forgive him!" said the clerk.

"A very curious story, Hatcher," Mark observed, as they went away together, and got into a lonely part of the road.

"Very," answered Joel, who had remarked that his present companion had been his best listener. "I thought you'd like it."

"Curious stuff that must have been, too. What did you say it was?"

"What do you think I said it was?" Hatcher asked in reply, quite aware that he had given it no name, for the simple reason that he had none to give it.

"I don't recollect. I've a bad memory for things with long names."

"Long or short," responded Joel, "you never heard it from my lips, for I don't know it."

"Oh!" said Mark, with some confusion, which the darkness was good enough to hide. A few steps further, and they parted.

CHAPTER XI.

Howlet and Hatcher parted, but Mark did not go home alone. Everybody knows the beautiful ballad of Uhland's, ending with this verse :—

> "Take, O boatman! thrice thy fee—
> Take! I give it willingly :
> For, invisible to thee,
> Spirits twain have passed with me."

Spirits twain, also invisible to the naked eye, passed with Mark Howlet, all the quiet way home. One took the form of his mother, as she looked when she knotted his hair into her own : this spirit told him anew of his sister's injuries, and reminded him once more that they were unpunished. The other spirit (more shadowy, but if truth must be told, rather more interesting to Mr. Howlet), was the very fetch and double of himself— a new, improved, and elegantly-bound edition of himself—with a gentleman-like bearing, and arrayed in a manner most genteel. And so it ought to have been; a Brummel of a spirit, a "rst gentleman in Europe of a ghost, considering the calculation, the pains, the thought bestowed upon its training and its toilette by the bodily Mark; for it was the shadow thrown before of a future and a sublimated Mr. Howlet. The bodily Mark had thorough grounded his ghost in calisthenics; it walked elegantly. The hands of the spirit were much whiter than Howlet's own hands; they were white as a lily. His hair, too, was a little curlier than the bodily Mark's, and his whiskers had that je ne scais quoi appearance which is rarely attained by cultivation, though sometimes it is catching, like epidemics (to which whiskers are peculiarly liable, by the by). But then Howlet had endowed his double with plenty of time, and a dressing-case replete with washes, unguents, and macassars many. As for the double's attire, that was a difficult matter, in which Howlet never could resolve this most elementary question :—How many pairs of boots a gentleman of small but adequate means ought to have in wear at one time? To-day he fixed upon the number four, and to-morrow, seven; upon the whole, five satisfied him most. But—asking pardon of the ladies—trousers constituted the great difficulty. This is accounted for by the peculiar instincts and cultivation of Mr. Howlet. Naturally superior to his class, he had some natural taste and some by observation. He knew that trousers were the key-note of harmonious attire—that to these must the tailor attune himself; and when he looked upon his ghost, and considered how he should start him as a gentleman of (as aforesaid) slender but easy means, he experienced strong mental struggles. Given the due number of trousers, their various hues and patterns selected, it only remained to match or contrast them with a dozen of gloves, and the walking gentleman was complete. Coats naturally fell into the arrangement; they had no choice. But the aforesaids?

It is very ridiculous of Mr. Howlet : but we cannot find it in our hearts to laugh much, neither you nor I, dear reader ; for we ourselves are equally ridiculous every day. We also have our doubles always walking by our side—prosperous, rich, handsome, generous (how generous to be sure!), much considered. We have built that well-loved ghost a mansion in a park of you know how many acres! and it has lawns, and terraces, and trees, and a walled fruit-garden, and flower-pots, and aviaries, and a fish-pond, the number or dimensions of which need not be set down, for you have counted them twenty times, and have measured them to an inch. Mine is a red-brick affair, combining all the elegance of the Elizabethan with the comforts of the modern or Cubic style of architecture. Of what fashion is yours? My drawing-room is 32 feet long by 24 feet broad. At one end you pass through hangings into a little chamber full of rare books, and prints, and pictures, and masterworks in gold and silver, and iron and ivory ; it is possible for one cigar to be smoked there. (I have known Macaulay to take two cigars there ; but then he was so interesting on the subject of Colonel Blood, that my prosperous double consented to break the rule.) At the other end is another little apartment, soft, rosy, full of a well-illumined dimness! it is not possible to smoke there—the impious weed would expire for shame. Unfortunately, however, after seven years' consideration in the intervals of business, I have not yet decided upon the tone, style, or material of the wall decorations. You are more fortunate, I hope. Whether I shall have them finished by the artist's pencil, whether I shall hang them in velvet, beaded into arabesques by golden threads ; whether—— but our space is limited.

Moreover, our business is with Mr. Howlet's double, as he walks there by the bodily Mark's side, elegant and at ease. This spirit, like Mark himself, was born of the other spirit. He was the child of her love and her youthful life ; it of her wrath and her death. For the long and short of it is, that respectable and thriving ghost, the shadow cast before of a future Mr. Howlet, is the embodiment of this idea ; that with filial duty might be combined personal advantage ; with business, pleasure ; that it might be possible to avenge the injury his family had sustained, and at the same time put money in his purse ; and thus one ghost would be laid, while he would undergo a blessed transfiguration, and become the well-to-do party of his daily dreams. And so both phantoms walked by his side, whispering all the way.

But, indeed, after Mark's first intense fury against Keppel had abated, he took no view of the subject from which some possible advantage to himself was excluded. He was meditating some stroke which should attain both objects, when Mr. Keppel offered to make a (gentleman's) gentleman of him ; and ever since since then he had been waiting for some grand opportunity. Up to this time he had only made himself acquainted with his master's affairs, and no definite scheme had as yet been suggested to him. He was an inert man, and his inertness was like that of a stone, which, once set rolling, rolls heaven knows where.

Now, to-night as he went from the Goat and Boots, the stone, urged by the spirits twain, began to move. He walked slowly ; his chest heaved slowly, and at long intervals ; and before he went to sleep that night, something like a plan was formed—a plan that should fulfil the mad prophecies of his mother almost to the letter.

To understand it, the reader must be made acquainted with the position in which Keppel at this time found himself, and in which Mark found him.

When this smart young man was about to marry, he refused, with a great show of unselfishness, to receive any information as to the conditions upon which Sophy Butler held her fortune ; the fact being, that he had already made himself acquainted with the circumstances of the case, and had no better alternative than to accept them. It has been said that old Butler's great ambition was to transmit his property to descendants of his name. Therefore, when he devised his well-loved property, he gave it all in trust for his daughter ; " whom heaven preserve," added he, "for she is a good girl, and all the joy and pride of my life, though delicate." But Sophy was to enjoy only a moiety of it till she married, and even *after* she was married, unless she bore a son. In that most desirable event, the entire property was to pass under her husband's control (save a small reserve for her private use), on condition that he took the name of Butler, and called the boy Daniel. But if Sophy bore daughters only, then the bulk of the property was to be held for *them* on similar terms. Meanwhile, if Sophy died without issue, the estate to pass to a poor nephew, Charles Butler, or his heirs; or if she died during the minority of a child, her husband was to enjoy a moiety of the property, until the child reached its majority.

Keppel's hold upon any of the property, on his marriage, depended therefore upon the life of his wife, or upon the lives of any children she might have; while if she gave birth to a son, then by resigning his ancient name, the property became his wholly.

Now the young man would have been better pleased had his wife been left in uncontrolled possession, but as it was, he accepted her very cheerfully, and prayed for a son. When there appeared good prospect of the satisfaction of his hope, who more gay, who more happy, who more affectionate than he? Nor, frank, happy man as he was, did he take any pains to disguise his satisfaction, or to mince his hopes. On the contrary, he kept Mrs. Keppel so constantly alive to them, that at length she regarded his demonstrations with a feeling akin to misery. He had already shown that he could be unkind; and what if the expectations he nourished with such extraordinary jealousy should be frustrated? Once she ventured to hint at such an eventuality; he said nothing, but he looked at her in a manner which convinced her that such a thing was not to be thought of.

With fear and trembling, then, rather than with joy, the poor girl awaited the birth of her child. At length the hour arrived. There was an infant Hercules—in bronze—on her mantel-piece; there was an infant Samuel—on canvas—over against her bed; one little Cupid stood on a bracket over her toilette-table (his companion, Psyche, had long been banished), and another was actually instrumental in supporting the curtains of her bed. But for all that her baby was pronounced to be a beautiful girl.

"Poor little creature!" said the mother, with a pitiful smile, as she kissed the infant stranger.

"Confusion!" said the father, with quite another expression of countenance, when the news was announced to him; and the door being closed, he further vented his feelings in language so strong that his man, who was present, suspected there was something more than met the eye in this little arrangement of Providence; and so started his investigations.

"Well, what did he say, nurse?" asked Sophy, with a feeble voice and an anxious heart.

"Don't ask *me*, mum!" the nurse exclaimed, plunging a spoon into a bowl of cordial as savagely as if it contained the heart of her worst enemy.

"Tell me, or I won't take bit or sup from you!"

"He said 'Oh!'" replied the nurse.

But Keppel answered for himself. His room was immediately below that in which his wife lay. The door opened for a single instant, and Sophy heard him shout these words:—"As if in spite, by ——," and then the door closed again, so that she heard no more. No matter. The tone in which was uttered what *had* reached her ears, and the noise of Keppel's feet, as he marched up and down, were enough: from that moment she began her slow dying.

Here was another aggravation for Keppel! This poor creature, this wretched daughter of the rabble, wandering about the house with that pale face of hers—not only bore him no more children, but endangered his prospects and tortured his existence by falling into a delicate state of health! Perhaps there was a remedy for this misfortune, in kindness; and, indeed, Keppel tried it now and then, not unsuccessfully. But it is a long cure for a bruised heart and a faithless spirit. Keppel's attentions were not followed by immediate convalescence. If she laughed a little more, there was a sad doubtful echo at the end; if her eyes looked brighter, and her cheeks took back a little of their lost bloom, these were almost as much the signs of fever as of happiness; and she had a bad trick of trembling, too, whenever he

was very kind. Ah! those little soft, suffering, ruthful women, what understanding they have also, and what a foolish use they make of their wisdom! They know every notch in the knife that wounds them; they know all the keener and the blunter places better than he who wields it; and yet the silly things not only desist from expostulation or any defensive armour, but they haven't even the sense to express a preference for either edge of the blade: that which cuts or that which bruises. Whichever you please, my dear, they say in their hearts, if they say anything, and when the lord has made his daily slice at the lady, she presently takes his arm, and goes to see what the last prettiest thing in bonnets may be. Upon the whole, however, Todtleben, with his earthworks and forts of mud, never devised a more masterly scheme of defence than these ramparts of gentleness and long-suffering. It is true, the defenders often yield at last. The shots go *through*; and the end is that the brave garrison becomes exhausted. You go pounding away leisurely, for the fort seems able to stand anything; when suddenly, Piff! all goes down together. It is a thing that will happen in the best-regulated families.

But Sophy Butler was not plucky, as other women are. We have seen how she bore her little matrimonial cross, fainting by the way; and how she could not be restored to health—much less to happiness—by the kindness of a day. She was rejoiced at his kindness, nursed it, believed in it, trembled at it (the little light that shone so far back, so little forward!), doubted it, dreaded it, and then took it to heart and rejoiced in it again. But she didn't get well. Her appetite was not improved; a result which so much disgusted Keppel, that he forthwith plunged back deeper into the mess-room style of life, to no good end. These little episodes were frequent. At such times, Keppel, not always sober, was then always peevish; often drunk, he was then brutal. Meanwhile, his wife, who lost all her happiness long before she lost an atom of her love, faded away, and at length slipped uncomplaining out of the world.

Keppel was now in this position: He depended for money, which he did love, upon the existence of a little girl whom he had never loved, whom he rather hated, as the sign, if not as the cause, of his disappointment. As she grew in health and strength, he was reminded that in a few short years she would take possession of all about her: when she fell sick, he was in a terror of apprehension, for with her last breath his last cheque would be drawn. Sick or in health, she pleased him not; she was at all times the centre of his blackest musings; and as the child grew day by day in grace and innocence, while he grew day by day more reckless and graceless, he saw in her at length a living reproach as well as a living disappointment. The one gave rancour to the other.

This, then, was the state of affairs when Mark went meditative home—he and his familiars; and this state of affairs he meditated. Not that he had never conned it over in his mind before—he and his familiars; but, to-night, from some cause or other, he seemed to take a clearer and more comprehensive view of the subject: and now and then he made short, abrupt gesticulations, as if he were coming to a resolution. "As iron sharpeneth iron, so a man sharpeneth the countenance of his friend." Perhaps the conversation in the parlour of the Goat and Boots had something to do with Mr. Howlet's sudden inspiration?

His proceedings, from that night, were as strange as the inspiration was sudden. He took to literature; in which the excellent library at Keppel Lodge gave him rare advantages. But though Mark's studies were very earnest, they were also very restricted. No romance, no poem, no history, no biography, no homily, did he ever look into; but there were several books of medicine, chemistry, alchemy, and magic, and these he read with a deep and secret avidity. What did he seek in these learned pages? Ten thousand readers guess—not ten guess rightly. But what he sought he found (after painful search and putting this and that together) in one of the great old volumes of alchemy. A few days after, Keppel went to town; his man attended him; and, ere he returned, added two little well-corked phials to his personal effects.

This addition to his property, however—like many another—seemed to afford small satisfaction to its possessor. While he had those tiny glass vessels in his pocket he feared to walk, to ride to stand, to sit. He dreaded to be jostled in the streets, as much as if his clothes were lined with fish-hooks; he dared not cross a road while there were two carts in sight, and he almost fainted whenever he tripped against a stone. Accidents occur so readily; and should any accident happen to him, and he be taken to some hospital or workhouse (as he might be), and then be searched (as of course he would be), the bottles would be found! Even this was what he dreaded—lining his clothes with fish-hooks, loading his feet with lead, filling his head with care, and fevering his blood with hot apprehensions.

When he got the innocent-looking little bottles of terror home, and secreted them where they enjoyed congenial company —in his razor-case—Mark was not more at his ease. The very first day of his return he pleaded fatigue, headache, "regularly knocked up, sir," and was allowed to keep his room, and the company of his razor-case. How many times he locked and unlocked it with that little key!—sometimes taking the bottles out to look at them, at others only peeping at them as they lay at the bottom, in the dark corner. So afraid of surprise, yet so rashly exposing himself to it! Why, when the neat-handed, but in this case unceremonious maid Madge walked in with his dinner, he had the box open on the bed, whereupon he was sitting, in a listless attitude but with by no means a careless face. He started, turned pale, and dashed down the box-lid.

"Good Hevins! Mr. Howlet! you arn't going to cut your throat!" the girl exclaimed, turning as pale as the party addressed.

"What put that in your head?" he growled.

"Over that clean bed! Well, then, give me them nasty razors; come!"

"You be off, and don't be a fool. I'm going to shave!" And taking out one of the razors, he whetted it upon his palm with such energy that the girl, sitting down the dinner-tray, scampered off to sound an alarm in the kitchen. Mark divined her intention, of course, and perceived the only means to extricate himself from the situation. Two minutes afterwards, when the affrighted butler put his head in at the door, Mark was coolly lathering his chin. The butler looked foolish, while the three or four faces which crowded over his shoulder assumed a ludicrous expression of mingled relief and disappointment. Mark lightly laughed, and invited his visitors to step in and witness the end of the operation. This they declined, and as his fellow-servants, growling at each other, went down-stairs again, Mark returned to his looking-glass, and quietly concluded the business he had begun.

He was never afterwards known to be incautious—quite the contrary. For the present, he put the razors away, took up a pile of old newspapers, and occupied himself for the remainder of the day in reading all the murders.

But at night, at bed-time, he locked his door, and again took forth one of the bottles, terrible and tiny. Placing it on the floor, he proceeded to prepare for bed. When he was wholly undressed, he sat down, took up the bottle nervously, drew the cork with extremest care, and then dipped into the colourless liquid the feather of a new quill.

"Now for the test," he muttered. He lightly applied the feather to the sole of his foot, eagerly watching the effect. In ten seconds, a yellowish spot appeared; in twenty seconds, the spot became purply blue and ineradicable.

"The thing!" he cried, in a loud whisper, starting to his feet, and gazing with an odd, fixed, half-frightened stare at the opposite wall.

The stare presently hardened into the hardest of smiles, as he heard his master leave the dining-room, and go plunging and rolling against the bannisters, singing meanwhile a song that was meant to be Bacchanal, but which was only maudlin.

"God of thunder!" roared he, having rolled long enough in one corner to sing the song out. "Body of Bacchus, chief of gods! things are coming to a pretty pass. Where's my dog? Keeps his room with headache, while his master, whose head's bad too, can't find *his* room at all. Hi, Simkin!"

"Yess'r."

Thus was addressed, and thus answered the butler, who, having the fear of a conflagration before his eyes, had already charged himself with the care of Keppel's candle.

"Simkin, undress me, and you're a made man. You shall have a new and spotless choker, old Purity, and then there'll be no excuse for not hanging yourself with that old one."

The butler respectfully but firmly bundled him into his bed-room.

Mark, who had softly unlocked his door to listen to all this, gave another hard smile as the last words were spoken, and then went to bed with his plan.

"Howlet, you a-bed?" breathed the butler through the key-hole, some ten minutes after.

"Ye-es," drawled Mark in the drowsiest manner.

"I say," remarked the other, putting his head in at the door, "there he is again! A bottle of port, a bottle of claret, and brandy no end to follow. I say, there'll be a axident one o' these times. What do you say?"

"Shouldn't wonder."

"That's what *I* say. Good night."

"Shouldn't wonder at all," repeated Mark to himself, cuddling the plan.

CHAPTER XII.

WOPPITS'S FLITTING.

It was a late vestry at Latherwell, and party-spirit ran high. The question in debate was this: did the pump really need a new sucker. The opposition warmly insisted that it did; that as it at present stood the parish pump was a sham—a mockery, a delusion, and a snare. That was the expression of Mr. Tike, the opposition leader, who furthermore declared that he would contend with his last breath against any such infringement of the people's liberties; any such tampering with the charter that was wrested from the hands of the tyrant. He would give the imbeciles who now held the reins of office to know that the days of magner carter were not yet passed; that there were yet men who could stand up for the liberties of a down-trodden country, and for the interests of a suffering parish; and the aforesaid imbeciles were never more mistaken in their lives if they imagined he would consent to a compromise on this question. He was for the sucker—the whole sucker—and nothing but the sucker!

The Gorelam party, on the other hand, took their stand on the ground of economy, and taunted the opposition with reckless expenditure and disgraceful jobbery. It was a very exhilarating row, and as the majority of the vestry-men, like whales, are under the necessity of imbibing before they could spout, and had made very liberal provision accordingly, it required all Mr. Tweakle's tact to keep the suckers and the anti-suckers from actual warfare.

How the dispute would have terminated, had it taken its natural course, is still a matter of speculation in Latherwell. Taunts and sarcasms of the most undisguised character were pelted backward and forward. Mr. Gorelam, getting on his legs for the fiftieth time, had declared that he could not express his disgust and indignation in words, and had inquired if Mr. Tike called himself a man? Mr. Tike had replied in a most cold-blooded manner that he was, and that if Mr. Gorelam would just step out, he would prove it to the honourable gentleman's satisfaction. But at this moment an incident occurred which can only be paralleled in the "Iliad" of Homer. Gorelam had risen to reply to the challenge of Tike, his white waistcoat, expanded to the full, gleamed like a cuirass; his hand was deliberately raised, his forefinger was extended, and levelled at the undaunted bosom of Tike, whose own forefinger rested on his nose, when a porter from the House rushed in: terror was in his eyes—horror in his hair—the whole man looked dishevelled and distraught as he approached the chair.

"Gentlemen," said he, solemnly but firmly, conscious that he bore intelligence that must obliterate all mere party squabbles "a boy have hooked it!"

There was a dead silence instantly. Men looked at each other in confusion. Tike's finger was withdrawn from his nose unconsciously; Gorelam's extended hand fell to his side, as he turned his countenance from his foe to the messenger. Then arose a murmur like the gathering of the waves upon the shore into one mighty wave. Every mouth was open, everybody was about to burst into an opinion; but the mighty wave was arrested even while the foam raged over its crest. Gorelam waved his hand. His face beamed with inspiration, like the face of a seer; and a grim, grim smile flickered over it. Then he suddenly darted his forefinger at the messenger, and—

"Porter," said he, in a low voice, which yet was audible in the furthermost corner of the room. "Porter, that boy's name is Woppits?"

The man, shrinking before the accusing eye, replied—

"It *is* Woppits, sir. Took his other shirt, and his stockings, and a clean handkercher, and is gone, sir."

Mr. Gorelam slapped his thigh, swept the meeting with one triumphant glance, resumed his seat, and blew a great blast with his handkerchief. He did not wish to seem elated by this well-timed proof of his sagacity, but it was not lost upon his supporters; while as for the opposition, they felt the stroke so keenly, that they never forgave the man who had furnished Gorelam with so telling an opportunity. That porter was discharged under the Tike administration.

Besides, the sucker question, which was going all in favour of the opposition when the messenger entered, was now virtually shelved; and the Gorelams were saved. Faction was extinct in Latherwell, for the time at least. Every ratepayer found himself robbed, bamboozled, and the pump of controversy was absorbed in the fact. Here had they been keeping this boy Woppits for fourteen or fifteen years, during which period, as Mr. Tike calculated on the spot, he had consumed 5746 pints of gruel, 3117 pints of soup, 4921 ounces of meat without bone, and 6263 lbs. of bread, to say nothing of vegetables, clothes, and Catechisms. (This statement was received with loud cheering.) And now, having consumed so much capital in growing up to a useful size, here he had decamped, with property belonging to the parish : whereas the very flesh of his bones belonged to them, the ratepayers of Latherwell.

"Gentlemen," said Mr. Gorelam, with the urbanity of superior information, "that's the way with them all. Here's this boy been fattening——"

"Not werry fat, sir," mildly expostulated Tweakle. He stood in full uniform, staff in hand and in his official capacity, near Gorelam's chair. "Not particular fat, sir !"

"Well, then, tall, sir !" rejoined the chairman sharply. "He couldn't have it both ways, I suppose ? Perhaps you think he ought, Tweakle ?"

"No, Mr. Gorelam !" answered the abashed functionary. "No, sir! and he cert'n'y was tall. Tall as a lath, he was !"

"Well, here he is, been growing taller and taller at the expense of the ratepayers, without the least regard as to what it cost, and staying as long as he found it convenient. Then he's off! and if it did not luckily happen, very luckily happen, that he had taken our clothes on his back, he might snap his fingers at us if ever we caught him. But as his taking these things constitutes him a thief, why we'll have his precious legs on the treadmill before he's a week older." Mr. Gorelam said this with considerable relish and satisfaction.

The fact is—as we already know—Woppits was no favourite with the worthy chairman; he had never recovered the first step, or rather kick, he took in that gentleman's presence when introduced to the board, and which, by very much staining Mr. Gorelam's linen with ink, had even brought his memory into disfavour with Mrs. Gorelam herself. From that hour Mr. G. had perseveringly prognosticated that the boy would come to a bad end; and consequently would have been delighted to see Woppits verify his prophecy on the "mill." He always had been on the look-out for the boy's faults, always looked severely and suspiciously upon him : of course the subs of all grades took the initiative from the great man, and on the whole Woppits did not find Elysium in Latherwell.

But he had a great friend in the beadle. That soft-hearted functionary, on whom fourteen years had no effect but to make him an older and a better boy, still viewed Woppits with the eye of a big brother; and commiserating the snubbings and peckings to which the boy was subjected, endeavoured, by gifts of food, halfpence, and kindness generally, to ameliorate his condition, and render him contented in that state of life into which it had pleased God to call him.

Though Tweakle's hat vibrated on his head when he heard that his *protégé* had run away, he was not surprised on the whole; nay, though the good man felt a sort of pang at parting, he rather approved the step than otherwise, and felt delighted that the boy had exhibited so much pluck and self-dependence.

Nevertheless, when Mr. Gorelam talked of theft and the treadmill, Tweakle looked serious, and felt as he looked.

"Lor', he can't be fur off, sir," said Mr. Tweakle, confidentially; "I'll be bound I'll find him and fetch him back, the little villain. He's gone to London : all runaway boys do, except them that goes to sea, and he ain't one of that sort. Shall I put him in jail, or bring him here straight, gentlemen ? "

"Ah, Tweakle, your eyes are opened to that boy at last, are they ? " asked Mr. Gorelam ; you don't think it'll do to stand up for him any longer. He never deceived *me*—not from the first hour I saw him. Well, if you think he's gone towards London, you had better be after him the first thing in the morning." They never were in a hurry at Latherwell.

But Mr. Tweakle did not wait till the morning. True, he went straight home, but that was not to go to bed, but merely to cut a huge slice from a leg of mutton, which, with a hunch of bread, he wrapped in last week's Latherwell "Lynx," and placed in his capacious pocket.

"Poor fellow," muttered he, "I don't believe he's got a ha'penny in the world, and he's had nothing since the morning, I'll bet anything."

It was late when the beadle started, but it was a beautiful moonlight night, and as pleasant walking as at noonday. As he went along, Tweakle argued with himself thus: The boy was off to London—no doubt of *that*. But he would hardly go by the high road—which was the most direct way—but would skulk along by byefields, and lonely places, which would make the road longer. Again, he would pause and hide, whenever he heard footsteps, or was likely to be seen. Considering these circumstances, and that the boy had not left Latherwell till late in the day, Tweakle came to the conclusion that he could not have gone farther than seven or eight miles, and that he would then probably take refuge for the night under a rick, or in a barn.

So Tweakle, hailing a carrier who overtook him at about a mile from Latherwell, rode some five miles further, and then stepped out determined to beat up all the ricks and barns near the next two or three miles of road. If he failed he would stop at an inn, rise early, and prosecute his search more vigorously.

It happened that the first likely place that Tweakle came upon was a sort of shed, belonging to a blacksmith and wheelwright, which stood at a little distance from Fuddle-cum-Fry. And it happened that this was the place in which the boy Woppits, weary and excited, had resolved to pass the night. The shed was nearly full of lumber, old wheels, old tubs, etc., etc., which rendered it all the more eligible for Woppits's purpose. It was snugger for the lumber ; and a good roomy tub, with an armful of straw in it, is not the worst lying, perhaps. So thought Woppits, at any rate, when he lighted upon that convenience : but then his taste was spoilt in infancy by sleeping under hedges and on ricks. Rejoicing much at his good fortune, he turned the good roomy barrel length-wise upon the ground—shifted it, with an infinite number of jerks and wriggles, till its mouth was brought to the wall, and then so arranged himself that he could reconnoitre in the direction of danger through the bunghole ; to which aperture he also kept his best ear.

The beadle looked into the barn about half an hour after these arrangements were completed, when the well-lodged Woppits had gone to be the equal of Imperial Princes in the republic of Sleep. Tweakle stuck his foot into an old wicker hencoop, which Woppits had placed as a snare near the open end of the shed ; and being stout, and unable to stand on one leg for any length of time, it was not without some eccentric evolutions that the beadle released himself. This, of course, aroused the boy, who, in fear and quietness, applied his eye to the bunghole, distinctly recognising the beadle. The good man poked about for a few minutes, assisted by the moonlight, and then called the runaway by name. "Woppits! Hi! Woppits! It's only me!" But Woppits stirred not, and Mr. Tweakle then went away, satisfied that the boy was not there.

Woppits's first feeling was one of terror, and he accordingly lay as quiet as a mouse; but the beadle had not long left the shed when the boy began to reflect that it was sheer ingratitude not to trust to his old friend, and a folly too. Besides Woppits's belly had also recognised its benefactor, Tweakle, and yearned towards him with hungry confidence. Thus seconded, Woppits

MARK CHARGES RUTH WITH BEING THE MURDERER OF HIS CHILD.

hesitated no longer, but, gathering himself out of the tub, turned out of the shed, and ran after his pursuer.

Great was Tweakle's surprise when, pausing to sniff at a blooming field of peas, he first heard rapid footsteps behind him, and as his own name was borne down by the wind from the same direction. The beadle's eyes attained the widest development ever known, when Woppits stood panting before him. His notions of cause and effect were completely upset at finding the boy running after him.

"Why, Woppits!" he exclaimed.

"Oh, sir, you won't split, will you?" cried the boy, with an imploring twist in his tone, and a corresponding twist of his entire body.

"Where did you come from?" asked Tweakle, severe at first.

"Out of that tub. I was watching you all the time—through the bunghole."

"Whose tub? what bunghole?" asked the bewildered beadle. "You ain't wandering in your head, are you?"

"Oh, yes; and in my legs and all the rest of me ever since yesterday; and I'm so jolly tired and hungry." And he chafed his nose severely with his cuff.

"Poor boy! Sit down under the hedge along of me. I've got some bread and meat in my pocket."

They seated themselves accordingly; and the next moment found Woppits devouring the cold mutton with an assiduity which brought to the mind of Tweakle pleasant memories of his own sweet, undyspeptic youth.

"You *must* have been precious hungry," he cried, as his young friend made a gutter of the paper, and poured the last remaining crumbs into his mouth.

"I just was. Why, Mr. Tweakle, I've had nothing atween my gruels this three days."

"Nothing between your gruels! What's that?"

"Nothing from breakfast to supper."

"Why, how do you make it out?"

"Because I had no luck, and never won!"

"What's your luck got to do with your dinner," asked Tweakle, "when you are under the protection of parochial authorities?"

"Well, I'll tell you, sir," replied Woppits. "You know Pankey?"

"Pankey?" repeated Tweakle, reflectively.

"You know him as took the oatmeal. Well, me and Pankey never could get nothing *staying* out of them dinners—not one of 'em—for we used to toss up who should have the two, his and mine: and I lost three days running."

"And that was the reason you ran away?"

"That was one of 'em, Mr. Tweakle, but it warn't all, sir," answered the boy, moodily. "Another of 'em was Mr. Gorelam, what always had me out, and stared at me o' visiting days, as if I'd been a-thievin'; but it was mostly short grub and too many pulls of the ear, which I couldn't stand it no longer. Would you ha' stood it, sir?"

"Where was you thinking of going?" asked the beadle evasively. "Don't you think you'd better go back with me?"

"No, I don't," said Woppits, decidedly, with that defiant look in his eye which had often irritated Mr. Gorelam.

"If you had the fortitude to bear it a bit longer, I think it would be better for you."

"What's forty tude?" Woppits asked, abruptly.

"Well, the patience—the pluck, you know."

"Oh, then, I ain't. Bless you, Mr. Tweakle, what's the use of forty tude against Mr. Gorelam and them? A feller might have a hunded and forty tude, and then he couldn't stand being half-starved all his life!"

"You'll be something more than half-starved before long, if you don't look sharp. Do you know how far it is to London? Near twenty miles!"

"Oh!" said the boy.

"And how are you to live on the way?"

"Well, I can get along on that cold mutton a good ways," replied Woppits, tenderly patting its sepulchre; "it was werry nice."

"But what will you do when you get there? You arn't got no money, and the clothes you've got on arn't yours, you know. Anybody can see that."

"I should think they could!" said Woppits, grinning at the large portion of his calf which protruded through the leg of his trowsers. "They'd think I stole them from my little brother. I wish I had a brother, or a mother, or something!"

Woppits began with a grin, as we have said: but when he wished he had a brother or a mother, he looked very grave, not to say unhappy, that it quite went to Tweakle's heart.

"Well, well," said he, "we must see what's to be done. You musn't go back, because if you do they'll put you into prison."

"What for?" asked Woppits, opening his eyes very wide.

"For not pulling all your clothes off before you started. You see, they're the property of the parish; and the fact is, you've thev' 'em. Now, I'll tell you what: I don't exactly know what I've got in my pocket, but I'll lend it to you, whatever it is; and then, when you get to London, and have earned a little, you must buy some more clothes, and send these back to the house."

Mr. Tweakle rummaged his pockets, and found twelve and threepence in them.

"Here," said he, piling the money on the ground, "there you are, Woppits, my boy! and there's many a man has built a mansion on fewer bricks to start with."

"What! am I to have the whole lot?" stammered Woppits.

"The whole lot!" Tweakle answered, complacently, enjoying the boy's surprise.

Woppits looked from the little heap of money to the large beadle with a painful face and glistening eyes.

"Oh dear!" he cried, catching the big hand of the beadle and squeezing it between his own, much to that functionary's distress. "You are a reg'lar good man, you are a stunning good man, to be so good to a poor cove like me."

And the overgrown workhouse boy sobbed, and the fat beadle consoled him in a manner ridiculous to see, unless you looked at them in a certain point of view.

"Come, this won't do," said Mr. Tweakle, when the boy's emotion had somewhat subsided; "let's talk about what you're to be up to."

"What do you advise, sir?"

"Well, I was considering. The last time I was in London I saw a man with baked potatoes in a can."

"What was he doing to 'em? Eatin' 'em?" inquired Woppits.

"Oh no, selling 'em. Baked per-taters, all-l-l-l 'ot!" piped the beadle. "That was it, nigh as I can recollect. What do you say to them, Woppits?"

Woppits shook his head.

"No?" said the beadle. "Why not?"

"No," replied Woppits, "musn't be wittles—I don't feel ekal to it. Lor' bless you, sir, a can of taters wouldn't last me no time! It must be something I couldn't tuck into."

"Well, suppose we say hearthstones?"

"That's better."

"Chickweed and grunsell! That's the very thing! You've only got to buy a basket, go into the fields and fill it, and there you are—stocked and started. I've heard," continued Tweakle, looking rather anxious and doubtful, though, "that a very good living is to be got out o' chickweed. Birds is scarce in London,

and the people is so fond of 'em that they can't give them too much chickweed, or grunsell neither."

"That'll do, then, Mr. Tweakle."

So after the good man had imparted all the advice he could master at the time, they parted affectionately in the middle of the road, Woppits for London, there to commence life with a basket of grunsell, and Mr. Tweakle to Latherwell, there to report his total want of success in overtaking the fugitive.

CHAPTER XIII.

THE PHIALS OPENED.

THERE are two sayings which I hold to be very wise. Alas me! I have much experimental knowledge of their truth. The first is Dr. Watts's saying, "Satan finds some mischief still for idle hands to do." The other, "Where there's a will there's a way." For a subtle link of association and consent exists between these proverbs, as you see when you apprehend the true signification of the latter one. But it is an abused proverb. I have heard that a journeyman hatter, sworn to devise something new for the season of 1601, seized the proverb, and applied it to his own bad case; and thenceforward it has been harnessed to material, and vulgar, and impossible uses. "Where there's a will there's a way," says Napoleon Bonaparte (who had much of the hatter in him), as he points his way up the Alps. "Where there's a will there's a way," says Heelball to me, though I demonstrate the impossibility of settling that little account. "Where there's a will there's a way," says Mr. Adam Bell, the great dust contractor, who, though he once handled the shovel himself, is now worth ninety thousand pounds, and wants to know why all the world cannot do likewise. No; in this sense, our proverb is a blind and brutal proverb, and is seldom used but to stab. Not but that it shines and sounds well; though there are some kindred sayings that shine and sound better, and are yet worse. "It is impossible, sire!" says one of Napoleon's generals. "Impossible! impossible!" replies that great soldier, revealing all the hatter that was in him; "blot that word from your dictionary, sir! Nothing's impossible!" Now that is generally regarded as a fine strong thing to say, and people have spent their time in licking it into the neatest, most epigrammatic, and most barefaced shape, for their own private use. Ah! divine little man—great *petit caporal*, king of kings, and conqueror of Europe—has not your shadeship amended that saying by this time? For my part, I wonder that you, a man of war, with that strategical head of yours, could dare to fight the great war of life without a Reserve, as you did! Did you really think, then, that *yours* was the kingdom, and the power, and the glory, and beyond you there was *no* Reserve?—You, *petit*, that a greatcoat could cover, and a little to spare? *You*, with your twopenny star—mostly visible on bloody days—rising as high, and as high, and as high as—the column of Austerlitz! Comrade, much is impossible in this world. You were a great man, and did great things; but that word is in the dictionaries notwithstanding. Indeed, it had already found its way back to its place among the I's, by the time you arrived at St. Helena; about which time also, say the almanacs, Providence, which had been regularly abolished by an act of Convention, began to reign again.

No; but this is where, if there's a will, there's also a way—a will to do good, or a will to do evil. Conceive a thought to do good, and you shall certainly behold a path that will lead to its fulfilment. Imagine some ill, some unaccustomed vice; it is at your elbow, there to revel in, if you please. And when vices are so fair to look on, as many are, and virtues are so ill-favoured at first sight, who can wonder that the former engage our contemplation oftenest? That is why our temptations are so many; and thus it is that the proverb is so considerable.

You find inclination—the Devil will find opportunity: there you have it in little. It was exemplified in Mr. Howlet's case; for Mr. Howlet having fulfilled the former condition, the other party soon furnished the latter.

Two or three days after Woppits's memorable flitting—that is to say, about a week after Mark went to bed cuddling his plan—he, Howlet, was sent on a confidential mission to some London money-lenders. He returned the same evening, and duly relating the most unsuccessful results of his journey, betook himself to his room without farther ceremony. He looked very dull and thoughtful that evening. While he changed his dusty apparel, he fell into a brown, hazy argument about affairs in general, which the business of undressing and dressing interrupted only in a brief, interjectional manner. Now he sat down to think of it, with only one arm in his waistcoat. He took one boot off, and dangled it for several minutes between his knees before it occurred to him that the other should be taken off too. He brushed one whisker, and then leisurely rubbed his ear with the handle of the brush, at once to allay an itching and (apparently) to promote the flow of ideas. But that is exactly what he could not do; for in fact he was not thinking at all, and his ideas would not flow. For why? Because there were cross currents, only resulting in a formless, shifting swirl; not noisy—not rude—but profound as the depths of good and evil. Good and evil it was, in fact, dim as was the perception thereof in Howlet's mind. Better minds than his fare no better in the same case. How often, and for how long a spell, has your heart or mine been torn by the conflict of good and ill, which, meeting there, have made it the mere battle-ground—wondering, distracted, half-unconscious we. Day by day the fight goes on, never pausing for nightfall, while the poor battle-ground—hurt by every spear that is thrown, shaken by the shock of that thunderless artillery, burdened by the slain, bathed in the blood of every wound—scarcely knows friend from foe, nor why the fight goes on so fiercely. Only when it is over, and the parties have retired, do we understand all about it; and happy is he who, counting the graves, finds Good the victor; happy the heart, happy the battle-field, that is not desolated by the conflict, which grows greener for all that bloodshed.

Now, Howlet's heart was harder and less informed than some folk's, and consequently he did not feel the struggle so much; but he did feel it, and was bewildered and uneasy, according to his kind. It was a contemplative sort of uneasiness, of course; and when he was refreshed, he lighted a cigar abstracted from his master's choicest box, and wandered into the park; or rather, he wandered into the park, and lighted a choice abstracted cigar.

Under these circumstances, he could only walk in the less frequented parts of the place, of course; and when he came to the boundary wall, he stood there awhile, gazing over into the meadows and the copse beyond. His mind was so preoccupied, that though his eyes were directed to the copse from the first, several minutes elapsed ere he observed a gang of gipsies pitched upon its borders. The Enemy had found his opportunity; the whirl and the swirl of ideas was stilled *instanter*, and began to flow pretty smoothly. While they gathered themselves together for the flood, Howlet took the cigar from his mouth, and stood still as a stone—his lips parted, as if inhaling some new, surprising notion as it came wafted from the carts, and the donkeys, and the ragged tents. Then—

"Eh?" he said to himself inquiringly, and turned back towards the house.

That he was not merely struck with the difference between the habitations of nomadic and civilised life, the dear reader will presently discover; but he certainly scrutinised that part of the house where the windows opened out upon the sloping lawn and its flower-beds with peculiar interest—glancing, too, from time to time, over the ground that lay between this portion of the house and the vagabonds. The scrutiny seemed to satisfy him. It was all good elastic sward, from the house to the boundary-wall, excepting only the flower-pots; therefore, no footstep could be traced upon it, the *absence* of any footstep could not be shown.

Pleased at having made this observation, Howlet retraced his steps, and in a few minutes was in conversation with the gipsies. In fine, he made a bargain with them—a very simple and innocent bargain—in the name of his master. Mr. Keppel, he said, had no personal objection to the neighbourhood of gipsies—they knew that already; but he expected a lengthened visit from a friend, whose wife had a foolish dread of them; this lady might arrive at any time; and if, when she did arrive, they would kindly pack off at once, there was half-a-guinea for them. If not, there were the constables and the stocks for them. The gipsies chose the money, and Mr. Howlet then explained that he was not a hard man, nor was his master a hard man. They need not depart till the last moment, when he would give them a sign.

This little piece of business completed, Mark strolled back to the house, flattering himself that the plan was now complete.

Quick came the opportunity. No other personage than Simkin suggested that the hour had come the moment Howlet appeared in the hall.

"Oh, I say, here you are!" exclaimed Simkin. "I've been looking for you everywhere."

"Well, what is it?"

"What is it? Why, here's the governor at it again! Something put him out, and he would have it; and he's got so dreadfully elevated, there's no holding him down. He's talking awful."

Keppel, savage with the disappointment his man had brought home from London, had taken to Burgundy; and, under the inspiration of that treacherous comforter, was muttering curses, deep and audible, against all the Butlers that ever lived.

"Well," said Mr. Howlet in answer to Mr. Simkin, "what's the use of troubling me? I can't help it. Let him talk awful; it's *only* talk—as yet!"

"No, but Mark, you know, you can do more with him in these tantrums than any one; so I thought if you'd just go in —— Not but what he is swearing about you, too! Says you're a blundering donkey, ordered Jenkins to saddle his horse, and swears he'll go to town himself this night."

"And stop at the first tavern!" sneered Mark.

"Well, see if you can't get him to bed, then. It's near ten o'clock."

"When he gets drowsy I will."

"I say, he'll be awful elevated before then, you know."

"Water his wine," growled Mark, "and let's whack the difference. I've no objection." And so he turned away.

Not half an hour elapsed, however, before Keppel was found drowsy; and accordingly Simkin, and Mark, and the neat-handed Madge with the candles, assisted him into a chamber on the ground-floor. This chamber communicated immediately with the room occupied by Ruth and her nurse; its windows (like Ruth's) opening upon a terrace which was a child's leap to the sloping lawn. It had been fitted up as a bed-room because Keppel, who had, of course, a most deadly anxiety about his daughter's health, liked to be near her whenever she showed a symptom of sickness; he was conveyed into it now because it was easy of access from the dining-room.

The neat-handed Madge had no sooner placed the candles down, than, with every mark of affrighted delicacy, she rushed from the room. There was no very imminent danger, however, for her master, rousing from his vinous lethargy, refused to be undressed, declaring that he must and would be in town before daylight. So, assisting him on to the bed, they left him in the dark, never doubting that he would sleep till morning.

A grave face wore Mr. Howlet, as he followed Simkin into the hall—a face changed every moment by the clouds of doubt and the brightness of resolution—as he weighed, and measured, and cast about in his mind. The moment had arrived. He had counted upon such a concatenation of circumstances as now presented itself; he hardly expected it so soon, and it might never happen again. Should he defer the chance? Mark having now arrived at the hall door, stooped under pretence of tying his shoe-string, but really to ask and answer this question. The answer was No! The thing was already half done to his hands.

How is it to be explained? When Mr. Howlet entered the kitchen he had a nobler air upon his countenance than ever it had worn in all his life before. Perhaps it was because he had resolved to do at once a dangerous, daring thing; which, however evil, is always great. Miss Tupper (little Ruth's nurse) particularly remarked this strange, grand look; and though—coming, as it did, from no noble source—it speedily passed away, it gave prestige to the attentions he bestowed upon her as they sat at supper. Mark had been rather attentive to her for some time past; to-night his manner was particularly agreeable. He sat by her side, he laughed and joked with her, he handed her meat and drink. Chiefly on her behalf, he provoked Simkin to bring forth a bottle of brandy; and when the careful butler produced a bottle more than half empty, the contents of which afforded only the weakest glass of toddy all round, Mark gallantly ascended to his room, and bringing down his private flask, reinforced the tumblers of all the party. Miss Tupper's glass he behaved toward most liberally; Simkin's received an almost equal mark of attention, more for appearance sake than on any other account, for the butler was a very heavy sleeper naturally; the same may be said of the housekeeper; but Jenkin, though he was only a footman and sat apart, Mark much delighted to honour on this occasion: Jenkin was notoriously known to sleep with one eye and one ear open. From all which the reader infers that Howlet's flask was medicated: with the contents of one of the terrible little bottles, perhaps. It was; very carefully and shrewdly medicated, according to the books in the library, so that while the sleepers should sleep well, they should not slumber *too* deeply or too long. That would only excite suspicion.

Nor is it to be supposed that Howlet allowed his fellow-servants to drowse and nod in each other's faces: he had huddled the plan to no such purpose. While the tumblers were full he laughed, and joked, and romped, in order to give the feast some of the character of a symposium, and thus keeping his fellow-servants alive for a time, and furnishing an explanation for heavy sleeping afterwards: but scarcely was "the goblet drained," than he suddenly cried "Hush!" assuming a listening attitude.

"What's the matter?" inquired several.

"Is any one up-stairs with Mr. Keppel?"

"No."

"I thought I heard him moving about there! He's on his way to London, you may depend." And Mr. Howlet laughed.

But Miss Tupper thought she heard a noise, too, and fearing for her little charge, whom she was strictly enjoined never to leave, she bustled up to her room, escorted by Jenkin. Simkin immediately followed, to lock up; and in ten minutes everybody was a-bed, or a-bedroom, and all was quiet.

Howlet, for one, was not a-bed, *he* was only a-bedroom; where he sat between a palpable Past and a scarcely mistakeable Future. He looked backward, he looked onward; there were signs of a renewal of the battle aforesaid; but upon the whole his resolution never faltered. Nevertheless, he trembled as he took the first decided step in a path which certainly had a jail in it, whether he should succeed in escaping it or not: and this though that first step was of itself innocent enough. It was simply the lighting of a second candle—and the placing it, with the other, in his window close against the panes. There they burned, as different to all concerns of men as any candles in the world, for full five minutes. That was a long time to Mr. Howlet, who meanwhile peered out into the dark from behind the shelter of a curtain, sullying the glass with his anxious, low-drawn breath. At length an owl hooted. "To-who-o-o," cried the melancholy bird, if, indeed, it were not a melancholy night-watching gipsy; for the hooting was raised in the direction of the camp.

Drawing a hearty breath again, Mark hurriedly removed the candle, and in half an hour the camp was broken up. March was the word. Not a gipsy remained.

Now Mark felt that he was fairly on the road with a jail in it. Not, however, as Howlet, valet, but as an independent person arrayed in superfine cloth, with a good gold watch, and a purse full of guineas; as a gentleman who had avenged his sister's wrongs on another gentleman. Forward, then! Midnight it is, and all clear!

The young man's next proceeding seemed scarcely so innocent as the first. What did he? He took a little cup, and he took the phial with the contents of which he had hocussed the brandy. Three or four drops from the bottle he mixed in the cup with some water; he had tried milk—that wouldn't do. A little syrup sweetens this draught. Then he takes a pair of new white gloves and the other bottle: and with these and the cup he quits his room.

The stairs do not creak much in a general way, but Mark thinks they make a detestable groaning to-night, though he treads them very tenderly in his stocking feet. Not only so, but the bannisters which he does not touch creak and click ever and anon, suddenly; and now there comes a cold whiff of wind past his head, as if a door had opened. These admonitions, these small signs and tokens, fail to move the valet from his purpose, but they put fear in his heart, palor in his face, and trembling into his limbs, so that it becomes rather a journey from his own room to that in which little Ruth and her nurse are sleeping.

First, however, he looks in upon his master. There lies the Kepple, his limbs thrown wildly, but still gracefully, upon the bed; his beautiful black hair streaming from his temples—yet as white and serene to see as if they were the Temple of Innocence; his forehead bathed in perspiration, his brows set hard, as if he were engaged in some deadly struggle. For the rest, he is fast asleep. All right then: we simply close the curtains about him, and then we close the door.

That is to say, the outer door. The inner, that which separates Keppel's chamber from Ruth's, we open. Miss Tupper's proverbial modesty, however, forbids the assumption that that is an easy matter. The door is provided with both lock and bolt on the inside. On the other hand, Howlet's shrewdness, and his opportunities for exercising it, equally forbid the supposition that he has now to force that door like a clumsy burglar. He simply introduces a duplicate key into the key-hole; but that, it appears, will not do. Miss Tupper's own key is left in the lock. Very well. Mark now takes a sort of skeleton key from his pocket; it catches a ward of Miss T.'s key, and they softly turn in the lock together. As for the bolt, that is of no consequence. The screws which hold the hasp have been previously drawn, and the holes which they filled in the door-post so judiciously worked with a gimlet, that though the screws themselves are nearly replaced, they have no bite at all; so, when Howlet sharply applies his knee to the door, it opens forthwith, the hasp falling dead upon the carpeted floor.

The noise of it falling aroused the child.

"Is 'at you, Mark?"

"Hush—h!" replied he, impatiently, and violently trembling: for if he loved any one he loved her. "Hush! don't wake good nurse. I thought you wanted some drink."

"So I do," said she, whispering, and smiling an arch smile, as if Mr. Howlet's appearance there was a joke.

"Well, here's some for you!" And Mark trembled more than ever as he held the cup to the child's lips.

"Oh, it's nice—isn't it?" she exclaimed, still in a whisper, when she had drunk.

"Is it? You shall have some more to-morrow if you lie down now, and make no noise to wake nurse."

"Shall I?" said she, well pleased, disposing her pretty head upon her pillow; and in two minutes, with the story book of "Little Red Riding-Hood" clasped in her hands, she slept as soundly as the dead.

Howlet would have given a thousand pounds to have had the potion in the cup again, as, smiling on him, she turned upon her bed. Now, however, it was quite too late. The draught insured her a breathless slumber of at least twenty hours. "Go on, or betray yourself," said the Enemy, in Howlet's ear. Accordingly he went on.

His next proceeding was to put one of the white gloves upon his right hand. The next to take Ruth's pale and rigid little form across his knees. The next to wet all the fingers of the gloved hand with the contents of that other bottle. Lastly, he threw back the child's head and its beautiful curls, and took her by the throat with a soft grasp, and with the gloved hand. In two minutes purply-black finger-marks appeared. Little Ruth was to all appearance strangled.

For a moment Mark looked aghast at this little stroke of business. What a scene for Miss Tupper to open her eyes upon! He looked quickly, savagely round upon her, almost expecting to meet the glare of her horrified face. No; she slept. Howlet *knew* she was safe locked in slumber for hours to come, though the heavens fell. Click! What if that were the click of the lock of Keppel's bedside pistol—Keppel awake, and watching him from the darkness beyond, through the half-open door! A swift glance in that direction also, a straining of the ear to listen! Ah! he snores like a pig. It was a noise in the wainscot.

"Now, loiterer!" whispered the devil in Mark's ear again.

He, Howlet, passed into Keppel's room with the child. Down upon the floor at his bedside he placed her—breathless—with her dress disordered, with her face pale, with her throat black—as if she had been thrown there by an assassin. And then he passed out, leaving all dark behind him.

KEPPEL THROWS LITTLE RUTH INTO THE LIMEKILN.

CHAPTER XIV.

DREAMING AND WAKING.

KEPPEL's people did not put him to bed comfortably, but quite otherwise. His pillow was rather on his head than his head on his pillow; therefore he dreamt, and a curious dream he dreamed.

Far above him were clouds like the sea in summer, with golden waifs like the galleys of Cleopatra and little white clouds like the sails of a fleet of fishers. In this sea was an island—glorious with woods, and meadows, and streams—full of riches—covered with flocks, and fruits, and sweet garden patches, wherein, one white palace lay shining in the sun. The aim and labour of his life, he dreamed, was to reach this island, which, drowsing in the soft airs that blew over the sea from every side, awaited his coming, to wake into broad life; and the only way to reach it was by a ladder, the rails of which were the dead effigies of all the enemies he ever had or had made. Not at regular intervals were these rails placed: some were far apart from others, so that he could barely touch them with his finger tips: therefore the ascent was slow and painful. Moreover, the dead image of the enemy on which he trod took life, became man or woman, and tugged at his feet, and clung about him, sorely hindering his upward progress. It gave them exquisite pain when he kicked them off, but what of that; Excelsior!

Beginning with the bottom rail, in which he recognised his father (this rail was a terrible distance from the rest), he worked himself up higher and higher, with more or less difficulty—past Lucy—past Butler—and then on again, until at length he had succeeded. One foot was actually planted on the precious soil—one hand grasped a knot of flowers, the eyes of which were sapphires and emeralds, while the broken stems anointed his hand with sleepy juices, and their crushed leaves breathed ravishing airs: his eyes were already fascinated by a group of beautiful women, stone hitherto, but now slowly waking, as under the trees they lay; when suddenly, straight over a hill came a child—his own daughter—and thrust him headlong down again with one touch of her little hand.

In other words, Keppel's head slipped from the pillow, and fell full two inches. However, the shock plucked him, insensible, from the deep wine-sodden sleep into which he had sunk. Starting suddenly off the bed, without a single idea yet returned to his skull, he sat down on a chair, casting his red and vacant eyes upon a moonbeam that now shot into the room, as if searching for something. Three or four times his eyes blinked, like an owl's in the sun, as they followed the beam from the chink where it entered to that spot on the floor where it rested. After the fourth blink he stared with more method at the spot on the floor. Then first an idea *did* stray back into his head; the idea being that there was a frog in the room, and that the moonbeam was tickling its back. This tickled Keppel's fancy, too—what there was of it awake—and blinking once more, he smiled a feeble smile of amusement.

Wonderful it was to see by what fine gradations this smile hardened off into a look full of bewildered horror, as now nearly awake, he glanced down again. *Was that a frog?* Was it not rather a little human hand? He went down upon his knees, crawling towards it, reached forth his fingers, and touched those other fingers as fearfully as if they were bathed in fire instead of by the cold moon. A thrill shot through his veins when his own hand was revealed too, and as he touched that innocent white palm. He was quite awake now, and more than half sobered; nevertheless, it was with a staggering step that he approached the window, tearing back the thick curtains. In the moonbeams streamed, in a flood, straight upon the body of little Ruth; they seemed to have found what they had been searching for—what they had been lurking outside to reveal; and now gathering about it, pointed out its every lineament to the terror-stricken Keppel. If the first beam that shot into the room had transfixed him, like an arrow, he could not have stood more pale, more breathless, so unutterably like one dead and condemned to eternal death. Howlet, peering in (he was waiting outside), saw that figure in the dim light.

As he stood with his hand pressed upon his mouth, this conviction pierced him through and through:—he had risen in his drunken sleep, full of murderous dreams; and in his blind hatred of the child, he had taken her from her nurse, and killed her. The door was open there, and all was quiet—quiet as death. Yes, it must be so. Nor was this the first time he had played the part of a somnambulist (a fact which his man very well knew, by the by). Yet the child might not be past recovery! Instantly he pulled the bell which communicated with his man's room (which bell the latter had muffled), and then made for the door, intending to alarm the house.

On the threshold he came face to face with Mr. Howlet, who had thrown off his waistcoat and neckcloth, and had all the appearance of having hurried precipitately to his master's assistance.

Keppel started back at the suddenness of this apparition; his man glided into the room with his candle, and shut the door.

"I've been reading," said he, in a whisper, "and had only begun to undress when you rang. Ah! Hush!" He suddenly placed his hand on his master's arm, as, pointing to Ruth's body, Keppel convulsively opened his lips to speak. "What! a murderer! Hush for your life!" He crossed the room on tiptoe, and closed the door leading to Ruth's apartment.

A gallows rose before Keppel's imagination. His lips worked convulsively, and he sat down, helpless.

Meanwhile Mark knelt by Ruth's side, felt her wrist, listened at her bosom, placed his hand over the tiny still beating heart.

"Dead!" he exclaimed in a low tone, "dead enough!" But as if unwilling to believe his senses, he again listened for her breathing, and even looked for a moment as if he detected the presence of life. Keppel, forgetting the gallows, caught at the hope which this artful expression inspired, and muttered in a hoarse but resolute voice—

"Go for a doctor!"

"Mr. Keppel," answered Howlet, deliberately rising and facing his master, "if I leave the house, I shall go for a constable. At the same time let me advise you to speak low—you might commit yourself!" Mark pointed towards the room where the nurse slept.

"Rascal!" rejoined the other, taking care, however, to observe Mark's advice, "do you dare to imagine——?"

"Yes I do, sir, and it's my opinion you shammed being drunk last night (you're sober enough now), and that you knew what you were about when you wouldn't be undressed! And what about that talk of going to London?" Howlet muttered all this so threateningly, eyeing Keppel the while with so much coolness, that his little bit of bluster was extinguished at its birth. With a stupified, melancholy look, he sat down again at the foot of his bed.

After a pause of a few moments, rendered intolerable by the steady, insolent gaze of his servant, Keppel rose with the same stupified air, and moved towards the door. Howlet instantly anticipated him—taking his stand with his back to the entrance, his arms folded.

"You mustn't go, sir, till I understand you!"

Mr. Keppel waved his hand before him in the most helpless way.

"Mark," he said, "how can you suppose such a thing? Me! My own child, on whose existence my very bread depended!"

The valet shook his head. He was, or seemed, touched.

"Master," replied he, "if I am wrong, the consequences to me would be something awful, but I can't shut my eyes to the plain facts. Your hatred of this child has been the talk of the house, and all the village knows your mad, passionate ways. Haven't I heard how you talk when the wine's in? Haven't I heard you curse that child a hundred times? And now I find her strangled in your own room, and you standing over her! You go to bed too drunk to help yourself, and three hours after you're as sober as I am! If I'm mad in thinking you guilty, where will you find a sane judge or juryman in England?"

Keppel turned his face away. He was growing a month older for every minute that passed.

"What shall I do?" he muttered, in a weak, despairing voice.

"Well, sir," replied his man, after some cogitation, "I've thought of it, and I'll tell you what I shall do. If I stand talking to you much longer, *I* shall get in for it. Who knows whether one of 'em (meaning his fellow-servants) isn't watching us now. I shall rouse the house!"

Howlet opened the door, apparently to carry out this purpose. His master glided towards him.

"No, no! For Heaven's sake! my dear fellow! my good friend! I haven't been unkind to you, Mark!"

Now Mr. Howlet could not resist this appeal to his gratitude; and besides, he was anxious to conclude the scene. Relinquishing the door-handle, he turned and looked through the window with a tear in his eye.

"There is some terrible mystery in all this," whispered his master, going to his side. "I swear to you that I know no more how the child came here than you do. Unless, indeed——"

"What?" asked Mark, turning hastily.

"Do you think it possible for a man to do murder in his sleep?"

"I think he'd find it precious hard to find any one to believe him, if he said so. Why?"

"Because," replied the other, passing his hand over his eyes, "I've a dim recollection of some murderous dream—about Ruth, too! And people have been known to do strange things in their sleep. They've been known——" he proceeded, reflectively.

"Mr. Keppel," interrupted Howlet, who by no means desired that his master should reflect upon this or any other subject at present, "don't be a fool, sir! Who'd believe such a tale? And if they did, it would be much the same thing to you. The child's death makes you a beggar, and you might as well hang as starve—a gentleman like you!" This was an artful thrust.

"Ruined—ruined! Dead done up!"

There was a pause—filled in at last, so far as Howlet was concerned, by a little pantomime of relenting. He sniffed the morning afar off, and felt that this stage of the business must be terminated forthwith.

"Well, sir," he said, calmly, "you reminded me that you've been kind to me, and so you have. I'll believe that you *did* do this in one of your sleep-walking fits; and to save all the house from destruction, I'll help you out of the mess!"

The frank, superior way in which the valet offered the gentleman his hand, and the humble, grateful, speechless manner with which the gentleman took it, was a sight to see.

"Now," continued Mr. Keppel's master, "I'll risk my neck for you; so you must please let me risk it my own way. Agreed?"

"Willingly; and you're a made man, Howlet, if you succeed in helping me through."

"Very well," answered the other, in a significant tone. "Now sharp's the word! The nurse!"

Keppel's heart sank within him.

"Now, if she's been listening all this while!" suggested Howlet. "Go in and see, sir."

"No—no! You go, Mark!"

Accordingly, Mr. Howlet stepped into the room—really to replace the hasp upon the lintel. Keppel waited and listened, full of a new terror. Suppose he had murdered the nurse, too!

"All right!" exclaimed his man, locking the door by the same means which opened it. "You left your cap in the room, sir;" and Howlet threw down a piece of velvet head-gear, which Keppel had worn when he was carried to his room. This new proof of his guilt, or misfortune, settled any doubt that might possibly have lingered in the mind of the unhappy man. Of course, he had no suspicion that the person who found the cap by the nurse's bedside might have placed it there. It was a great relief, however, to know that nurse was alive: and when the valet said, "All right!" the gentleman breathed again.

"Now," continued Howlet, "do as you said you'd do. Off to London!"

"But what about the—the child?"

"Ah! Just watch by it till I dress. I will then go out with you, dispose of the body, return, go to bed, and account for Ruth's absence in the morning. Leave that to me. All you've got to do is, to know nothing about the matter when you come back, and to go mad for the loss of the child. You'll look mad enough, though—so you needn't say much, mind! I've got my plan all right, and will give you the cue when you return. Say to-morrow night, *late*: at about eleven. And mind you *do* go to London, and be seen by some one who knows you."

The whispered conference was ended. Stooping, Howlet gently took the story-book from the child's hand, and quitted the room.

Before he could return, Howlet had to carry out several little details necessary to the plan, and which could not well be proceeded with till this stage of the affair was successfully passed.

In the first place, he went quickly to his room, returning with a pair of boots like those which farm labourers commonly wear—very old, clumsy, and large. These in his hands, and Little Red Riding Hood in his pocket, he crept stealthily out of the house. Where he emerged there was a gravel walk: beyond that, he would be visible from the windows, and his figure *might* be seen (there was almost light enough) by any of his fellow-servants who might happen to be star-gazing. When he got to the lawn, therefore, he stooped low down, and so ran swiftly and lightly in the direction of the gipsies' camp. He had not gone many yards, however, before he stopped, put the boots over his slippers, and then turned back toward that side of the house where Ruth's room lay. With long strides he strode clean through the flower-pots, leaving a great coarse foot-print at every step: and then on to the lawn where it sloped up to the terrace upon which the window of Ruth's apartment opened. He climbs the terrace—that's an easy matter. He stands before the window (where also great foot-marks will be found to-morrow), takes out a knife, and noiselessly splinters the frame-work of the casement. Then, between its leaves, he adroitly inserts the blade, and the well-oiled and otherwise prepared bolt shoots back. The window *had* shutters and fastenings impregnable; but, in the memory of man, there had never been need for them, and so they were neglected; as Mark knew as well as any one.

Softly pushing back one leaf of the casement, he thrust in his head, and attentively listened: the nurse still breathed heavily. Into the room stepped he, and shot the bolt of the door which opened into Keppel's apartment, where that gentleman was now shivering in a panic of apprehension at Howlet's long absence. This last little feat accomplished, all evidence of that door's having been opened from the outside was destroyed. Congratulating himself on that fact, Howlet went out at the window, closed it, leapt the terrace, and went crushing through the flower-beds again, and on to the elastic, printless turf, as before.

On his way he dropped Little Red Riding Hood.

Nothing was now to be done but to take off the boots, and go back in the slippers: which was successfully accomplished. The reader, remembering a passage in the last chapter, sees the object of all these manœuvres, and of the bargain with the gipsies: it was to make it appear that Ruth had been stolen by these poultry-loving wanderers. Charmingly was it done, and all in the space of fifteen minutes. The church clock chimed two as Howlet re-entered his bed-room.

CHAPTER XV.

WHAT IT IS TO BE WICKED.

KNOWING that his master could not endure to be left in the dark, and at the same time anxious that a light should not be seen in Keppel's room, Howlet placed his candle on the floor in a corner, when he went away to complete his arrangements. It was sorry comfort—that dim, blear-eyed, goblin-like flame, flickering in the corner like a witch's eye in an hour of wickedest inspiration. Rising, falling, wavering, it made that idea substantial which (if *I* have any experience in such matters) haunts all murderers in common—namely, that for them the secure laws of nature are dissolved: that all elements and senses are unloosed; and though they *may* keep their seats from custom, or go coursing in their circles as before, still waver, waver, and giddily threaten upon the verge of a thousand vagaries. Providence no longer provides for them: not that their eyes shall see as other men's, or their ears hear, or that the earth shall be solid under their feet; that the sun shall warm them, or the winds give them breath, or water flow over their lips; that walls shall not fall on them, or streets close and crush them; that darkness shall hide them; or that, though they cut their tongues out, they shall not cry their own guilt at the street corners. So, as this candle wavered, the walls rocked, the floor heaved, the ceiling fell and rose again, under the shadows. Now the room expanded big as a church; now it collapsed narrow as a tomb. How Keppel's head swam as he began to feel all this, though only in little as yet.

Now he endeavoured to take refuge in pitiful and sentimental thought, which to do him justice, was not altogether got up for the occasion. "Poor little creature!" he thought; but was any good angel near enough to him now to *hear* a thought? That seemed so doubtful; so he repeated in a loud whisper—"Poor little creature, I loved her after all! My own little daughter—an angel in heaven now, and perhaps looking down with pity on her unhappy father—who has been the innocent cause of her death, and who is well punished for all his unkindness to her." And the poor wretch looked round the shadow-haunted room, as if he hoped to see some recording angel taking down his words. He saw nothing of the kind. He saw only the walls moving like walls of smoke, and the ceiling rising and falling, and that blear, witch-eyed flame blinking in the corner. The only stable thing in the room was the body of the child; that seemed as fixed as his fate and the type of its irrevocability. He would have touched her kindly, to prove to himself and the recording angel (if any) that he had no malice or guilt in his heart; but the thrill that trembled through his blood when their hands met in the moonlight, had scarcely subsided yet. Hardly dared he look on her, indeed; for the candle had an eye on her, too, hovering over her face like a bat with phosphorescent wings, and clothing all the little body with fantastic shadows. Nevertheless, he could not restrain his eyes from wandering to the spot where she lay, though at every glance his eyes seemed to take up the shadows and lay them on his heart; as a certain party took Peter Schlemihl's shadow by the heels, and rolled it up, and put it in his pocket. At last, while he looked, the light leapt up—fell—expired; and then, as the moonbeams came in again, they revealed, in their own dim, ghostly way, not the face of his murdered daughter, but of the murdered Lucy!

This shock he was utterly unprepared for. His head swam and but for fear he would have fainted; as it was, he went tottering out of the room; he could remain with no such horrors any longer. Outside there, he leant against the wall waiting Howlet's return—full of heats, and breathless fumes, and shiftless unrest—like a man in the prairie, and fire closing down upon him on every side. Now this is the way he was punished, in a crime of which he was innocent, for that he *had* been guilty of. Ah, what did that poor old Widow Howlet know of the ways of Providence? Or what do *you* know, if it comes to that?

Recovering somewhat from his last shock, Keppel began to reflect that Howlet was a long time absent. A long time. It must be at least half an hour since he left the room. So he imagined in his bewildered mind, while in fact scarce more than five minutes had elapsed. Henceforward every moment was dragged out to the length of a dozen—every minute seemed to be another hour—countless hours of suspense. He listened with such strained attention, that at some moments he was deaf as a post; he glanced about him with eyes that magnified or overshot all that fell within their range; and he had already approached a climax of apprehension when the noise of Mark's knife on the window-sash of the nurse's room whispered into Keppel's hollow ears.

"Hark!" He stood the image of dread attention, like a stag when the scent of the hounds first comes down the wind.

"Again! that was certainly a footstep!" A moment after, and he heard Howlet jump from the terrace and run from the house.

"Treachery, by heaven!" exclaimed Keppel, in a voice dangerously loud, "Here I stand, while that smooth villain, Howlet, traps me, and bargains for my carcase. No, you scoundrel, it has not come to that yet, maybe."

Full of sudden resolution, he re-entered his room, threw on a hat and a large cloak, which luckily lay there, since some night excursion, took from his pocket a key which gave ingress and egress by a private way, and prepared to fly.

"And leave you behind?" pondered he, turning back to look on little Ruth. "No. By British law no man's a murderer till the body's found; and it shan't be found here."

Carefully taking up the child, whose senses Howlet had so securely locked in sleep, Keppel folded her in his cloak and departed. His step was as light and as soft as his man's. By a fortunate chance he avoided the flower-beds, leaving only a light trace of his feet on the gravel-walk, which was so much the better, since it was to be supposed that he had really gone to London in his drink; and in a few minutes he was out of the grounds. Then the church clock chimed two.

Now whither? Keppel did not ask himself this question till he was full two miles away from those long-desired, ill-bought possessions of his. Then, breathless and exhausted, he sat down to rest on a wayside bank—that very bank on which Lucy lay stretched so many years before, at the mercy of heaven and Mrs. Jolliffe's dog. He had no knowledge of that as he rested there—thankful for the cool rain, that he now noticed for the first time, as it pattered against his hot face; but it is true, nevertheless, that as the rain-drops fell soothingly about him, whispering among the leaves with a thousand sweet tongues, he went back for a few moments into a soft oblivious dream of the times when he used to walk there with that other one—almost an innocent man. How blessed it was—even a moment of even such dreaming! I believe in the communion of spirits—upon the earth as well as out of it. I know I lose mine sometimes—not only when my carcase is asleep, but awake; and I believe it (the spirit) goes to some one whom I love and have wronged, and settles that little matter with the *other* spirit, or comforts my friend; or warns him; or bids him be stedfast, assuring him of my faith; or even sometimes puts bad thoughts out of his head. Other people's spirits do the same by me, I am sure. In this way I account for "curious dreams," and revelations not otherwise accounted for. Now suppose Lucy's spirit—on the earth or out of it—visited Keppel in his trouble, and itself soothed him with these dreams; what a good faithful little spirit that must have been! And (supposing her to be still above the earth, of course) how she must have wondered at some new sensation of gladness presently, when the spirit came back with ever so vague a hint, that to think of her might be not the most ungrateful thing to Keppel, after all.

Certainly it was not. There he sat, almost drowsing in that dream for several minutes—his hat off, the clasps of his cloak loosened, that he might feel more of the wind and the cool rain, and with Ruth safely wrapped, and stretched upon his knees.

Oh, that burden on his knees! When he glanced down at it, his old reminiscences vanished, the rain was no longer cool, nor the wind. That burden must be put away, whatever became of the burden on his conscience. But how? Bury it? He had not even a pocket-knife wherewith to turn up an inch of sod. Take it into a wood, and bury it with grass and leaves? While the winds blow, and old women go gathering sticks, and boys go nutting and nesting, there is no security in any such hiding-place. Throw it into the pool where he and Lucy had parted? He ejected that idea as soon as it entered his mind. But if not the pool, the river? That was the thing. Judiciously weighted with a few

stones, his secret would lie concealed there for ever; and, you know, no man's a murderer till the body's found.

This was Keppel's conclusion, as, clapping on his hat and adjusting his cloak, he rose from the bank and briskly continued his journey.

His eyes bent upon the ground, he went doggedly on for full half an hour (it was three miles to the river), always by by-paths. Presently he heard the crowing of a cock, and looking up, saw the morning coming up upon his right hand, and the night rolling away upon his left. Thereupon he thought of the division of the just and the unjust, "as a shepherd divideth the sheep from the goats;" and gazing upon the retreating clouds, he half expected to see his own image there, floating away into eternal darkness. Then the grand and awful march of the "Dies Iræ" sounded through him, and again he plunged along, with his head down.

When he lifted it again, he saw straight before him, between the light and the darkness, a white glare—sickly fainting off upon the right hand, standing in a pale, sullen column on the left. In Keppel's present state of mind, everything had power to alarm him. He had an image of terror for every object that met his eyes. And when he saw this pale, slow-moving glare rising between the night and the morning, he had another sad thought, of the legions of death and the mists of the pit. This vision corroborated the other. Stopping dead in the middle of the path, he stared heavily before him, and some minutes elapsed before he discovered the true nature of the object that had terrified him.

"Pooh!" he exclaimed, "the lime-kilns, of course!"

The lime-kilns, of course. But that hardly seemed a sufficient explanation for Mr. Keppel. For, after making the discovery, he did not fall again into his rapid walk, as might have been expected, but rather "hung fire," as they say. Nor did he carry his eyes towards the ground again, but kept them fixed on the steam and smoke of the kiln, as he went loitering about it, skirting it at a distance.

At length he bethought him that he was damp and chill; that it was warm by the kiln, and so persuaded himself to go up there. As he turned into a path that led thitherward, the hot breath of the lime-pits came to meet him. Then he trembled anew, but still he went on. Forward through melancholy patches of vegetation, black—stifled by the hot breath of the pits; past melancholy bushes, whose naked branches stood bleaching, and beyond where there was no green thing at all, and no living thing but the living fire; where no sound answered his footsteps; where the ground lay soft and white; while around was the spectral gray of the morning, and before him rose the smoke of the kiln—indistinctly, like the robes of a ghostly host rising skyward. What sort of figure Keppel made, standing there in his great cloak at the border of the kiln, like a dark statue amidst all the spectral light, I leave the reader to imagine. Also I leave the reader to imagine what his thoughts were, while he eagerly watched a rag as it was blown upon the burning lime in the pit. While he watched it, it was utterly consumed, leaving not a vestige behind. What Keppel then *did* was unequivocal, whatever his thoughts had been or were. He loosed the clasp of his cloak once more, wrapped it about the little body it had hitherto protected from the rain, and rolled the bundle in!

We are told that, in cases of sudden accident, the crushing of a limb or what not, the sufferer has at first only a confused sense of pain—that the anguish is keener an hour after than at the time of the injury. So it was with Keppel in the severer calamity that had befallen him. At first his mind was crushed and numbed; but as soon as he had disposed of "the body," an agony of distincter meaning took possession of him.

His first feeling, when he turned away from the kiln, was of extreme lightness in his limbs. He saw that his arms swung at his sides—but, for any other sensation, they might have been the arms of somebody else. His legs—though, as if by some mechanism of their own, they bore him swiftly along—seemed no more substantial than shadows, controlling him, rather than he them. Another sensation he had, sufficiently unpleasant: all things seemed apart from and distant from him. The tree there—it seemed miles away; that hedge was as dim to his sight as the far horizon; between his vision and the very grass at his

MR. KEPPEL AT BAY.

feet appeared an impassable region of atmosphere ; it was all as if he were suspended alone in space, thousands of miles away, and only saw the familiar things of this world through a glass. A terrible sensation, representing the solitude which belongs to consummated, utter, irremediable guilt.

Nor can it be said that he now heard the rustling of any tree, or the singing of any bird. He was only *conscious* of the sounds, and they had all one meaning. The glorious red of the eastern clouds had that one meaning too. The rain had ceased ; but when a wind shook the boughs, it whispered " murder." When the boughs scattered the rain-drops to the ground, they pattered a little volley of accusations, and " murder" was the burden of them all. In the corn-fields, the ears nodded to each other, and he could see the murmur run along, as each after each bent to listen to and to repeat one low-hinted sound, " murder." Started a lark from the meadow, shrilly crying out the word—rising with it, higher and higher, round and round and higher still, till at length it was only a fluttering speck ; but down to earth and up to heaven went the terrible cry—clear !

His shadowy, unstable feet quickened, as these sounds echoed in Keppel's heart, empty of all consolation. They even made a bound forward when the lark burst upward at his side, and henceforward they went pattering along to the same awful tune. Right foot and left, each took up a syllable of the dread word— mur-der ! mur-der ! mur-der ! mur-der ! That was the still-repeated sound of Keppel's footsteps, right and left. Then his arms, alternately swinging, took it up : they motioned it to each

other, as one makes words by the mere motion of the lips. Then the blood swelled into a vein in his temples, and *it* began to beat the same devil's tattoo upon his brain. And they all went quicker and quicker together.

From a walk the unhappy man broke into a convulsive trot ; then into a run ; and at length, hounded by the louder-baying echoes of his own footsteps, lashed by the vein that beat faster on his skull, mocked by his swinging arms, he dashed forward as if he would run clean off the face of the earth. The wind ran by his side, low laughing ; a bough dashed his hat from his head with a half-jeering, half-vengeful whistle ; he saw the field la-bourers pause on their way to work, and point at him—heard them pursue him, or so he thought. On he dashed, leaping ditches, plunging through new-ploughed land—always straight ahead and full in view, till there was no more strength in him. At hand was a ruined cowhouse. Into this he sprang, banged to the rickety door, piled against it what lumber lay there, and stood panting with his back against all. No one followed him. In the pain of those last minutes, he had been visible only to the Eye that sees all, and beholds always. Peering through the chinks, he became assured of this ; so, sitting down on a rickety trough, he wiped his damp forehead, and thanked Providence for his escape.

The shed looked out upon a meadow, where an after-growth of hay was ripe for the scythe. Presently came the haymakers, brown, freckled men and women, and children laughing and ragged ; he plainly saw that there was no chance of his quitting the place without detection till evening came, and the labour of the day was over. And supposing the haymakers should have occasion to enter his hiding-place? Then comes discovery. To guard against this, he took away from the door the lumber with which he had barricaded it, and erected a sort of screen at the further and darkest end of the shed, where he might hide on occasion.

It all proved as Keppel anticipated. After working awhile, the haymakers came in a body towards the shed, leisurely, laughing. Keppel instantly retreated behind his screen, crouching in a corner; but the labourers came no further than the threshold of his hiding-place, content to prepare their humble breakfast just within the shelter of the roof. Coarse bread, and morsels of cheese and bacon, commonly formed the repast, as Keppel could plainly see through the chinks of his prison; but the labourers ate as men only do who have first to earn their food, and, washed down with beer or milk, it disappeared in the swiftest, happiest, heartiest manner. All this while, the men roared out their rude jokes, and the women laughed, and said what appeared to be very smart things, and the children gamboled like good-humoured little suckling bears, who proverbially have all their troubles to come. Keppel viewed all this with the studious eye of envy. What would he not have given to have been from that time forward a haymaker, too!—to have forgotten, in daily toil and hard fare, his wealth and his gentility, the lodge—and little Ruth!

One of the labourers had with him a small, wiry-haired, fierce-looking dog, who, tired of tumbling with the boys and girls, had lain down, with leisure to look about him. Presently he saw Keppel's two eyes twinkling through the chinks of his barricade, and made so sudden a spring towards them, that their owner recoiled in alarm. But Keppel was fortunate. Though the dog still leapt at him, barking fiercely, the owner of the animal merely called "Rat! rat!" and no more came of it.

All the weary hours of the morning did Keppel remain cramped in his hiding-place; his terrors, from time to time, renewed by an occasional razzia on the part of the wiry-haired dog. The afternoon came; down fell the rain anew, and the labourers left the field. Keppel gladly watched their retreating figures; but they were hardly out of sight when he wished them back again, almost. If he had lost the fear occasioned by their presence, he had also lost the excitement of listening and watching for them, which had occupied him all the morning, staving off reflection somewhat. But now, when he ventured to look out, there were the big wet fields spreading out so dreary and quiet—with not a sound to break the silence save a sheep-bell monotonously tinkling at a distance. Within, the prospect was no more calculated to cheer a guilty and miserable man. The rain oozed through the broken tiles, and, trickling down the walls, grimy with age, and black with many showers, dropped, dropped, dropped, as if measuring eternity. And those cross-beams overhead, what were they like?

Then came the reflection, had he not been too hasty? Was he sure that Howlet was treacherous? Where was the proof? By his impatience and folly, might he not have thwarted the plans of the faithful fellow, after all? One thing was certain, however, whatever may have been Howlet's plan for disposing of the body, it could not have been more effectual than that he (Keppel) had adopted. Comforted by this reflection, Keppel went on thinking, soothed and saddened at the same time by the dropping of the rain. He had vaguely determined to remain in the shed till dark, and then—see about it.

CHAPTER XVI.

MERITORIOUS CONDUCT OF A CHARITY BOY.

NIGH unto the spot where Keppel had found so secure a sepulchre for his child, was a spacious recess cut in the chalk, where were stowed trucks and other gear used by the lime-burners. Scarcely had Keppel disappeared, when slowly rising from the vehicle nearest to the mouth of the recess a human head, wearing a towzled crop of hair, made its appearance. The human head was followed by a pair of shoulders enveloped in linsey-woolsey, well dusted with chalk. Then a long leg, partly clothed in parochial gray, was lowered over the side of the truck; and,

finally, the whole form of our young friend Woppits dropped to the ground.

Three days had passed since our young friend parted with the good Tweakle, who this very night had gone to bed in the secret and fond belief that the boy was in London, meditating—if, indeed, he had not already solved—the grunsell question. Nay, at that very moment, Tweakle was dreaming that the basket of canary-food was already launched upon the town, and had discharged full two-thirds of its cargo—that the bird people of Bethnal Green and Whitechapel had taken to his young friend so kindly, that he was already risen in favour with the citizens, who delighted to honour him; and at length, in that sweet vision, Tweakle saw his *protégé* in a gorgeous green and canary-coloured chariot, with an immense bunch of chickweed emblazoned on the panels and on the hammercloth. Also the coachman wore a bouquet of grunsell; likewise the footman.

It is impossible to say whether this dream might not have been realized at some distant day, had Woppits given the thing a fair trial; but what are the plans of a beadle and a parish boy against the manœuvres of her Majesty's dragoons?

It happened on the evening of the day when Woppits and Tweakle bade good-bye, and just as the former was about to turn in under a hayrick for the night, his ears were assailed by the mighty tramping of horses. Looking down the road the unhappy Woppits beheld the approach of a strong detachment of cavalry; which, in his ignorance of the workings of our glorious constitution, and in his unbounded belief in the power of Mr. Gorelam, he concluded had been despatched in search of him. His apprehensions were confirmed on seeing the soldiery marching straight toward London! The very road on which he was travelling was filled with them.

Creeping round on all fours to the back of the rick, Woppits lay as still as his trembling limbs would permit till the detachment had passed. Oh, how long they seemed in passing! how dreadful was the clanging of their sabres in his ears! Not till this fearsome sound had altogether died away did he venture to move. Then assured that no carbine was levelled at him round the corner, or over the hedge, he scampered off across the country. Afraid to ask his road, he had on the night on which we again find him arrived at the limekilns, where he determined to take up his quarters. On leaving Tweakle, he resolved firmly not to expend a penny of the borrowed money till he started in trade; but stirred thereto by hunger, he actually gave threepence for a loaf the day after. No more could possibly be spared, not another penny; so he made his supper off a large juicy turnip before he stole in among the trucks, to pass the night.

"Well, I'm blessed!" ejaculated Woppits in his thought of thoughts, looking after Keppel. "He's gone, has he? If I didn't think it was that there old Gorelam's milingtary after me again! I wonder what he chucked into that hole?"

Woppits cautiously approached the edge of the pit.

"Well, he must be a funny man," continued he, from this situation, "to go pitching his togs about like that. Why, that's a stunning blue cloak! Got a scarlick linin' too, it have. If you ain't spoilt with the lime I'll hook you out."

Nodding his head at the bundle, Woppits ran back to the cave, and in a moment returned with a two-pronged fork which he had previously observed standing in a corner. "Now, then, out you come!" said he. Leaning over the pit, he twisted the prongs of the fork into the loose folds of the cloak, and endeavoured to land it. He did move it a little towards him, but the quicklime had already commenced operations, and the bundle was heavy. Woppits thought that was because it stuck to the lime and making a vigorous effort, he rolled it completely over in the direction of land. As he did so, a little white arm became exposed.

Woppits dropped the fork and his lower jaw at the same time, terror-stricken. However, he was a genuine British boy at bottom, and his first terror was instantly followed by a more active one—for the child's safety. Grasping the fork again, he applied it with such dexterity that in a second of time he had succeeded in lifting Ruth out upon the bank. As for the cloak, it fell from her, already half consumed, and lay consuming.

A beautiful religious awe was spread over the boy's kind, simple face, as he knelt by Ruth's side. He lifted up her hand: it was supple, but it fell heavily when his fingers released it.

"Our Father which art in heaven," said he, little knowing how truly it was his sister upon whom his tears fell. And then, when he felt better, "You poor little dear, you don't mean to say you're dead," said he. "To be sure, you don't seem so cold as young Dick at the House was. Oh, dear! So it was you as he chucked in, was it? The jolly great coward! What harm could *you* do him, I should like to know? Why didn't he chuck in somebody his own size? Why couldn't he——? Eh, why gracious mercy!" exclaimed the boy, as he caught sight of the marks on Ruth's throat, "if you ain't been strangulated!"

Woppits sprang to his feet. Gazing at the horizon a moment with bewildered eyes, his first and most natural impulse now was, to run off and give an alarm. Indeed, his fleet legs were already carrying him away from the kiln, when he suddenly stopped, and thus addressed himself—

"Hulloa! what are you up to now, Woppits? A goin' to make yourself public in this way, are you? A goin' to put yourself in the papers, for old Gorelam to see, are you? So as he might fetch you back, and get Mr. Tweakle into trouble; and wery likely old Gorelam to say it was you what pushed her in? Woppits, I wish you may get it."

The boy turned back, violently shaking his head, as if he had cleverly frustrated somebody who had designs upon him. He retraced his steps but slowly, however, pondering the really serious dilemma into which he had fallen, and trying to make up his mind as to what was best to be done."

"It's a precious fix," muttered the boy, as, the better to deliberate, he seated himself on the ground at a little distance from Ruth. Purely out of reverence for the little still body, did he keep aloof from her, and not at all out of fear. "It's a precious fix," said he; "and a precious fix it is. Of course I ain't sorry I hooked you out, you poor little dear; but, upon my word, I do wish I'd never knowed anything about you! 'Twouldn't ha' made no difference to you, you know! What *am* I to do? I can't leave you like that, for sure. I could—well, of course, I could!—but lor, how could I, after all? Pitchin' you back agin would be being as bad as himself, almost! S'pose I was to dig you a little bit of a grave, and put some grass on the top? I can't make you a coffin, but I can put some nice bits of slate at the bottom for you to lie on."

So thinking, Woppits awfully took the little creature up in his arms, and, with a true perception of what belonged to the innocent dead, carried her out of all view of the kiln into the pleasantest of green and grassy hollows. Here he laid her down, and presently commenced digging her grave with a sharp broken piece of slate which he had found near the kiln.

It was not a cheerful occupation, as poor Woppits felt. He tried whistling, to keep his spirits up; but the very first note startled him as much as if it had broken from the lips of some insensible being at his elbow, instead of from his own.

"Serve yer right," he said to himself, half aloud, and nearly crying with vexation. "If you must whistle over a little young un's grave, couldn't you think of nothing more solemner than 'All round my hat?' Young heathen! Ain't there no psalm tunes?"

Thus rebuked by his better self, Woppits, applying himself with new vigour to his work, struck up the "Old Hundredth." Very soft and low were the first notes, and cruel was the effort to get them out; for as his heart was now quite full and his eyes brimming over, it was only with the greatest difficulty that he could keep his lips properly screwed up. However, Woppits felt that it was a sort of duty—something like consecrating the ground or reading the Burial Service; and so he went manfully on, firmer and louder at every bar, with a glory on his pauper face, and his pauper heart aching with pious grief, till he had fairly got through every verse—one of the most comical, beautiful, laughable, and heart-rending bits of music that ever was performed.

If it didn't consecrate the ground—if it was not equal to reading the Burial Service (which I've my own opinion about)—it at least did Woppits a world of good. As he performed a shake on the last notes, and they died away on the keen morning air, he felt the load lifted from his heart, and he dug away almost cheerfully: that was his reward. He even began to meditate on his own affairs, and presently fell into quite another sort of soliloquy.

"My eye," said he, knocking off the mould that clung to his awkward spade, "I'm a comin' on in the way of history and adventures. All in three days! First, I runs away, and turns the blessed parish upside down. Then I stows myself away in a tub, like a Hi-talian brigand in a cave, and Mr. Tweakle comes a chasing arter me, and a lendin' me twelve and thruppence. Then I goes in for chickweed, and am prewented by the milingtary. Then I gets a poor strangulated baby thrown upon my hands, and now I'm a sexton. And a werry wet sexton I am too," writhing in his clothes, more than damp with the rain which had again fallen. "But lor, there's luck in all things; for if it hadn't been for the rain a soaking the ground, it would ha' been werry slow work with this 'ere slate!"

Slow work it was at the best; but Woppits had by this time excavated a hollow of about two feet deep, and was on his knees grubbing away, when, judge of his astonishment, form a notion of the galvanic action of his limbs, as a small voice cried in his ear—

"Papa!"

Woppits, still kneeling in the little grave, clutched his trousers in terror, opening his eyes in an alarming way. There, revived at length by the rain, was little Ruth sitting upright, and vigorously rubbing her eyes.

"I'm thirsty," complained the small voice.

There could be no doubt about it—she was alive!

"I *am* blowed!" ejaculated Woppits, as soon as his tongue would wag. "You ain't strangulated after all, but alive and kicking in spite of the choking and the lime-burning, and in spite of me willainously diggin' your grave before your very eyes! Then all I got to say is, Hooray!" And the boy sprang to his feet, tossing the extemporized spade high into the air.

Now Ruth, thanks to the rain and the rude handling she had received, was sufficiently awake to look about her, and was not a little frightened at her strange situation, and her equally strange companion. Accordingly she began to cry.

"Bless your heart, don't cry," Woppits said, "You needn't be afraid of me, and as for the old bogey in the cloak, he's gone. I ain't used to nussin', but I'll try and nuss you, little dear. There, there!" and Woppits took the child in his arms, and tenderly wiped its eyes with his cap. Then his eye lighting on a large dock leaf, in which the rain had accumulated, he was reminded that she had complained of thirst. Going to a little torrent that rushed along hard by, he caught some water in the big leaf, and gave the child to drink.

The little creature took it eagerly, and then put her arms round the neck of her rough nurse and kissed him.

Now it happened that never before in Woppits' recollection had he been kissed by man, or woman, or child. Ruth's affectionate salute had, then, an extraordinary effect upon him. His face burnt crimson; he felt utterly ashamed of himself; and a big something swelled in his breast. I find it impossible to describe how he looked, and little can be gathered from what he said. It was—

"Oh, I say, jigger that you know—leastways I don't mean jigger it, but you hadn't better. I've seen it done, but it ain't good for poor fellers like me." Nevertheless, he hugged her up closer, walking slowly on with the child in his arms.

"I say," spoke the boy after a silence, "do you know what your name is, young un?"

"I'm Ruth," she answered.

"Ruth? Why then you're a gal? My gracious! this *is* adventures! Well, what else besides Ruth?"

"Miss Ruth."

"Oh," rejoined Woppits; and another short pause ensued, during which the puzzled nurse scratched his towzled head twenty times at least.

"Are you going to papa?" the child asked at length.

"What, him in the cloak, you mean, perhaps? Not if I knows it!" answered Woppits, vehemently. But seeing that his manner alarmed his small *protégé*, he went on to say, "Leastways, not yet, my pretty chaffinch. We're now going to have some breakfast." An idea which only at that moment entered his head, and so they trudged on.

"If anybody asked me what I should like," mused the boy,

"I should say, just to drop on Mr. Tweakle. He's the cove. He'd advise me what to do in no time. I'm sure I don't know what to be after. I gets further and further from that there chickweed every turn I take. Of course it's no use thinking about such nonsense, but I should very much like to keep this poor little gal; and if I could stow it anywhere, and earn enough to buy it wittles, I'm blest if I wouldn't. Howsomever, she shall have one breakfast with me, and out of the chickweed money too. So I tell you what it is, little Ruth," continued he aloud, as they came to a close-grown copse, amply sheltered, "you stay here for a minnit—only a minnit, mind—and I'll run and get you some wittles."

It actually never occurred to the boy, till he was out of sight of the fact, that Ruth had only a nightgown on—and that that was drenched with rain. Immediately after, he remembered that he had left his bundle in the lime truck, where he had taken up his quarters. Swift as a buck he darted off for that precious "other shirt," the socks and the neckerchief, and great was his satisfaction at recovering them. Back then he hied to the copse, where Ruth sat shivering, but otherwise quiet as a mouse.

"Here!" said he, "I've brought you such a lovely rig out! Let's have that wet gown off. There it comes, and now you're going to be as fine as a duchess—leastways as dry."

Woppits wrapped the poor little body in his coarse warm shirt, tying it down into some degree of shapeliness by means of the spare neckerchief and that which he then wore. As for the socks, they were woollen, and drew up over Ruth's knees; so that, upon the whole, though she did not look pretty, she looked pretty comfortable. Woppits seemed rather to admire the *tout ensemble*. Stepping back a few paces to obtain a better idea of the effect, he put his head on one side, exclaiming, "That's capital! Now for the wittles!" And off he ran again.

Boldly he walked into a thriving little bit of a town, the inhabitants of which had just opened their various eyes and their various premises. It happened that the first shop in the row was a china repository, the boy appertaining to which was leisurely hanging some brown stone bottles on hooks driven into the doorway.

"The very thing," thought Woppits. "How much is them bottles, my man?" rattling the money in his pocket, so that the repository boy should hear the assuring chink.

"How long have you had a man, Charity?" coolly rejoined the other.

For the sake of little Ruth, Woppits suppressed a violent inclination to fight the China one on the spot, and again and more meekly asked the price of the bottles, at the same time exhibiting a shilling.

"Well, the quart uns is sixpence to you, sevenpence to poor people," the youth graciously responded.

"Then I'll take a quart." And Woppits, having tendered a shilling, and received a bottle and his change, scampered off to a cowhouse, bought a quart of warm milk, and finally a nice white loaf.

"There goes one!" sighed he, as he made his way back to the copse. "It goes werry much agin my feelin's, but I do think somehow that if Mr. Tweakle had found the poor little thing hisself, he would have done the same."

Seated on the knees of the workhouse runaway, who himself sat on a brick, Miss Ruth Keppel took her breakfast. She seemed to be quite recovered from her unhealthy sleep, and the manifest kindness of Woppits had already won her to content. An earthen jar is not quite so handsome as a porcelain basin, nor were Woppits' fingers so delicate as a silver spoon; nevertheless, the child made a hearty meal of the long slips of bread steeped in the warm milk, and presently looked so cheerful and affectionate, and talked so prettily, that Woppits resolved not to part with the little maiden, come what would. "'Ceptin' allus that I ain't obliged," said he.

CHAPTER XVII.

MASTER AND MAN.

MARK's plan, then, was too nicely elaborated; and complicated plots, like all other complicated machinery, are terribly liable to derangement. Not but the scheme went to admiration so long as Howlet had the guidance of it in his hands; and, when, after successfully forging a burglarious entrance into the premises, he returned to his own room, only one necessary part of the undertaking remained to be performed. That was an important one—the disposal of little Ruth; for did she revive in Keppel's presence, the whole plot would be discovered. What he proposed to do with her was, to take her to some monstrous kind old lady (with whom he had already made an arrangement provisionally) to be nursed. This motherly old person had only to be informed that the happiness of two noble houses depended upon the child's being brought up in seclusion, to enter into the business with a degree of satisfaction which no pecuniary arrangement alone could impart; but at the same time, it was understood that she was to be well paid.

Let us, then, imagine Mark's surprise and mortification when, on descending once more into Keppel's room, he found its late occupants gone. Keppel's hat and cloak he missed at the same moment, and at once comprehended the whole truth. This was the end of his precious plan! He was defeated; and nothing seemed to remain at present but to heap upon his own and Keppel's head curses deep—anathemas more remarkable for earnestness than elegance. Then he sneaked to his room again, and sat down on the side of the bed to ruminate.

Here was a lively state of affairs, he said to himself. Keppel, alarmed at his long absence, had carried off the proof of (what he supposed to be) his guilt, and now, what would come of that? Either that presently the child would wake in his arms, or he would bury it alive! These alternatives were dreadful to think of. In the first case, he, Mark, would be found out; in the second, he would virtually be a murderer. That was what would come of merely playing at assassination. Mark was aghast at this terrible conclusion; and the more he pondered, the more he feared the worst would happen—that is to say, that Keppel would take the first opportunity to rid himself of his lifeless burden. But *was* it the worst alternative? Wonderful is that law of self-preservation, which is said to be the first and most powerful in nature. Howlet, as we have said before, loved Ruth, if he loved anybody in the world; but, considering that if her father hastily buried her out of the way, his own fraud, and his master's chance of securing himself from imputation, would also be buried; while, if she revived untimely, he, the young man then at liberty in his own chamber, would probably be transported beyond seas—when Howlet pondered all this, I say, he began to hope almost that Keppel had sunk his child in some pond or river, or found for her a grave that would never reveal its secret.

"You see," said Howlet, in continuation of these terrible reflections, "he's such a coward! A fellow of any spirit would come straight home, and say, 'Now, look here, Howlet, the child's dead and buried, and you know all about it. Perhaps you helped to do it—perhaps not. At all events, it *is* done; and if, from this time, you ever open your mouth about the matter to me, I'll knock you down; if to anybody else, I'll declare that we killed her together, and leave you to clear yourself if you can!' A fellow would have something to lay hold of then—something to set his head against; but he'll do nothing of the sort. He'll find courage enough to throw her into some river, I dare say, with as many stones about her as would sink a seventy-four; but then he'll go shirking about afterwards with his white face, ready to fall on his knees to the first officer that looks hard at him. Well, there's nothing I can do just now, except seem to be doing nothing; so I'll just slip into bed, and see what turns up in the morning."

To go to bed is always much easier than to go to sleep, as Howlet found many a night after he took to making Plans. He had lain some three or four hours, and had barely got beyond a doze, when his ears were assailed by a great clamour at the doors. Instantly broad awake in every sense, he exclaimed—

"Who's there?"

"Oh, pray, Mr. Mark," exclaimed the voice of Mrs. Buskett, housekeeper; "here's a pretty to do! Oh, get up!"

Howlet was heard tumbling out of bed most distinctly.

"Open the door a little way, and tell me what's the matter."

"Oh, dear, whatever shall we *do*?" responded Mrs. Buskett, incoherently. "The stupid, snoring, lazy creature!"

"What stupid, snoring, lazy creature?" Howlet returned, thinking that a little virtuous indignation, no matter about what, would do no harm at this juncture. "Who are you calling names, ma'am?"

"Oh, not you, Mr. Mark! The pretty creature! Ah, that dratted Tupper! and the window wide open, and those wretches getting in and stealing her away, the precious! Oh my! oh dear!"

Mark could hear the old woman's knuckles crack as she wrung her hands. Another thing he heard, more interesting than the housekeeper's grief: she had said "those wretches;" she meant the Bohemians; and it was clear that she at least was misled by the evidence he had so industriously created to account for the child's loss.

"Now, what's it all about?" said he, by this time dressed and out upon the landing.

Of course he was very much shocked when he heard the particulars of little Ruth's abduction, though his feelings were rather expressed by looks than in words. However, he sharply questioned Miss Tupper, who stood the mute image of despair, with very red eyes and the corner of her apron in her mouth. Poor Tupper was as innocent and as bewildered as a new-born babe.

"This must be seen to!" exclaimed Howlet, with decision. "Tupper, you must tell the governor; that's your business!"

"Lord bless you, he isn't at home. He went off in that drunken fit as he said he would."

Howlet, lifting his eyelids, gave a grunt of dissatisfaction; and then, seeing that he was on all hands expected to take the lead in the family crisis, went gravely down-stairs to examine Ruth's apartment. Here he met the butler.

"Sad thing this, Howlet, very sad," said Simkin, with the one sad tone, and the one shake of the head, with which he moralized on all grave events, from the fall of a chimney-pot to the death of his relations. "Well, I always said so; I always said that some'at would happen one of these days. It's a judgment! that's what it is!"

Howlet made no reply, but busily examined the windows, and traced with his fingers the footmarks on the terrace.

"Now, sir?" exclaimed Mrs. Buskett, inquiringly.

"Oh yes, ma'am, you're right. Gipsies, decidedly." And, followed by Polly Tupper and another of his fellow-servants, he pursued the track he had so skilfully forged until it was lost on the turf. While this examination was going on, Tupper made a sudden spring at a piece of paper that lay in the path.

"That's the darling's book!" she screamed, tearing the sodden leaves as she eagerly turned them over. "The darling's book it is, that she took to bed with her."

"Then it's clear that she was carried off in this direction, and that's where those thieves have been pitched for near a month," ejaculated Howlet, pointing his forefinger like Napoleon when he crossed the Alps.

Wilkin, who had already been reconnoitring in this direction, returned at that instant with the intelligence that the camp had been broken up, apparently in some haste. The evidence was unanimously pronounced complete.

Still the question was, What was to be done? Mrs. Buskett suggested telling the constable; Mr. Simkin suggested alarming the village; Mr. Wilkin thought a Bow Street runner should be called on the scene instanter. Mr. Howlet, however, thought that no definite steps should be taken, and no uproar made in the matter, till Mr. Keppel returned: "and," said he, with a melancholy shake of the head, "I pretty well know where to find him."

"Then that's what you'd better do at once," was the opinion of all.

"And you won't make any stir till I come back, you know?"

Ay, and no stir should be made till he returned.

So Howlet retired.

Now of course he knew no more where to find his master than the guilty know how to find peace. That indeed was his great difficulty; and he found himself compelled to acknowledge that, unless he at once overcame it—i.e., unless he immediately re-established communication with Mr. Keppel—he stood in imminent danger. So it was with a doubtful heart and vague intentions that he set out in search of him whom he scarcely

hoped to find. The valet again and again pondered the chances of the child's waking, or of her being buried where she would never wake again; but the more he reflected the more could he come to no conclusion. It was only clear that it would be well, in any case, to fall in with Keppel alone and speedily.

Howlet had been walking the horse slowly round the park wall all this time, and had kept a scrutinizing eye upon the path, notwithstanding the intensity of his reflections. As he approached a certain spot which nearly faced that side of the lodge in which Keppel's private entrance was pierced, more eager were Mark's glances; at length they fastened upon two footmarks printed in the recently-moistened ground. The heels were to the wall; it was here that Keppel had leapt it. Howlet eagerly searched for a repetition of the footprints, but there were no more; his master had evidently stepped at once from the path into the harder road. But there was a piece of straw flattened to the ground for about the breadth of a man's foot-sole. This was as you turned to the right, supposing you had your back to the wall. This was a most important discovery. It showed the direction Keppel had taken; for the road was the high road, and there was no other near the village. It was true that the fugitive gentleman could by and by strike off into the fields, but still, in the main, this was his track.

With something like hope, Mark now rode speedily on—often standing up in his stirrups to overlook the country, and keeping a keen eye about him generally. Straight was the road for several miles, but at length it branched out to the right, to the left, and to the left again. Again Mark hesitated, and desponded. There stood the finger-post, pointing with charming impartiality in all three directions—but which? The choice was simply between east, west, and south-west. Mr. Howlet's bridle hand relaxed upon the rein, and his horse, taking advantage of the circumstance, swerved off to the racks and water-troughs of the Mayflower, crowning the rise where the roads diverged; perceiving which old and tall hostel, Mark obtained a new idea—not a bright one, but safe and determinate. Here would he put up, and here would he remain for the day, in that corner room there (evidently a public one), which with its two great windows overlooked the whole country in almost any direction.

"Now," said the valet to himself, "if the child revives before he has an opportunity of destroying it, he will come tearing back by one of these roads—with a constable, perhaps. If he returns at all, I shall probably meet him in this neighbourhood: if he doesn't, then I am off: or I go back to the lodge, innocent and unsuccessful, and prepare myself for the worst."

Accordingly, Howlet alighted. As he touched the ground, an odd spasmodic expression was apparent in his countenance. The truth was, that a little bundle, which he had carefully bestowed in the great pocket of his coat, bumped against his legs; and the bundle contained the two wicked phials, the gloves, and the boots—the latter having been cut into shreds. These were to have been disposed of, one by one, and bit by bit, on the way; but now the journey was ended. Howlet's command to the servant who bustled out of the inn, was therefore, "Just put my horse in the stable, and give me some breakfast. If it's convenient, I should like it in that room (pointing to the apartment already mentioned), and I'll just take a stroll while it is getting ready."

In about twenty minutes he returned. The bottles were broken, and the fragments scattered among the dense rank grass that grew by a ditch-side. The gloves, torn and smirched with mud, were thrust into a little fissure in a tree, which scarcely betrayed how hollow it was at heart. The boots—already cut in pieces, as aforesaid—were scattered broadcast over a close wild patch of gorse and furze.

Howlet had scarcely concluded the hearty plain meal which the innkeeper, with an innkeeper's penetration, knew would be most welcome to a man of Howlet's quality, when heavy clouds appeared overhead, and gave him an excellent excuse for tarrying. The innkeeper too, and all his staff, were people new to the country, and saw nothing remarkable in a man with Howlet's half-grown half-gentleman appearance, putting up for a few hours, at his discretion; again, therefore, Howlet was fortunate. Breakfast being over, he called for a newspaper, and pretended to make himself comfortable. But as soon as the waiter was out of the room, he commenced a series of migrations from one big window to the other, much too frequent and anxious to accord with any comfortable idea. Then as the morning wore on, he ordered a mug of strong ale—none but the strongest; then noon came, and he had beans and bacon; after that came another mug, which not being quite strong enough for Howlet's taste this time, was followed by brandy and water; and then down came the rain that drove the labourers away from Keppel's neighbourhood, and dripped and plashed about the shed where he was hiding.

Whether it was that the Mayflower had little company that day, or whether the Mayflower's customers preferred the homely comfort and homely drink of the tap below, is not recorded; but this is, that no man drank in Howlet's company the whole day. Awful work it was, walking from one window to the other, hour after hour, all alone, with no company but his own restless reflections, his glass, and some pictures of beeves, horses, pigs, fowls, and other the living delights of the agricultural mind; but, upon the whole, Howlet wished for nothing better. Tim, the waiter, visited him periodically, under cover of a dusting-cloth, whenever, in his opinion, the gentleman's measure required replenishing. On every such occasion the young man remarked: "Showery day, sir; very showery, to be sure. Do a deal of good, though. Same again, sir? Wery well, sir." A style of remark which, though unobjectionable in itself, fails to be interesting after the third or fourth repetition. Howlet took the same again several times, and remained sober only because he had so much to think about. Nevertheless, fatigued from long excitement, to say nothing of the sleepless night last past, he began to doze towards sunset. Indeed, he fell asleep at length, but was roused by the fall of the newspaper, which he had still retained in his hand for appearance sake, and to employ his wandering fingers. Starting up, "This won't do!" he exclaimed, and rubbing his eyes, and throwing his hair back, he crossed over to the other window, staring out into the dusk.

A hundred times that day had his eyes rested, momentarily, on a shed which stood at some little distance from the inn, though not more than fifty yards from the tree where he had hidden the gloves that morning. Now he saw a man cautiously turn the corner of this shed, and, with a hasty glance about him, strike into the south-west road aforesaid. Not only could not Howlet discern the features of this man, but the dusk and the distance disguised his garb and his gait; but the valet had not a doubt of his identity. Instantly Howlet's hand was on the bell; at the same time, the man, breaking through a gap in the hedge that skirted the road, walked rapidly along the inner, or field side, so as to be hidden from view.

"My horse, directly," cried Howlet to the waiter who answered to his summons: and then, endeavouring to appear cool, he dragged a great watch from his fob, glanced at it, and added: "I must be off in two minutes; let me have my horse in that time, and you may divide five shillings with the hostler." All the while the rain drizzled miserably.

Rather under than over the specified time, the horse was at the door. Meanwhile, Howlet discharged his reckoning, and jumping into the saddle, rode away—not quickly. As he departed, the landlord made a remark which would not have pleased Mr. Howlet, had he heard it. Boniface imparted to the group around him an opinion he had all along entertained, it seems, that the guest of the day was no other than Nailer, the celebrated Bow Street officer.

If the day had passed heavily with Howlet, as he sat watching for Keppel at the Mayflower window, drearily had it passed with Mr. Keppel, watching for nightfall through the chinks of the shed. Not that he had any idea of what he should do when night came, except get away from his hiding-place, and go somewhere; which in fact meant, into another hiding-place. Happy would he have been to have slept that night at the Lodge, if only Howlet were faithful; and over and over again the unhappy man asked himself whether he had not been too precipitate—whether the sounds that had so scared him, were really the signals of his servant's treachery. But, now that he had fled, what was more likely than that Howlet should reveal the whole affair? And now that he, Keppel, came to think of it, he had given his man not too many reasons to feel any great attach-

ment for him. The servant had never received more than his hire, except what was given as a reward for keeping silence about some little private transaction not necessary to be known to all the world. Yes! he had on two occasions received an undeserved kicking; and, if it came to that, how about his sister Lucy? But that had nothing to do with the present difficulty. Yes it had! Did he not see her face in the moonlight, which at the same time revealed the murder of his child? Great heaven! suppose that, Lucy being dead, her soul had been sent back in the body of Ruth?

The little conversation Keppel was having with himself, was here interrupted by a sudden start. Then he asked what was the use of reviving old grievances? None whatever, answered he. But the old grievances came thick and fast for all that—thicker and faster as the evening approached; old evil acts, long smothered up and hidden away, sailed in from all sides as the shadows gathered round him. It was not dark out of doors, but the old shed seemed full of darkness—darkness alive and full of grim associations; so that he was fain to press his face against a chink in the wall, so that his eyes might see nothing but the quiet evening falling over the fields.

It *must* be getting towards night now! He had become so impressed with the gloom within the barn, that the light without was exaggerated to his eyes. Therefore he would go at once into the fresh air; where he could better resolve on some course of action—his mind being more composed.

Accordingly, he came out (as Howlet saw him)—finding that it was indeed near night; and he crossed the field, struck into the road, and again breaking through a gap in the hedge, rapidly walked on the inner side.

Although Howlet mounted so hurriedly, he rode slowly from the Mayflower, willing to give Keppel three minutes more time, in order that he might get so much further from the inn, and that nobody might witness their interview. Then he put his horse to a trot; and soon after Keppel heard the sounds of its hoofs pattering along the road.

Now he had crossed an angle of the field—an angle formed by the main road and a lane which led out of it, and down which he proposed to travel. Consequently, when he turned at the sound of the horse's feet, he beheld his rider flourishing his whip in token of recognition, and evidently bearing down toward him. Keppel's face assumed a terrible expression; and instead of running off into the open meadow, he rushed to the hedge, whence, with all the strength of desperation, he tore a heavy stake.

By the time he had well poised this in his hands, the horseman had approached the spot where he stood.

"Mr. Keppel," cried Mark, who reined in immediately opposite his master, the low hedge of the lane dividing them, "Mr. Kepple! I say, it's me, Mark!"

Horace made no reply, but stood panting at the rider, clutching the stake with both hands.

"He's mad," thought Howlet, drawing close to the hedge. "Let's see. They say you must be firm with mad people, and they're cowed directly. So here goes!"

"Come, come!" said he aloud; "let's have none of this nonsense."

Keppel had now no doubt that his man's intention was to seize him; and maddened at the idea, he sprang up the bank of the hedge, clutched at a branch with one hand, and made such a desperate cut at Howlet's head with the stake, that, had it taken effect, Mark's own skull would certainly have been cracked, in whatever condition was Keppel's at the time being. As it was, however, the point of the club descended on the pommel of the saddle. Howlet instantly seized it; and the horse giving a start at the same moment, the weapon was jerked out of Keppel's hand.

"Confound you, you idiot!" exclaimed the other, "is this the way you serve your friends? I've half a mind to leave you to get on as you best can!" And while Keppel, struck by this remark, hesitated, Howlet rode to the gate, which he now first noticed a few yards ahead, backed his horse, leapt it, and in two minutes was dismounted, with his hand on Keppel's arm.

"Now then, look at me, Mr. Keppel!" he said. "Do I appear like an enemy?"

"Mark," replied the other, "this is killing me."

"Of course it is—and me too; for if you persist in this sort of folly, both our necks will be found in a halter in a very short time. Yours will, at any rate."

"Then there's no *immediate* danger," faltered Keppel, somewhat cooled.

"I can't say, for certain. But what have you done with the —the child, sir? Where is she?"

"Where no one will ever find her."

"You must tell me directly, if you please. Is it far from here?"

"Oh yes, miles and miles away! I can't show you—I can't tell you where now, Mark."

"Look here!"

And Howlet rapidly detailed all the measures he had taken to avoid discovery, and to set the household and the world generally upon a false scent. "Now, sir," he concluded, "you see you can place confidence in me; and if you had done so from the first, you'd have saved yourself the danger of absenting yourself in this way. So I ask you again, and I hope you'll give me a true answer—What's become of little Ruth? where's the body?"

"There is no body!" answered Keppel, shuddering.

Mark was confounded: his limited imagination could suggest no possibility of truth for such an answer, which yet seemed made earnestly and truthfully enough.

"*Is* none?" he echoed.

Keppel was silent.

"Mr. Keppel," Mark deliberately said, shifting his hold on his riding-whip, so that it swung heavily with its weighted handle downward, "listen to me. You know what I have done in my anxiety to cover up this affair, and you know what comes of taking the reins in your own hands, even when you've got your own neck to save. But, like a stupid, I've got myself in for it too. Now, though you're very welcome to do what you like with your own life, I'm cursed if I don't look after mine. 'Tain't too late to haul you before a justice, whereby I'm safe, as I ought to be, for I never killed so much as a dog in all my life. So now, sir, tell me where Ruth is at once, or off you go. You'd better!"

"Off I go!" repeated the other; and, stepping back a pace or two, his clinched hands and flashing eyes gave him a very dangerous appearance.

Howlet, for his part, swung the heavy whip backward and forward, pendulum-fashion, the thong twisted in his fingers; and so the two men regarded each other for several moments. But neither was in a position to indulge in hostilities, and presently the men's countenances softened. At the same instant, and from the same cause, Keppel's hands were unclinched, and Howlet again took the whip by the right end. Then—

"It's gone," said Keppel. "That's all I can tell you."

"Gone! Gone where?"

"All gone—every shred and sign of it."

Howlet's face blanched, and the eyelids quivered so painfully that tears came into his eyes. This was murder with a vengeance! and a very pretty end to the plan, too!

"For heaven's sake how?" he ejaculated.

"Ah, *you* could not have managed better. I threw it into a lime-pit."

"Throw it there! the live —— into the live lime?"

"Why not?" replied the other, attempting to cover, with an air of practical philosophy, the horror which was reflected upon his countenance from Howlet's. "The dead feel no pain, you know, Mark!"

"True, sir," replied the other, and turned away, sick at heart.

Late that night, master and man returned—the former in a hired chaise. Keppel's guilty agitation passed for grief, especially when it became generally known—as Howlet took care it should be—that upon his daughter's life Keppel depended for his very bread. The country round was scoured for gipsies; but these people are put in possession of any news that affects themselves without the aid of newspapers or the "Hue and Cry;" and almost before the search was commenced, the band in question had quietly dispersed themselves among other companies. Conscious, too, that any investigation into their affairs was undesirable, and knowing that no account they could render

of themselves would be believed, they said nothing. Moreover, as they really had not stolen the child, it could not be found among them; and to stir, therefore, was more dangerous than to be still.

Meanwhile, until Ruth's death was proved, as long as she could be living, Horace was safe in the enjoyment of her property; especially as Ruth's heirs (the poor Butler cousins aforesaid) were by no means in a position to engage in doubtful litigation.

And now we see the power which Howlet has obtained over the man who injured his sister. Mark speaks, and Keppel's property, if not his existence, vanishes. The valet keeps silence, and bestows life and riches on his master. Under these circumstances, Howlet thinks that a handsome annual allowance should be made him; though Keppel has to let the park as grazing ground, and perform other acts of economy, in order to meet the demand. But there is balm of some feeble sort for every sore, and hereby he obtains the reputation of a just steward and an honourable man, who, so far from injuring the property, now that the existence of his daughter is uncertain, rather labours to improve it, and to increase the hoard she shall enjoy if ever fortune restores her to her father's arms.

As for Mr. Howlet, he has this idea: He will take his allowance for a few years, carefully hoarding it. Then he will announce to Keppel his desire to go to America; giving out in public that he intends to invest his little savings in business in London; and requiring that gentleman to compound for all future payments by one handsome sum—say four at years' purchase, or, in round numbers, a thousand pounds.

We shall see what Providence has to do with that little scheme. Meanwhile, we renew our acquaintance with Mr. Hatcher.

CHAPTER XVIII.

MR. HATCHER DOES BUSINESS.

WE have already enjoyed a glimpse at Mr. Hatcher's residence, at Old Sleaford; but that was at night, when the shutters were closed, and when little could be made of it.

Behold the residence, then, as our indefatigable Joel takes the shutters down, and the morning beams come streaming in, revealing its treasures. Now, he brings forth two boards, which he hangs on their respective hooks in the doorway. On one is inscribed, in cruel red letters on a pea-green ground, "Rents collected; debts legally recovered;" on the other, "Sworn broker; levies and distraints made on the shortest notice;" though never but once in all his existence had Hatcher been called upon to exercise that branch of his business: and then it was only because the well-to-do saddler had a quarrel with the ill-to-do saddler, in consequence of a dispute between their little boys with respect to the proprietorship of a pop-gun.

With a watering-pot, Joel now sprinkles the path up the middle of the shop (which is a new-fangled operation), and then is ready for inspection a small quantity of second-hand furniture, which has a dismal effect upon the mind. There are sturdy family tables, beneath which, year in and year out, who knows how many little feet have clustered—now for the Christmas feast, now to partake of a tear-moistened loaf, too small for so many mouths. That is mother's rocking-chair. There, when she was a beautiful young woman, she laid her new baby across her knees, and looked at it, rocking to the tune of her own joyful emotions; and there she rocked to another tune when she was small and pinched and gray, and news came that her baby—now six foot one in his boots—had died at Quatre-Bras, with a Frenchman at the end of his bayonet. There are the decanters which dear Mrs. Chitling loved so well, not for themselves alone. There is the work-box where Polly kept her love-letters—poor Jack's letters, whose mother wouldn't let him marry Polly, and who afterwards kept a "fourpenny shop," and got idle and fat unknown to Polly, whose dear unsuspicious little heart broke long before. Those dear women! There is a meat-jack: itself poetry, when you recollect that it was with that very jack that young Spencer, the curate (who couldn't afford to keep a regular servant), himself roasted a partridge for his wife when she lay ill one day, and carried it up-stairs to her himself; and she laughed and couldn't eat it, and then cried and couldn't eat it, because her husband looked so awfully red and serious, and had spent his very last shilling in the bird, as she well knew. However, let me tell you that young Spencer became Dean Spencer from that day (the Greek he knew was bewildering) ; and, what's more, his wife loved him just as much as ever, though she wasn't a bit prouder of him. And when you consider those leather breeches—but we will go no further into these particulars : we are violating the sanctity of private life.

Especially as Hatcher himself viewed these objects strictly with the eye of a broker. His father had been a broker in town. He had two sheriff's officers of brothers, through whom, indeed, he chiefly obtained his stock-in-trade. Hatcher's father was a very remarkable man. He it was who obtained admission into the residence of Captain Blogsville. He treacherously waylaid the captain's charwoman in the disguise of a lover, when she ran out one evening for whisky and cigars, and treated her with so much rum that he was enabled to divest her of her gown, her shawl, her false front, and her bonnet, without a struggle. Accoutred in these, he deceived the gallant captain, who himself admitted him. This exploit was much talked of among the profession, for the captain was a wary man, and had kept at bay half-a-dozen seedy lurchers with hooked noses for the two preceding months. But, as old Mr. Hatcher used to say, it takes a Christian to perform a feat like that.

We must not forget to mention that to Joel's business of broker was added that of marine store dealer, i.e., he dealt in old rags, old metals, bottles, broken glass, etc. etc. ; he stopped short at bones, however. Indeed, I'm not sure that bones was invented at that period, as an article of commerce, save among resurrectionists and slave-dealers.

Beyond the shop, and at the end of the little path, was the living-room of Joel and his mother—a queer, dingy little place, the principal furniture in which consisted of a black cat, a few old-fashioned chairs, and a rickety card-table, the top still adorned with a sheet of baize, once fair and green, but now for the most part yellow, pot-stained, and tattered, like a ruined old gamester as it was. On the mantel-piece, a shepherd, with one arm piped to a shepherdess with one leg, a headless dog following in their wake. There was a flute suspended by a piece of red cord. This was the flute Joel used to play, when, at eighteen, he fell in love with Miss Figg ("Green Figg," she was sometimes called, in allusion to her complexion) aged thirty-seven. There was a tea-caddy of satin-wood, inlaid with shells ; there was a "Woodman's Return" (a piece of very brilliant water-colour) on the walls ; but above all, there stood in a corner a huge hall clock, impressing you more than anything else with the meanness of the place, by its sonorous and highly respectable ticking. The peculiarity which I have observed to distinguish other clocks of its ancient and well-descended character, belonged to this. It seemed, as it ticked there in its grand loud manner, to tick in its sleep ; and the hands, majestically moving over the silvered dial, appeared rather to record once more the time that *had* been, rather than the time that was. For my part, I wonder how anybody can go by such a timepiece. I could only stop by it—pause and linger by it contemplatively all my life through. If it ticked in my bed-room, I should never get up ; in my library, I should never go to bed, but read for ever books of the period of Queen Anne, with intervals of Palestrina on a spinnet. But if, instead of being a young man, I happened to be an old woman, I'd give the world for one of those old clocks with their silvery faces and their low humming pendulums. Then, if it pleased to record once more the time that had been rather than the time present, why so much the better, and so much the more companionable a clock for me. When I told my old stories to my grand-daughters—how their poor, dear grandfather looked when he came courting me, with his rich brown hair, his man-like eyes, his laced shirt and his hessians—when I related my strange dreams, and how my little Arthur's pigeon forsook the cote when he died, and afterwards was found roosting on a tree near his burial-place—the hum of the pendulum should fall in with the tale, and confirm it. When, alone of a winter evening, I should cast my old eyes now and then at the dial, and as the minute hand went round—click ! click !—I should again await my husband's return, with his brown locks and his beautiful eyes, and hear him at the door

stamping the snow from his feet as the bell struck. And when I thought of another time, I should look fearfully at my old timepiece, dreading that it would again stop as it pointed the moment that my husband died ; for I'm a superstitious old woman, and I'm human, and my past sorrows are my pleasures now.

Talking of old women, a question occurs to me, which, as Mr. Hatcher has not yet done sweeping his shop, I may as well mention. It is this. How is it, that though, when we look at an old man, no matter how old, we may easily repeal the work of time and labour—the weariness, the fever, and the fret of fifty years, and behold him young, handsome, gay, and twenty-four—an old woman baffles all imagination in that regard ? Mopus is seventy-eight—he is hard, keen, cold, thin as a hatchet. His figure is a wry figure ; his old nose and chin are red as a lobster's claw, and as cruel ; his face is furrowed, not like a ploughed field, but as with flywheels, cogwheels, bobbins, spindles, and that sort of inhuman-looking money-grinding thing. Yet not only can you believe that he was once five feet eleven, with twelve stone of bone and muscle, that he was the best rider in the field, the jolliest dog at the table, the most generous spendthrift everywhere, but you can see it in him ; you can recall his ruddy complexion, his delicate mouth, and laughing eyes. But Mrs. Mopus ! Dear old woman, sitting for ever in that big chair of hers, with her wrinkled face, her little faded eyes, and her false "front"—how am I to believe that she was once the loveliest woman in the county ? They say her hair, black and massy, crowned her with grandeur ; that her eyes were large, and soft as night ; that her figure was like a palm ; that her singing was a proverb, and her dancing the most wonderful stately thing ; that young men crowded about her, and one went to the wars in Spain, and got shot, for her. It is hard to believe. Not a sign of it is visible—not only in the poor old girl's appearance, but, alas ! in the sad deposition from all that crowding about of young men they talk of. But then Mrs. Mopus is no relation of mine.

I should inquire into the cause of all this ; how far the neglect of the young men aforesaid is to be accounted for by my own sentiment, or want of sentiment, in the matter ! why (mystery of mysteries !) young women seem also to be afflicted in the same manner ; and whether the utterly cruel and senseless use of "old woman" as a term of reproach and contempt, is to be thus accounted for. But the broker, our friend, has completed his arrangements for the day.

Opportunely, an immense black bonnet lurches through a partially-opened door leading into the shop, and out of the depths of the black silk cavern issue these words, quavering—

"Breffas is ready, Joly dear !"

Those women again ! Here's one of them addressing herself to our ferrety friend by endearing diminutives. She calls him "Joly dear !" He grunts in return. He says, "Very well, I'm coming ;" and the great black bonnet retreats respectfully, carrying the old woman, Joly's mother, with it. The old woman was never out of that bonnet, except in the privacy of her bed-chamber. The moment she divested herself of her nightcap it was replaced by the bonnet ; and when she retired for the night, its monstrous reflection might be seen on the chamber-curtains up to the very moment of applying the extinguisher.

"Well," says Joly to the old woman—though how he managed to aim the words into the bonnet, so as to reach her ears, is hard to understand—"Well," said he, as he sat down to his tea and his bacon, "how do you find yourself this morning ?"

"Oh, no great shakes !" sighed the widow. At the same time shaking her head with such emphasis that the extreme borders of the bonnet described a semicircle. "I've got it right down my back this morning. Ah ! I'm going home, Joly, I shan't be a burden to you much longer."

As, with little variety, this was the answer Joel received to the same inquiry at the same time every morning, it did not much affect him. It occurs to me now that this strong presentiment about going home may account for her always wearing her bonnet.

"Ah !" replied Hatcher, taking up the teapot, "you're always worse on Mondays and Thursdays. I wish that Skinner would get a flock somewhere else !"

The person thus disrespectfully spoken of as "that Skinner,"

HATCHER IN PURSUIT OF USEFUL KNOWLEDGE.

was a preacher whom Mrs. H---her used to sit under on Sundays and Wednesdays. He was not a cheerful preacher, it must be confessed; in fact, he was proud to call himself "a startler," from the vigour and dexterity with which he scattered fire and brimstone amongst his flock, and from the unmistakeable force with which he proved that they were all going to the burning headlong. The consequence was, that he kept his congregation in a state of religious wretchedness from week to week, much to his own satisfaction. Not that I mean to say he was not in earnest. He was one of the honestest men in the world; and if he failed to turn many sinners to repentance, he ofttimes stopped them suddenly in the broad road, took them by the calf of the leg, as it were, and gave them a terrible shaking. Peace be with him!

"Ah, he is a beautiful man, he is," says the widow. "He's a rouser, if ever there was one; and if you'd only sit under him, he'd open your eyes to the road you're going; I'm sure he would!"

"Oh, he's very well, I dare say, mother," answered her son, knowing of old how unprofitable it was to provoke any controversy on the subject. "But I've got enough on my mind just now. There's that Mrs. Cubley not sent her instalment again."

"What's the use bothering over them people? Why don't you go in, Joly?"

"Ah! why don't I? Because the old man and one of the children's got the fever!"

"Oh, stuff, you know!" rejoined the widow with a worldly flash in her eyes which would have astonished the beautiful man. "That won't butter parsnips, you know!"

"What won't?"

"Your going on excusing 'em because of that!"

"Who excuses 'em? What's the use of me seizing, and bringing the fever home here in the beds and things? Eh?"

"Ah, well, you knows best," said the widow, with a sigh. "Coming!" cried she, in answer to a tapping on the counter. "Shop, Joel."

Joel put down his cup, and rose to attend upon the first customer of the day; a youth evidently employed in the preparation of chalk, and proud to carry the signs thereof over the surface of his garments.

"You buy brass, mister?" inquired the boy.

"I buy anything honestly come by. What have you got?"

The boy exhibited a heavy pair of clasps, much discoloured. They were not of common device—two swans, whose necks locked into each other. Joel took them gingerly, turning them over with some interest. He had seen them before.

"Where did you get them, my boy?" Joel asked, at the same time throwing the clasps carelessly into one scale, and a small weight into the other.

"Found 'em in one of our kils!"

"Found 'em in a kiln, did you?" echoed Hatcher, blandly, looking among the halfpence in the till to take time. "Dear me! How the live lime does blacken and corrode things! Was they as discoloured as this, now, when you cut 'em off?"

Hatcher's head was bent over the till as he said this, but

from beneath his heavy brows he shot a concealed glance at his customer.

"Cut 'em off what?" asked the boy.

"Oh, I thought they might have been on an old cloak collar or something," returned Joel, at length raising his head, and handing the boy a penny.

"No," said the lime-burner, "that's just as I found 'em in the north pit yesterday mornin'."

So saying he quitted the shop; while Hatcher, instead of casting his late purchase into the receptacle set apart for old brass, took it from the scale, and walked thoughtfully into the little back room.

"What's that, Joly?" asked Mrs. Hatcher, as her son, instead of reseating himself to his breakfast, set about polishing the clasps.

"Silver," answered he shortly.

"But we don't buy silver?"

"Yes, we do, when we can get it at sixpence a pound," rejoined Joel, rubbing so vigorously that all his hair was aroused and in motion.

"'Pon my word, I thought so!" added he, after a pause, and eyeing the article attentively as it lay in his broad palm.

"What?" cried the old woman, eagerly, hoping to hear that the silver proved to be gold.

"Yes, there they are, as plain as the nose on his face. Here, old woman," handing her the clasps, "look and tell me what you see here."

Mrs. Hatcher adjusted her spectacles, turned her face to the window, and examined the objects that so much interested Mr. Joel. "Well," said she, "there's two letters on 'em; one's a H, and one's a K. What does that stand for? They won't be owned, will they?"

"Well, no," replied her son, "perhaps not. As for what the letters stand for, I think I pretty well know; because, you see, I had my suspicions as to who the things belonged to from the first. But how on earth they came there—?" And, moving to the mantelpiece, Hatcher rested his elbow upon it, and commenced kneading his chin. Mrs. Hatcher knew by this that her son was "studying," and accordingly troubled him with no more questions.

But however Joel studied, he could not solve the question he proposed to himself—How did Mr. Keppel's cloak, which was new and handsome, get into the lime-pit? He ferreted up the question this way and that; down into this corner, and it escaped; into that, and it was gone. The only conclusion he could come to was, either that the Lodge had been robbed, or Keppel himself had got into the lime in one of his roaring fits of dissipation. But if either accident had occurred, surely it must be talked of in the village.

After some further cogitation, therefore, Hatcher put the clasps into his pocket and his hat on his head, and wended his way towards the great exchange of gossip, the Goat and Boots. As he approached the house, who should he see but old Tittypee, the gardener, just entering at the door.

"Ah," said Joel, "he's the fellow."

A group of gossipers were assembled round the bar, with beer in their hands and consternation in their faces.

"Hallo!" cried Tittypee, as Hatcher entered, glad of an opportunity to tell the news once more. "Heard of our loss, I suppose, Mr. Hatcher?"

"Good heavens!" Hatcher exclaimed, his whole nervous system titillating with excitement (for he thought his more dismal conjecture the right one), "so it's true, is it? Poor fellow, poor fellow!" and he fumbled in his pocket for the clasps. Indeed, he had nearly produced them, when some one of the company observed—

"Yes, poor fellow! His only child, you know. He must feel awful cut-up about it!"

Mr. Hatcher drew forth his handkerchief instead of the tell-tales, and buried his face in it with a loud report, in order to hide his shame and confusion at having been so nearly betrayed into a precipitate, unbusiness-like step.

"Oh, it's shockun!" exclaimed another. "If you have a young un die, why, o' coorse, that's bad enough; but to have un stole off by a passell of gipsies!"

"I dun know," chimed in a third. "The little girl may be

all right, after all. The gipsies what took her 'll bring her back again, some day, when the wust of the wind's blowed over, and if her father 'll pay down hansum. That's their game, of course it is!"

Hatcher now quite comprehended the position of affairs, and thought he might safely trust himself to break in with a question. "When was it?" said he.

"Night afore last, or yesterday mornin', maybe."

"Gipsies, eh?"

"Ain't no doubt about it. They were there by the copse that very evenun; and in the mornun they was gone; and there was their tracks right up to the winder; and the winder was broke open, and the child were gone."

That certainly seems to be a pretty clear case, thought Hatcher. Then he asked aloud, "Didn't the rogues steal anything else?"

"Well, Mrs. Buskett, she missed the master's cloak last night, but how they got at that nobody knows, and nobody can tell. He says he didn't take it wi' him."

"Where?"

"Oh," explained Wilkin, who stepped in at that moment with his finger to his nose. "He got—" and then Wilkin, the wag, rolled about like a drunken man; "only he got dead drunk, and had to be carried to bed; and he wouldn't be undressed, swearin' he'd be off to London before mornin', which he was. He's always at them mad tricks."

"And when did he come home?"

"Last night. Howlet found him out in town, told him all about it, and home he comes in an awful way. The beadle and the constable are set to work, and a hundred pounds reward is offered for any clue to recovering the child; but there ain't none."

Hatcher involuntarily felt the clasps through his pocket, and was of a different opinion. His idea was that some one had a clue; and muttering, "Well, God help us all!" sauntered back to his residence. Here he locked the clasps in his cash-box; while to his mother he said, "Whatever you do or say, now, not a word about those silver things. It might transport you!"

The old woman wagged her bonnet so near Joly's face that his nose was in imminent danger of being swept away. She looked at him closely with a strange glitter of fondness and avarice in her eyes; and "Ah! Joly," says she, "you needn't tell me. You needn't put your old mother up to being keerful of her clever Joly's interest, nor you needn't let me into your affairs more'n you wish. A nod's enough for an old ooman like me. Now you go in to Mrs. Cubley, dear, and tell her you'll have her sticks in ten minutes if she don't pay ten shillin' down."

CHAPTER XIX.

HATCHER, MORALIST AND PHILOSOPHER.

"Ah, this is better!" sighed Mr. Hatcher, as, on the evening of the day which dawned in our last chapter, he sat alone in the grim little room behind the shop. Not that the room was by any means so grim as usual. It was dark without, and would have been Egyptian dark within; but a cheerful fire glowed in the grate, carpeting the hearth with cloth of gold, and flinging soft draperies on the walls. The dun furniture was tipped and pointed with brightness. Dull, solitary, old chairs, the melancholy survivors of once numerous and genteel families, came out in quite a social manner; they seemed to gather closer round the fire, to blink at it in company. A tea-kettle bubbled musically on one hob; on the other stood a teapot, wherein the cup that cheers distilled leisurely. Mr. Hatcher was in no hurry. Half reclining on one chair, with his heels elevated on another, he contemplated a stack of toast simmering in its own butter before the fire, and realized the bliss of being comfortably alone—locked up as he was, and barricaded from the outer world by his stock in trade. He had taken great pains for himself this evening. He had studiously made himself thus cosy, partly because he wished to celebrate the acquisition of those little bits of silver, but more because bodily ease is good for reflection. And having seated himself with the teapot and the toast and the poker all within easy reach, he launched out into the calm waters of contemplation.

"This is better," said he; "I couldn't get on at all before; couldn't fix my mind, no how. Precious glad I persuaded the old girl to go out to tea! Hope she won't go talking about those what's-its-names though. Not that there's much fear—only tell the old lady that there's money hanging to anything, and that's enough. Awful fond of money the old lady is, to be sure. Can't make it out; I can't. Some people's never satisfied." Whereupon Joel, shaking his head, took up a second slice of toast, opened his jaws, and bit it to the backbone.

"Hullo!" continued he, as he for the first time caught sight of a large white cat poised upon the hearth, with all the selfish gravity of cats in general, "you here? Well, old fellow you're an animal after my own heart; and you're company's welcome, even on this occasion. Good cat! good cat!"

As both Joel's hands were engaged, one with toast, the other with a teacup, he lowered from the chair on which it reclined one of his bluchers, wherewith to stroke the beast.

"Ah!" mused Joel, affectionately caressing Nick's back with the toe of his boot, "it's a wonder to me how men can persist in their liking for dogs. I wonder they can stand such a reproach as them animals are, always following at their heels, watching 'em as they eat and drink, waiting for 'em on the door-mat whenever they go in or out. Why, half the dogs alive are better than their masters! Catch a man sticking up for his young uns as a dog will! Do dogs ever cut away and leave their little uns to starve? Catch a man serving another when he's sold up, and ain't got a feather to fly with! Catch a dog leaving his master, though he didn't get an ounce o' meat a-week for his pains! Now I sees nothing about master and servant, or the haristocracy, and the way they goes on; neither about lawyers, nor parsons, nor overseers, and them; but, considerin' the matter in a animal point of view only, I do think it's wonderful cats ain't more in favour. They go along with the world in a much more easy and sensible manner. They are quiet and sedate, like all respectable parties in this here centery. Never in a flurry; always jolly keen and cautious; not over fond of light, but no objection to warmth; don't want any fun except caterwauling and catching mice, which is all the nicer because the other parties don't like it. Who'd care to win, if nobody lost? Not cats, tho'f they do look as meek as the milk they're so fond of! When they see a lamed bird falling from a tree, they pounces on it, crunches its little bones, and then looks round as innocent as wegetarians. When they see danger they run. That's the way, ar'n't it, Nick?—you sleek, fat, grave, shiny, cunning-looking villain! If you could talk, now, you're just the chap I should like to take advice of, under these circumstances."

Nick purred an acknowledgment, and getting up to stretch his limbs, arched his back, threw his fore-legs forward, and out peeped the cruel claws.

"Lor'!" continued the philosophic and ameliorated broker, who, like many men of his kind, was wonderfully and fancifully loquacious to himself—"Lor'! it's just impossible to be too thankful for a natural talent for business. There's lots of dull dogs, now, who, directly they had got those bits of silver, would have dropped them in the melting-pot, cleared their five shillings, and thought no more about it!"

It might have occurred to Mr. Hatcher that there were dogs duller yet, who would have declined the opportunity of clearing even that paltry sum. But it did not occur to Mr. Hatcher. It was not comprehended in the boundaries of things possible for Mr. Hatcher.

"But leave me alone," pursued he. "I've got my eyes open!"

(Here he winked.)

"Always keep 'em open, my Christian friends!"

(Puts his finger to his nose.)

"Had 'em open for years!"

(Raises his eyebrows to full cock, throws up his chin, gently passes the tip of his tongue round his lips, and then, sharply pulling some unseen trigger, down come the eyebrows. All which intimates—"What do you think of that, my friends? Not that I take credit for it—I'm used to it." Then he dives for more toast; but before the bit has reached his mouth, he breaks out afresh.)

"Now, I flatter myself I'm a man of observation, and a citizen of the world, as Goldfinch says. Well, among other observations which I've made in our little vale below, this isn't the worst nor the least valuable. I've observed Tom making money, and Dick going to the workhouse; and, keeping my eyes on 'em, I asks myself, How is it? Dick's not particular bright—but Tom's a fool. Neither of them can read; neither of 'em's had friends to start 'em, or to keep 'em back; one's as ugly as the other is; and whereas Tom's got two boys and five gals, Dick's got five gals and two boys. Now, where's the difference, I ask? How is it, says I, looking at 'em, that one rides out in his shay, while the other never rode in his life, except when they took him to the House on a shutter! Why, here it is! Nick, you villain," cried Joel, quite gleeful over his sagacity, "listen, for it's something in your line. Tom licks, Dick kicks!

"Well, why not? Tom doesn't lick to the end of his days, but only till he has licked together a nice little heap of money; then he sits down on it, and other Thomases come and lick the ground all round about.

"Again, there's such a thing as strainin' at a gnat, and swallerin' of a camel, as the Scripture tells us. Now, Dick strains at a very little gnat when he refuses to take advantages that Tom snaps up like a hawk; and he swallows an awful big camel when he and his children go on to the parish. Accordingly, I'm for Tom's plan; whereby I've licked together a hundred and thirty-seven pounds ten, all snug in my box up-stairs. But that ain't all I've got there. In that box there's a precious nest-egg now, that I'm a nidjot if I don't hatch into a golden hen—a hen that shall make her nest of bank-notes, and lay no end of gold and silver. Gold and silver, Nick!" repeated Hatcher, warming at the prospect; "gold and silver, you precious villain! and you shall have a silver collar, as sure as you're a tom cat!—if I can get one cheap.

"Now," continued he, pushing back the tray, settling in his chair anew, and taking his chin in his hand, "let's see how things stand. H'm! H'm!"

Having got thus far, and finding he could go no farther, he rose, looked round, cogitated or seemed to cogitate, had some doubts apparently, some internal struggle. Finally, he seemed to have succeeded in diverting his own attention from the matter in hand; and seizing the opportunity, he went to the cupboard, tossed off a glass of brandy, hastily wiped his mouth with his hand, and resumed his place on the hearthrug before the other Joel had time to look round. There was evidently some suspicion between them, however, for the Joel that had the brandy looked very confused and ashamed.

But the blush soon passed away, and again Hatcher said to himself—"Ah! Now let's see how things stand, in a quiet scientific manner. Hi! Nick. Here, go out, sir!" Joel opened the door for the cat, who quietly stole out, licking his jaws. "Couldn't stand anything listening after all; and cats are superstitious animals. Now, then," and down sat Mr. Hatcher again; again took his chin in his hand, and so proceeded with the case before him.

"This Mr. Keppel—no, stop: we'll call 'em A's and B's. Well, A's a gentleman—of a very poor sort. He marries B, a lady of property. A likes the property very well, but doesn't care a fig for B: nevertheless, he finds that while he's got B fast enough, he has precious little hold on her money. But if A and B have a boy, then A does pretty much as he likes:—considering that I went to Doctors' Commons and had a look at the will as soon as his wife died, under what I thought circumstances of suspicion, I ought to know that. Well, they don't have a boy: they have a girl, C; which makes things awful inconvenient and disagreeable to A. A never cared for B: C was only a sort of judgment on him; so he couldn't like C—in fact," said Joel, putting his head on one side, and contemplating the case for a moment—"I shouldn't. But C's valuable too. So long as C lives, or till she comes of age, A's all right—pretty fair, at any rate. So soon as she dies, farewell departed greatness—the spirit-stirrin' drum, and the piercin' flute as A's been playing such a pretty tune on since he married B. That's how matters stand, then; if you throw in the fact that A takes his liquor rather strong, and what's more, takes plenty of it—gets bold, gets reckless, gets what they call essentric, I believe; but which, for short, I call rum.

"But here comes in a circumstance!" said Joel, at this point

51

of the soliloquy, began kneading his chin with renewed interest and vigour. "A circumstarnce which I shall now proceed to take the liberty of inquiring into, in my little way. C, the child, all of a sudden disappears. The plaintiff—no, the defendant—says she was stole away by gipsies; but, gentlemen of the jury, that point is a *hex parte* statement—that is to say, the other party mightn't think so; therefore, it goes for what it's worth at present. Meantime, I say, she disappears, suddenly *and* mysteriously."

Here Joel drew himself up, refreshed himself with a snort, and then proceeded in the judicial vein which his mind naturally adopted on such occasions.

Every man is imaginative when he is on his hobby; when a man is alone, and pleased with himself, and comfortable, it is wonderful what boyish, playful whims he indulges; in what odd ways he harangues himself or anybody else of whom he may be thinking; and how gravely he acts the part of this character or that, like an actor at rehearsal. So Mr. Hatcher, as he warmed, fancied himself addressing a jury.

"Now, gentlemen, the *other* party as I referred to—which his penetration does him great credit, and his father was a very valuable officer—don't say that C *wasn't* carried away by gipsies—what he says is, Was she? and, What for? He challenges that *hex parte* statement; and if nothin' comes of it, why there's no harm done, I hope. To proceed.

"The defendant's case isn't bad. The gipsies were there that evening; they were gone in the morning. There are coarse footprints leading from the camp to the room where the child slept; the door of which was locked from the inside when found missing. A little book which the young un took to bed with her was found in the park, in the direction of the camp. Gipsies have stolen children; and A might have been up to some of his tricks with one of the gipsy people, which they revenge accordingly. But more than all, it doesn't seem reasonable that A should desire to get rid of C in any way, looking at the provisions of the last testament: that's an important point.

"Now comes the other party. He thinks it remarkable, first, that nothing should have been said about the loss of the little one for about twenty hours; and then, that all the town should be so jolly welcome to go and look at the footmarks and the broken window-frame. If you say that A's absence accounts for no stir being made in a hurry, the other party says that A's absence itself is got to be accounted for—leastways, it isn't quite clear, though there seems to be no doubt that he went to bed dead drunk; and if he rose in the night must have rose drunk, and just capable of doing any mad thing he said he'd do. But how comes his cloak in a limekiln? If the gipsies stole the cloak, they'd have kept it: it is as easy to hide a cloak as a child. Perhaps you argue that, though they did keep the garment, they were afraid to keep the clasps, because of the letters on 'em, and so cut them off and threw them away. But gipsies like trinkets, they are first-rate tinkers, and in two minutes the clasps could have been hammered into a bracelet or perhaps a nose-ring. But, says you, coming to the point, do you think it at all likely that A himself would go and get rid of the child, knowing what we do? No, says the other party—no, gentlemen of the jury—not if he was in his right mind. Not if A's brains never got fuddled with drink; not if he wasn't, in consequence, a anxious, nervous, timorated man—liable to run his head against a danger he couldn't see, to avoid dangers that anybody else would snap their fingers at, if they existed. But I tell you what I *do* say," continued the broker, resigning his judicial character, and speaking as plain as Mr. Hatcher—"considerin' that A's been thinking of nothing but this property—how to get it and how to keep it—for many years; considerin' that what with loose free livin', etcetera, he's got to be eccentric; considerin' he never cared about the child; considerin' that he goes in fear of losing his indulgencies one day by measles, and the next by hoopin' cough; and, lastly, considerin' that there's nobody in the way to hinder him, I say A might do *this*; he reasons to himself—'I take the child, and have it brought up quiet, making it seem to be stolen: then I'm safe for near twenty year. If people make a row while the young un lives, I produce it, and all's square; if the child dies while it's away, then they've got to *prove* its death, which would be jolly difficult, and isn't like to be tried!'

"Now, that's what I say!" and Joel paused, looking hard at the fire. "Then the verdict is, that Mr. Hatcher has good

reason to ask—*Was* Ruth Keppel stole by gipsies? And he'll be foolish if he don't look into it. But *now* the clasps ain't accounted for! And another thing I've left out of the reckoning: A has a valet, D, and D seemed to know where to find A when A went off that night. Now D, when I come to think of it——"

And Joel went off into a study even browner than the last.

CHAPTER XX.

HATCHER, MARINER, AND FRIEND OF HIS SPECIES.

NEXT morning, Joel found himself in his best clothes at the lime-kilns; and, what is more, straying quite accidentally, of course, past a group of the workpeople, then engaged in discussing breakfast, in the very hollow where Woppits had found shelter on a previous and memorable occasion.

The eyes of all the lime-burners were immediately turned on Joel; not that visitors were very unfrequent, but they were always ragged, houseless creatures—tramps, and other human waifs and strays—who crept there for the sake of the warmth. Joel had a good coat, comfortably buttoned; his hat was on one side; his walking-stick was flourishing; his toes were turned out; he was a gentleman of curious habits, taking the air—apparently. And if the lime-burners exhibited some interest in Mr. Hatcher, Mr. Hatcher was not annoyed thereat; on the contrary, he regarded the workpeople with a most affable countenance, and hummed a little tune as he went his way. This being the case—

"Mornin', mister," said the ganger, or overlooker.

"Good morning!" blandly answered the curious gentleman taking a walk. At the same time, pulling up, he smiled the smile which he had observed among the characteristics of philanthropists and friends of their species. "Warm work yours, my men!"

"You may well say that, sir," replied the other, who didn't mind being patronized by kind gentlemen, as they generally stood something. "Wery warm," said he; "and what's more, it's a sort of work as parches your throat like an old stick."

"Oh, I know, my friend, I know. The dust of the lime rises, and lodges in the epithalamum, which it tittles [here several lime-burners cough], likewise the capricorn! [Another fit of coughing; after which one of the men adds faintly, 'Oh, my poor capricorn!'] The result is obvious. You are—ahem—you——"

"Get jolly thirsty," said the ganger.

"Exactly. Makes you drink a good deal, no doubt! Always can drink, I suppose?" said Joel, playfully, and munificently fumbling at his watch-guard.

"Yes, sir, thank you," responded the ganger, the gang looking on in momentary expectation. "Will you drink with us, sir?" and he offered Joel his mug of beer.

Mr. Hatcher replied that nothing would give him greater pleasure; that they were not to think him proud; that, in fact, he was a working man himself; he was, indeed, he said, elevating his eyebrows, and looking as much astonished at the announcement as the ganger pretended to be. It seemed as if the gentleman had never got that view of his position in society before, and as if it rather amused him. Nevertheless, he sipped the ganger's beer in a very delicate and unworkmanlike manner; and a little shudder ran through his frame as he handed back the mug, obviously because he was not used to drink beer. However, there was a half-crown in the mug when he returned it.

"Perhaps," said he, "you won't mind drinking with me?"

"Cert'inly, sir. Thankee, sir," said the lime-men all.

"Not much troubled with visitors, I suppose?" remarked Joel, feeling more at his case.

"Not many this weather," was the answer. "Have a goodish few in the cold weather, though. A kil's a God-send to a poor tramp as can't find a lodging, you see. It's a precious time now, though, since we had one of 'em here; I suppose things is getting better."

"Yes, we had, Joe," broke in one of the men; "he warn't a tramp, though, wor he? That workhouse one, you know, two or three nights sin'."

"Oh, ah, I remember now; but he was off again afore daylight."

"WOPPITS, YOU'RE WANTED!"

"Queer card he was," continued the other, contemplatively swinging his empty mug between his knees. "Wonder he didn't stop till mornin'—speshly as you said you'd give him a bit o' breffust."

"A Sleaford lad was that?" inquired Joel, quietly.

"Oh, no, sir; he warn't like the Sleafords. He had on a gray smock and green smalls—that's what he wore. Don'no wheres he come from."

Joel made a note in his mind of the gray smock and the green smalls, carelessly remarking, "Some runaway 'prentice, I dare say. And so that's the only one you've had for a long time, eh?"

"As fur as I see," replied the ganger.

"And of course some one of you's always here, and you keep a look-out."

"Well, we do pretty much; and it's quite as well. Some poor devil comes and lays down by the kil; he shifts nearer and nearer in his sleep, and mebbee in he goes. All over then, sir."

"Never escapes, eh? Did you ever find one that died in that shocking way, my man?"

"Find 'em? Not a bit of 'em! If they happen to have metal buttons on their clothes, or iron tips on their shoes, or a knife in their pockets, or summut o' that, we find it; or mebbee a tooth or so, if we look sharp, and they don't bide in too long, but as for anything else—! But, as I said afore, one of us is pooty much here, and we keeps a sharp look-out. That night Charity was about, we all knocked off, though, if you wants to know partiklar."

"Wasn't you afraid to trust a stranger here? I mean, didn't he walk off with anything?"

"Walk off with anythin'? No? He warn't the sort," replied the ganger, giving a furtive glance at Joel's not too prepossessing countenance. "Besides, there was nothin' to walk off with, 'cept these tools," and the ganger waved his hand comprehensively. "We did miss a prong out of here, but we found it over at the north pit!"

"Which do you call the north pit? What do you call a prong?" asked Joel, looking eagerly around, and rubbing his chin, no longer dimpled with the smiles of philanthropy.

"There," answered the ganger, rudely jerking his thumb over his shoulder. "Them things with wooden handles, and bent irons at the end."

"Oh, indeed! Dear me! Now, what could the boy want with the—the prong?"

"Who said he wanted anything with it?" rejoined the ganger, coarsely. He was tired of Joel's interrogations, didn't like his appearance, and had got his half-crown. "Who said he touched it? I didn't! Some of us left it there, I dessay."

"Ah, no doubt, no doubt," rejoined Mr. Hatcher. "You would naturally leave your prongs about after the fatigues of the day, wouldn't you? H'm?" There was no answer; and seeing that he would gain nothing by tarrying longer, Mr. Hatcher distributed a cheerful nod among the company, adding, "Well, I'll get on a little further—your kilns here attracted me out of my way."

"Werry kind of 'em," grunted the ganger, "much obliged to 'em, I'm sure."

"Good morning!"

No answer. And off walked Joel Hatcher, once more a gentleman taking the air.

"Gray smock and green breeches there that night. Gone before morning. Prong carried over to the north pit—where the clasps were found. Gray smock! my green smalls!—I must look after you! You're a runaway from Latherwell, you are—I know your livery. Humph! A runaway workhouse boy getting up before daylight to run away from a breakfast! Don't seem sensible—can't see him in that light. Suppose he didn't get into the kiln himself! *That* wouldn't account for the clasps. No, my nimble smalls, you're running away somewhere at this moment, unless they've caught you, and placed you in Latherwell stocks. I wouldn't mind occupying the same situation at your side. I'd give something considerable to have you by the ear for just ten minutes; and you've got to be found, that's certain!

"What time like the time present?" Mr. Hatcher then asked of himself. He had no pressing business on hand; his mother could look after the shop for a little time, at a pinch; he had four guineas in his pocket; why not send up a message to the old woman, and pay a visit to Latherwell at once? No sooner said than done. He steps into a wayside public-house, writes three or four careful lines to the Bonnet, and gives a loiterer sixpence to convey the message. The thing's done.

That same afternoon, Hatcher was in Latherwell; his journey thither was not so painful or so roundabout as Lucy's. Concerning a parish runaway, he was referred to Mr. Tweakle, beadle, 22, Pump Street. Having an attack of gout, that functionary was invalided, and received Mr. Hatcher in his bed-room.

"I've come," began Joel, with something of his judicial manner, "concerning a lad which, I believe, ran away from the workhouse, here!"

"Have you, though?" exclaimed Mr. Tweakle, forgetting even the gout in his anxiety for his young friend. "Dear me! Have you now? Just shut the door, sir; will you be so good? And if an elderly party should happen to come in—a person in black, sir—change the object of conversation. *You* know! natural like."

Mr. Hatcher winked and shut the door.

"Thank you. Now, how is the boy? Did he send you?"

It was clear, then, that the runaway had not returned to Latherwell, or been carried back to that cradle of his infant years. Hatcher's object now was, to obtain a description of the boy. Meanwhile, taking his cue from Mr. Tweakle's mysteriously interested manner, he boldly replied that the boy had sent him, and was quite well.

"Oh, I knew he was all right," said Tweakle proudly, "from his sending back the clothes. The carrier left them at the House only last night, I'm told."

"Sent the clothes back? What clothes?" Hatcher asked, rather off his guard.

"Hush! his House-suit, you know, sir; what he had on when he ran away."

"Oh, ah!" Mr. Hatcher began to think there might be some mistake in identity. "How many boys have run away from this parish, now?" he inquired.

"Only Woppits, sir! God bless you, there's not another boy in our place with pluck enough to do it. He's the only one that has run away since I've been beadle, which is now seventeen year and a-half, come Michaelmas."

"And he's sent his clothes back, has he, the honest lad!—his gray frock and his poor green smalls?"

"And his shoes, and his cap and his shirts, sir—one of 'em couldn't expect the other, perhaps. He promised to send 'em back, and he's kept his word. But how comes it that you didn't know about it? Who may you be, if I'm so bold as to ask?"

Mr. Tweakle began to fear that he had been putting weapons into the hands of an enemy.

"Me!" exclaimed Joel, clearing his throat to make way for the large lie he was about to eject. It was the first that came to hand, and he had no time to pick and choose. Well, the fact is, I'm mate of the *Black Bull*, the ship in which Woppits has taken a berth as cabin-boy, bound for China and the islands of Oozly. We sails in a few days; and the voyage being long, with contrary winds in general, it ain't likely that you'll hear of Woppits for some years to come! I didn't know about his sending his togs back, d'ye see! I found him his sea-going rig; that's all I know about it, mate."

And to further his nautical pretensions, Mr. Hatcher rose from his chair, and hitched his trousers up one leg at a time. Then he sat down again, and looking Tweakle hard in the face, began to chew imaginary tobacco.

"Goin' to Chaney, is he?" sighed the beadle. "Well, Chaney ought to be proud of him, that's all I got to say to Chaney, or them islands either."

"Yes," returned Hatcher, "he's a fine fellow—make a good seaman, I warrant ye. Furls a bobstay naturally, he does; and as for clewing a reef——!" Hatcher whistled the admiration which he found it impossible to express in words, hauling in the atmosphere, hand over hand, to illustrate his meaning. "D'ye see, mate? That's a' operation Lord Nelson himself never got the reg'lar hang of. But that boy!—I say, he looks older than he is, though. How old did you say he was, Mr. Beadle?"

"Fifteen, about, sir," answered the unsuspicious Tweakle, "and not a flaw about him except that scar on his cheek, which was done one bitter day agin' Mr. Gorelam's railin's, as he was sweeping away the snow."

"Ah, he told me about that."

"I say," remarked Tweakle, after a few moments' reflection, "I tell you what, I don't exactly know whether Chaney's the forrin part I mean, but I know there *is* a forrin part where the natives barter diamonds, and gold and ivory, and that, for pen-knives and glass beads. Now, if you'd be good enough to take charge of it, I should like to invest a pound or so in them articles for my young friend."

Hatcher replied that he knew the natives in Chaney didn't trade in that way, and he wasn't sure about the Oozly Islands, because, d'ye see, it was his first voyage in them parts. However, he vowed to keep a sharp look out for Woppits's welfare generally; and, freighted with many precious messages from the good beadle to his friend, the disguised craft Joel Hatcher set sail from Pump Street. How grim it looked as it steered round the corner!

CHAPTER XXI.

EXTRAORDINARY METAMORPHOSIS.

THE Blue Raven, perched on the Dover road, was a bustling and a thriving hostel, forty years ago. In those piping times for coaches, the Lightning and the Defiance stopped at the Blue Raven, which changed the horses, gave beef and beer to the passengers, and rejoiced in the scarlet presence of coachman and guard. Alas for the Blue Raven! When I knew it some twenty years ago, its glories were all departed. It was even then as empty and melancholy as last year's nest. The sign-board, struck with a rusty order of paralysis, had ceased to swing; the water-trough, inconsolable for the loss of the pigeons and other fowl which used to perch about it, cheerily and home-like, of old, refused to hold water any longer; one of the seats in the porch, seeing no further use for itself, had given away altogether; the chimney-stack, from which the smoke of so many roaring winter fires once soared, had collapsed; Crummels, the landlord, had grown deaf: his housekeeper was deaf too; and Bob, the only remaining hostler and serving man, had contracted so confirmed a habit of shaking his head at the times he lived in, that at length it became a disease: he shook his head from morning to night.

By this time affairs have changed. Crummels went quietly to his grave several years ago; the housekeeper quietly followed, as if by pre-arrangement; Bob, never to leave the road, went to live with a tollgate-man for the remainder of his days, which were brief; and lastly, the Blue Raven, deserted and alone, committed suicide by spontaneous combustion.

I am very sorry for that, because I could have described to modern passengers by the Dover road the very seat outside the inn, where once upon a time, and in the evening, a woman sat shearing away the curls from a little girl's head. Crummels had been waiting for a customer all day long, when this woman presented herself at the bar, and called for a pair of scissors. Crummels was incredulous; but that was all she *did* call for, humbly, and for charity's sake.

She was no beauty, this woman—much the contrary. Her face was coarse and freckled; her eyes lacked timidity, which is so excellent in woman; her hair was short, and of an uncertain mouse colour, and little neatness was exhibited in its arrangement. It had evidently no fixed idea of a parting, and a large portion of it, actuated by an indecent curiosity, was poking out of a hole in the crown of her bonnet; which was blowsy, but fashionable. Her dress generally was unprepossessing. The bonnet I have mentioned. The gown, of cambric chintz, arrested the passer, no less by its extravagance of pattern than by the violence of its colouring. This gown was short in the waist (though, as the woman had nothing that corresponded to a waist, that was of little moment) and low in the neck; therefore the fair shoulders had to be covered, which they were, with a huge cotton kerchief, emblazoned with the death of Nelson. Modesty called loudly for another kerchief to be stitched round the skirt of the gown, which was inordinately short; but modesty called in vain in this case, as in many others. And there were the young woman's legs, bare almost to the knees; or they would have been, save for her blue worsted stockings.

The toilette of the little girl was scarcely superior. Her bonnet was many sizes too large, but this disadvantage had its advantages; for the fair face was shaded from the sun and sheltered from the wind. Then she had on an old drab gingham cloak or pelisse, with a large cape, and a large kerchief was wound about her throat; so that, taking away the head, she presented a miniature image of a hackney coachman.

"You know," says the awkward and disreputable-looking female, as she saws away at the child's curls, depositing each ringlet in the bosom of her gown, while the child looking up wondering; "you know, I'm werry sorry, my little darling, to go a cropping of you in this way, but what's to be done, my precious? What with the werry suspicious way I walks, with these things flipper-flapperin' about my legs, and what with your pooty shiny curls a bobbin' about, and making you a little lady in spite of your clothes, why we'll get bowled out; and you'll get sent back to the bogey in the cloak, while I shall be took to quod. That's prison, don't you know."

It was evident that the child had heard before of the bogey in the cloak, and it was equally clear that the mention of him brought back to the child's mind recollections not directly connected with bogies. "Oh," she said, beginning to cry, "I want to go home! Ruth wants to go home!"

"Well—we're a-goin' home, ain't we?" answered the female. "We're a-goin, where there's a big garden—oh, ever so big!—where there's flowers, and cock-sorrel, and all that in it. On'y don't you cry!"

The little creature was quieted for a while—until the young person had shorn off all her ringlets, giving her fair head a most unhandsome appearance. Then she broke out again fretfully, crying for some bread and some drink.

"Good heavens!" exclaimed the female, with a bewildered air, "hungry again, are you? Well—I dare say you are, my precious. You see I'm so full of worrit that I don't feel hungry a bit.

"I ain't got another farden," she mentally added; "but I'll see if the old cock as was kind enough to lend me the sithers will give you something. I wish I could come up with them hop-fields that I was told of yesterday."

Rising to go into the house, the woman was for the first time aware of the presence of a third party. This was a spare man, buttoned up in a snuffy-brown coat, and who had been leaning against the empty trough, craning his neck in the direction of the sheltered seat which the disreputable-looking one now rose to quit. The trough was at some distance, but the evening was still and the stranger's neck was long. As soon as he saw that the woman had discovered him, he crossed over toward her, and spoke.

"Good evening, ma'am," said he, stroking his chin, and looking like a gentleman taking a walk. "Wish you good evening, ma'am."

To which madam replied in considerable confusion, "Oh, pretty well, thank'ee, I am," and, with a dexterous sidling movement, planted herself before the child.

"And how is your little charge, ma'am?" pursued the stranger, endeavouring to get a glimpse at her under the arm of the young person. "Perhaps she would eat a piece of gingerbread?"

"Perhaps she would," responded the awkward woman, at once disarmed by this opportune liberality.

The snuff-brown stranger produced a square piece of gingerbread, and motioning the young woman aside, presented it to the child. As soon as he looked fairly into the little face, he snorted with a sound of self-congratulation, and seating himself, muttered, "At last, by Jingo!"

"What's at last?" exclaimed the young woman, with an angry start of surprise, and with not a little consternation pictured on her countenance.

"Oh, it's all right, ma'am" (a peculiar emphasis on "ma'am"); "you needn't mind me: not a bit of it. It's all right, my dear."

And the snuff-brown man pawed his chin, and inter-wriggled his fingers alternately, in the great satisfaction of his soul.

"There!" said the young woman, seizing the cake from the child's hands, "you'd better take your gingerbread and go. I dunno as we want your company."

"Oh, that's it, is it? Well, I daresay you don't; nobody expected you to." Suddenly, Mr. Hatcher placed his hand on the young woman's shoulder, adding, in a low tone—

"Woppits, you're wanted!"

The gingerbread and the lower jaw of the disreputable-looking person dropped simultaneously at this information. Sinking on to the bench, and throwing forward one leg in a defensive attitude, Woppits tremblingly ejaculated—

"Who-o-o wants me?"

"The law, and I'm its officer!"

"Well, what does the law want with a poor cove like me? I ain't a lawyer! I ain't done nothing to the law! Never touched it!"

"Oh, that's your opinion, is it, my man? What do you call thieving, then? Who stole clothes from a workhouse? I say, where did you get this child from?"

This was said in a sharp imperative voice, the speaker's eyes keenly searching the interior of the young person's bonnet meanwhile.

"Picked it up," answered the lad, who had no interest in concealing the truth, if it came to that.

"Picked it up, eh? Come now, young feller, it's no use trying that story on with me, you know—not a bit of it. Because it's seven years' transportation, if you do."

"Who's trying on? I did pick it up. Raked it out of a lime-pit after a feller threw it in. That's where I got it from."

"What a story! In them clothes it's wearing now? Be careful, young man, be careful."

"No; in no clothes at all—she had only a bedgown on, 'cept the cloak she was wrapped up in."

"Oh, except the cloak she was wrapped up in," repeated Mr. Hatcher, shivering with satisfaction. "But you needn't talk so loud, my boy—I ain't deaf. Well, go on! Where's the cloak she was wrapped in?"

"Same as she'd ha' been if I hadn't seen her throwed in, pretty dear. Burnt up and cooked!"

"How did you get these women's things?"

"Bought 'em."

"Oh, that is easy said, that is! And pray where did you get the money from?"

"Well, if you must know, a gentleman lent it to me," answered Woppits, growing still more uneasy.

"Now, what sort of gentleman?" asked Joel, eagerly.

"What sort?"

"Out with it! What sort?"

"Did you say what sort of gentleman?"

"I tell you what, young man, if you prevaricate with me, you're handcuffed and hauled off to jail in a jiffy! Answer, immejate!" Woppits's evident uneasiness on this point piqued Mr. Hatcher's curiosity to the utmost.

"Here, mister!" cried Woppits, rising, a tear glistening in his eye and determination bristling out at every joint of him. "Fetch out your handcuffs! Haul me off! I'll see you and the law at Jericho before I tells you that gentleman's name, or anything about him. Come on!"

Hatcher was rather staggered at this outburst, and, what is more to the purpose, was alarmed at the high voice in which the workhouse runaway defied him.

"You young blockhead!" exclaimed he (if you can exclaim in a whisper), "what are you shouting like that for? You're in for it safe enough, I can tell you ; so you needn't be so anxious to be took up. The gentleman be hanged!"

"You let him alone, then, mister. He knows nothing about this young one, at any rate."

"Very well, then; that's enough, my lad, ;" replied Hatcher, in a conciliatory tone. This broke Woppits down again. After an uneasy pause, during which Hatcher kneaded his chin into an inexpressible variety of shapes, the boy said :—

"I say, mister, what do you think the law'll do to me?"

"Well," answered Hatcher, "for the clothes I should say about twelve months breaking stones on bread and water."

"Why, I sent 'em back!" cried Woppits, opening his eyes to their widest.

"What's that got to do with it ? Well, then, for the child, goodness knows what you'll get for that ! It's a hanging matter, generally speaking."

"And what's to be done to the feller that threw her into the lime, then ?"

"Oh, come, now," replied Mr. Hatcher, adopting a different tone, "you're a 'cute young man, I daresay, and a nice young man ; but you ain't got a character from your last situation. *We* know all about it. The fact is, you run away from Lather-well, get hard up, see this child alone, steal it, sell her good clothes, and perhaps jewels, and her hair, too—I see you've been cropping it—and so rig yourself out as a beggar with a large family. You see, my lad, it's no use trying to fiddle me. I'm too old."

Now, truthfully to account for the purchase of his female attire, Woppits must have again brought up the subject of the gentleman that lent him money. Woppits therefore contented himself with declaring that he had no intention to fiddle anybody, and stood with one of Ruth's hands grasped in his, and his eyes sadly fixed upon the ground.

"Now, I'll tell you what," said Hatcher, after another pause, filled in with reflection on either side. "I'm not a hard man. I've got a heart in my bosom, young man, like others of my speshus ; and can feel for the unfortunate. If you'll just step in and bring out a jug of ale and something to eat, we'll sit down, and you shall tell me all about it, from the time you ran away from the workhouse and Mr. Gorelam (you see I know pretty well all about it), and then we'll see what can be done."

Had Woppits been going forth to execution, the prospect of something to eat and drink would have soothed him. Straight-way marched he in, taking the child with him by the hand. In a few minutes, he returned with a huge dish of cold beef, an uncut loaf, and a jug of beer generously overflowing with rich foam—all which he eyed with a demure twinkle, as he placed them on a rude table before the benches outside.

"I say," remarked Mr. Hatcher, looking ruefully at the beef, "I meant bread and cheese."

"Well, I *thought* you might ; but you didn't say, you know. Shall I change it ?"

"Oh never mind."

And they fell to—Woppits looking up the tender parts for Ruth, but rather preferring, for his own consumption, good hard indigestible slices, and plenty of them.

"Oh my! oh dear!" he cried, as, blundering most dexter-ously, he whipped a long juicy slice about three-quarters of an an inch thick to the ground, "there's a lovely piece all spoiled with the dirt! What shall we do ? Here!—the landlord's look-ing!" and in a trice he had it safe in the recesses of his gown.

"Don't do that again!" said Hatcher. "Now, then," con-tinued that artful one, wiping his mouth long before Woppits had any idea of bringing the meal to a conclusion, "just tell me how you *did* get the infant. One gentleman to another, you know."

"Told you the truth before ; found it choking in a kiln, and it came to arterworks," answered Woppits, shortly, masticating his words and his beef at the same time.

"Eh! what's that about choking ? You said nothing about that before. Come now, no gammon, young fellow."

"Very well, then," answered the boy, indignantly ; "take that hankercher off her neck, and see if it's gammon!"

Hatcher seized the kerchief in a manner so rough and eager that the child cried, and clung to her protector.

"Come, I say, mister! gently, will you! That ain't the way to handle a baby! Let me take the pin out, my precious!

There now !" said he, exposing the terrible finger-marks, which were as distinct as ever. "Now, what's gammon ?"

What with the beef and the beer, Woppits was quite at his ease now.

Hatcher stretched both his hands across the table, and lifted the child over to his side. Heedless of her cries, and Woppits's flourishes of apprehension, he proceeded to examine the marks with the greatest eagerness—holding her close to his dim-looking eyes, then gnawing at her throat, as it were, with those same eyes, at arm's length—turning her this way and that, as though she had been an anatomical model rather than a living child. Then taking out his handkerchief, he dipped it into the beer (to Woppits's infinite disgust), and twisting a corner round his fin-ger, commenced rubbing at the marks as he had rubbed at the clasps. The child winced at the smart, and cried so piteously that the sound thereof entered even the dull ears of Crummels.

"Stow it !" shouted Woppits, rising with his knife in his hand, " or else I'm blessed if I'm not handcuffed for somethin'."

"Won't come off !" the other muttered, " and yet I'd wager my life it's *on* the skin, not under it." Hatcher restored the child to her seat, took his chin in his hand, looked at her, and pondered. He knew it was impossible to compress the throat leaving such marks, and also leaving the child alive. His next reflection was that the finger-prints were of the same colour all over ; whereas, if the child had been really strangled, they would have been fainter at the edges, and not so well defined.

"Now, then !" exclaimed Woppits. "Didn't I say so ? Isn't she been strangulated ?"

"Well, my young friend, you may think so, but I understand these things ; and that place round the little gal's throat she was born with. You've heard of people being marked, I suppose, haven't you ? Now, that place in your cheek : that ain't a na-tural born mark—done with the blade of a scraper, that was, I can see."

If this mark had no other value, it gave Woppits an almost superstitious notion of the sagacity of the snuff-brown stranger. It was clearly useless to endeavour to keep any secret from him.

"Then," said Woppits, whose common-sense never deserted him under any circumstances, "there'll be no occasion to keep this blessed great hankycher round her neck."

"Why not ?"

"Oh, the cat's out, you know."

"Don't you talk so precious loud," whispered Hatcher, look-ing round suspiciously ; put the hankycher on, and never mind whether the cat's out or no. You just go on and tell me all about it."

Beginning at the boundary wall at Latherwell workhouse, Woppits recounted all his adventures from the time when he dropped from that eminence, always excepting what had passed between Mr. Tweakle and himself. For that part of the story he substituted the following :—

"Well, as I was going down the road, I meets a gentleman. Ses the gentleman to me, ses he, 'Woppits, my boy, if you'd like to borrer twelve-and-threepence off me you're werry welcome.' 'Thank'ee,' ses I, for I was werry ill pervided. So he did."

"And you spent all the money the gentleman gave you to buy these clothes ?"

"Not quite ; but it's all gone for them and wittles."

"Bless my soul !" Hatcher exclaimed, very much affected. "What a noble-minded lad you must be! What a generous young youth !"

"Oh, I don't know !" said Woppits, blushing up to the crown of his bonnet. "You needn't mention it. 'Tain't much I've done for her after all ; and I'd just like to keep her alto-gether, only there's that jiggerin' law, I s'pose !"

"And do you never think of the drag she'd be upon you everywhere you went ?"

"No, I never did ; and I'm not goin' to begin to think any-think of that kind."

"But you'll never be able to get along with her, at all," replied Hatcher, humanely and reflectively, "unless somebody helps you—somebody with a heart in his bosom."

"Lord bless you, sir !" answered Woppits, the hinges of his speech oiled by Crummels's ale, and his fear of the law banished by Joel's apparent mollification, "you're innocent, sir. She's no trouble. She's been well brought up, she has !"

AN INCIDENT IN MR. YALLOPS'S KITCHEN.

"How do you know?" and Hatcher looked up suspiciously.

"Why, because she's got such a lovely way when she says 'thank'ee' and 'please' and that—which she always does. Besides, she never goes to sleep without saying all she knows of 'Our Father!' She gets as far as 'Deliver us from evil,'" said Woppits, inclining his head, and whispering in Hatcher's ear, "and then she makes a hitch, and can't get no further."

"Does she now?" amiably answered the other, blinking unpleasantly on the child with his ancient and fish-like eyes.

"Yes, she does, and shall say it to you, if you like. Ruth, my pet, say 'Our Father' to the gentleman!"

After some further coaxing, the child began the old-fashioned prayer, peeping slyly at Hatcher all the while from the depths of her dreary bonnet. The voice was so low and sweet, it seemed scarcely so near; and both Hatcher and Woppits had to bend their heads to hear it. She went on very bashfully until she saw land, in the shape of the last words which she knew of the prayer, then with sudden clearness she cried, "but deliver us from evil!" and stopped, and cast up a frightened glance into Woppits's face; and Woppits looked at Hatcher, and Hatcher coughed, and looked hard at a donkey browsing at large in a neighbouring ditch.

"There you are, you see," said Woppits, again inclining his head confidentially towards Hatcher. "That's where she always stops."

"Won-der-ful!" exclaimed the other, still gazing abstractedly at the donkey. "Upon my soul," mused he, that little affair having awakened with a weak flutter in his breast, "that's curious! One would almost think she'd stopt there till she met me. She'll learn the rest, now, I shouldn't wonder!"

"Won-der-ful!" he repeated.

"I say, mister, I ain't the willin you took me for—am I?"

"Young man," replied Hatcher, solemnly taking Woppits's hand in his own great pale, cold, soft paw, "your conduct has been such as must command admiration and respect!"

"Do you think so?"

"Think, sir! Have you been tried, and have you been found wantin'?"

"You don't mean wittles?"

"I refer to your immortal part, my friend!"

"Oh, well, I don't know as I have."

"You're a honour to your speshus. You've got a heart in your bosom!" and Hatcher turned away.

"Then you'll put us in a good word with the law, won't you, mister? Eh?"

"I'll do more," replied Mr. Hatcher. "I can appreciate your affection for the little girl, as much as here and there one; and sorry should I be to be the means of parting of you—it would haunt me to my latter days. Stoop down here, young man. I know I'm going contrary to law—and the law, mind you, wouldn't believe a word of your story, which prisoners it never does believe—and I know I am going agin' my duty. But the voice of duty I will be deaf unto. I will follow the dictates of my heart, be the consequences what they may. Go! go, my young friend, and may you be happy!"

"Go where?" asked the matter-of-fact Woppits.

"Just wherever you please," answered the magnanimous Hatcher.

"I say, mister, what a parson you'd make! Did you ever try that line?"

"My young friend, don't allude to happy days long past!" sighed Mr. Hatcher. "But no more of that. I said, just wherever you please. But you can't go wherever you please, as you're situated; so look here!"

And Mr. Hatcher drew from his pocket a small canvas bag, throttled with a piece of twine. So tightly was its throat tied up, that it was a work of several minutes to remove the string. Time well spent!—plan for carrying money most happy! Here you have not only the purse itself strangled, but also all maudlin promptings to humanity, as they call it. You carry a stupid gaping purse, ready to fly open at a touch. Moved by a sudden impulse (and sudden impulses are always dangerous), you resolve to bestow a crown upon somebody; out comes the purse, open flies its mouth, and you're five shillings poorer before you can say Jack Robinson. But carry your money in a well-tied bag, and ere you can get at its contents you have thought twice; your impulses are arrested in their mad career; you remember that you have some coppers about you, or a loose sixpence in your waistcoat pocket! and you rescue four-and-sixpence from the Moloch of mistaken charity!

With more of a business than of a benevolent twinkle in his eyes, Joel patiently unbound his money-bag, and taking out a golden piece, held it between his finger and thumb.

"Here you are," said he; "that's to help you on your way!" He paused for a moment, looking with one eye into the bowels of the purse, like the familiar but untiring image of a magpie peeping into a marrow-bone. Then, withdrawing his eye, he dipped his fingers in and fished up another golden coin, smaller than the first. "Here—take this likewise. What have you got to put 'em in?"

"Oh, I've got a pocket!" answered Woppits, tumbling up his gown in a most abandoned manner. "I can take care of 'em—if that's all. But you don't mean 'em both for me?"

"Yes, my young friend, both for you. And now, what do you mean to do? If you're caught after this, it will be a bad job for you—and for me, too, for that matter. But that's what comes of having a heart in your bosom!"

"Oh, that'll do you no harm, mister; and you needn't be afeard of me."

"Well, if you're the lad I take you for, you wouldn't like to get me into trouble, after what I've done for you."

"What I said afore I ses now: Don't you be afeard of me."

"All right, then. But I can tell you, you'll have to be very careful, though, when I come to think of it, the law's so awful particular: no, I'm afraid, after all, I can't let you off!"

"Come, don't go playin' with a feller," cried Woppits, the tears starting to his eyes at this sudden change in the wind.

"I don't know what to do, my friend. I didn't ought to lose sight of you, at any rate. Give me those curls you cut off."

"What curls?"

"That you cropped from Ruth's head just now!"

Woppits gave them up ruefully: Hatcher placed them in his pocket-book. "Now, you heard what I said," continued he. "If I let you go, I mustn't lose sight of you. You must report yourself to me once in three months, or else I'm down upon you, and into prison you go!"

"Werry well, I'm ready."

"Be here, then, this day three months, with the child; and maybe I'll give you something handsome to help you through."

The proposition perfectly restored Woppits's self-possession. He swallowed a great draught of ale, first looking pleased, and then contemplative, as Hatcher looked pleased and contemplative too.

"I say," murmured Woppits, after a few moments thus passed, "what do you think your name would be, mister, if you was a parson?"

Mr. Hatcher was for once surprised. "What do you think it would have been?" said he.

"Bellows!" said Woppits.

"Come, you be more serious, young man. This is a serious matter. I was just going to say you can't do better than keep to that disguise—to those clothes—only you'll have to brush your hair up, and put yourself straight a bit, if you want to pass for a young woman."

"I'll buy a brush! I'll buy a pair of them combs to stick in at the sides of my hair. I've got plenty of money!" and Woppits slapped his pockets and laughed loud. I am afraid the boy was rather intoxicated, judging from his next exclamation, which was a loud "Hooray!"

"Hush! what a noisy chap you are! Why can't you speak soft, like I do?"

"Because I never was a parson, nor the reverend William Bellows! Because I'm so jolly glad that me and little Ruth will give the law and old Gorelam the slip yet. Mister, shall we have some more beer? I'll pay for it."

"Hold your confounded tongue!" Hatcher whispered fiercely, putting his hand over the boy's mouth.

"They can't hear anything!" whispered Woppits too, making up in expression what emphasis was denied to his voice; "they're as deaf as milestones, both of 'em!" and he jerked his thumb in the direction of the Blue Raven.

"How do you know?"

"Because when I borrowed the sithers, and when I went in for this beer, he put a funnel thing into his ear, and I had to holler."

"And ain't there no one else about the house?"

"I didn't see anybody else."

"Then," said Hatcher, cautiously stroking his chin, "I think we will have another mug of beer. Don't disturb yourself, my friend—I'll go for it myself."

As Hatcher approached the bar, Crummels took up his trumpet, and placing the smaller end to his ear, turned the larger toward Joel, motioning him to pour his orders in there.

"Another mug of ale, if you please."

Crummels nodded.

"And two beds."

Crummels looked.

"One for that poor young woman and her child, and one for myself: do you hear?"

Another nod.

"Can I have 'em?"

Crummels took the horn from his ear, and handed it to the housekeeper, who stood hard by. When people are deaf, they have to depend very largely on observation; and on the principle that two heads are better than one, the housekeeper was never far from Crummels, nor Crummels from the housekeeper, when any business was going on. The good dame placed the trumpet to her ear, and turned to Joel with exactly the same melancholy pantomime which Crummels had performed.

"Can I have 'em?" roared Hatcher, who was getting impatient, and didn't like to be subjected to the scrutiny of the quiet keen eyes which rested upon his countenance.

"Can you have what, sir?" asked the dame, in such a small kind of voice that Hatcher actually felt ashamed of himself.

"Two bed-rooms, if you please, ma'am," he replied.

"Yes," said the housekeeper, with her little deaf voice. Thank goodness there were still two beds to spare in the old place.

Hatcher returned to Woppits with the foaming mug.

"Drink, my boy!" he said; "it's long since you had the chance, and it mayn't come again soon.

"Ah," said the lad, as he drank, "that's werry good ale. I say, mister, you'll excuse me if I offended you at first startin'."

"I've got nothing to excuse, and I only want to set you right; that's all I want;" and putting the beer to his lips, he took a very sparing draught, and again handed the jug to Woppits.

Little Ruth was by this time asleep, her head resting on the table. Woppits having seen the bottom of the mug, with little help from his good companion, soon grew drowsy too.

"Come, it's getting late," said Hatcher, at this juncture of affairs. "I've engaged a bed for you, and I think I may as well turn in here myself for to-night."

There had been little rest for the ear-trumpet since Hatcher had ordered the beds. The housekeeper expressed her opinions through it to the landlord, and it was the medium by which the landlord unfolded his ideas to the housekeeper, as together they peeped through the window at the strange party. The conclusion was, that the farther the queer-looking man and the "owdacious" looking young woman were placed apart the better; so a room on the first floor was appropriated to Mr. Hatcher, and an attic in a remote corner of the house was prepared for Woppits and Ruth.

The cosiest, sleepiest four-poster that ever was built, stood in Hatcher's room; the plumpest bolster and pillow, and the whitest linen, garnished the bed. On one of the pillows was a snowy night-cap, in case the lodger was so addicted. It was a sin and a shame, but Hatcher flung himself on this beautiful bed without even performing the ceremony of taking his boots off—soiling the delicate counterpane, and crushing the pillow out of shape in the most reckless way. He remembered that every innkeeper was his own washerwoman. As for the night-cap, he simply wiped his face with it.

"I've had a narrow escape!" grunted he, as he adjusted his arms beneath his head. "A little more, and I should have trusted that booby to have gone off with the child, and blow upon the whole business the first time he got a pint of beer into his head. Not that I'm particular concerned as to what he does with the little 'un, so far as I can see—for it seems to me my business is with Ruth Keppel dead, and not Ruth Keppel living. Still—don't know yet. What a wonderful providential thing that everybody here seems to be deaf! Well, I know what I shall do—I'm in for it, and mean to go through. The stupid young brute is tipsy enough, and snoring like a brewer's pig by this time, I'll warrant. However, I'll wait awhile, and then, Miss Ruth K., you go along with me. I'll adopt *you* myself; though what I'm to do with the little imp, with her precious praying and shrinking, and deliver us from evil, is more than I know at present. However, I'll stow her away somewhere. As for him, he'll be glad to hold his tongue for fear of Mr. Hatcher and the law."

But it happened that the stupid young brute for whom Mr. Hatcher had such profound contempt, so far from snoring like a brewer's pig, was not snoring at all. On the contrary, he was wide awake; nor was he tipsy. He *had been* intoxicated, I sorrowfully admit; but the boy had never tasted ale twice in his life before; and, therefore, while at first it encouraged and tipsified him, it presently made him ill. Recovering therefrom, he was now merely qualmish, headachy, melancholy, thoughtful. He, too, was yet undressed; but sat on the edge of the bed, his aching head held in his hands, and musing over the events of the evening. By the force of re-action, perhaps, he took an unfavourable view of those events. He took an unfavourable view of the snuff-brown stranger; in whose whole manner, equally with his generosity, Woppits now saw only suspicion. Certain looks and tones which passed unnoticed at the time, he now beheld through the exaggerated lenses of fear and prejudice; and the result of his reflections was, that he had better fasten his door.

On proceeding to put this idea into practice, however, Woppits found that the door had neither lock nor bolt, though a rude and efficient fastening was contrivable with an old shutter bar, which dropped into hasps at the door-posts. Into the hasps Woppits dropped the bar, and then resumed his seat and his reflections.

In a few minutes he started up again. "I tell you what, my little blossom," whispered he, addressing the sleep-closed ears of Ruth, "we'll cut this. I don't like it at all. Fust, I'll creep down and find a way out, and then we'll be off before we get into mischief. He's a snake in the grass, that reverent Mr. Bellows is!"

So saying, Woppits noiselessly took down the bar. As the door swung gently open, he heard a creaking of the stairs, and he heard a footstep which accounted for the creaking. Up to the attics came the footstep—lightly along the passage toward his room. The boy trembled in every limb. Then looking round upon the sleeping child, her beautiful little arms spread over upon the quilt, all the trembling rapidly oozed out of his fingers and toes; and he felt himself shoot up, as it were, a good two inches, his arms stiffening. Licking one hand after the other, he grasped the bar firmly, saying to himself all in the

same minute, "You've come for no good, mister—and you shall have it."

A hand from without gently pushed at the door. Woppits slipped behind it, in the profound dark.

A head was put in, very slowly and deliberately. Woppits dimly saw a hand go up to the chin, and had no doubt as to his visitor.

With cat-like stealth and steadiness a body and legs followed the head into the room, screening Woppits behind the half-opened door.

"This must be the room," said the intruder, softly, but yet audibly, all was so still. "Ah, I thought so; here's the young one, but where's the boy? eh? But that makes no difference to me. I don't want *him*! He may hang himself!"

Quietly Hatcher stripped down the bed-clothes, and, taking out his handkerchief, was just about to throw it over Ruth's mouth, when down came the shutter-bar upon his head, crash! Hatcher lurched to the floor without a groan.

How fortunate it was the landlord was deaf, and had lodged Woppits at the top of the house!

"Hist, my darling! if you say a word now, you dunno what'll happen!" said the boy, as he huddled her clothes upon the wondering, frightened child. "Put your arms through, there's a precious! We're going away, Ruth. We mustn't stay here!"

"Is it the man in the cloak come?"

"No, no, not him, but a friend of his, I'll be bound."

Woppits took Ruth in his arms, reached the door, looked back on the prostrate Hatcher, and remembered that the child's curls were in that gentleman's pocket-book. Soon they were replaced in the bosom of his own gown. Then he descended the stairs, found his way to a back door, unfastened it, and so off and across the country, feeling five years older than when he had first cast eyes upon the snuff-brown stranger.

CHAPTER XXII.

MR. HATCHER IN A NEW ROLE.

THE sun saw many things when he rose that morning; but few more ridiculous and pitiful than awaited him in the attics of the Blue Raven. There lay Joel Hatcher on the floor, his eyes and mouth only partially closed, his wound gaping, and his heavy under-jaw resting on his chest. His countenance was bloody—bloody in strange blots and streaks; but it was pale also, and therefore afforded a contrast which would have delighted those parties who are engaged on "Edith Finding the Dead Body of Harold." He was, in fact, as much like a dead body as possible; and well would it have been for certain persons of our acquaintance had he been decently washed, dressed, and buried forthwith. However, that was not to be yet. It will come right in time, no doubt. Scarcely had ten minutes elapsed from the time when the sun discovered him, when he slowly emerged into consciousness—not with a start and a sudden bound to his feet, as villains left weltering in their gore (in novels) generally do, but one eye at a time, one limb at a time, and without stirring so much as the half of an inch. As the young man's face was toward the wall, and the wall was of the same colour as that which decorated his own dormitory at home, he languidly shut his eyes upon it again, unconscious of the difference. Then he had a notion that the confounded roof was leaking again, and that the rain had been trickling through upon his head. Then he raised his hand, and passed his fingers through his hair, and held them before his eyes, and saw them smirched with blood.

Instantly the events of the preceding evening came trooping into Hatcher's mind in double-quick time. He recollected everything, from the time when he crept from his own room in the inn, to the flash of light which started out of his eyes as he was felled to the floor whereon he lay at present. It was rather an awful time for Mr. Hatcher, the few minutes which followed these reminiscences. Still he did not stir, but lay gazing at his bloody fingers, meanwhile perspiring with terror. He had not lost much blood, but that he did not know. He only felt it thickening in his hair, stiffening on his face, clogging his eyebrows, and he thought to himself, "Perhaps I'm dying! I don't feel any pain, but that, I've heard, is sure to leave you

59

before death! Oh, deliver us! Dyin's awful, and I'm sure I meant to be prepared; and if I did say anything agin' Mr. Skinner, I'm sure it was out of no ill-will to the gentleman! Away from mother and everything! Knocked on the head like a mad dog, and left to die in a public-house—by a boy, too. Oh, if I had him here! but I know it ain't Christian! I know a man in my circumstances ought to pray for him;" and Hatcher groaned in spirit as well as in flesh.

"Has he gone, I wonder, or is he grinning at me now?" was his next thought. Slowly turning himself over, he discovered that he was alone; at the same time, he felt a rush of pain into the back settlements of his skull (a phrenologist might call them the convict settlements), which must have been very consoling, did he really believe that pain goes not over the threshold of death. The little flood of agony did indeed appear to have a reassuring effect. Hatcher got upon his knees, felt his head solicitously, shook it tenderly from side to side, and hearing nothing rattle, began to think matters might not be so bad, after all. Then he worked his shoulder-joints, and otherwise patted and poked himself, his countenance becoming less anxious every moment. At length, with a sigh of relief, he got upon his feet, and looked about him.

"I don't believe," mused he, "that I'm much hurt, after all! not anything serious. It takes a good deal to kill some people! while other some, poor snivellin' wretches, if they get a tap, where are they? *Mine* was no fly-kick! I wonder what the young villain——"

"Did it with?" he would have added; but his eyes at the moment encountered the shutter-bar—the end of it significant with a spot of blood.

Hatcher immediately felt worse.

"The murderous ruffian!" he faintly said. "It's a merciful thing I'm spared, I'm sure. Pretty hands for Mr. Keppel's daughter to get into; and my one pound ten, too. I'll stop the villain! He can't have got far; he'll be noticed wherever he goes in that costoom, and I'll track him, and have him apprehended and——"

Hatcher had stepped across the room, and was about to leave it.

"And make a confounded fool of myself," continued he, turning back. "Upon my life, I shall begin to think I *am* seriously hurt if I go on like this! Let him go, hang him! I don't want him, nor the brat either, for that matter; I want 'em to get out of the way, and to keep out of the way. It's all for the best as it is. Suppose I had had my own way—got the child clean off from him, and he'd made himself scarce through fear! Well, then, suppose I'd been found *with* the brat, and no ways to account for it—pretty set-out that had been! While as it is, he's off, and he'll take precious care not to betray himself now, for his own sake. People who don't know but what they may be wanted for a murder, don't make themselves very public in general. By George! it's worth a knock on the head to have things brought about so comfortable; and I shall do the trick yet, or my name's not Joel. Why, I know enough to lay my hands on *him* in a week, if I wanted to, the young ruffian!"

Compared with this reflection, Balm of Gilead was as nothing, as a plaster for Mr. Hatcher's wound.

"Now, let me see what's to be done (my poor head!). It's now about four o'clock, and I don't suppose the old moles below are stirring yet. Better be certain, though!"

Softly opening the door, Hatcher protruded his face over the bannisters, and listened. I wonder what good Mrs. Lupin, the housekeeper, would have thought of it, had she looked up at that moment.

"All quiet enough at present," whispered Hatcher, creeping back into the room. "Now, I'll tidy this place up a bit, before I go down to my own room. It won't do for them to know of my coming here, or of the reception I met with; which I think my skull's bust now!"

Where Hatcher's head had lain, there was a small red pool, spread over a surface about as large as a man's hand. As he looked upon it, this fearful reflection swept through his mind: that pool of blood there, his own hands bloody, the bar blood-stained, Woppits and the child unaccountably gone, his own bed tumbled, indeed, but bearing evidence enough of having never been slept in after a Christian fashion; what would be inferred, if

these circumstances were discovered—if he were found there in that room? That he was a murderer, of course! At the best, he would be lodged in jail till he accounted for himself; and a pretty figure he should cut when he had done so! But there was a chance that he would not be believed; that Woppits would never again turn up; that affairs might so complicate themselves, that he would be hanged!

Deadly sweat broke out upon Mr. Hatcher's forehead as this idea flashed through him, red hot!

With trembling anxiety—agony, though, is the word—he drew out his handkerchief, wiped up the little pool, and went to the hand-basin to rinse it for further operations. He saw the error in time.

"Oh Lord, that won't do!" he cried, in a bewildered, despairing tone. "I might as well go and put it under their very noses?"

Folding the handkerchief, then, so as to bring an unstained part uppermost, down upon his knees he went again, rubbing at the blood-marks. Rub he did. He rubbed till his arms ached; till his handkerchief was chafed into holes; till he had brought the crimson stains to a high state of polish, and an apparently fixed determination to remain. Then, in an awful frame of mind, he ventured to dip a corner of the kerchief in the ewer, anointed it with soap, and applied himself anew to his most melancholy work. A hundred pulses throbbed in his wounded head; big drops trickled fast down his face; and still he scrubbed and rubbed, the stain scarcely moving. "The infernal thing!" said he, grinding the words between his teeth, "I seem to rub it *in* rather than out." Nevertheless, the wetted rag was more efficacious than the dry one; but then he had moistened all the unstained corners by this time, and, as he said, *that* game was up. Looking about him in despair, he spied a row of flower-pots, and an old sandbag, such as is used to keep the draught out of windows; and two brilliant ideas entered his head at the same time. Now he had no objections to using the water. He poured a little more into the basin, and boldly washed the blood from his handkerchief, leaving it well moistened. The red water he then tilted into the flower-pots, where it sank, and was lost in the mould. Then he ripped up the sandbag, put a little of its fine contents upon his handkerchief, mixing it with soap, and once more scoured at the sullen spot. At last, he had the satisfaction of seeing it fade out; and the floor being already as white as it possibly could be, he was under no apprehension that his handiwork would contrast with good Mrs. Lupin's. His next proceeding was to wipe the bar, and stand it carelessly near the door. Then, observing that the bed bore but one impression, and that only a little one, Hatcher threw himself upon it, and tossed and tumbled till he had manufactured very good evidence of an adult person having slept there.

All was clear so far. Mr. Hatcher now descended to his own room, and had the satisfaction to be greeted by the reflection of own countenance the moment he stood within the door:—that is to say, a satisfaction it might have been; but then his countenance was at once so white and so red, so pale, so bloody, so dirty, weary, anxious, and wild, that for a moment he recoiled in horror. Here was a new difficulty; for if his own room boasted a looking-glass, which Woppits's did not, it had no bow-pots, as the attic had. Of course there was nothing to prevent his going out into the yard behind, where there was a copious pump; but on the contrary there was nothing to prevent his being observed by an early bird who had risen with an eye to the neighbouring worm. There stood an ewer of fair water, there hung two snowy towels: what would he not have given for a row of flower-pots also! How he longed to plunge his throbbing head into the water, to remove the sickening stiffness that lay upon his features like a varnish! Nor was it possible to make an appearance in that plight. What was to be done, then? His handkerchief was already grimed and soiled beyond precedent; and he had no other resource——yes, he had; and he was not the man to stick at any means to help himself out of a dilemma. Mr. Hatcher washed his face with one stocking, and dried it with the other! He then rolled them together, and clapped them into his pocket. The thing was done. He was a respectable-looking man again; and there was nothing left but quietly to await the announcement of "half-past six, if you please, sir," at which time he had desired to be called.

Consulting an old-fashioned watch which he never failed to

carry, he found that he had nearly an hour to spare. "An hour's sleep," said he, "would do me no harm;" and down he lay. He closed his eyes, but they opened again a moment after, as wide awake as ever. Says he, "I'll count a hundred!—One, two, three, four, five—ah! and I'd give twice five in gold guineas to have these questions answered: what could have been Keppel's motive in throwing his child into a lime-kiln—and how came those marks about her throat?" To the first problem he could give no solution, except that some scheme by which Keppel would have benefited had been concocted, but that it had failed at some inopportune moment; and that it had been proposed to cover the bungling attempt in the lime-pit. As for the other riddle, he had to give that up, whichever way he took it. It was a hedgehog of a riddle, which there was no getting at, from any side. Weary of the matter, and sleepy too, Hatcher's mind at length wandered off—first to murders at home, especially strangulation murders, and then to Thugs and lasso-murderers in Indian wilds. Thuggery, British and foreign, at length merged amicably the one into the other; and Hatcher's eyes closed lazily. His bed seemed to rock, and then he drowsily fancied he was swinging in the hammock of an Indiaman; then he came out of his slumber a little way, and thought of William Ray, who was mate of an Indiaman. Then he recalled how he had told that story, and then—he started broad awake again! He recollected the audience that listened to that story, with its stain more like a pinch than a bruise. He remembered the deep interest one man had taken in the tragedy, and the questions that one man had asked concerning it. When he, Joel Hatcher, had got as far as this, he found that he had risen from the bed, for there, in the glass, he saw reflected his own compressed lips, his own dilating eyes!

Came a rap at his chamber door.

"Come in!" shouted Hatcher, inwardly cursing whoever knocked, for smashing into the splendid train of reflection in which he was running. "No, no! don't come in," he added, recollecting himself, "I'm dressing."

A few minutes after Hatcher made his appearance in the little bar-parlour, looking rather disreputable. His eyes were staring red, like charcoal: that was the consequence of his exalted and elated reflections. His face was ghastly pale: that was the result of his blood-letting. His clothes hung loosely about him: that was habitual. And his hat was cocked formidably over his forehead; which couldn't be helped, considering the terrible gash which ensanguined the bump of self-esteem, behind there.

Both Crummels and Lupin were in a state of deaf indignation already. When Mr. Hatcher put his ferrety face within the door, their wrath became seasoned with fear and disgust.

"That woman's off, sir," said the landlord, in a high tone; but, after all, only speaking like a loud echo. "She's off; and I don't half like it." With that he adjusted his ear-trumpet with a degree of impatience and fuss quite odd. There he stood, with his horn poked at Hatcher, like an eccentric unicorn.

"They've been gone since four o'clock!" bawled Hatcher. "She told you she'd have to go—I heard her; and she said she didn't want to disturb you. She's gone to Dover to meet her husband: seafarin' man, you know. I'm a seafarin' man myself!" concluded Hatcher, hitching up his breeches with the manner that had imposed upon old Tweakle.

Crummels retailed the information to Mrs. Lupin in a much lower voice, whereupon she seemed somewhat mollified. She declared, however, that she didn't hear the young person say she was going away so early, but then she was rather hard of hearing.

This explanation was, however, scarcely sufficient. Some other question was evidently lurking in the minds of the landlord and his quiet old housekeeper.

"Did you say you were a seafaring man?" asked Crummels, mildly.

"Oh, yes," replied the bluff Hatcher, chewing that imaginary quid again. He had a momentary idea of doing a little bit of a hornpipe: it luckily occurred to him, however, that he did not know how to do it.

"Oh!" nodded Crummels; "perhaps you are acquainted with the young woman's husband?"

"Acquainted?" (a heavy sea appeared to have struck Mr. Hatcher at this point, for he rolled dreadfully). "Sailed the world round with him! Been to Chaney and the Oozley

Islands in the same ship—and that's more!" Carried away by the charm of lying, he deftly threw back his hat, really intending to perform the first steps of a hornpipe this time. But the rim of his castor, raking over his forgotten wound, struck agony through every fibre of him, and the intention was modified. Dance he did—like mad; while compelled to give voice to his anguish—"Yo! heave! he—o—o!" yelled he, grinning so horribly that Crummels's tongue looked out of his gaping mouth, while Mrs. Lupin started back with uplifted hands.

Seeing the effect of this exhibition, Hatcher hastened to compose his features, which he did most hideously.

"That's how we do it at sea!" he remarked, with another grin in Mrs. Lupin's direction, at the same time crossing his legs. This latter manœuvre was also nautical, ostensibly; but, in fact, Mr. Hatcher found it necessary to grind one foot under the other, in order to suppress any further demonstration.

Crummels thought he'd better come to the point at once; so he said—

"Because the young person hasn't paid for her bed, that's all."

"Oh, I'll pay for her," shouted Hatcher, quite heartily, glad of an opportunity to roar again. "Tell me how much it comes to altogether, and I'll be off."

That was exactly what the old people desired. The reckoning was made and paid; and Hatcher, with his head dizzy and full of pain, his mind vague and full of his clue, took the rapidest means of getting back to Old Sleaford.

Widow Hatcher was soon in amazement and in tears at Joly's melancholy plight.

"Ask no questions now, mother," languidly replied the son to the mother's interrogations. "I'm going up to have a few hours' rest, and then I shall set to work in earnest. I've got a nest of guineas in my skull, and then I shall count 'em."

Hatcher pushed the anxious old woman aside, and went upstairs slowly, and rolling from side to side, like a drunken man. When he came to the landing-place leading into his room, he paused, a wild-looking perplexity peeping from his eyes. He glanced to the left, to the right, furtively; and finding nobody looking, gazed fixedly at his legs. Then he pawed his chin. Then he said to himself, with extraordinary deliberation, "Licked at a hornpipe! Joel Hatcher, son of the celebrated orsifer, can't do a hornpipe when needs be. Gentlemen, I have the greatest confidence in Mr. Hatcher. He'll try again."

Accordingly, Mr. Hatcher did so. One hand resting on his hips, the other flourishing in the air, he proceeded to perform such demoniac flourishes with his legs, as would have consumed a dervish with envy. He cut a "pigeon's wing;" he shuffled; he whirled on one heel, stamping furiously with the other; he kicked up behind; he kicked up before; he danced the dance of a demon.

Scared by the unusual sounds, up rushed widow Hatcher, like an old whirlwind.

"Joly, Joly," screamed she, midway on the stairs.

"All females are ordered to leave the court!" replied her son, waving his hand with dignity, and pausing to give due weight to the announcement. Then shooting forth a leg recommenced his saltations, winding up with a flourish, weird, wild, sudden. (This step I afterwards communicated to Mr. Robson, who appalled people with it in the "Yellow Dwarf.")

All this while, Hatcher was smiling in his most agreeable manner. When he had concluded, he pleasantly bowed to the wall, saying—

"Gentlemen, Mr. Hatcher's done it!"

And forthwith walked into his bed-room.

Poor Mrs. H. walked out of it a few minutes afterwards, filled with the sad conviction that Joly had been forgetting himself: i.e., that he was intoxicated. She had serious thoughts, therefore, of sending for Mr. Skinner; but before many hours passed away, she found it necessary to send for the doctor instead.

Doctor Mangles arrived, and found Hatcher apparently asleep. The widow detailed the symptoms of the case; and the doctor turned to leave the room, saying something like "leeches," and "get his head shaved." Then it appeared that Hatcher had not been asleep; and that he was in a lucid interval.

"Doctor," he exclaimed, startling that gentleman, at whom he looked point-blank, "what's the matter with me? What's my head to be shaved for? Am I out of my mind?"

"Tut, tut, I thought he was asleep," said the doctor, in an aside. "No, young man, I hope not; but these fevers, you see, sometimes affect the brain; and render it necessary——"

"Very well, doctor. Good night!" and Hatcher turned his face to the wall. Doctor Mangles went home forthwith, in a tall gig, navigated by a lank horse.

"Mother," said Hatcher, "come here."

The widow obeyed.

"You know them silver clasps?"

"I've seen 'em, Joly, dear."

"Then sit down, and I'll tell you the value of 'em."

Then he related clearly all he had discovered within the last few days. "Now if I get delirious," added he, "I should likely talk about what I don't want a stranger to hear. So you nurse me; and keep close to me! and if I should die—of course I shan't, you know, but it's as well to be prepared—take the clasps to the Lodge, just say that you know the secret that belongs to 'em; and that he can have the lot for five hundred pounds. He'll buy em."

CHAPTER XXIII.

WOPPITS IN LONDON.

TIRED as any number of dogs was Woppits, as he struck into the Dover Road, Southwark, three days after we last parted with him. Troubled was he also for little Ruth's sake—whose head, reclining on his shoulder, had grown heavier all day long—who was sick and feverish, and refused all food. Woppits would have taken her into one of the many apothecaries' shops he looked so wistfully at in passing, but fear of the wisdom and penetration of the faculty restrained him; for, as he said, he "felt convinced that a doctor would see through his sext as soon as he put his head inside the door." So, wearily, he went on up the Dover Road till he came to the end of it, there by St. George's Church, where he stopped, bewildered by the traffic and the bustle upon which he had so suddenly debouched.

By the side of the church ran—and, indeed, their career is not yet ended—two narrow streets: Long Lane the one, Kent Street the other. The meanest capacity, capable only of following its nose, had no difficulty in discovering to what branch of commerce the former was devoted—an intolerable stench of raw, dressed, and half-dressed hides, settling that question at once. The odour which pervaded the other thoroughfare told loudly of fish, rags, oil-lamps, and gutters. Fish was abundantly exhibited to the eye also, on shop-boards, on wayside stalls, in baskets and barrows, and dangled on the forefingers of blowsy women, just emerged from a warm pickle of vice and strong drink. The oil-lamps blurred out upon the thick atmosphere, with a chill, blood-shot glare, as if they, too, were hard-drinkers of gin, instead of oil. Rags there was no end of—on the fish-venders, on the blowsy women (who, however, had all a large and splendid handkerchief over their shoulders), on lines stretched across the street, hanging in bunches for sale at the doors, choking broken window-panes, trailing after the legs of little children, whose tiny souls were already ragged and fishy, too. At the corner of this street stood an old man, with a hot stew of eels and whelks for sale, by retail, in cupfuls; and in so fatherly a manner did this old man dispense his ha'porths among a crowd of boys, that Woppits was drawn towards him.

"Wilks?" inquired the old gentleman, "or eels?" And he whipped off the lid of the kettle with a flourish, releasing a seductive odour.

"Are they good for a baby that's poorly, mister?" asked Woppits, who happened to be the only customer at the stall at the moment.

"Well, wilks ain't, missus, but eels is. The eel's a werry healing thing to the stomach. Try some wirrout the winegar."

But poor little Ruth was not to be tempted by stewed eels, with or without vinegar. When the cup was presented to her, she turned her head away with a shudder, and nestled down upon Woppits's shoulder again.

"Ah, she won't, you see!" said Woppits, with tears in his eyes. "She ain't eat a bit of anythink since yesterday."

"Wot's the matter with it?"

"I only wish I knowed."

"Take her up to Codlings," said the fatherly whelk-man; "he's reckoned good at young uns."

"I don't know Codlings," replied Woppits. "Where is it?"

"Don't know it? Not Codlings? Then you're a stranger about here, mum?"

"Yes, I've just come from—from ever so far, and don't know what to do. I haven't got no lodging yet. Can you tell me where to find one, mister?"

By this time a new bevy of customers had flocked round the board, with demands at once facetious and imperative; so that the old man was too deeply engaged to hear this last question. One of the customers heard it, however, and with a large white whelk embarrassing his utterance, he remarked—

"Lodgings? Yes. Go to Yallops's."

"Where's that?" Woppits asked.

"Second lamp on the left—'Lodgings for travellers' on it," said the youth, bolting his last whelk, and with the gravest playfulness draining the cup down his nearest neighbour's back. After which he went a little aloof, slid his hands into his pockets, and as gravely performed a dance in the face of the injured party.

Past a rag-shop, and a gin-shop, and a shop for the sale of baked sheep's heads—and the first lamp is reached. "Beds," says the lamp, in stumpy red letters, dimly illuminated from within by an oil-fed light, which rose and fell in the night air, so that the red letters appeared and faded in a suspicious and skulking manner. Past another rag-shop, a toy-maker's, another gin-shop, a fish-shop, a beef-steak-pudding shop, and then Woppits comes under the second lamp. It stands out from a barber's shop, over which is inscribed the name "Whiffins;" so that Woppits thinks there must be some mistake. However, casting his eyes down in dejection, he sees written over the kitchen-window, "Yallops's lodging-house;" next he observes several people of sufficiently miserable aspect enter the passage of the house; and as they do not turn into the shop to be shaved, Woppits rightly concludes that they descend into the Yallops's regions.

Woppits joined the company in the passage, and with them proceeded down a short flight of stairs. Here was revealed a sort of watchbox; and in the watchbox sate a dark young man, perspiring freely and taking the money. The young man had a turn-down collar, a hooked nose, and greasy locks painfully twisted into ringlets; he wore a great signet ring on his little finger, another ring confined his neckerchief, and the people called him William.

Said William, when Woppits's turn came to pass the watch-box, "Now, how many on yer?"

"Two," Woppits replied.

"Cook?" further inquired William, holding up a tin ticket.

"Cook what?"

"'Ow do I know?" said William, with a convulsive and savage movement of the nose. "Fourpence! Come, fork out—you're a blocking up the passidge."

Woppits handed fourpence into the watchbox, and presently found himself in a spacious kitchen. Round the sides of this room were ranged long tables and forms, which were nearly all occupied; for Yallops's kitchen was famous, and his house a thriving one. Several lamps descended from the ceiling, which had been recently whitewashed; and in fact, considering the locality and the company, the place was surprisingly well ordered and cleanly in every respect. A capacious stove, fitted with an immense boiler and oven, occupied a niche in the wall. Over against the stove was a large locker, containing the knives, plates, forks, etc., of the establishment. Upon the locker was seated a man proportionally large, with a bullet head and a furrowed nose; he was dressed in a shooting-jacket, and wore a clean white apron. This was Mr. Yallops, ex-prize-fighter, and present proprietor of the lodging-house.

Busied about the fireplace was a meek-looking woman, young by her shining black hair, her white teeth, her unwrinkled forehead—old by her hollow eyes and the mouth thinned by care. As she silently moves about, brightening this, arranging that in order, she sometimes presses her hand to her side, and sometimes coughs; observing which, you find it no longer difficult to account for the brilliancy that frets in her deep-set eyes, nor for the delicate blush which rests on her white cheek, down here in a Kent Street "kitchen." This is "Yallops's Gal!" If she has any other style, title, or designation, it is unknown here, even to

Yallops himself. When any lodger requires her services, he calls out "Hi!" or "D'ye hear!" but among themselves, or out of the establishment, she is known as "Yallops's Gal," and nothing else.

Ask Yallops who she is, and if he happens to be in a good humour he will answer, "Goodness knows! She kem here three years ago for lodgin' one night, and sat by herself all alone in that corner, looking plain enough that she didn't want any talk, nor to give any. Lots o' gals will come in and sit like that, when they has fits of derjection on 'em, and nobody takes no notice—I don't. Howasever, this one was unkimmon handsome—unkimmon handsome she was then, and one of the fellows here took it in his head to go over and chaff her—untie her bonnet he did at last, I b'lieve. Well, you should ha' seen what followed. My eye! she got up straight as that there toasting-fork, and set back her head, and took her under-lip in her teeth, and blazed at him with them eyes of her'n, sich as I never see in all my life, and I seen a pooty good deal, I have. Now, that cowed the feller, rayther suddent ; and then he began swearin' at her, and gives her a sharp lift back into her seat. Now I never allows nothing o' that sort here ; so I jest crossed over and knocked him down. Well, they brings him to, and he has his supper, as usual, and I thought no more about it ; but when I fancied they'd all gone off to roost, out she comes, and catches hold o' my arm, and swings down upon her knees, begging o' me to let her stop. Says she—on'y I ain't no scholar, and can't say the langwidge as she did—'I don't want any wages—not a penny ; but I'll scrub, and cook, and wash—on'y you let me stop, I implores yer. For mercy's sake let me stop, I implores yer,' ses she ag'in. Well, you know," Yallops would add, in a less impressive tone, "seeing she'd be werry handy, and a savin' to me, I hadn't the heart to say no—so here she is ; and here she stops, cookin' and doin' about. Besides, that ain't all : sometimes I have a gal or a chap took so sudden sick that I can't have 'em moved, and then she comes out strong, she do. A good gal—a werry good gal!"

When, released from prison after dislocating the spine of the Brompton Bison in a pugilistic encounter, Yallops resolved to take a lodging-house, he made up his mind that it should be respectable of its class. That is to say he determined that it should be no harbour for thieves that were "wanted." How he got the information nobody knew, but as soon as any one new to the business showed his pale face within the kitchen, or any "old bird" entered, with brazen, scowling visage, and hands yet warm from some illegal exploit, Yallops would ejaculate from his seat on the locker, "Not to-night." Then straightway he of the warm hands would give a nod of intelligence and depart ; or if he took no heed of the warning, his burglarious dreams that night were sure to be disturbed by the gleam of an official lantern ; Yallops observing, as the warm hands passed out in iron wrist-bands, "I told you so, you know !"

As Woppits sat in a corner of the kitchen, his eyes and ears equally engaged with the strange people and the strange conversation around him, his simple face and strangely-attired baby attracted the notice of Yallops's Gal, who went over towards him. With a woman's instinct, she saw at a glance that the child was ill.

"What ails it ?" she asked.

"I don't know, I'm sure. P'r'aps you'll be good enough to look at it, mum."

Yallops's Gal did so—and felt its pulse, and placed her hand on the little hot forehead. Then she went out, and presently returned with a medicinal powder.

"Give this to the child," said she.

"I wish *you* wouldn't mind, mum," supplicated Woppits : "you'll do it ever so much softer than I shall."

So the woman took Ruth upon her knee, and administered the medicine, and kissed her tenderly afterwards.

At this moment, the young man with the turn-down collars made his appearance, and simply ejaculated—

"Full !"

"Shut up, then," said Mr. Yallops, rising from the box. "Now, then, who cooks ? Chops and steaks fust !"

Nine steaks, and about half a dozen chops started from their seats, and were handed over to Mr. Yallops, each with a tin ticket, which was numbered.

Yallops made a slit in the chops and steaks, inserting in each its appropriate ticket, and delivered them to the girl for spitting.

"Who give me these sossages ?" exclaimed Yallops, indignantly.

"Me, mister !" replied a voice from the crowd.

"Then, jist you fetch 'em back, and wait till the last !" said the despotic Yallops, flourishing his long fork. "When I ses steaks, I means steaks. I'll call sossages, when they're wanted."

If the chops and steaks were not up to the mark established at the city taverns, that was the fault of the various proprietors, whose habit it was to order the butcher to "give it 'em solid-eatin' ;" as to the cookery, it was unimpeachable. At exactly the proper moment each supper reposed in a clean plate, and Mr. Yallops, calling a meeting of the shareholders, made successful distribution.

"*Now* sossages—sossages and rashers !"

Now, as sausages mustered pretty strong, and as they were all cooked in one gigantic pan, a difficulty might have arisen as to the proprietorship, since not every sausage could be ticketed. But Yallops was an ingenious man, and the difficulty was obviated by a process at once simple, unfailing, and expeditious. Each bundle of abominations was run upon a skewer, and kept together by a little linch-pin.

"Now, then," cried Yallops, when the sausages had been delivered, in an embrowned and bursting condition—"bloaters !"

The rising was terrific. Poor, indeed, was the individual who could not afford to sup upon a herring, considering that supper is with the miserables of this class the great meal of the day. Twenty hands were at once thrust forward, and in every hand was a bloater. Tickets were not allowed with herrings ; the woman simply went round with a large tin dish and collected them indiscriminately. "Mine's a big 'un with his tail off," cried one. "Mine's a soft roed un, so mind yer !" muttered a moody youth of fifteen, who had notoriously been crossed in love. "Two for me," said another briskly, "I'm the cove as allus has two, you know." But the woman collected them without a word of remark, and pretty much as if she were a machine invented for the purpose.

As Woppits was not in a condition to respond to any of the cook's invitations, he amused himself with wishing he had been, and with watching the proceedings. At length, not even these amusements could keep him from the arms of sleep. Yielding to fatigue, he dropped his head upon his chest, and slumbered.

Now, all because of the hard dumplings he had experienced at Latherwell House of Industry, Woppits had contracted the vulgar habit of snoring. To-night he snored ; and, during the silent consumption of bloaters, the sound of his snoring was but too audible. Many were the eyes directed towards him therefore, and many the comments elicited by the poor boy's strange appearance.

"Green !" muttered one.

"Jolly green !" responded another.

"Pooty kid !"

"Wonder where *she* found herself ?"

"Wot a 'ead of 'air !"

"I say, Foxey" (this was said by a bulky, bullet-headed youth, who had brought in three large slabs of pudding on a cabbage leaf, and several baked potatoes in his hat—and had consumed them) ; "I say, Foxey, there's a beauty—just about your style, Foxey !"

Foxey was the moody youth, who had not only been disappointed in his love, but in his bloater ; for, in the chances of distribution, he had got a hard-roed one. Foxey looked up with a scowl.

"Not quite so big as Polly, though, she ain't—which she *was* too big for you, wasn't she, Foxey ?"

"My name's Finch, George Nagle, and you'd better hold your jaw," replied the other."

"Werry good busk she had, mind yer. I allus admired her busk," continued the bulky boy with a bulky sort of humour.

"And she goes and throws that there busk away on a crockery hawker," chimed in another youth, "while my henterprisin' friend Finch is a pining of hisself to death ! Not but what the crockery cove could lick him any day," carelessly added the speaker.

"Would he?"

"Would he, ah! Look at his calves! Look at his whiskers!" replied the other, demonstratively.

"Ah, you should look at them, don't you know," calmly said the bulky boy.

The face of Mr. Finch was red—was white—was green, as he rose.

"Yallops!" he cried, appealingly.

"Stow it!" said Yallops, addressing the bulky one.

"Stowed it is," replied Nagle.

"'Taint a subject for chaff, arter all, is it?" whispered his compatriot, in a confidential and soothing tone. "You've loved yourself, you know."

"I have; and it's a werry delicate subject in-deed!"

Yallops brought his eye round to the playful young fellows at this period, and the conversation ceased.

Nobody seemed to think it at all remarkable.

There followed a silence, in which the snoring of Woppits was again most distinctly audible.

"I say, Pippin," remarked the bulky boy to his confederate, *you've* got a moosical ear. Why don't you stick up to the young ooman?"

"'Cos my taste don't lay towards serrynades," answered Pippin. "Who is she?" continued this youth, a keen, clean-limbed straight-backed lad of sixteen, with impudence and intelligence enough for a prime minister. He was, in fact, the cock of the kitchen, and a great favourite of Mr. Yallops's. "Landlord," said the Pippin, "d'ye know her?"

"Tramp," answered Mr. Yallops, whose business it was to know everything and everybody, and to communicate all that he properly could.

"Well, tramp or no tramp, she can't be allowed to kill herself with appleplexy, right afore our eyes. Hi! young woman!" and, followed by two or three others of the company, he walked up to the snoring figure, and patted it on the shoulder.

But the young woman only responded by flinging her head back, snoring much louder than before in consequence thereof. A stray ringlet was seen peeping out of the bosom of the gown.

"Hallo!" exclaimed the Pippin, abstracting the entire curl with marvellous dexterity. "Why she's a travelling barber! Here, Foxey, you want your hair cut."

The young man's hair was still bristling in indignation at the jail scissors.

"You let Foxey alone, and then Foxey'll let you alone," snarled Mr. Finch.

"Werry much obliged to Foxey."

"Has she got any more of it in her buzzum?" asked a by-stander.

The Pippin gingerly inserted his hand, withdrew the entire packet from which the one lock had escaped.

"Now, Pip," cried Yallops, "stow that, you know. Put it back."

"Only a lark, 'pon my word! Just to see how she looks when she wakes. Here, Nagle, you're the cove. Come here. Bring Nagle a chair, somebody."

Somebody brought Nagle a chair, in which he disposed himself; and the Pippin having borrowed some hair-pins from some of the women, proceeded to affix Ruth's curls to the autumnal stubble of Nagle's head.

"Now," said Pip, "all come round Nagle's chair, and snore pooty."

The concert opened with remarkable spirit, and speedily aroused little Ruth, who awoke with a look and a cry of affright. The next instant Woppits was on his feet; at the next he spied Ruth's curls on Nagle's head; another moment, and his fist plunged heavily between the bulky boy's eyes, and over he went, chair and all.

"Bravo! pluck!" cried Yallops, the professional; "fust blood for the young woman! Oh—it's all over!" he continued, as the bulky boy recovered his legs, and began to "square up."

"The lark's over—hope you liked it. Give the young woman back her hair, and let her alone. But if you *want* a round with somebody, I'll oblige you!"

Remembering the fate of the Brompton Bison, Nagle declined, and order was again restored—the company retiring, some to their seats, but most of them to bed. As to Woppits, he

retired to a further corner of the kitchen, to gather together the precious curls, and to soothe little Ruth. So intently was he occupied, that he started with surprise at length to see almost every one gone but the Pippin, and that young gentleman close at hand, scrutinising him narrowly with those keen black eyes of his.

CHAPTER XXIV.

A LITTLE CONVERSATION.

"WHAT'S trumps?" inquired the Pippin, whispering across the table.

"How do I know?" Woppits answered, in considerable ill-temper. "Arks somebody as lives here, if you want to know partickler."

"Lor, don't be huffed at nothing—'tain't flosophy! It was only a joke; and werry glad I was to see you give that bad boy such a topper. But here, come! what's your lay?"

"I know nothink about what you're talking—about trumps, and that there. If you wants to talk to me, talk like a Christen cove, will you!"

"Oh, that's all my eye! You've got a lay, you know!"

"No I ain't; or else I shouldn't ha' come here, should I? At the same time, I expects one. I paid fourpence for it at the door, and the sooner we begin it the better," said Woppits, who thought he had found the solution of the mysterious word.

"You're a joker, ain't yer?" said the Pippin, after a pause, and with a bit of a frown. "Well since you won't tell me what you are, I'll tell you what you ain't. F'r instance, you ain't a woman!"

"Not a woman, ain't I?" (Woppits blushed like one, at all events.)

"No more'n I am."

"How do you know?"

"How do I know? Why, by about ten different tokens, mate. The first thing that put me up to it was the way you hit out—straight from your shoulder, don't you know. A gal, my friend, throws her arm up, and then brings it down summut between a hit and a claw. See?"

"Very well, s'pose I do?"

"Then you see another thing; you see it ain't no use tryin' it on any furder. Lor! you're right with me. Out with it! Wot's your game?"

"You won't split?"

"S'help me never!" replied the Pippin.

"Then," said Woppits, "I ain't a woman. I'm a cove."

"Cert'in'y you are, mate. Go on."

"Runnin' away, I am, with my little sister, as her father was cruel to, which I couldn't abide."

"Werry good. Well, where are you runnin' to?"

"Ah, that's it!" sighed Woppits, ruefully. "That's what I should like to know!"

"I dessay you would. Well, so far you're a fool. Now, what about that hair?"

"Cut it off because they shouldn't know her again. That's what I bought those togs for, o'course."

"Oh, you had some brass then?"

"Blowed if it's any use talking to you," cried Woppits again, indignantly. "What do you call brass? Is that brass?" And whipping up his petticoats in the reckless manner which had characterized him on a previous occasion, he drew forth a little rag parcel, and threw it on the table with much clatter.

"Now, then, what are you up to, Billy Green?" exclaimed the Pippin, in a hurried whisper. "I'm jiggered if you won't go a committin' sewercide next! Put it back, can't you! It's too late now, I shouldn't wonder. Is any of 'em looking this way?"

The Pippin's back was turned to the company—the few that yet lingered.

"On'y one—a tall gentleman with one eye!"

"Barker! Well, you count what you've got. Thump it down hard, and count it loud."

Woppits obeyed the direction. "One pound three and six-pence," he exclaimed, in a voice which startled Yallops's Gal, who was making gruel for a sick tramp.

MR. HATCHER MAKES AN UNPLEASANT PICTURE OF HIMSELF.

"That's reglar!" said the Pippin, loudly and cheerfully, and facing round to the company, while he placed it in his pocket. "Ask me for it in the mornin'. It's safe now," he added in a whisper to the bewildered Woppits, "otherways you'd have found werry little of it by to-morrow, arter they once seen it."

"Oh! How's that?" said the boy, opening his eyes in amazement; "ain't they a good sort of people here?"

"Good sort? of course they are! On'y, for the most part, they're thieves, that's all. You'll be a thief before you've been in London a month."

Woppits looked so astonished and incredulous, that the Pippin shook his head emphatically, and repeated the prophetic words, "Ah, you will, and no mistake!"

"But *you* ain't a thief, are you?"

The Pippin frankly and quietly admitted that he was.

"Then just give me back my money; come now!" Woppits cried with much consternation.

"I didn't say I was a swindler, did I?" rejoined the Pippin, indignant. "D'ye think I'd sneak away a feller's last shilling, under these here circumstances? If I'm 'bliged to be a prig, I ain't 'bliged to be a rat, am I?"

And while he jerked out these interrogations, the Pippin looked so much like injured honour, that Woppits was silenced for a few moments.

But—

"I don't see much difference," said he at length.

"None o' you 'spectable coves can! Not when you preaches to us!"

"Well, and what do you see in my face to make you so precious kind arter my welfares?" Suspicion was again rising in Woppits's bosom.

"I d'n know! 'Cause you're plucky, I s'pose, and ain't got no friends; and then, ag'in, a man can't bring wuss luck upon himself than by hurtin' a young 'un!" And the Pippin seriously pointed to Ruth.

"Well," remarked Woppits, after the pause that followed the thief's satisfactory explanation, "I mean to be honest."

"Do yer?" sneered the other. "I mean to take out that there patent o'mine for livin' without grub, and lodgin' without a roof, and being, oh! so jolly kind to my neighbour what'll see me go to the dogs with the greatest pleasure arterworks."

"Honesty's got nothin' to do with your neighbour—whether he's kind or not."

"*Ain't* it?"

"No!" answered Woppits, valiantly; "and I never mean to be a thief. Besides, the other thing'll come handier to me I know how to be honest, and I dunno how to thieve."

"Ah, we all knows our own business best!" yawned the Pippin. He did not quite relish the conversation, at its turn.

"Oh, you know, honesty's the best policy! Mr. Tweak that is a friend of mine—taught me so. Did you ever try it, mister?"

"Can't say as ever I did. Never lay in my line. But I dessay, as your friend Mr. Tweak says, it's a werry good thing when you're used to it!" The Pippin again yawned. "I say, 'hough," he added, "how are you going to come the honest dodge, eh?"

"Well, the friend I was speakin' of advised chickweed. What do you think on it?"

"Stale—werry stale!" answered the Pippin, gravely shaking his head. "Let me see. Why, there's two, there's—ah, there's four of 'em sleep here now."

"And ain't there room for another?"

"Well, it's accordin' how you works it, you know. That's everything."

"What! works the chickweed?"

"Ah! There's two ways of doin' it now—one is to sling your basket over your shoulder, borrer a couple of kids—yours and another would just suit—and chant up and down the big streets 'William at the Garding Gate,' or 'Roger Ranstead,' or summut o' that. Howsever, that dodge ain't the best—it don't pay as well as the other."

"What's the other, then?" asked Woppits, who was amused as well as instructed.

"The derjected rustic dodge. This is how it's done. You get your basket o'chickweed, and a few bulrushes, or some pheasant's feathers, which you can get in Leadenhall. Then you throw open the front of your smock, jest to let the benevolent see that you ain't got no shirt on; then you bleaches your mug, and stands jest off the kerb-stones hanging of your head, and looking werry much ashamed o' yourself. The benevolent likes to see a cove looking ashamed of hisself."

"And the people come and deal with you?"

"Yes, they comes to deal with you," replied the Pippin, with a grin.

"What do you put in the mug?" asked Woppits, his interest increasing.

"What mug?"

"The one you bleaches: do you stand your bulrushes in it?"

For a moment the Pippin looked as if he could scarcely believe his ears, and then he suddenly exploded in a fit of laughter.

"Lor!" said he, as he gradually recovered his breath, "you're as good as a play, you are. It's no use talking to you like a fellow-creetur, you're so precious iggerant. Why, your mug's your countingence, ain't it?"

"Not that ever I heerd on," answered Woppits, innocently. "Then what do you mean by bleachin' it?"

"Why, you wouldn't be so blessed innocent as to try the dodge I've been telling you of, with a jib like that! You must go and make yourself up for consumshin—whiten your cheeks and darken your eyes. There's a reg'lar hartist in that down here—does it beautiful; gives you a holler eye for twopence, wot you might put a walnut in. Sunk and wasted cheeks is a penny more; and he throws in a arctic flush for a brown."

"I'm blessed!" exclaimed Woppits, bewildered anew.

"There's some coves that can't take the consumshin dodge at all—Nagle couldn't, you know. Well, this here hartist as I'm telling you of, he does 'em a sore leg—a stunner—quite a picter it is—for about sixpence. A bad leg's a werry good dodge too in the winter, when the rheumatiz comes on to the old ladies and genelmen. 'Bout May's the time for consumshin—the spring and fall."

Woppits stared at his informant long after he had thus concluded, without uttering a word. So the Pippin continued—

"Well, it's a lucky thing you tumbled over me, I can tell you. Now, what might be your game with the chickweed?"

"Sell it, and live on the profits: that's what my friend advised."

"What—Tweak?"

"That's him."

"Very well. Did your friend ever try that lay?" contemptuously pursued the Pippin.

"Don't think he ever did; leastways, I know he didn't. He kept a tripe-shop: sold calves' feet, and trotters, and cowheels, you know."

"Then why didn't he advise you to go into his own line?" rejoined the Pippin, quickly. "Here! will you take my advice?"

"Wot is it?"

"Well, you try trotters and calves' feet. The best game out, with a small capital. Trotters cost threepence a-dozen at the

biler's, and you get a ha'penny a-piece for 'em. Besides, you wouldn't have to drag the young 'un about at that game. No occasion to go out till evenin', arter she's a-bed, you know."

"Where'd I have to go to sell 'em?" Woppits asked.

"Oh, round to public-house tap-rooms and bars. If you've a mind to try 'em, I'll put you in the way."

"Well, I should, because trotters is something you can eat if you can't sell 'em; and then they'll keep me in mind of my friend, and that'll do me no harm."

"Werry well, then. Now, I'll put you right about the togs, to begin with; for if you're caught in London in them winmen's things, you'll pooty soon find yourself behind a grating—I mean to say, in prison."

"Lor!"

"Yes, that's it, and nothin' else. It's agin the law, and so off they must come. Now, how much can we spare for a jacket and trousers, and a hat? Well, I'll go and see," said the Pippin. "It ain't werry late yet, and I knows about your measure."

And the kind-hearted rogue, after talking with Yallops for a few moments, left the kitchen.

Half an hour had elapsed, and all but Woppits had retired to the dormitories, when the Pippin returned with an entire suit of masculine apparel.

"Now," said he, "let's try 'em on. Off with these here."

Woppits, blushing up to the tips of his ears, pointed to the Gal.

"Oh, ah," responded the other. "Werry true. Yallops, be so good as to send her off for a few minutes; and p'raps she'll take this little kid with her."

"There you are," he continued, as the young woman retired. "Now let me unhook you. Don't be bashful of Mr. Yallops—he won't retire, but he'll shut his eyes, if you're timid. That's the ticket—what I call a fit. Now the coat,—hat! Beautiful! Lend us your shaving-glass, Mr. Wy! There, how do you like yourself?"

"Werry nice!" answered Woppits. "The trousers is loose, though—feel as though I should slip through 'em."

"Ah! that's because of the spikiness of your legs; it ain't no fault of the trousers. You'll soon fill 'em out, if your trade prospers. In the mornin' we shall see to the basket and stock. Arter which you'll be 'spected to stand one pot of 'arf-an-'arf, and an ounce of 'bacca."

The woman and little Ruth were re-admitted. The former was too used to behold the performance of miracles in that kitchen—the blind to see, the lame to walk, and the dumb to sing comic songs—to be much surprised at Woppits's metamorphosis. As to little Ruth, she was too sleepy to observe anything.

"Shut your eyes and go to sleep, dear," said our young friend, as on the following evening he bustled about the comparatively decent little room in which he was lodged—the decentest in the house, thanks to Yallops's Gal, who had taken to the child. "Hush to sleep, my dear," said he, tucking in little Ruth, "and I'll bring you home another Jim Crow with gold legs;" and then he proceeded to tie on his white apron and sleeves.

"And will you bring me back the lady that nursed me, and carried me such a long way?" asked the child, solicitously.

"Did you like her, my precious?" returned Woppits, laughing an odd sort of laugh over his basket.

"Oh, yes. I do love her very much. Let her come again—bring her here again, please."

"Oh, I'll look after her," cried Woppits, giving the child a final tuck in, and a kiss into the bargain. "You're sure you love her, though?"

"Oh, sure!"

Woppits looked not only happy, he looked triumphant, as he emerged from Yallops's passage, and went out into the drizzling rain that evening.

CHAPTER XXV.

ONE TOO MANY.

"ONE hundred pounds reward!" The line was printed in the most bare-faced type, and still impudently shouted from the placards affixed to Mr. Keppel's gate-posts. It looked, that placard did, as if it knew it lied, and was resolved to brazen it to the utmost, and to the last. It fluttered now in tatters on either side of the gate; but it held on desperately, in spite of the hail that battered it; of the rain that pelted it; of the wind that tore and tugged at it, now from this corner, and now from that, as though indignant at the deception. But, ragged as was the placard, it never abated a jot of its pretensions to earnestness and justice. There was, at least, the great line "a hundred pounds reward!" and there was another, from which the way-farer, often with much labour, gathered that somebody wished somebody else to be lodged in one of his Majesty's jails. A line of much meaning this to Keppel, who never failed to read it as he passed in or out.

Which was now but seldom. Not that he was an eremitical man; not that he had any peculiar relish for the seclusion of home, but rather because he hated the whole place, with every-body and everything about it. That for one reason. For another, his valet would not often allow him to wander from the hated house, in every closet of which he had a skeleton. Howlet's motive for this is obvious. His master went to still further excesses when abroad, and then said things which were not wholesome. At length it came to this:—Howlet never permitted Mr. Keppel to go out alone; and established himself in a room contiguous to that which his master commonly occupied, under the pretence that he had contracted a nervous disorder, that rendered necessary an unremitting attendance.

So it is a winter day, solemn and quiet, because of the still-falling snow. Watching the flakes as they fall upon his trees and upon his lands sits Horace Keppel, in a grand carved chair, in a sumptuous and perfumed room, with wines and fruits at his elbow; in his mind this bitter sick longing that something like snow would fall upon his heart, covering up its memories, numb-ing its pain. For some moments this reflection gives such a touch of melancholy to his face that he becomes poetic, and we regard him with a little tenderness even; but the melancholy soon becomes gloom again, the valet of his valet swallows a great glass of wine at a gulp, and turns and scowls at the fire.

At this moment in walks Mr. Howlet. After glancing steadily from his master to the decanters, comparing their rela-tive conditions, he takes up the latter and coolly returns them to a buffet; moreover, he turns the key on them, places the key in his waistcoat-pocket, and goes quietly to trim the fire.

Keppel watched these operations in a white heat of shame and wrath. The cool manner in which Mark trifled with the poker, after he had put the wine away, provoked Keppel beyond bounds. Lunging forth his right foot, he kicked the valet, as he bent there over the fireplace, clean into a corner, where he lay curled up like a hedgehog.

For a moment neither of the men stirred. Howlet lay pant-ing, and wondering at his master's new-found temerity; while Keppel, panting also, wondering at that same inspiration. Then Mark, setting his features to "calm," though that was by no means the actual state of the weather, uncurled himself, went to the fireplace, and resumed the little duty that had been so suddenly interrupted.

Now this did not at all suit Keppel's humour—this silent and meek submission was not to his taste; so, though he was rather afraid of opening anything like a discussion, he burst forth with—

"Do you mean to repeat this insult *every* day?"

"I *did* intend to pursue that course; but——"

"Well?"

"Now I'm not sure whether it's at all equal to the case."

"You cold scoundrel, what are you threatening now?"

"A lunatic asylum! A nice quiet madhouse!" replied How-let, standing upright this time, with the poker in his hand.

Keppel stared in abject astonishment.

Mark nodded.

Keppel burst into a shout of derisive laughter, not altogether genuine. It ceased abruptly; and in the strange silence which followed, Howlet whispered these words:

"I tell you what, Mr. Keppel; if you think *that* can't be done, or that I won't do it, if you repeat the trick you've just played, I can only say that you're confoundedly mistaken."

"Good gracious!" exclaimed Keppel, a moment after, turning his bewildered face to the fire, "where is this to end?"

"Where your folly ends; which at present is bound straight for the gallows. End it here, sir, and all you complain of is ended too."

"I wish my life were ended! I wish I were dead."

"Supposing *that* to be the end of it, I daresay you do!" rejoined the other, with severe pleasantry. "But it's hardly consistent to suppose it would be. There's a good deal to come after that."

"Oh, I'm to have a chaplain as well as jailer, I perceive! Let me warn you that you're too ambitious; you take much too high ground, my wise serpent and my faithful jackal. Beware!"

Howlet bowed much as if he had received orders for dinner.

"*You* preach!" continued the chafing gentleman, again work-ing himself into a fury. "Who's the gainer in this business?"

"Oh, I'm the gainer, of course," answered Howlet, putting his hands together, and marking the periods of his speech by gently rising and falling on his heels. "It's gain to be the servant—companion, if you will—to a man already riding in the gallows cart; it's gain to know that you have so served him that the rope that hangs him will choke you; it's gain to pass sleep-less nights and anxious days in order to save him from wantonly throwing away his life as well as your own. Oh, yes—I'm a gainer."

"You have scarcely said all out, Mark. You don't refer to that little salary of yours."

"Well, find some one to keep your secret cheaper. I'm heartily tired of the bargain. Ring for Wilkin, or Jenkins; turn it over to one of them. They're needy men, and might do it at a reduction."

"There must be an end to this," cried Keppel, determinedly. "I'm not so much in love with my life as to keep it on these terms." Here he rose and walked to the window. "I'll not submit to be treated like an imbecile in my own house, nor to be walked out and home like a valuable dog with the mange. Either you or I must quit this, Mark."

Howlet's eyes glistened for a moment. "We shall both quit it, if you're not careful," said he.

"I've heard enough about that. Now listen to me. You are not particularly attached to any one in this part of the country, I believe?"

"Except yourself, Mr. Keppel."

"Of course, of course. Well, you would have no objection to leave England?"

"It's my native land, sir!" rejoined Howlet.

"Your native humbug! Come, seriously, Howlet, what do you say to finishing your life in America?"

"Which it would not take long to finish with my present re-sources. What on earth, sir, should I do in America?"

"Nothing. Keep quiet. Marry. Live at ease."

"What on?"

"A thousand pounds, which I'll give you the day you sail, over and above all expense. And—— Who's this, Mark?"

For several moments Keppel had been watching a strange-looking male figure, which came creeping up the avenue by the assistance of a stick. His eyes were bent on the ground, his hand trembled even while it rested upon the staff, and his hobbling gait, and the frequency with which he paused, betokened an old and infirm man.

"A beggar, I think, sir," answered Mr. Howlet.

"Beggars do not often come up that avenue, and his dress is not a beggar's."

Some tall shrubs now screened the old man from view, and Keppel took up the conversation where he had broken it off so abruptly.

"Well, what say you to the proposition?"

"Must respectfully beg leave to decline, sir," returned How-let, composedly. "I must look to my old age, sir! and, at the rate of a hundred a-year, the sum you name would be gone, interest and all, and my savings into the bargain, long before I was fifty."

"By Jove, that's a cool view of the case. It's clear to me, Howlet—Come in! Well, what is it, Jenkins?"

"A gentleman below wishes to see you, sir."

"Did he give you his name?"

"No, sir; said it was important business, sir!"

"Bring me his card. I cannot be bothered now."

The servant retired, and presently returned with some six square inches of pasteboard, bearing the name and occupation of Mr. Joel Hatcher.

"Hatcher—who's Hatcher?" mused Mr. Keppel.

With sudden and singular distinctness, his man remembered the story-telling night at the Goat and Boots; since when he and Hatcher had never exchanged a word.

"A broker—old store dealer in Sleaford here, sir, I believe."

"Send him to the housekeeper, Jenkins—I'm busy;" and Keppel threw the card into the fire.

He looked towards his man as he did so, and the latter (not altogether to Mr. Keppel's surprise, for he had observed and obeyed similar signs before) humbly signified, "No."

"Stay," then said Keppel, as the footman was leaving the room. "Now I reflect, I think I saw the man coming up the avenue. He seemed ill; is he?"

"If I might make so bold," answered Jenkins, whose sentiments on the subject were brimming over, "I should say he was the most singular and extrordinary person—here he is, sir."

And the man gave a sudden skip aside, as he became aware of the "extrordinary" presence behind him.

There he was, with his hat under his arm, and his newly-shaven head bound about with a green handkerchief, for warmth's sake—the kerchief contrasting hideously with his sickly blue-white features, his scrubby eye-brows, and the scanty red beard which hung limp and dull from his chin, like dead hair. The man had evidently not long left a sick-bed; and the nipping cold of the day by no means improved his personal appearance.

The obeisance he made Mr. Keppel was the most grotesque thing of the kind ever seen, I suppose; he was so anxiously respectful, and so miserably unused to the ceremony he had ventured on. Also he bowed to Howlet; and afterwards stood simpering and chafing his lean hands on the threshold. It was as if he had risen from the grave, and felt doubtful whether people would recognize his existence any longer. So grim and fantastic was the appearance he presented, that Keppel's nerves were rudely shocked; and he would have ordered him away instantly but for the strange look of humility in the man's eyes.

Certainly, there was great expression in those eyes—to Howlet, who had a side view of their cadaverous owner. A fox-meeting-a-farmerish sort of expresssion it was: and as men feel the approach of thunder, the valet felt the coming of mischief.

At a look from his master, Jenkins retired. "Come in, my man," said Keppel to Hatcher; "take a chair, if you've anything to say to me."

The pale man lowered himself upon the extreme edge of a chair, and forthwith began to swallow a series of little speeches, as fast as they rose to his lips. Then from time to time he stroked his head, bringing his hand forward from the crown in a most supplicatory manner. Meanwhile he threw an occasional glance at Keppel—a glance so humble.

Howlet retired to the adjoining apartment, in which were a series of little holes drilled, commanding every portion of the room which his master almost exclusively occupied.

"Well, sir," said Horace, tapping the table with the nut-crackers. "How can I serve you? What's your business?"

Very aggravating! Often as he had amused himself, a-sick-bed, rehearsing the scene that was to take place between himself and Keppel, here he was as unprepared as ever. As soon as he had got the first word of that speech upon his tongue, an unknown power compelled him to gulp it down again. However, with one great effort, and one great gulp, and a still more deprecatory stroking of his head, he unbuttoned his great-coat, drew out a pocket-book, and broke the ice.

"Oh, I—I beg your pardon, sir, I merely called, that is, I wished to know—but I'm an ignorant man, sir, I haven't the gift of——"

"Come, out with it, my man. You merely called—so I see. You wish to know—what?" and Keppel brought him up sharp with another rap on the table.

The rap jerked Joel's hand out of an inner pocket, into which it had strayed, and from which he drew a small packet, wrapped in fine paper. The sight of this small object infused fresh life and courage into Mr. Hatcher's heart. He ventured to clear his throat, he even so far indulged himself as to lick his lips, as he advanced to the table with this magical little packet in his hand. Drawing his chair after him, he deliberately seated himself, and unfolded the paper, displaying its contents with the air of a conjuror.

There was a slip of paper with writing on it; there was a carefully folded sheet of paper, which, when properly displayed, proved to be a clean and perfect copy of the placard at that moment fluttering in rags at Keppel's gate-posts; and there was another little packet, sealed at the ends.

Keppel viewed these preliminaries with momentarily increasing apprehension. His lips twitched—so did his eyebrows; and by some occult process, the cadaverous hue was transferred from Hatcher's face to his own. Having arranged the contents of the packet to his satisfaction, the broker encircled them with one arm, that he might sweep them up in a moment, if necessary; stroked his head with increased deference, felt his chin, and then in a sweet voice said—

"Three months ago, sir—I think I'm correct—(consulting the placard)—yes, three months and a week ago, you had the misfortune to lose your little daughter. Ah! sad is the loss of a little daughter! I once—I'll lock that door, Mr. Keppel, if you've no objection." he added, abruptly.

"Pardon me, Mr. Hatcher, the door does well enough. Come, what else have you to say?" Keppel looked as stern as possible, as a means of appearing self-possessed. "How does my loss concern you?"

"Well, sir, if you'd been thrown upon your back for three months in consequence of it, and thankful to get up at last, notwithstanding you're such a scarecrow as you are—I mean as I am—you'd be of opinion that it concerned you a good deal."

Neither Keppel in his chair, nor his man in the ante-chamber, could make anything of this speech; and the hearts of both began to beat more quickly, soothed by the hope that the intruder was only a lunatic after all. As the broker sat there, nodding, and grinning, and stroking his head, under the impression that he had given his answer rather a humorous turn, Keppel became confirmed in this idea, and acted upon it.

"Well, well," said he, "I'm sorry, Mr.—a—Hatcher, that your sympathy for me should have led to such melancholy results. Preyed upon your mind, eh?"

The grin shaded off into such a blank stare, that Keppel was still more encouraged—in one sense. Shifting nearer to the bell-rope, he continued, in a louder and more majestic voice—

"Anxiety so great that it threw you on a bed of sickness, eh? Very much obliged to you, I'm sure, Mr. Hatcher. If we had known it, we should not have allowed it, of course; we should have got another little girl, you know."

"No occasion, thank'ee," said Hatcher, who didn't like to be talked to in this manner.

"Oh, you're all right now, are you, Hatcher?"

"Yes, and so are you!"

There was more meaning than madness in this remark, Keppel thought; and he looked keenly at the broker while he said slowly and absently—

"Oh, yes, I'm all right."

"Oh, yes!" nodded the other, stroking his head again.

Naturally there was a pause after this.

"Mr. Hatcher," then said Keppel, "I think you had better go home. You are either wandering in your mind or playing the fool; and in either case, this is not the place for you."

"I beg your pardon, sir; but I was never more sensible in my life. When I say I'm all right, so I am all right. When you say you're all right, that's what I say. And I'll prove it too!"

"What do you mean, sir? Say at once, for I'm about to ring the bell."

"Well, look here!" replied Hatcher, leaning over the table, with his arms extended, and fixing his ferrety eyes on the fascinated gentleman. "You can take these bills down from the gates!"

No reply. Keppel turned his face to the mantelpiece.

"You need never have stuck 'em up."

No answer. Keppel's hand was upon a magnificent lustre, the pendants of which trembled and clinked together.

"Why, pray?" he asked at length, with the voice of a thirsty man.

"Because," replied Hatcher, in a low voice, but so distinct in the breathless silence of his listener, that every word sounded as clear as the echoes from the smith's anvil, "because she was dead before a line was printed! Murdered, and that's more!"

One of the lustrous pendants fell upon the hearth, and was shivered into fifty pieces. Hatcher, who saw Mr. Keppel's awful face reflected in the glass, smiled a smug smile, fondled his chin, and proceeded to disembowel the packet that was sealed at the ends. His attention roused by the noise of Hatcher's movements, Keppel now watched _his_ reflection in the glass, and saw those thin cold fingers slowly reveal the blackened cloak clasps. He recognized them; he saw how they were regarded by the broker, turning them over and over in his palm there so tenderly, and he writhed back into his chair without looking around again.

At this moment Howlet entered; he was a little at a loss.

"Ah! come in, Mark," cried Mr. Keppel, anxiously.

"Ay," thought Hatcher, "come in, Mark. I wonder it wasn't 'come in' before this. Well, I've got three shots for you, my noble champion, and down you come."

"Well! why, what's all this, Mr. Hatcher?" said the valet, in well-affected surprise, looking from one to the other.

"Not too loud, Howlet," exclaimed his master. "Shut the door."

"'Tis shut, sir."

"Draw the blinds then! Confound it, draw the blinds! and take everything dangerous out of my reach!"

Hatcher stept softly across the room to obey these directions—he would have given them himself under similar circumstances. As he went a little out of ear-shot, Howlet bent over the table, and whispered "Courage!"

"But the clasps!"

"Yes," said Mr. Hatcher, who had caught the last words, "there's no getting over them, you know! There's as pretty a link in the evidence as ever I see! Who'd have thought they'd ever be a link of that sort, eh?" at which little joke Hatcher again stroked his head.

"What clasps are these?" asked Mark, innocently. "It seems to me that you're a little bit gone, Mr. Hatcher."

"Thank you, Mr. Howlet; but considerin' that I haven't drunk anything but barley-water for twelve or thirteen weeks, that isn't likely. No, sir, it's you that's a little bit gone. As for the clasps, if you wish to know, they belong to a cloak of Mr. Keppel's—a cloak that was lost when _she_ was lost."

"Ah, I see! Now, no more nonsense! You stole the cloak and the child too. You're the very man we want!"

Sidling swiftly up to Joel, he seized him by the collar.

"Ah," said the broker, keeping his eye steadily fixed on Howlet's, while their hot breath mingled together, "keep your hold there, on my collar, that's a good fellow. Don't let your fingers touch my throat—they might leave a mark, you know."

Howlet's hands fell nerveless from the rampart of snuff-brown cloth which defended Joel's grisly neck. Did this fantastic monster, with his lean jaws and greedy eyes, hold _his_ secret too? The broker fairly snapped at his chin with his finger and thumb, so great was his satisfaction, and smilingly assumed his chair with the half-audible exclamation, "Shot number one!" Louder he said—

"Mr. Howlet, I'm surprised—I'm astonished—that you should have such an opinion of me, that never stole not even such a thing as a hint in all my life; and, I'm sure, we've passed many hours together—hours of refreshing from the toil of life—at the 'Goat,' you know, with the friendly glass, and the cheerful pipe, and the flowing can, and stories! Why, the very last time we were there together, you were amused, I'm sure! Ah, I see you remember the night I speak of, a very cheerful night, and a very queer story! You didn't think me a thief then, Mr. Howlet, or you wouldn't have drank with me, I'm sure!"

Shot number two. The noble champion staggered for a moment, and then foundered. Joel, who by this time was as cool as a cucumber, took up the placard and commenced its perusal, like a political old gentleman over his favourite morning paper. Howlet whistled at the window; Keppel glared at the fire.

The longer the silence lasted the less inclined was any one of the trio to break it. At length Keppel, who was the most impatient, struck his fist heavily upon the table, exclaiming—

"Well! Now your object! Your object in coming here, sir?" and he turned savagely upon Hatcher, who exhibited a scared countenance over the top of the placard.

"Object, sir?" echoed he, shocked at a word so opprobrious. "Come, we won't talk like that, sir. I've no object except to make it all right and comfortable."

"Let us come to an understanding," rejoined Keppel.

"Ah, let's come to an understanding," repeated the other, fondling his hands.

"You fancy you've made a discovery?"

"Very much so."

"What are you going to do with it?"

"With the discovery? Lor' bless you, nothing!"

"You haven't recovered your fever, that's clear," replied Keppel.

Now Howlet struck in. "If this gentleman would be good enough to step into the ante-room for a few minutes, I think I could explain——"

"Thank you, I'd much rather not," interrupted the gentleman in question. "I—I haven't got time. I promised mother I'd be home by eight o'clock, and if I'm not there, she'll be sending some boy to inquire for me, or something! We'd better settle it at once!"

"By Jove, then you'll have to summon back a little reason. I ask you again, what are you going to do with this discovery?"

"And I says again, nothing. I don't know anything about a discovery—at least not at present. All I want to know is, will you buy these clasps?"

Howlet understood the proposition immediately. "How much do you ask for them?" said he.

"Well, I ain't a greedy man—let's see, there's three of us. I'll take my fair third."

"What's that? How much money does your fair third represent?"

"Well, I can't say, till I've seen your steward's books, can I? But among gentlemen—you wouldn't object to submitting 'em to my inspection, of course."

Keppel penetrated his meaning, and, rising up, he said with an air of determination never before visible in him, "Take yourself off, sir. In one minute it will be too late, for I'll kick you through the window!"

Mr. Hatcher was equal to the situation.

"Well, well, we won't quarrel. You're master here, and you shall be obeyed. I'll get home, then. You see," he continued, as he leisurely folded up the placard, the clasps being already safe in a breast pocket, "you see, I'm rather weak as yet, gentlemen, and can't stand the night air. I'm sure it's a wonder and a mercy, as the Psalmist says, that I'm alive at all." (Here he stooped to pick up his hat, which he had placed under a chair.) "I didn't tell you, Mr. Howlet, did I, how I got into this bad way? You see, the night after I saw Mr. Keppel throw the child into the lime, I went over from my place to see how things stood there, and found the clasps and one or two other trifles; but in coming home somehow I stumbled, and fell upon my head, which received a hawful wound, fever follerin'. But, do you know, Mr. Mark" (here the speaker's eyes sought Keppel's averted face, and his voice sank into the distinctest of whispers), "I don't think it was the blow so much as what I'd seen. So dreadful, you know!—such a gentleman too! Good day, Mr. Mark—good day, sir!" Taking his stick, he hobbled forthwith to the door.

Mr. Keppel looked round, catching Mr. Hatcher's eye as the latter glanced over his shoulder. Keppel laughed bitterly.

"Ha! ha! he does it well! He even beats _you_, Mark!"

"Come, Mr. Hatcher," said the person thus addressed, who had scarcely recovered the shock of shot number two, "don't go off in that stupid way. Between men of business, you know——"

ILLUSTRATED CIRCULATING LIBRARY.

"Never fear," said the unhappy gentleman, again laughing: "he does not intend to go over the door-mat."

"I beg your pardon, sir; I'm going straight; and if you want to know my *lowest* terms, I can state 'em in two minutes. Two hundred and fifty pounds a-year, paid in advance—half-yearly—reversion of one hundred pounds a-year to mother in case of my early death. I know pretty well what you can stand, and I've kept within the mark. Perhaps you'll consider these terms, and send word. I shall remain at home for twenty-four hours."

Mr. Hatcher bowed—and a very pretty picture he made, framed in the doorway, with the gloom in the background. Without awaiting an answer, he was gone. The momentous visit was concluded; as for the result, the reader anticipates it. Ere twenty-four hours had elapsed, a check for a hundred and twenty-five pounds reposed in Mr. Hatcher's cash-box, and the clasps were where Keppel would alone confide them—in the deep sea."

CHAPTER XXVI.

A HAPPY FAMILY.

Woppits prospered. This was all the more remarkable because his calling left him an immense amount of spare time on hand; and Dr. Watts has told us how prone is the father of evil to find employment for idle people. A fortunate circumstance contributed to this good state of things. Miss Wheezer's circulating library was round the corner. True, the literary provender there provided was not very delicate, but then no more was Woppits's appetite, while his love for the marvellous added a charm to everything spectral, bloody, adventurous, and enchanted, that fell in his way. Books of this kind he bolted entire—that is, with the exception of all words over three "synables;" and if, like the ostrich after a luncheon of nails, he was little the better for them, he was at any rate none the worse. Meanwhile his digestion was exercised; by and by he even began to have a literary palate, and would deliver into the ear of the Pippin criticisms almost as charming as those of a Wilson or a Croker; for they were intensely savage, though generally erroneous. Woppits's discrimination was especially exercised on the drama. Miss Wheezer had several volumes of plays of all kinds: Woppits knew them by heart.

But do not suppose all the time set apart from business was so construed. There was the place to "do up," for instance; and meals, to be eaten, must be cooked. Now, Woppits delighted in cooking, and so did little Ruth, for that matter; and our young friend, who felt all the responsibilities of his position, never lost an opportunity of sowing in her infant mind the seeds of that domestic knowledge which might be so useful to her in after-life.

"Now, my precious!" said he, tucking up his sleeves, with the air of a conjuror, "observe me. I'm going to give you a lesson on taters—which I've got before me. When you come to cook the taters—which is the fust branch of domestic edication—mind you take out all the eyes! That," said he, pausing and looking Ruth in the face learnedly, "is indispensable. Do you know what that hard word means, my dear?"

"No; tell me."

"It means, my precious! you can't do without it. That's what indispensable means. Werry well. Then with the pint of your knife, you fetches out the eyes—so. Werry good! Now to the second part. When——"

"But what do they have eyes for, Woppits, dear?"

"What——? Well, that's a question of natural philosophy (Woppits had been extending his reading lately), or else it's a dispensation of Providence. Now, if it's natural philosophy, the tater is a sort of machine or ortomyton, which is obliged to grow eyes, and can't help itself. If it's a dispensation of Providence, He causes them eyes to come there, out of which springs other taters, for the food of man. If I was to be asked my own opinion, all I should say is, first you may depend upon it the tater couldn't do without 'em. Hows'ever, we'll leave that branch of the conversation," continued the boy, flourishing the knife which he held in his hand, and evidently talking with a consciousness that his only listener was a child. "This is weal! Weal, Ruth, is a little bullock, you know! and weal's a tickler

for the inexperienced housekeeper. You ought to be very suspicious of it—for of all meat to go, weal's it! Now, you stir up this batter, dear—all one way, you know, and without splashing of your pinafore. I'm going to cut this meat into small pieces. Observe—one eye on me, t'other on the batter."

"Why, it is going to be a nice ——?"

"Toe-in-the-hold, my precious!"

Other occupations furnished other illustrations. At this time he had all the duties of a housewife upon his hands—down to curling Ruth's hair, and the laundry work into the bargain. While engaged in the latter occupation, about this period, the Pippin made him a visit.

"Now you very naughty child, you know that's my sarcer, that I stand my iron on. Bring it here this minnit. What, you're at it again? You've knocked down that cheer with your nice clean perricots a-airing. And now—Hallo, here's Mr. Pippin, and me in all this muddle! Come in."

"Well, my dower," said the young gentleman, in a patronizing tone, from behind his long pipe and his formidable collar, "hard at it, then? How goes it?"

"Oh, werry well, if you mean business. More'n ironin' does. What with all the blacks, and the starch sticking, and that naughty gal, I'm worrited a'most to death."

"Naughty, eh? We won't have that. Come here, little shiner. That's what I call you, Little Shiner! See what I got for yer."

Ruth came forward accordingly, and the Pippin, with much formality, presented her with some hardbake. With fewer ceremonies Ruth proceeded to devour it.

"Ah, you'll spile her, if you go on like that!" exclaimed Woppits, crashing down the iron in an almost professional style.

"Spile her!" answered the other, gruffly. "Spile me—that's what she'll do. I never comes here but I goes home a wiser and a wusser man, as Hamblet says. Gets quite soft and spooney, I do. Feels as if I wants to go home to my mother. What do you think o' that?" and the Pippin laughed—a laugh too loud and short to be as humorous as he meant to be. "When it come to *that*, you know, I turns in and goes to bed; which it's pooty near time."

"Ah, I knows the feeling," responded Woppits, shaking his head. "You feel ashamed of yourself—that's what it is. Why sometimes I catch myself sayin' some rough word I hear outside, and I look at her and she looks at me, and I feel just the same. All over, it is."

"That's it. Now cut it! So you are rubbin' on pooty comfurble, are you?"

"Yes, we are," answered Woppits, with a grateful countenance. "Last week I earned fourteen and eightpence: and I can tell you I never tots up on Saturday nights without feelin' in a very thankful way to you, that has been my friend."

"Get out!" exclaimed the Pippin, flourishing his pipe with an expression of disgust. "What have you got to thank *me* for? Why it was as much for a lark as anythink, that I advised you to sell trotters at all—just to see how you'd go at it, and how you'd look when your money was all gone. That's up and down straight, my boy! I ain't goin' to tell no lies to you."

"Ah, but, you know, the money *was* all gone, once, and you lent me 'arf a suvering to start afresh. Eh? You forget that! But lookee here! it's time for me to be off."

"Oh, I say," exclaimed the Pippin, suddenly, "I've been talkin' about you!"

"Have you, though? Who to?" asked the other, anxiously.

"Well, you see the gal at our place—you know the gal——?"

"I do, but I don't see that she's a gal at all. She's old enough to be my mother."

"Well, what if she is? At all events, gal or no gal, she knows I come here now and then to see you; and—well, the fact is, I've been and told her all I know about you!"

"What did she say?"

"Not much—never does, you know. But when I went to say that o' course you must ha' had no end of trouble with young shiner here, washin', and dressin', and cleanin' house, and that, for the last two months, she says, 'Well, ask him,' says she, 'whether I shall come and help him, 'casionally.'"

"I'm sure I'm werry much obliged to her. But the money. Fourteen shillings a week won't go to it."

"As if *she* wanted money! Never has any! Never asks Yallops for any, 'cept now and then for clothes! Besides, she seemed to want to come. 'Tell him,' ses she, 'I love the child, and shall be glad to do anything I can for her sake.' There! what more do you want?"

This chapter is to carry us over five years. Therefore, I shall only say that "Yallops's Gal" was permitted by the gallant Woppits to make herself useful to him and to Ruth, and great were the changes she introduced into Woppit's humble lodging. How wide were the eyes of Woppits opened to the shortcomings of his own domestic economy, it is impossible to describe. Now, hitherto he had been rather proud of it than otherwise; and therefore it was almost with a grudging heart that he beheld undreamed of comfort rising about him. This, however, was only for a time. Then arose a new subject for fretfulness. Ruth's affection for the stranger who talked to her so prettily, and dressed her so neatly, and taught her to sew and to spell, grew day by day—so that Woppits became jealous, and sometimes went so far as to wish that the visits of "Mrs. Bell," as she was presently called, would cease altogether.

Happily, they did not: on the contrary, they became still more frequent. Otherwise, what would Woppits have done in that terrible fever? What if she had not dared to wait on him day after day, night after night, eating, drinking, sleeping in the midst of pestilence? Then there was the Pippin. The Pippin's conduct at this time was such that I firmly believe, had he been properly taken in hand—properly, I say; not by that sad sort of persons who used to assault him at street-corners with printed forms, in which he was asked, in the most daring type, whether he knew that he was damned, or flatly informed that eternal torment awaited him; these only made the wicked boy sneer, and "chaff," and swear. But had even our poor friend Woppits been aware of his influence, had he used it with decency and discretion, the Pippin would have become a very good man, as the world goes. But Woppits never knew his power: and whatever good his influence exerted over the young thief, was soon dissipated in the company of his coarser companions. In the end, he died in Australia and a convict's uniform.

I found my belief in the Pippin's convertibility on the following circumstance:—

Woppits, I have said, was sick; therefore Woppits was poor. This inevitable consequence struck the Pippin at once. So one evening he marched up to his friend's lodgings, took off his hat, walked in, and taking his patient's attendant into the shadow of the bed-curtains, drew out a handful of silver.

"Get him a nice neck o' mutton," whispered he (Woppits was insensible), "and a jolly stew of taters: that's wot set me up. Put a glass o' port into it. I've heard *that's* good."

The woman shook her head.

"Well, give him the wine neat, then; I ain't partickler."

"You don't understand me," said the woman, kindly.

The Pippin looked keenly at her; his eyes fell; he turned red; and said he with a queer grin, as he shambled out of the room.

"Oh, you're a rum un, you are!"

Under the circumstances, he might naturally have laughed in her face, and gone to tell the story in company to which so nice a reading of the law of mine and thine appeared preposterous. The Pippin did nothing of the kind; he took a walk to Hyde Park, and did not cease to take a walk there till the clock of Westminster Abbey struck eleven. Next morning he rose at least two hours earlier than ever in his life before, and not content with that innovation upon his habits, he went down to the river and did a hard day's work there. He helped some lightermen to unload a barge, and so well did he work, that at the close of the day he received half-a-crown.

The Pippin turned that coin over and over in his hands—bruised by unwonted labour—with strange and mingled feelings. All day long for *that* miserable piece of silver, when he had a dozen in his pocket at the moment, all "earned" yesterday in the twinkling of a pocket-book! But what a nice-looking half-crown it was! What a solid, hearty, heavy, respectable half-crown! It looked as if it would buy—ay, a hundred times as many comforts as those others there, in his pocket. "But of course, you know," said the Pippin, wagging his head at himself, "that's all my eye! That's all imagination, that is."

Which it wasn't.

However, the Pippin kept the half-crown in his hand till he again arrived at Woppit's door. "Here you are!" said he to Mrs. Bell; "perhaps this'll do! Look here! Down at the river it was." And having displayed his broken and blistered hands in satisfaction of her scruples, he retired.

I don't pretend to say that he slept the sweet sleep of industry that night. What with his aching limbs and aching thoughts about that mother of his, he scarcely slept a wink till morning. But he went down to the river again, nevertheless; and the next day and the next, for eleven days, sneaking away from his companions to his noble piece of work, as a man hitherto honest would sneak away to thieve. Every evening he carried the half-crown to Woppits, with one exception. Then, as he pondered over the hard-earned coin, and compared it with several others less honestly obtained, and saw more and more that the one was different to all the rest—(how, heaven only knew)—he resolved to cheat his friend. He kept the wholesome half-crown for his own use, and, not to give Woppits exactly one of the stolen coins, he changed it for two shillings and sixpence—a little piece of Jesuitism which we will pardon him. Next day, the Pippin ate the first piece of honest bread that ever passed his lips; for his father was a thief, and his mother weaned him on a stolen pound-cake. Of course when I write bread, I write figuratively. I mean that the Pippin ate his first honest slice of roast pork, with cabbage and potatoes. Again it was imagination, of course; but the Pippin thought he had never tasted such lovely pork in his life; certainly he never remembered to have been served so liberally with crackling.

I knew all these circumstances at the time, and augured well from this abundant service of crackling: but the augury was falsified that very night. The Pippin that night was "taken." He was sent to prison for six months; and never turned his hand to honest courses again.

Meanwhile, Woppits had recovered. It was during the time of his recovery that he told his nurse all his story—about the finding of Ruth, and about Mr. Tweakle, and all. Yallop's Gal cried. She put her hands to her face, and rocked to and fro, sobbing—especially at the Tweakle part—and long after Woppits had vacated his pillowed chair for his bed, she sat at the window and wept, and plainly was full of wonder.

Now, she had never been known to cry before; and she seemed so much more cheerful afterwards—not for a day or two, but for ever afterwards—that Woppits for one, and I for another, thought it was a pity the spring had not broken sooner in her barren, drowthy heart. The very next day she actually read one of Miss Wheezer's books to the convalescent Woppits—laughing at the laughable parts, too, in a quiet way.

From that time all went well. A strange old gentleman came upon Woppits one day as he painfully crept out to take an airing, eking out what was left of his strength by a stick. The old gentleman was doing exactly the same thing with two sticks. He cried "hallo!" to our young friend with much abruptness; and entered into conversation with him, when what should happen but when the old gentleman quoted Shakspeare, which he did fifty times a day, Woppits quoted the poet also. The old gentleman tried again; Woppits followed with six lines badly accentuated, but thoroughly appreciated. The old gentleman stared savagely. "Boy," said he, "when you're quite well, come to that address at half-past eight in the morning."

The morning arrived. Woppits went to the house indicated on the card, was shown into the bed-room of the old gentleman, who immediately thrust a newspaper into his hand. "Now fire away," said he, "begin with Music and the Drama." When Woppits had read on for about an hour, the old gentleman checked him with a ferocious grunt, unfastened a knot in the top of his night-cap, drew out a shilling, and flinging it at Woppits, ordered him to go down and get some breakfast, and then be off. "And mind you come again to-morrow," added he, nodding fiercely. "Hi! hi! boy!" he roared, when his reader was half-way down the stairs. "Hand me that violin! If you let it fall, I'll strangle you with the bow, by all that's good!"

"When music, heavenly maid, was young!"

sang he in the same breath, though sick only at its last extremity.

And as the boy closed the door, he heard this strange old gentleman's fingers making music the sweetest and clearest that ever had greeted his young ears. I can tell you that duchesses had listened to that fiddle.

The end of all this was, that Woppits's income was henceforth reinforced by no less than seven shillings a week; and in addition, one meal of every day was sure and unlimited. A great thing that. Nor did it end there. The old gentleman discovered by and by that Woppits had a taste for gardening. He knew a weed from a flower the moment he set eyes on it: and whenever he took a spade in hand he worked with such a will that it seemed as if the plants were to be sown on the *other* side of the soil, down to which Woppits was working. This was enough for the strange old gentleman. Woppits was ordered to appear an hour earlier, and remain an hour later; *i. e.*, to luncheon. So the meal was called, but when Woppits looked upon it, the best feelings of his nature revolted at the term.

"Well, sir, you've had your luncheon, I suppose," roared the old gentleman in an accusing voice, that morning.

"*Dinner*, sir!" answered Woppits, firmly.

"Luncheon, sir! Say luncheon, if you please."

"Sir, I'm afraid. It's tempting of Providence!"

The old gentleman raged like a bull.

Woppits's wages were, henceforth, half-a-guinea a week; and as he still took his evening's walk with his white sleeves, and his white apron, and his white basket, he really began to look upon himself as a prosperous young fellow. Happy he was as a king, or as a sandboy (much the same thing, so far as happiness goes), especially as his friend from Yallops's had at length quitted that establishment altogether, and had cast in her lot with him and little Ruth. They had now apartments in Bulger's Gardens, Kennington, which Yallops himself assisted to furnish.

"Is that your resolution, mum?" said he, when his "Gal" communicated her desire to leave his service.

"Yes—thanking you for your kindness and protection."

"Well, I'm werry sorry; that's all I got to say—werry sorry! Howsever, I can't say nothing ag'n it; and I don't know as I ought. I think I'm up to your game. You've took to that young Woppits and the child, and you're goin' to be a mother to 'em. Good luck to yer! But how are you going to start. You've no money!"

"A little; but I intended to ask you for a little more."

"Did you?" exclaimed Yallops, with quite a bright look in his eyes. "Well, old gal, how much is it to be? I've a neat little stock of shiners, which you've helped to put together more'n you think. And you might ha' had your share on 'em—on'y I felt it was no use arsking you—you wouldn't be Mrs. Yallops, of course; I know THAT. Well, a temp'n note's at your service, and another fiver, if you ses the word. And werry cheap you've been at that!"

Mrs. Bell, as she now began to call herself, had no scruple to say the word; and almost as soon as Woppits's health was re-established, she began life anew as a sempstress, under the same roof with him and with Ruth.

How this strange little family fared from day to day for five years, it would be tedious to recount. One day, and one Sunday, cut from the middle of that period—when Woppits's young ambition dwelt on collars, and Ruth was grown a tall, lithe six-year-old, and Mrs. Bell had softened down into a quiet peace—will fairly represent the whole.

Evening—shades of evening—Woppits discovered brushing his hair before a looking-glass; a basket covered with a very white cloth on an adjoining table. A knock.

"Come in! Oh, it's you, Mrs. Bell. Thought our little madcap hadn't taken it into her head to knock. She's late, ain't she?"

"It is only just past the school hour. She'll be in by the time I make tea."

From a cupboard in the room (which, by agreement, was reserved as a common sitting-room, Woppits sleeping in a sort of garret, which being only eight feet by six, and rather "troubled with rats," had been thrown in cheap by the landlady) forth came a bright teapot and other table furniture. The tea being made, the teapot was placed on the hob, to shine in the firelight comfortably. Then Mrs. Bell proceeded to employ herself in cutting bread-and-butter—no light work in Bulger's Gardens.

"Here she is!" cried Woppits, as a chirping and a footstep is heard on the stairs.

And there she was, her bonnet thrown back upon her shoulders, her cheeks glowing, her curls tucked impudently behind her ears—a pretty creature, and full of grace. Her first act on entering the room was not that of a well-bred child, however. She flung her school-bag to the floor, tossed down her bonnet and cape in the same unceremonious manner, and walking up to the table, seized a slice of the fresh-cut bread-and-butter.

"Well, I'm blowed! That's pretty manners, ain't it!" says Woppits. "I shall have to send a note to your governess, miss. This ain't the thing, you know!"

"No more is saying 'blowed!' Governess says so, and so does mother. Let me eat this one little piece, Woppits dear, and then I'll put away my things and say 'good afternoon.' I am so dreadful hungry!"

The compromise is accepted, and tea proceeds. This over, Woppits goes out, and Ruth remains with Mrs. Bell till bed-time, repeating her lessons, or reading, or sewing, while her kind "mother" cheerfully stitches. At eight o'clock, when Ruth has been a-bed an hour, Mrs. Bell puts her work aside, and sometimes reads, and sometimes flits out for a stiff walk round the common; but oftener, placing her feet on the fender, and shading her eyes with her hand, enjoys a long, sad, profound reverie. At about ten o'clock, she too retires to her room, where Ruth lies. At eleven or twelve, Woppits comes whistling down the deserted street, with his basket slung at his shoulder, softly lets himself in, and, if it is wintry or rainy weather, invariably finds some savoury little mess simmering on the hob of that humble sitting-room. There's a small white cloth on the table, and a clean plate, and a bright knife and spoon, and a tumbler turned down, and a teacupful of ale close kept in a decanter, where, in the candlelight, it really looks like wine. Woppits contemplates all these arrangements with wonderful satisfaction. He says more could not be done if he were a gentleman; and he behaves accordingly. As for the morning, Woppits was enduring the fury of the strange old gentleman, Mrs. Bell was engaged in household matters, and Ruth was of course at school.

So the working days were spent:—then there were the Sundays. These were not unlike the Sabbaths in Bulger's Gardens generally. Materfamilias had much cooking and dressing to go through with; Paterfamilias had to help his hard-pressed mate by cleaning the knives and forks, polishing the little boots, inking the white places on them, and perhaps cleverly patching them here and there. Then the door of the rabbit-hutch wanted a nail; or the wind, which Tommy had taken out of the bellows, had to be restored; or the scarlet runners wanted stringing; or the washing-tub was to be caulked. With such affairs would father occupy himself till the eventful moment arrived when mother, coming forth in a clean cotton gown, and a cap with some ribbons in it, and with a tin ticket in her hand, says: "Now, father, I'm goin' for it!" which means for the shoulder of mutton, then at the bakehouse. No more work for Paterfamilias that day. He comes out of his bed-room with a highly shining and respectable countenance, with a bright, clean shirt on—cuffed—collared; and henceforth he is good and grave and idle. Dinner over, he solemnly takes his pipe and his newspaper, sitting out in the garden, it may be, in view of his rabbit hutch and in the shadow of his sweet peas. Thus in contemplation, and surrounded by nature, he is happy till tea-time. After which he flecks his Sunday silk handkerchief round his Sunday hat, and tells mother how she looks, as requested. I don't say that he then always takes her to church, but sometimes he does, and might go oftener if those hard, close, narrow free seats, did not give him the idea that he was getting his religion—as he will never accept his bread—like a pauper.

Woppits spent the forenoon of Sunday over a heap of old magazines and odd volumes—ay, a hundred-weight of them, which the strange gentleman had given him—and in this mass of reading Woppits revelled for five or six hours of a fine Sunday morning. Ruth was never there to behold this misuse of the time. She was always at church with Mrs. Bell, and only returned to find him dressed in his best, and ready to carry her off to Brixton Hill; then home to tea; then all to church; then literature and the drama till bed-time, except when Woppits varied the evening by attempting hymn tunes on an eighteenpenny flute.

TRIUMPHANT SUCCESS OF THE NEW CROCODILE.

Thus five short years, and all sufficiently happy, passed away. Woppits was growing all this while, and at length became a proper, tall young man, with a certain air about him sometimes which pleased rather than puzzled Mrs. Bell. Ruth was growing, too, in grace and sweetness, as well as in stature. Every year brought more love into this strange little family; and if I were asked who Ruth loved best—or Woppits, or Mrs. Bell—I should only get bewildered.

CHAPTER XXVII.

THE OFFICER TURNS UP AND IS PUT DOWN.

THERE was no mistaking him. It was a dark drizzly night, but the street was narrow, and he was leaning with his back to the wall, the light from a lamp falling full upon his features, upon his fish-like eyes, upon his scrubby eyebrows, upon his big chin, and upon the fingers that were employed, as usual, in kneading it. The officer of the law had turned up again.

Woppits trembled. The officer was not likely to forget or forgive that blow with the window-bar—and what as to Ruth? Not solicitude for his worldly goods saved Woppits's basket from falling to the ground, but the terrible power of the officer's eye, which seemed to shoot a magic current across the street, fixing lip and limb in the position it touched them in. Had Woppits been asked an hour before to describe this man, he would have drawn a very sorry portrait; but with the face before him it seemed not an hour since he had last looked on it.

The years that had elapsed since that time were wiped away. He forgot the broad shoulders and brawny arms that had now become his, which was a great pity: but there stood Woppits, feeling and looking pretty much as he would on that memorable night had the soft-hearted officer walked down-stairs with the gash in his head to intercept his flight.

The two eyes, glowing like phosphorus, came across the street, and the officer's hand was suddenly placed on our young friend's shoulder. Then a well-remembered voice said in his ear, "Woppits, I believe."

That broke the spell. Woppits saw that something desperate must be done to free him from a desperate situation. He remembered his arms: more to the purpose, he remembered his legs. Dexterously raising one of those legs, he threw it behind those of the officer, and with a smart blow on the chest down fell the enemy. Down fell Woppits's basket also—the salt-cellar audibly striking on the officer's teeth, and shooting its contents down the officer's throat. Swiftly Woppits turned the corner, and walked and ran, and ran and walked, by all known bye-ways home.

The lights out—all a-bed. If little Ruth be dreaming a pleasant dream, it is to be hoped that she'll finish it within the next minute.

Time's up. Woppits is at Mrs. Bell's chamber door.

"Mrs. Bell! Mrs. Bell!" violently whispered he through the key-hole. "Oh, do open your eyes! Mrs. B-e-l-ll!"

Ruth awoke. "Mother," cried she, "some one's calling at the door."

"Oh, you're awake then, my pet," continued Woppits through the keyhole. "Do you get up, then. She ought to know better than to sleep like that."

"Oh, it's brother! There's something wrong, I'm sure."

"Now, mother," shouted the young man—still through the keyhole—"as quick as you can."

Mrs. Bell also thought there was something wrong. She feared that her constant advice and his own good resolutions had failed, and that Woppits was intoxicated.

"Go to bed, dear," she answered. "I'll see you in the morning."

"In the morning!" ejaculated Woppits. "Just hark! Mother, I don't know whether you're aware of it, but you're wasting precious time. I shall have to open the door if you don't."

Hastily clothing herself, Mrs. Bell opened the door, and beheld Woppits standing there, with beads of perspiration dotting his forehead.

"Now," said he, "dress her as quick as you can. We must be off. He's after us again. Close at our heels, he is."

"Who?"

"The ferrety man I told you of—him that I knocked down with the bar. He's round the corner—knocked down again; but he'll be up here straight, as soon as they tell him where I live."

"Let him come!" said she, with her cool woman's head. "Why need you fear him or any other man?"

"Let him come!" roared Woppits. "Is the woman mad! Let him come—and me nearly murdered him once! Let him come to put me in prison, innocent or guilty, and to take *her* away from us! There! well! don't mind me, only at the same time don't talk like that any more, that's a good soul. Just help us to get off as soon as we can; we won't go far, and you'll see us as soon as it's safe."

"And what shall I tell him if he does come?" asked the woman, bustling about to fill an old carpet-bag.

"Why!" answered Woppits, who still talked dreadful English, whenever he was excited; "this is what you tell him. He's had it twice! Let him look out for the third time. Because if he don't, it mayn't be good for his health—not for a precious long journey! That's what you tell him. Tell him officer or no officer, if he comes a persecutin' and a prosecutin' me, as never did any wrong to anybody, which you knows—I'll stick him!"

"Oh, Woppits, dear!" exclaimed Ruth, who was dressed by this time.

"Won't I?" said Woppits, looking at the child. "Well," added he, after a few moments of gazing on her sweet face, while his own underwent a gradual change, "that's accordin', of course. But if I don't break his head for him—! Mrs. Bell, tell him this, that you know nothing of me nor the child either. 'I never saw her,' ses you, 'and I don't want.'"

The preparation was completed when Mrs. Bell, going to an old inlaid tea-caddy, took out three sovereigns—all the common stock, save one great crown piece with a hole in it—put them into a purse, and slipped them quietly into the carpet-bag. She then went to the door to see if any one was watching in the street; and finding all clear, gave her children a hurried embrace, and they parted. "You'll hear from me soon," said Woppits, as he turned away.

Hatcher had come to London with the most general and commercial ideas. His uncle the sheriff's-officer had apprised him that the household effects of Lord Soppit were for sale, and ought to "go for a song;" and our friend had come to town to attend the auction. Now, it was not often that Hatcher found himself in London; and on this occasion he resolved to spare himself no pleasure which the city afforded. He was a rising man—he had store of gold; and so assured was he of the eye of the auctioneer who was to sell up Lord Soppit, that he felt he might freely indulge in a little dissipation. To-night, he thought, he would just walk through the "slums" of which he had read in the "Swell's Guide to Funny Places," in which necessary work Mr. Hatcher had expended one shilling. As for Woppits and the child, he thought no more of them than of the Babes in the Wood. This adventure, therefore, took him completely by surprise; and as he lay there among the ruins of

Woppits's stock-in-trade, he found it difficult to collect his scattered senses.

At first, he was not nearly so certain of Woppits's identity, as Woppits of his; but the suspicion alone brought him up suddenly to the wall, against which he was leaning when the young man first perceived him. Woppits's subsequent behaviour set the suspicion beyond a doubt; and it troubled Mr. Hatcher. He had long accustomed himself to the idea that Woppits would never turn-up again, after what had happened at the Blue Raven—that he would keep out of the way—that he was dead, perhaps; or, better still, that Ruth herself had comfortably and naturally deceased. However, here he was—lively enough; and who knew whether Ruth herself was not living? or that Woppits, stirred up by this sudden encounter, might take some step or make some revelation, which would sink the prosperous barque of his fortunes? For, of course, it had only to be breathed that Ruth was alive, and down would go that gallant craft.

"Then," said Hatcher, who thought all this in a second, "since I've been fool enough to reveal myself to him, I'd better follow him up, find out his actual circumstances, and watch his movements. Besides, the youngster may be dead after all; what with the measles, and the hooping-cough, and scarlet fever, and other diseases incident to infancy. Now, where does he live?"

This he almost immediately discovered.

A large man, who in his youth must have been very much like Nagle, sidled up with his hands in his pockets. "What's the row, mister?" said he with a grin, as he contemplated Hatcher rising from the debris of the trotter basket.

"Really I don't know," responded Hatcher. "The poor young man was jostled by a rude fellow just as I passed him; his basket fell, it struck me, I tripped, and fell too. I suppose he has run after the rude fellow. Poor young man! All his wares spoilt! Do you happen to know him?" And Hatcher put his hand in his pocket, whence was heard the gentle sound of silver chinking against silver.

"Know him!" echoed the stranger, looking suspiciously at Hatcher. "I b'lieve I do! What for?"

"Oh, I thought I might have repaired his loss; that's all."

"Well, I have heard his name—it's Woppits; and if you're a friend to him, and I dunno as you can be anythink else—he lives in Bulger's Gardens—this side o' Kennin'ton Common."

"Thank you! Well, if *you're* a friend to him, you'll pack up his goods and take 'em there. Here's a shillin' for the trouble."

And with a benevolent smirk he walked off. "Now, Bulger's Gardens," said he, pausing in a dark corner to enter the address in his pocket-book, "where are you? But, no! I'll not go there for a little while. I'm—I'm in such a white heat, that if I was to see him now, I might do him a mischief, I might indeed! I won't even go in that direction yet awhile, but just take a turn and cool myself, and consider what course to steer." He and that gallant barque—his fortune.

Accordingly Hatcher piloted himself thoughtfully up this dark street and down that secluded alley, but, in spite of his resolution, could not help stopping now and then to inquire the way to Kennington Common, and insensibly, and by roundabout ways, nearing that locality. At length, as he approached Bulger's Gardens, he came suddenly upon the man to whom he had been indebted for his information as to Woppits's whereabouts. It struck the astute Hatcher that he might be able to imbibe a little more intelligence from this person.

"Hallo, there you are, then!" cried Hatcher, coming softly behind the stranger.

"Here I am," responded he, nervously, not immediately recognizing the kind-hearted gentleman with whom he had so recently spoken; "who wants me? Oh, I beg your pardon, mister. I didn't know you for the minnit. But you do walk gallows like a cat, you do!"

"Oh, never mind me, friend. You took home that poor fellow's basket, I suppose?"

"Cert'n'y I did. That's where I just come from."

"All right?"

"Don't know; not bein' at home, he couldn't say. She took 'em in!"

"She told you——" said Hatcher, his voice appearing to be wrenched all manner of ways—"the girl told you he was not at home, eh?"

"Who said the gal? It was the woman."

"Ah, his mother, I suppose!" returned the other, carelessly.

"*He* got a mother! Never had any as ever I heard on. No, it was the woman who went from Yallops's to keep house for him."

"Dear me," cried Hatcher, making a noise which, however it might pass for a laugh in London streets, would have been set down as a howl by any traveller in the neighbourhood of hyenas, "dear me! he must be drivin' a good trade, to be keepin' his housekeeper as well as the other one!"

"Why, she's a little un—his sister, I believe—and missis keeps herself. So I've heard. I dunno much about her—nobody does."

"I thought," returned Hatcher, artfully fumbling in his pockets once more, "I thought you said she came from Yelper's."

"No. I ain't so iggorant as that. I said Yallops's—that's what I said. Yallops's is a lodgin' crib! She used to look arter things there."

"Ah, I see. And now she prefers private life," laughed the broker, who only asked about the woman to give an air of generality to his inquiries, and that they might not be thought to point too directly at Woppits and the child. Whether, however, the big man had grown suspicious, or whether he was disgusted that no pecuniary advance followed that fumbling in the pocket, I do not know; but Hatcher got no farther reply more explicit than an "Ah," or more satisfactory than a grunt. So he wished the man good night.

Mr. Hatcher did not go to Bulger's Gardens that evening. He was unnerved by the events of the last few hours, and as he wended his way to his lodgings, he blundered along pretty much as if he were intoxicated. There could be little doubt about it: Ruth was still alive—Woppits was still her protector—and he had all the threads of a story which, if related too freely, might result in his—Mr. Hatcher's—conviction for complicity in a very pretty swindle. Of course, this chance had always existed, but he had never met it face to face from the time he made the bargain with Keppel to the present; perhaps it was on this account that it now out-stared him at every turn of his thoughts. He cursed his fortune for having ever fallen in with Woppits again; for in the excitement of this rencontre nothing was more probable than that the latter would talk about the affair to his intimate friends, and that might lead to an explosion. It was clear that he must gain some new ascendancy over Woppits, and contrive a scheme to get him out of the country. Then he, the astute Mr. Hatcher, might enjoy his pension in peace.

Next morning, with a good purse of gold in his pockets, with an official-looking stick in his hand, and with a subdued smile on his countenance, he sallied forth from the Saracen's Head, and soon the population of Bulger's Gardens were aware of his important presence. One of the inhabitants was asked, in an important voice, where Mr. Woppits lived; and when informed, he rapped with an important knock on Mr. Woppits's door.

"First floor," said a voice, who responded to the rat-tat.

Mr. Hatcher accordingly stole up to the first floor, putting as much vigour into his legs as they could stand, that the sound of his footsteps might seem important too. He rapped loudly on the door of the front room, and before any reply could be given, he turned the handle, and opening the door, thrust his head into the room.

"Good morning, ma'am," said he, rather taken aback by the comfortable and well-ordered appearance of the apartment.

"Good morning, sir," answered Mrs. Bell, taken aback, for her part, by the suddenness of the intrusion and the ugliness of the intruder.

"I believe you keep house, or something of that, for a young man that lives here."

"Yes; for Mr. Woppits." She knew the man with whom she had to deal at a glance, and was as cool as a counsellor.

"Of course," answered the intruder, ferreting into every corner of the room with his eyes. "Well, this is an unfortunate affair, ma'am! Very unfortunate, upon my word!"

"What's an unfortunate affair?" asked Mrs. Bell, quietly.

"What, ma'am? What! why, this child-stealing business, of course. What else do you think brings me here?"

"I should really find it difficult to guess! Perhaps you'll be good enough to explain yourself."

"Certainly, ma'am," responded Hatcher, rather confounded by the woman's coolness. "These unpleasant jobs *are* best concluded as quickly as possible. Where's the child—the little girl?"

"There's no child here, sir!"

"Not——"

"That's all the answer I can give you, but you're at liberty to search for yourself." Mrs. Bell had taken the precaution of removing every scrap of little Ruth's clothing, her school-books, and all her little childish treasures.

"Well, I can see she's not here; I don't need to be told that. What I want to know is, where is she?"

"And I can give you no information. Your business is not with me, evidently; you had better call when Mr. Woppits is at home."

"Which, ma'am, he won't be, ma'am. for a considerable time," remarked Hatcher, with an ironical bow and a snigger.

"What do you mean?" Mrs. Bell grew pale.

"Lor now, it's very kind of you to try to screen him, and you do it very clever; but it's too late, you see, unfortunately. We've got him!"

"Got him!" echoed the woman. taken off her guard, "you've got him, and you come here to inquire for Ruth! Then indeed I know nothing of her, for she went away with him."

"Oh! Do you mean to say that they've gone off together! Where?"

The woman discovered the trap into which she had fallen, and happily did not fail to see how the stranger had put his own foot into it.

"I thought you said you had him!"

"So I—so we have," he answered in some confusion.

"Who are *we?*" asked she, taking up the interrogative, and actually looking down the cold eyes in her indignation.

"Who! Oh, you'll soon see! why the law, the prison authorities."

"That's false—I *know* it's false."

"*You* know!"

"Yes!" replied she, "and if it wasn't unnecessary, I'd prove it to you."

Hatcher was nonplussed. This woman evidently knew too much. He took a turn or two up and down the room, apparently in consultation with his chin. But his reflection became foggier and foggier in the presence of that calm, clear-eyed, self-possessed woman; and stopping suddenly before her, he stamped impatiently, crying, "Where are they?"

Mrs. Bell gave him a quiet look of surprise, but made no other sign.

It was clear that bullying would not answer Mr. Hatcher's purpose. He took another turn up and down, and then, slowly drawing a canvas bag from his pocket, counted out upon the table five pounds.

"Now, my good woman, where are they?"

The woman laughed, tapped the floor with her foot with an expression of impatience and amusement, and took up her needlework.

"She wants to make a good bargain," thought Hatcher. He placed the money in the bag again, which, with its entire contents, he then threw at the woman's feet.

"Now for it!" said he. "There's fourteen good sovereigns there, all I've got in the world."

"Just to tell you where this young man and his sister are to be found?" said she, placing her foot against the money-bag and toying with it.

"That's all."

"But then you're the law—the prison authorities."

"Oh, hang that, ma'am! It's all right. *He* won't come to harm, I promise you!"

"Ah! You are sure it *is* Woppits's sister you want?" continued she, still kicking the money-bag to and fro.

"Confound—! What are you drivin' at?"

"Let me ask you one more question, and then——Are you the man," said she, folding her arms upon the table before her, and looking steadily at him—"are you the man that threw the child into the lime-pit, or are you merely employed by him?"

"Hang you!" Mr. Hatcher began (we have softened the expletive), and all his self-possession gone, his face livid, his eyes bloodshot.

"Not another word, sir!" cried the woman, rising. "I've been obliged to live with thieves—*thieves*," repeated she, observing that he grew still paler at the word, "and no man ever addressed me in that way before. If you don't instantly leave this house, I'll put you into the hands of the police."

And therewith she advanced towards him with so firm a foot that the old tumble-down casement rattled again, and it really did seem as if she herself meant to collar him without further warning. The effect was instantaneous and decided—Mr. Hatcher backed towards the door, holding his official stick, with both hands, crosswise before him; happy he seemed to gain the staircase, where, turning tail, he made a hurried retreat from the house. Meanwhile, there lay the money-bag, and Mr. Hatcher's name and address was written on it.

CHAPTER XXVIII.

WOPPITS UNDERGOES A SINGULAR TRANSFORMATION.

WOPPITS, griping Ruth's hand, and tugging that little craft along with her bows half out of water, like a cockboat at the stern of a steam-ship, desisted, after about an hour's journey, and put up for the night at a cottage whose ambition proved its ruin. It aspired to an ale-house, and was only a comfortless, lazy, windy, beery hovel, very melancholy, as if afflicted with some hidden disease; and it had red curtains, that still were flaring where they were not dingy, and painted door-posts, and a glaring reeky lamp—all reminding you of those poor human creatures who come out of nights, and call themselves "gay." However, there was room and decency enough in the house, at a shift, and our friends passed the night very well.

As soon as daylight came again, Woppits and Ruth partook of a frugal breakfast and departed. Woppits had no very definite idea as to where he was to bestow himself for the few days which he proposed to spend "out of town," and now simply wandered along till he could fall in with a lodging sufficiently retired, convenient, and above all, cheap.

Presently he neared the hamlet of Tooting; the way thither Ruth thought the loveliest and most beautiful in the world. She had been very little in the country since Woppits first carried her out of it; and ever and anon, as they came to some big old-fashioned house, with its shrubberies and lawns visible through the stern iron gates, there arose in her mind and there dwelt upon her face a dim, placid, dreamy wonder. She thought she had seen them before, or had dreamed of them, or—what was it?

When Woppits turned about, he saw her wrapped in this wondering dreamy air, as she came slowly from some gate through which she had been peeping, he first looked savage, and then he looked sad. Perhaps it is hereby explained that as soon as he came to a green lane, the young man turned into it, abandoning the highway.

The lane was a long lane and a green lane; in these respects, not an uncommon lane. But it is not every lane that is ornamented by a house, black, yellow, red, and on wheels. Now this one was so garnished.

Half-way down the eminently English avenue, and drawn up on one side, beneath the trees, there stood the curiosity. There were evident traces of the canoe in its construction; the builder had also a coffin in his eye when he designed it, plainly; though its general outlines seemed borrowed from a trough, and the *tout ensemble* reminded you of Noah's Ark. Perhaps the presence of a large tarpaulin overhanging the roof had something to do with this effect—only the tarpaulin looked so much like a pall. Not that the machine was at all funereal of hue; on the contrary, it was painted the lower half black, the upper portion yellow, with broad lines of red here and there, as I almost said before.

"What a funny thing!" exclaimed Ruth, as they approached the monster. "What is it?"

"Well," answered her protector, with an air of perplexity, "I can't make anything of it. It can't be—and yet I don't know! See here, Ruth, at the reading on it. 'Richard Biddles, St. Alban's, Herts, common stage, 3044.' Ah! that's what it is!

It's a monniment to somebody. Come away, dear; somebody's buried there. Richard Biddles's family vault, this is. 'Common stage!'—that's the epicalf of it. It means, you know, Ruth, the stage we must all come to some day, which all the world's a stage. St. Alban's is where he used to live; and that's where he got hurt, it says."

"And what's the 3044?" pursued Ruth, demurely. "Was that his age when he died?"

"No, miss. *You* know better than that. And it isn't befittin' for a young lady to make game of such scenes. You ought to remember Methusalem."

"Hush!" whispered the child, pointing to an adjacent meadow. "There's some one there!"

So there was; but not a very visible object. Prone on the grass was somebody lying—his face buried in his handkerchief. Nor was he the only occupant of the field. A large white donkey, his harness trailing at his side, was quietly browsing at a little distance. Another reason why they did not sooner espy the man was, that he was a small man; and another, that he wore a coat the hue of which was like grass; while, to favour the illusion, here and there a bright brass button blossomed out of the garment like a dandelion.

"He's asleep!" said Ruth, softly.

The head in the handkerchief wagged dolefully, while the small portion of leg disclosed by the coat distinctly quivered.

"He's ill!" exclaimed Woppits. "He's in a fit!"

This observation was made in so loud a tone that it roused the object of their solicitude. Hastily raising his head, he jerked himself into a sitting posture, and faced towards them. He was weeping.

"B-be off!" he sobbed. "B-be off! There's no show to-day. You might ha' known that!" and he waved back the intruders with a powder flask (stopped with a cork) which he tenderly grasped by the neck.

The sight of the poor little man, with his weeping eyes, his face puckered with grief, smote sorely on the heart of the tender Woppits. As for Ruth, full of commiseration, she took up his old hat, which had rolled to some distance, and brushed the dust from it. That was doing something.

"Oh, don't cry, mister," said Woppits; "we arn't come to see no show. Can I do anything for you?"

"No, thank ye! Nobody can do anything for me any more. The sooner I'm in my grave the better! Good-bye!"

And taking his hat from Ruth, who eyed him with eyes full of wonder and pity, he pulled it with a despairing plunge over his forehead, and walked straight towards the sepulchre.

"I told you so!" said Woppits in an awful whisper to the child. "He's Richard Biddles, and he's goin' to get in ag'in!"

But for the present he didn't get in again. Turning his back when he had got within the shadow of the sepulchre, he raised the powder-flask to his lips.

Woppits saw the suicidal act. "He's going to blow himself up!" shouted he, and darted forward.

"Be off!" screamed the mysterious man. "Be off! be off! be off! It's rum, I tell you!" and elevating his elbow in a defensive attitude, he darted round to the other side of the mausoleum.

"You let me alone to my sorrow, young man," continued he moodily, "and get out of the way. I'm going to call my donkey!" whereat he whistled, and the donkey came trotting forward.

"Put yourself in the sharps, Jacob," said the little green man, with a profound sigh, at the same moment depositing the flask in the depths of the swallow-tailed coat. "We'll get on a little further!"

A light broke in upon the bewildered Woppits. "Well, I never!" he exclaimed, laughing aloud. "What do you think, mister? If I wasn't persuading my little sister that that travellin' house of yours was a family vault!"

"It *is* a vault, young man!" rejoined the other, in deliberate and hollow tones. "It contains all that remains of a dee-ar departed friend!" and throwing an arm round the neck of the donkey, as if there he found comfort and sympathy, again the little man gave way to grief.

"Poor fellow!" from Ruth, who turned pale.

"Oh, indeed!" from Woppits, who turned red, ashamed of

his levity. "And me laughing? Is it your brother you've lost, mister?"

"Oh, no," replied the little man, with a gesture which almost implied that he only wished it was.

"Not your mother?"

"My mother! Could my mother ha' done what *he* done?" And the mysterious man faced about impatiently.

"Well, you needn't tell unless you like. I'm very sorry for you, that's all. Very sorry."

"Are you! are you sorry, young man? Give me your hand!" Coming forward with a certain wavering of the legs, the little green man brought his palm down with a smack into the outstretched hand of Woppits, which he then vigorously shook, smiling wan.

"My friend," said he, keeping Woppits's fingers in his grasp, "you're a man! I'll tell you all! You won't betray me!"

"I should think *not!*"

"Then," continued the other, rolling his eyes, and faintly hiccuping, "I've lost my crocodile!"

"Your crocodile!"

"Drunk hisself to death!" continued the little man, dropping Woppits's hand to brush away a tear. "Died last night at twenty minutes past nine of dolorous trimmings!"

"How could he get drunk?" asked Woppits, in doubt and indignation.

"Now, how do *you* get drunk? How do *I* get drunk? By sitting and drinking! He'd sit and drink at any house we put up at of a night till he went to bed. All the wet weather through he'd sit and drink. What do you call that?"

Now Woppits had read about several crocodiles in his time, but he had met with no previous instance of that animal's betraying any objection to wet weather, or of his boozing at an ale-house. In fact, such a proceeding was clearly contrary to the known habits of the creature; and Woppits could not believe the little green man. However, he mistrusted his argumentative powers, and instead of tackling the showman on physiological or other abstruse grounds, he resolved to floor him with figures.

"Now, how many feet long *was* your crocodile, mister?"

Mr. Biddles (who had exhumed the powder-flask meanwhile) struck an attitude.

"Three-and-twenty feet from the tip of his snout to the extremities of his tail! Hi! hi! hiei! His scales of such extensive hardness that a cannon-ball ——"

"Never mind his cannon-ball and scales—just stop a minute! Twenty feet long, you said, mind you! Now, how could he sit down in a public-house?"

"Ah, that was his measurement with his skin on! Hang it all! you wouldn't expect a poor fellow to take his pint with the skin on, would you?"

This the showman said with so serious an air, that Woppits could only look, as he felt, amazed.

"Oh, I see how it is," broke in the little man, briskly; "you never suspected it! Nobody did! That's what I say! I shall never get another like him! It's no use keeping the skin, that I see, for nobody else 'll ever work it like he did; and after him, a bungler I couldn't stand."

Woppits's vision became clearer; but to disperse all doubt, he begged to be allowed to see this skin."

First looking up and down the lane, and across and athwart the field, to be sure that no scoffing eye was upon him, Mr. Biddles went to the sepulchre, unlocked a door at the back, and carefully withdrew the skin of a crocodile, who never dreamed, as he lay in the warm ooze of the Nile, that his tough integument would come at last to such base uses. Mr. Biddles unrolled this monster's scaly rind as gingerly as a haberdasher, spreading it forth upon the ground. Then opening a flap in the side, he invited Woppits to look in.

"There you are, sir! All my own design and invention! You see those two stumps in the front legs? Well, he used to pull himself along with them. Those two strings, as you observe, are worked upon the principle of a boat's rudder; they lead right to the extremity, you see, and enable the hannimal to wag his tail at pleasure."

"Oh, I see! It was the man who worked this concern that you lost by the trimmings?"

"Precisely. That's it precisely."

"And don't you think any one could do it as well as him?"

"No," said Mr. Biddles, with decision; "I don't."

"Then I do."

"Youth's alway's presumptious," said Mr. Biddles, sententiously.

"Well, let's have a try, will you?"

"*And* ambitious. Oh, yes, you can try, and a pretty mess you'll make of it, I'll be bound. However, help me to take the skin into the field, and we'll see."

Selecting a smooth spot, the hide of the scaly monster was again opened out, and Woppits, with Mr. Biddles's assistance, inserted himself in it—Ruth looking on. half amused, half frightened. When she lost sight of her brother altogether, the alarm predominated.

"Now, mister, what next?" cried a voice that seemed to come from the bowels of the earth.

"Crawl up as far as you can, and lay hold of the two handles. Got 'em?"

"All right!"

"Got the two strings?"

"One in each hand."

"Off we go, then. All you've got to do is to walk slowly up and down, and when I talk of your tameness, wag your tail."

"All right!"

"Yar you hev' the femous errrockerdile of the Nail, jest arreved from the river Egypt on the Gangers, who whale in his natif woods thinks no more of capsisin' a man-of-war with one lash Of his tail, than he does of devourin' the captain and crew afterwards! Cannon balls do bounce off his scales which is harder than adamunk five feet four long is each of his tusks which is serrated like a handspike. But hei! hei! ladies and gentlemen walk up and Observe the power of kyindness. This furrowcious beast after defyin' his Majesty's navy and ridgments of the laine was won over by the surgeon of his Majesty's flag-ship *Blunderbore* who egstracted a splinter from his foot, after which he followed the vessel peacefully into Portsmouth harbour, and is now *as* tame [wag], *as* harmless [wag] as one of our own specie! Hei! hei!—Oh Lor!—hooray! hooray!" continued Mr. Biddles, embracing little Ruth, because he could not get at Woppits. "Little did I think I should live to see it done like that again! Lord forgive me for saying it, but he does it more nat'ral than you, Tom!"

"Well," said Woppits, thrusting his head out of the side of the crocodile of the Nile, "is it all over? Did I do it right?"

"Do it right? Oh don't ask," replied Biddles. "You and me, young man, could make our fortunes at it; and I only wish you had nothing better to do."

"What! than to make my fortune? More I haven't!"

"You don't mean to say you're willing to go in for it, do you?" asked the showman, his eyes glistening.

"Yes," replied Woppits, resolutely, and looking at Ruth. "If it'll pay, I'll be your crocodile."

"Good!" rejoined Mr. Biddles, who, now that it had come to business, took forth the powder flask and locked it up in the sepulchre. "And your little sister?" added he, rubbing his hands.

"Well, what of her?"

"Can't she dance, or something? I've got lots of properties in there (pointing to the caravan); had 'em ever since I cut the drama, you know. My eye! If she only could! The Flower of Barbary! Dancing-girl of the Harem! or something like that, eh? We might make a mint o' money among us."

"You get out, with your Flowers of Barbary!" returned Woppits, evidently offended. "She's got nothing to do with it. She's a little lady, and never done anything but go to school: no more she shall yet awhile, if I can earn enough. And if I can't do that with being a crocodile, why I'll—I'll try something else; that's all."

"Oh, well!" cried Biddles, hastily, and in a conciliatory tone, "I didn't know that; there's no harm done, I hope. As to earnin' enough to support yourself and her, you only do as you did just now, young man, and there won't be much fear of that."

"Was that *all* I should have to do?"

"That's all, sir," replied the showman.

"Then I think I can give you a wrinkle. What do you say to a performing crocodile?"

77

"Eh?" ejaculated Mr. Biddles, under his breath.

"Ah! Can you play anything—any moosical insterment?"

"The fiddle, I can."

"Then bring it out, and I'm blow'd if I don't dance to it. I don't mean to say that I could venter on a hornpipe; I mean one of them walking dances, you know."

"My eye!" said Mr. Biddles to himself admiringly, as he turned to get the fiddle, "a waltzing crocodile! There's attraction for you!"

"Or," cried Woppits, carried away for the moment, "if you'd like it better, I could sing a comic song."

Biddles turned about. "That would be coming it too strong," said he gravely. "Crocodiles never do that, you know!"

"Not accordin' to natur'?—well, on consideration, perhaps it ain't. But the dancin's all right. That'll only be showing that I've quite recovered from my splinter, you know, mister. Ah! bring it along," he continued, as the fiddle appeared. "Now I'll show you how a genteel crocodile does it on the banks of his native Gangers."

So saying, Woppits once more embowelled himself; Mr. Biddles struck up an old, slow, stately minuet, to which the crocodile sedately paced.

"A little quicker," sighed the crocodile, who seemed to like it.

The fiddler's elbow jogged at a merrier pace, and still the beast kept time, wagging his head, and flourishing his tail in triumph whenever the music gave him a favourable opportunity. He grew excited, that crocodile; the fiddler also, he grew excited; and so did little Ruth, who, clapping her hands, screamed with delight. The tail of the beast waxed eloquent in its flourishings; an imaginative person might even have seen his eyes roll, as with still lengthier and bolder strides he capered on the green. The fiddler fiddled faster; his feet began to move spasmodically; and at length, carried away, Mr. Biddles also danced. At this point the minuet was abandoned; so bold had Biddles grown that he struck up "Jack Robinson" without a moment's warning. The amphibious monster was equal to it. Ejaculating a yell of defiance that spoke more of the Liffey than of the Nile, the crocodile threw out his legs with renewed energy, floundering over the field rarely. Now laughter brought Mr. Biddles to his knees, in which position he fiddled on, brave as the good Sir Hugh Witherington, of "Chevy Chase," who, "when his legs were both cut off, he fought upon his stumps." How Richard Biddles shuffled about on his knees after the dancer! But such exertions could not last for ever. Soon the exhausted beast gave in, rolling over on to his back in token thereof.

Several minutes elapsed before a word was uttered from any side. Then Woppits's head, red as the rising sun, slowly emerged from the slit in the crocodile's hide.

"What—what did you think of that?" panted he.

"Think of it!" echoed the other. "Beautiful, sir! Splendid, sir! Only say that you'll go in with me, and I'll give you a couple of pound to clinch the bargain, and we'll go fair halves as long as you like to stop."

"That's a bargain!" said the crocodile, with decision. "Just hand me the preliminaries while you think of it, and when I've fetched my breath, I'll get out and talk to you."

With the air of a man who knows that he doing a good thing for himself, the showman brought forth two sovereigns, and dropped them into the jaws of the beast.

"Now, then, young feller," said Mr. Biddles, when he thought Woppits had had time enough to recover his breath, 'as soon as you like to come out, we'll go and have a nice bit of something for supper. How are you going to manage about the little girl?"

"Well, that's what I've been thinking about," answered Woppits, resuming the perpendicular attitude of a man and a brother. "I can't do better than take her home. Eh, Ruth?"

"It would be fun to see you dance like that every day," said she, doubtfully.

"She seems bent on it!" whispered the showman to Woppits. "Let her stay. She'll be uncommon handy—go round with the plate sometimes. Folks like pretty faces!"

"Do they? Well, go round with the plate yourself, then," replied Woppits, angrily. "Ruth isn't to be bargained for. I told you so five minutes ago. I shall take her home."

"Oh, very well; no offence. Of course you know your own know best. Where might she live, if I might be so bold as to ask?"

This question brought new reflections to Woppits's mind. Was it safe to take little Ruth to town?—would it be discreet in him to appear in Bulger's Gardens yet awhile? These questions he finally answered with a negative.

"H'm! well, I've changed my mind, mister, for to-day," said he to Mr. Biddles.

"Very good; and to-night, young man, you will share my humble cot—my bread, and cheese, and beer!"

"Thank'ee," Woppits returned; "I've no objection."

"Very good," replied Mr. Biddles.

CHAPTER XXIX.

CROSS PURPOSES.

A DEFEATED prize-fighter when the sponge is thrown up; a gamester when his last stake is swept from the table; a plucked student when he first meets his friends; a convicted thief meditating whether he shall not throw his boots at the judge; a fox trapped; a hound fresh beaten; chanticleer torn, draggled, and driven from his own dunghill and from the bosom of his family—Mr. Hatcher was all these as he emerged into Bulger's Gardens after his interview with Mrs. Bell. Certainly he was not himself. He acknowledged it. He said as much, when, pausing at Mrs. Bell's door, he looked up at the house and then at the Gardens generally, and took off his hat and stroked his head in the old manner—half cunning, half distraught, wholly humble and deprecatory. After which he put his hat on again, and strolled away, humming a tune. And not only so, but he carried his stick jauntily, and walked with a light *staccato* movement—*con moto*, if I may so express it; and when he came upon some little Bulgers playing their innocent games, he stopped and grinned at them—*effetuoso*. But the plucked student, the ruined gamester, the trapped fox, the beaten hound—were in his heart for all that, and now and then you could see their pictures on his countenance.

In this confused state of mind, which is as much like drunkenness as anything else, Hatcher quitted Bulger's Gardens. The brisk air blowing down the main road seemed to sober his faculties; but, as sometimes happens among his fellow-creatures, his sobriety was much more disagreeable than his intoxication. The maudlin *effetuoso* grin by which he expressed his approval of infancy and mud pies, was preferable, with all its discords, to the solemn and more genuine scowl that followed it. While he kept the fox and the hound in his heart quiet, crouching, he was a much pleasanter object to look at than when they began to peep from his eyes and lay his teeth bare; and I rather think he was aware of it. But the road was wide; there were few passengers to observe him. Moreover, there was the green called Kennington Common at no great distance; and as he grew soberer and darker, he hurried on that he might be all alone on the Common, to grin, and chatter, and cogitate as he pleased.

He succeeded very well, as far as the grinning and the chattering was concerned, but reflection was still far from his mind. Mr. Hatcher, like many men of his kind, was liable to panic. The very circumspection and suspicion with which all his business operations were surrounded, rendered him painfully sensitive of any sign or sound that betokened a reverse. Creeping so stealthily that no one ever heard him, the faintest echo of an adversary's footsteps sounded to him like thunder; working always in the dark, any sudden or unfriendly ray of light blinded him—at least for the time. He belonged to the tribe of rogues whose only exceeding craft oft-times reveals them in the midst of their plunder—with the assassin's knife in their hands, and the victim's money in their breeches pockets. So it is that heaven orders these things—there, where all is clear, for us here, who, with our Diogenes lanterns of philosophy, our bull's-eyes of modern discovery, go groping for ever under a cloud. So cunning is the hand of him that most cunningly makes weapons against his fellow-men, that one day it wakes while its master sleeps, and forges for *him* the surest weapon of all.

But we must not anticipate Mr. Hatcher's career, or judge

him by other men. We do not at all know yet what the end of his game may be, for at present it is only checked; seriously checked, though, and seriously endangered; and he bewildered and desperate accordingly. As long as little Ruth's existence and possible production was undemonstrated, he lived happy and hopeful in the enjoyment of his pension. But when he saw that she was alive, and that Woppits was also in the flesh—when he discovered that their story was well known to another party, she being a clear-headed woman who knew well how to use her knowledge—he quaked for his pension's sake, for his liberty, and for the old woman his mother. He thirsted to be rid of his anxiety, and cursed himself for having thrust his hand into the hive, as it were, worrying and exasperating the bees, who were quietly making what honey they could, without retrospect, and probably without a thought for to-morrow beyond the bread thereof.

It was such an aggravation, too, to have lost his money—the twenty pounds that Mrs. Bell toyed with so prettily. And then to be beaten by a woman! Bless her! Might she rise alive and hearty next morning, and might heaven be her portion ultimately! As Mr. Hatcher muttered a prayer of this description, he thrust his stick to the roots of a poor briar, and dug it up, and kicked it before him on the common.

But we shall not follow Mr. Hatcher through all the various moods that possessed him that day. Enough that towards the end of it, he stroked his head less frequently, which was a sign that he had recovered his self-possession somewhat; and kneaded his chin more, which was a sign that the fox was busy in the trap; wriggling and gnawing himself out, with a more determined eye than ever to young ducks. His opinion was, as he cogitated at his lodgings in Lant Street, that now he had re-opened the business so far as Woppits and Ruth were concerned—now that they had taken alarm, and might have recourse to heaven only knew what proceedings—he had better not go home to Old Sleaford; but rather keep an eye on Bulger's Gardens, if that were possible, and regulate his conduct by the result of what he might observe there.

"By-the-bye," said he, "I wonder what they know of Woppits at the place mentioned by the man that took his basket home—where the young gentleman lodged. Let me see! Lappers? No! Pallers? Yappers? Yelpers? Yallops!—that's the name! Now, where does Yallops live, and what sort of a man is Yallops? That's worth inquirin' into!" added Mr. Hatcher, wagging his head, and placing his hat on it. Whereupon he sallied into the street—Broadway, Southwark, as it is now called.

His first endeavour was to find the street in which he had encountered Woppits on the previous evening. This, however, was a more difficult matter than he had calculated on. In the first place, he did not know the name of the street; and again, the neighbourhood in which he found himself was so ill-lighted; the ill-paved thoroughfares were so much alike, in their dirt, their darkness, their poverty, and their general blackguardism, that, after an exploration of two hours he found himself at his starting-point, exhausted and unsuccessful.

But Mr. Hatcher was not easily turned off the scent. Next morning he wrote a letter to his mother, informing her that there was a "screw loose in the K. business;" that he might be detained in town for some days, and that if any inquiry were made about him, she was to reply that he had gone to town to arrange some affairs, and that was all she knew about it.

When evening arrived, Mr. Hatcher set out in search of Yallops, in a more determined and prepared manner. He had got himself up in an official style for his visit to Bulger's Gardens—coat buttoned up to the throat, a tall black frock, and no shirt-collar; for everybody knows that a display of linen is considered incompatible with official dignity. Now Hatcher was aware that this pad-and-button style of attire would scarcely recommend him to the class of people amongst whom his inquiries were to be prosecuted—especially considering the nature of those inquiries. And, luckily, he had brought with him, for visiting his uncle the sheriff's officer, a large, honest, open-hearted, or open-breasted blue coat, of the true old English school; and it had brass buttons. Then there was his shirt, with the magnificent frilled front. What could be better? The landlady at Lant Street quite admired Mr. Hatcher, as, throwing his hat to the back of his head, walking rather wide, and

with his hands clasped behind his back, he sallied out in the dusk. This time he was more successful. He soon discovered the street in which he had discovered Woppits and his little white basket. There was the very lamp-post against which he had leaned; nay, there were the fragments of Woppits's salt-cellar, glistening in the kennel. He stopped, and seemed to take a strange pleasure in poking the bits of glass about with his stick, turning them over and over, and regarding them with vague but not unspeculative eyes.

Two young men—decent mechanics, so far as their habiliments and deportment went—but with something indescribable about their heads which denoted a different order of industrials, sauntered on the opposite side of the street.

"There's a mark!" exclaimed one to the other, looking towards the spot where Hatcher was standing.

"Where, Pip? What, him against the lamp? He ain't much. Look at his tile!"

"Ah! but his fluted dickey, my friend! Those articles generally travels in company of a gold snuff-box. Wait half a minute and I'll give you a pinch out of it."

"Ole 'ard!" replied the Pippin's companion, as that young gentleman turned to inspect a bunch of handkerchiefs hanging against a door-post, so giving his companion an opportunity of walking off without observation—"Ole 'ard! I know him! He's the feller that was asking so affectionately after Woppits the urrer night!"

"Sure?"

"Could swear to his mug afore a ole jury!"

"H'm! That's curious! I should like to make his acquaintance. You leave him to me. All square you know! What I earns off him we divide."

"Right," answered the other, and went his way.

Such an honest-looking, good-tempered face it was that looked into Mr. Hatcher's a moment after, and in such a cheery tone did the Pippin address him! "Have you lost anythink, sir?" said he.

"Y-yes, my man! I accidentally dropped a shillin'. But lor, it ain't of much consequence—a shillin', you know!"

"Poor innocent!" said the Pippin to himself. But he observed aloud, rubbing his hands, shrugging his shoulders, and looking into Hatcher's face with that frank, sad, but cheerfully resigned smile which is commonly considered to be peculiar to organ-grinders—

"Ain't it of no consequence! Well, not to such a gentleman as you, sir, p'raps; but to a poor young man wot's got no father nor mother!—You wouldn't give me half of it if I was to find it, would you, kind gentleman?"

"My good young man," returned Mr. Hatcher, tapping the Pippin's shoulder with his stick, "No! I'm a poor man's friend!—I've a heart in my bosom!"

"Oh poor gentleman! Don't it hurt you, sir?" wickedly interrupted the Pippin.

Hatcher looked keenly, and yet confusedly at the other; he was not sure whether the young man had misunderstood or was making game of him. Innocence! There never was such simplicity as was exhibited in the Pippin's countenance. Re-assured—

"You mistake me, friend!" continued Mr. Hatcher. "I say I'm a friend to the poor; I say I've a heart in my bosom. You know what a heart is, young man, don't you?"

"Oh yes, sir. I know what you mean now. It's something innards, and it feels for another!"

"Exactly. Now, I feel for another; specially for the working man. And what I ses, having studied the working man, is, that he oughtn't to find anything; that he ought to earn hard every shillin' he gets; otherways he gets into extravagand habits, and instead of looking after his lawful occupation, goes moonin' about the streets for gentlemen as may happen to drop shillin's!"

"Dear me, I never see it in that light afore, sir! Please, ain't you a parlyment man?"

"Not at present, my friend; not at present!"

"Beg your pardin, thought you must be from your amiable sentiments."

"No! But what I was goin' to observe was, that on principle—on principle, mind——."

"Oh, sir; you *are* a parlyment man, now! That's what they allus say!" The Pippin gave a little deprecatory wriggle, and smiled still more like a child of nature.

"Whatever I may be, young man," said Mr. Hatcher gravely (he did not like these interruptions—they kept him from the point) it is not your duty to ask questions about it!"

"Oh no, sir; I know that!" (How abashed the Pippin was!)

"Very well, then. To conclude what I was saying of, I object to your finding my shillin' and having half of it. But if you're a trustworthy young man, willin' to make yourself generally useful, and don't mind earnin' one, I've too much heart in my bosom not to say, Come to me, come to me, young man!"

Here Mr. Hatcher blew his nose, spreading his handkerchief abroad, so that his face underwent a total eclipse. The Pippin seemed to take an observation of this phenomenon, placing his thumb to his nose, closing one eye, and gazing intently along his fingers with the other. He had scarcely concluded, when Hatcher's benevolent countenance re-appeared again, to cheer and bless the world; especially the Pippin, who was in a glow of hope and gratitude.

Earn a shilling! The Pippin had a tremor of joy at the thought! Look at his hands, kind gentleman! They showed how long he had been wandering about without work, and without a mossle of bread! What was the job? Where was it? Only show it him! And the poor fellow eagerly tucked his wristbands up; his cuffs, I mean.

What a spectacle for the gods were these two rogues! And how completely one rogue was "taken in" by the other, though Mr. Hatcher had more than one suspicion that the young man was playing off a little scheme too. However, that could only be to gain a few shillings from a simple-hearted member of parliament, and did not at all interfere with that honourable gentleman's design. On the contrary, it proved the other party's fitness for carrying it out.

"Aha!" said the benevolent one, with a faint smile of superiority, "you don't know the person you've got to deal with! You want to see the job, do you? You think it's diggin', perhaps; or carryin' a parcel; or weedin' my garden; or cleanin' my plate. No such thing, young man. This is but the labour of man's hands. You would dig, for to dig you're not ashamed. You would carry my parcel; p'r'aps a light porter is your native business. You would weed my garding, and you wouldn't pick the flowers. You would clean my plate, and you would not steal a single spoon—"

"Oh no, sir, that I wouldn't!"

"—Because I should keep my butler's heye on you! No. I would employ you in a situation of trust, where I couldn't lose anything, and you might!"

"You're a downy card, sir!" interjected the Pippin, meaningly; "you're up to snuff, you are, if ever a gentleman was."

"I *am* a downy card, my friend," replied Mr. Hatcher; "and I'm up to snuff likewise, as you observe." He was pleased with himself, and sniggered accordingly.

"Well, I'm ready sir; what is it to be?"

"H'm! let me see!" Hatcher paused, fumbled his chin, and glanced seriously at the Pippin, who looked another way, somewhat in the manner of suspected innocence. "Yes," continued the other buoyantly, "that will do. Look here, my young friend, I *am* a parlyment man! And being the poor man's friend, I am engaged in inquiry into his condition; how he lives, and how he lodges, and that; espeshly those poor men as sell things in the streets."

"Oh!"

"Now, first, can you direct me to any place where they do lodge? I've heard of Robinson's, and Walker's, and Ya_pers's, for instance, in these parts."

"There's Yallop's, i—!" insinuated the Pippin, with a twinkle in his eyes, as if five-an'-twenty packets of drill d-eyed needles were sparkling in them.

"Ah! H'm! Yallop's. Do you know the vulgar place, young man?" As for Mr. Hatcher's fish-like eyes, they looked as if they had been kept too long, and shone phosphorescently, out of the dark of his shaggy brows.

"Know it? I lodge there myself, when I'm at home!"

"Do you indeed? Where is it?"

"Kent Street—just here. No. 362. Name of Whiffen over the shop. White lamp with red letters."

"You are right, young man!" said Hatcher, who could not fail to recognise the tone of truth, though he was sometimes deceived by clever imitations, like the rest of us. So fur you've not been found wanting. Bless you, I knew all about it! All about it!"

How spitefully the needles sparkled!

"Now the situation of trust that I spoke of. Be equal to it, and—but I say no more; only, remember, I'm your friend if you do, or you go your ways, and you're none the better and I'm none the worse. Do you know Bulger's Gardens?"

"Kennington Common; this side."

"Right again. Well, do you know the landlord of Bulger's Gardens?"

"No, sir; but I used to be a 'quaintance of a young party as lives there!"

"Not a young woman, I hope!" said Mr. Hatcher, severely.

"Oh dear no, sir; it was a young man. His name was Woppits!" And the Pippin shook his head—of all things the safest to do. It meant "Ah, that *was* a young man!" but it went no further. It did not imply that the party in question was very good or very bad. You took your choice of meanings, according as inclination led you. Mr. Hatcher took his choice, and of course it betrayed him.

"Dear me!" said he, with great concern, "I'm very sorry to hear that! You are acquainted with that person, are you? Oh dear! oh dear! I hope I'm not deceived in you, my young friend!"

"Oh no, sir; I don't speak to the party now. I soon see through him; and I says to him—that's three year ago come Easter Monday—'Woppits,' I says, 'I wasn't aweer as you was the character I finds you. You're deceitful,' I says; 'and you've a many wicked ways about you, which no proper conducted young man oughter countingance. So, Woppits,' I says, 'if it's all the same to you, I'd rayther not be seen along of you any more. Why don't you go down to the river like I do!' I says—them was my very words—'and do a honest day's work, which sweet is the bread thereof?' And so it is, ain't it, sir?"

"There's no sweeter, my friend—no sweeter."

"I knows it!" said the Pippin, moodily, and sadly, and angrily too. "Thunderin' well I knows it."

"Don't! Don't be severe on him! Then you don't keep company with this—a—Woppits—now?"

"Keep company with him now, did you say, sir? Oh dear, no! He's too wicked! You've got no idea how wicked he is, sir; you can't have, a genelman like you!"

"Oh yes, I can, my man! For, do you know, I'm pooty intimate with his history, being related, on his mother's side, to a friend of mine. Broke that mother's heart, brought his father's gray hairs with sorrer to the grave, driv' his aunt Matilda into the workus with three small children—one an infant in arms—and then ran away with his little sister."

"'Ow werry shockin'!" exclaimed the Pippin, solemnly, shaking his head.

"And him such a lad! Lor, when *I* was a *lad!*— Well, well, it is no business of mine; but, seeing I'm a friend of my species—I *can't* help it! I'm anxious about that little child. It would be good to pluck her brand from the burning!"

"And leave his'n where it is," remarked the other demurely. "Serve him right!"

"Oh, don't say that, my young friend—not quite that. Bad he may be, wicked he may be, 'bandoned he may be; which we've very good reason for s'posing he is. But I would be his friend, and do him good. At the same time, young man, I would rather be his sister's friend, and do her good. I s'pose you know her; have you seen her lately?"

"No, I ain't, sir. Have you?" asked the Pippin, rather painedly.

"Not for years," responded Mr. Hatcher, brushing his hand across his eyes. "Ah, if that child were mine, I should adore it. I should restore it to the bosom of its friends; we would bring her up to our own ways of thinking; and I would leave her two hundred and fifty pounds a-year. Come in here, young man; come in here!"

THE EFFECT OF MR. TWEAKLE'S COMMUNICATION.

The two rogues had been walking slowly along during the major part of this conversation, and had now arrived opposite the door of a coffee-house in the main road. The Pippin had no objection to a rasher, as, indeed, he remarked; and in they went. Mr. Hatcher threw himself upon a seat, resting his face upon his hands dejectedly. The Pippin, having ordered ham and eggs, sat upon an opposite bench, gazing at Mr. Hatcher across the table in a sympathetic and thoughtful manner.

"Oh dear!" he remarked, after a little while, "how affectin' all this here is!"

"Ah!" responded Mr. Hatcher, raising his head, and smiling a wan smile, "you see the effect of having a heart in your bosom, my young friend. I raly thought I should have burst into tears in the street, and that's why I came in here. Poor child!"

"Can I do anything, mister?" said the Pippin, who saw that the other was beating about the bush now, as much for the pleasure of the thing as for any reason he might have. "You was talkin' of my earnin' a shillin', and sitivations of trust. I'm willin'."

"Oh, you could—but then, again, what is it to me? Well, I might as well know what that bad young man is up to, and his little sister, how she is, and that; and do you know, I've reason to believe they're actually hiding somewhere! Actually hiding."

"You don't say so, sir?" replied the Pippin, with an odd look. "I wonder what that can be for."

"Don't inquire into that, my friend—pray don't; it would only give you pain. But perhaps you could discover his where-abouts, and what's become of that orphin child; upon receipt of which information, I would hasten to 'em; I would reclaim 'em; and I would give you 'arf a crown!"

"But s'posin' I was to find the party, and not the other?"

"'Arf a crown for the information."

"And s'posin' I was to find the youngster, and not the party."

"Take her!" cried Mr. Hatcher, rather too eagerly. "Take her, clap her into a hackney-coach, that no eye may see the good act, bring her to me, and I'll give you a pound!"

"Well, it cert'n'y mightn't be much trouble!" said the Pippin, on consideration.

"The risk is nothing, and the action good," chimed in Mr. Hatcher.

"I think I'll do it, sir—I think I'll be on to it at once!"

"As you please, young man. When shall I see you again?"

"S'pose we say ten to-night, at my lodgin' at Mr. Yallops's, sir. And please, kind gentleman, couldn't you drop a shillin' on account?"

"It's ag'in my principle," returned Mr. Hatcher, in his par-liamentary manner, "but I'll sacrifice my principle for once, my young friend—it may encourage you. There's the shillin'. Now, ten o'clock at Mr. Yallops's. Good-bye."

And the interview terminated.

Mr. Hatcher was so funny that evening—so peculiar—that he put his landlady all of a twitter. He invited himself into her room; and stood lobsters and brandy and water. He told stories (chiefly in the brokering line), and volunteered to sing a song, if she'd sing another, which condition was accepted. What strains were those is not known now to any breeze of my acquaintance; but Mr. Hatcher's song was a comic one, about undertakers; and Hatcher was so successful in it, that it gave the widow quite a turn to look at him. Her song was sentimental, and affected Mr. Hatcher to tears. It was then, I believe, that he confided the story of his first love.

CHAPTER XXX.

A RIFT IN THE CLOUD.

"Now, Pip," said that person to himself, when he had got fairly into the street, "there's summut wrong here! That nice old genelman in the frills is a do: Pip, he must be done! He's up to mischief about Woppits and that young 'un, which, I can plainly see, is a sort of Little Red Ridinghood; and I'm to pull the bobbin, and the latch'll fly up, and Frills is the wolf as'll go in and eat her up as innercent as my gran'mother. Here it is!" he continued, taking Mr. Hatcher's shilling from his pocket, and gazing on it—"the blood-money; for sich it is, I'm blessed if it ain't! Well," said he, turning the coin over in the palm of his hand, as if it were an entomological specimen, or something of that sort, "I've touched warious moneys, got it in warious ways; but I never handled one of this kind afore! Root of all evil? I knowed a 'arf-a-crown that was werry nigh bein' the root of all good; but this! what a pooty plant it would grow, to be sure, if it had been set in a different sile to mine! Fancy I see that plant! Fancy I see its fruits: young Ruth devoured by the wolf, old Woppits a-goin' about cranky looking arter her, Mrs. Bell frettin' herself to a shadder about the pair on 'em, the undertaker takin' her medjur, and me a bloated aristocrat on one pun' one! Not that I've knowed much about Woppits and them lately, or seen 'em either; but that ain't their fault, it's mine. Why shouldn't they keep clear of a kid like me, that could only bring 'em in disgrace, and perhaps the Noses about 'em whenever I was wanted? Besides, I'm ashamed to look 'em in the face, more'n they are me; and I keep out of their way more'n they do mine, arter all. So, Woppits, I'm not angry with you, and maybe I'll do you a good turn afore the night's out."

Accordingly, as soon as the great world of London had got its candles fairly alight, he appeared in Bulger's Gardens. Another person might have been seen wandering about near the Gardens. It was not Mr. Hatcher, but a friend of the Pippin's, furnished with a very accurate description of Mr. Hatcher, and warned to give an alarm if that gentleman approached. For of course the Pippin was not sure of Mr. Hatcher's manœuvres generally, and was wary of him. If the reader has any curiosity as to who the watcher was, I can relieve him. He had no less a nose than that of Yallops's money-taker, lent for the occasion by Yallops himself; to whom Pippin had confided his adventure, and who had such confidence in the integrity of Mrs. Bell, and of anybody whom she might love, that only for the necessity of carrying on his business in person he would have sallied out himself; and then, as he observed, the wolf might have "napped it," had he been found prowling in the neighbourhood.

For the same reason that induced the Pippin to set a watch, he carefully reconnoitred Mrs. Bell's apartments from the exterior before he approached the door. He congratulated himself on his foresight. There was a light in Mrs. Bell's sitting-room; the blind was down, and there was a portentous shadow on it. A male shadow; a bulky shadow; a shadow with a bald head.

Now, who was this? What did the shadow mean?

The Pippin cogitated. He was alarmed, but he was also courageous and expert. He was at the door, and within the door, and had his eye at Mrs. Bell's keyhole in about the time I take in mentioning it. How he accomplished this little feat is his secret; and also how he came out again a moment afterwards, with the same expedition and the same stealth.

He had overheard a conversation between a man unknown and Mrs. Bell, or so much of it as embraced the words "jail," and "law." And he had seen displayed upon the table a constable's staff. This was enough for the Pippin. He returned into the street, or rather into the Gardens, bade William go back to his avocation, and mounted guard himself.

To give every man his due, the shadow belonged to Mr. Tweakle; and his appearance is thus accounted for. Woppits had, of course, apprised Mrs. Bell of all his history—all that he knew of it; and Mr. Tweakle had as fair and as clear an image in her heart as in his. If I were to enumerate any hour since Woppits's memorable illness in which she had longed to see and to speak to that beadle, I should have to multiply every day by two, and every night by ten; and when I had found the total, I should also find the number of times she had dreaded to meet him, with a terrible dread. All things undefined are dreadful; and there are uncertainties of which no solution can bring comfort. Let them be. There's some comfort in *them*, depend on it.

But when Woppits was in danger, and little Ruth—when they were driven from her home, and it was no more home—when the old desolation stared at her from their chairs, and lay in their beds, looking in *that* wide ghostly way, consuming her breath before it entered her lips—what else was to be done? What but to write to Mr. Tweakle, and beg him to come to town at once, if he was still Woppits's friend.

The letter found the good man at his post as a public officer. He had seen the downfall of the Gorelam administration; he served in the memorable crisis which followed (when Gorelam made that famous remark of his, about "How was the king's government to be carried on?"); he held office under the Tike *régime*, and is believed to have taken an active part—though this is not generally known—in the restoration of the Gorelam party to power. But though, as a beadle, Mr. Tweakle was unaltered, his relations to society were changed as a man. A tall headstone in Latherwell churchyard bore the name of Mrs. Tweakle, and the beadle was a widower. Considering the number of graces and virtues recorded on the headstone, Mr. Tweakle bore his loss with wonderful fortitude; but perhaps the good man was not so able a judge of character as the stone-cutter; and those who are immediately acquainted with the sun say there are spots on *it*.

Obtaining leave of absence, Mr. Tweakle lost no time in presenting himself in Bulger's Gardens. How shall I describe his emotion when Mrs. Bell recounted Woppits's haps and mishaps since his residence in London—dwelt upon his self-denial, his perseverance, his courage, his love, in the matter of little Ruth! How shall I depict the rueful face of Mr. Tweakle, when Mrs. Bell described Woppits ill and like to die, his slow recovery, and his creeping about by help of a stick!—his dismayed and perplexed countenance when she came to Woppits's sudden flight, and told about the mysterious stranger who had scared him away, and how she in turn had scared the stranger!

"Why, then, ma'am," Tweakle observed, as Mrs. Bell brought her story to a conclusion, "he soon got over that voyage to Chaney! How did he get on there, ma'am?"

"*I* never heard of his going to China; indeed, I'm sure he never set foot in a boat."

"But he *did* go, ma'am," replied Tweakle, positively; "at least, he shipped for those parts, for the mate of the vessel he sailed in—the *Black Bull* it was, ma'am, to the best of my belief—came to me in Pump Street, and told me all about it."

"What sort of a man was he who came to tell you all about it?" asked Woppits's housekeeper, after a little consideration.

"Well, ma'am, he was a rum-looking man, rather. He had a large chin, and——"

"And blinking, deep-set eyes?"

"Blinky eyes, ma'am, and scanty red whiskers. You don't know him, do you?"

"He was here yesterday morning! It's the man I have told you of!" cried Mrs. Bell, in considerable excitement. "He and the man who gave Woppits the money at the country inn are one and the same person!"

"Dear me, I shouldn't wonder!" responded Tweakle, gazing in mingled awe and respect at the woman who displayed so much sagacity. "Perhaps you have an idea as to what he wants, ma'am?"

"To get possession of little Ruth."

"Did it never strike you, ma'am," replied the other, anxious to prove that, as an off'cer, he was sagacious too, "that it might be Woppits this fellow's after? We ain't at all clear about his parents, you know, ma'am."

Mrs. Bell's lips quivered. She plucked at the table-cover nervously, as she made some faint, wandering observation about Mr. Tweakle's having known Woppits when he was very young.

"Ah," responded he, "you are right, ma'am. If I was a superstitious sort of man, I should almost go so far as to say mine was the first eyes that ever beheld him. There I goes a gatherin' nettles for Jemmy Blake's little 'un, that were werry ill, to make tea of. There I goes, ma'am, down about a pool near our place, as innocent as may be, when all of a sudden I kicks a infant out of a heap o' leaves and grass; and there it was, the little dear! a-looking up at me, ma'am, and a-smiling in such a way as you ain't no notion of!"

Mrs. Bell, whose face was covered with her hands, groaned audibly.

"Ah, well you may weep, ma'am, and well you may take on! I said to myself at the time, 'Who's had the heart to do this?' I says; 'he's worse than the brutes!' I says; and if I hadn't felt savage myself, I should have begun to think there was no more human natur' in the world! Never mind, ma'am, don't you cry!" for Mrs. Bell was rocking backwards and forwards in dreadful distress. "He's all right enough now, or he soon will be; and as for them as 'bandoned him to the loaves and fishes, Providence has had it out of 'em before this time, I'll be bound. If not, I advises 'em to look out!"

"Heaven forgive them! Heaven forgive us all!" sobbed the woman, a word at a time.

"That's all right, of course. I don't go ag'in that, ma'am; it wouldn't befit a person in my situation so to do; and I see werry little mercy about, myself, except what does come from heaven. At the same time, I've got a nice little bit o' hevidence ag'in the parties at home, which it may be my dooty to bring forward one of these days, and I shall do my dooty. It's a shawl, ma'am! Red and white, and a long fringe hanging to it. Ah, many's the shine I've had about that shawl with the late departed! But I was firm, ma'am! I was firm! And I allers said, 'Henrietta!'—Why, bless my soul, Mrs. Bell!"

Mrs. Bell fell forward on her knees, threw up her hands, clasped them passionately together, and sank insensible. It was as if she had clapped her hands as a signal for her own execution, and fell—shot through the heart.

Tweakle's experiences with Henrietta had rendered him rather familiar than otherwise with such occurrences, so that he did not betray nearly so much alarm (nor sympathy, I am afraid) as might have been expected of him. He took the poor woman's hands within his own, chafed them, and patiently waited till she should "come to."

She did not "come to" for so long a time, that her spirit, her life, must have made a wide excursion, embracing who knows how many places, how many scenes, how many years! Her insensible body, lying there a-heap, with her head resting on a chair, and her hair flowing over it, it reminds me—I don't know why,—of the mantle that Elijah cast off when he entered the heavenly chariot. For though her spirit departed also in a chariot of fire—in a fiery passion of remorse and grief—it has not gone to heaven; on the contrary, it rather fled from heaven, in awe of it, in dread-full love and gratitude to it, as it pointed through humble beadledom her guilt, and to the rod that healed while it chastised. Oh! to know for certain that all she had inferred was true!—that she had not been wrapping herself so long in a false and stolen comfort, but that it was her's; that it had been prepared for her, perhaps, by that mighty, tender Hand, which would kill this whole calf of a world in rejoicing over a repentant son, rather than turn him from his gates.

But I wonder where the fiery chariot did carry this poor soul, while its torn trappings lay a-heap by the chair! Perhaps, touched by Mr. Tweakle's story, it got into that shawl—red and white, with the long fringe—and went and sat down by the pool that the beadle talked of, and wrapped a baby in it; and—but this is the merest speculation.

"Come! come," whispered Mr. Tweakle, as the woman sighed a great sigh, and opened her eyes to let her tears flow (if those drops upon her face were not so many splashes from the pond), "why didn't you tell me it was too much for you, ma'am? You shouldn't take on like that, you know! It shows your good

heart, to be sure; but that's all it's good for, that I'm aware on. Cheer up, ma'am! As I said before you went off, our young friend's none the wuss at this present speaking, so far as we know, and as for his unnateral parents ——"

"Don't! don't!" cried she, holding up her hands again, as if the firing party had levelled their muskets for another volley; "pray, no more. The punishment is over, I think, and I'm dying!"

So saying, she gathered up that worn body of hers, which hardly stood upright, however, as yet, and tottered out of the room.

"Poor thing!" ejaculated Mr. Tweakle, "faintin' does severely punish a person, I dare say. I'd sooner be knocked down with a wonner in my stomach, myself. But as for dyin'! My Henrietta allus said the same; but," added he, reflectively, "I generally remarked that Henrietta used to come up a good deal stronger for it, afterwards."

So Mr. Tweakle, unsuspicious man! again put himself in the exercise of patience; in which, despite his bulk, he had a fine opportunity of becoming a perfect gymnast and Bounding Brother, that evening; for minute after minute passed, and still Mrs. Bell did not re-appear; minute after minute, in which Mr. Tweakle exhibited increasing agility, shifting in his chair from time to time with extraordinary levity. At length, near an hour had elapsed since Mrs. Bell left the room (how that watch popped in and out of his fob!), and he could bear it no longer. He exhausted himself in a bound from his chair—wiping the hot blood from his forehead, as it seemed, when it occurred to him that Mrs. Bell's observation about dying might refer to an intention of hanging herself! Henrietta had threatened him with such a catastrophe several times; and on one occasion had permitted herself to be found suspended behind a door in her bonnet strings, just as she was about to give the fatal leap from a teacaddy. What if Mrs. Bell had made a felo de se of herself, and was now only waiting to be cut down? The idea was insupportable!

To nerve himself, Mr. Tweakle buttoned his coat to the top button, loosed a bundle that had accompanied him to London, and took thence his cocked hat, provided for possible emergencies of an official nature, clapped it on his head, and stole fearfully out of the room.

When he got outside the door, he found the door of an adjoining room partly open. It was dark within—or would have been dark but for the moon, which shone full into the apartment.

It taxed Mr. Tweakle's ingenuity to insert his head and the hat on it in the little space that offered itself between the door and the doorpost; but by a dexterous though painful twist of his neck he accomplished it, rather than move the door, against which he half expected to find Mrs. Bell hanging. It required even more of Mr. Tweakle's small stock of ingenuity to prospect round the corner, when he had got his head in, so as to assure himself whether Mrs. Bell was hanging there or not; indeed, there was a certain obliquity in his vision in his latter days, which I can only account for by the shifts he put it to on this occasion. However, he accomplished this feat also, and was rewarded by the discovery that only Mrs. Bell's bonnet strings, and not her body, were suspended behind the door. This emboldened Mr. Tweakle. Arranging his hat, which bristled on one side of his head in indignation at being worked into the room in so unofficial a manner, he stepped warily in, and looked about him.

In another moment the hat was off, and Mr. Tweakle, under his breath, said "Amen!" There was Mrs. Bell, on her knees by the bedside, her hands clasped over her head, her face upon the pillow, and resting piously. She was undisturbed by the beadle's entrance; he would not disturb her. She had been weeping, sobbing—he could tell that, for the prayer, or the thanksgiving, or whatever it was that she ejaculated in that earnest whisper, was broken into fifty pieces as it passed her lips. Why should I think of broken bread, as I record this?—of the bread that was broken and wonderfully multiplied on the mountain? Unless it be that her prayer, or her thanksgiving, was multiplied and magnified too, satisfying the multitude of angels.

Mr. Tweakle took himself out of the room. He took himself out of the room in a way that was odd to behold; it had so much of the ridiculous and of the pious in it. Gaining the door of the outer room, he skipped over it like a lamplighter, or rather like the stout and elderly Miss O'Bese, when she wishes to warn her lover that she's only a giddy thing, after all. Plumping into his chair, the beadle threw off his hat, threw out his heels, and clinked them together in the satisfaction of his spirit.

"What a religious party that is!" said he to himself, more than half aloud. "What a soft-hearted party! What a mother she would make to be sure!"

(Mrs. Bell stood in the doorway as he said this; she had walked in as unperceived by Mr. Tweakle as his own intrusion had been invisible to her. But there was not a shadow the more upon her countenance when she heard this opinion passed upon no other person than herself! She who— Ah! that red-blue shawl with the long fringe hanging to it!)

"Henrietta," said Mr. Tweakle, snapping his heels together with increased vehemence, "be you a sperrit in heaven, or whatever you may be—I was fond of you, and so I ain't ashamed of myself, though you often said I ought to be. But if you had been a party like this 'un—why——!" Mr. Tweakle rose from his chair to emphasize his sentiments on that head, when he beheld Mrs. Bell. She advanced towards him with a pale face, indeed, but with a lovely light beaming in her eyes—melancholy, but calm, clear, serene as the moonlight in which they had lately rested.

"Good evenin', ma'am!" said Mr. Tweakle, blushing to the roots of his hair (and his blushes had to flow over a wide surface before they reached those roots). "I hope I see you well, ma'am —well again. I—a—a was just remarking to myself as you came in—a—. You didn't hear anything, ma'am, did you?"

"Hear what?" she answered, quite cheerfully.

"Any allusion about a lamented party?"

"Oh, we'll have no more lamentation to-night! Don't you think me a very silly woman, Mr. Tweakle?"

"Do you ask me, ma'am, as an orficer, or as a man? As a orficer, I say you ought to control your feelin's—your dooty bound to control your feelin's. As a man, ma'am," continued Mr. Tweakle, getting very red again, and shuffling to the edge of his chair, "I says as a man, I says—the—my lamented Henrietta—she——"

Here Mr. Tweakle's voice meandered off into the distance; and, judging from his distraught appearance, Mr. Tweakle had already begun to meander after it; when, a sudden idea striking him, he darted up his wristband, and engaged with an ardour amounting almost to vehemence in the capture of a purely imaginary flea.

"Yes?" remarked Mrs. Bell, interrogatively, and smiling.

"I was going to—— You haven't got such a thing as a pipe of tobacco about, have you, ma'am?"

"You shall have some in one moment. I'll fetch it for you myself."

And before Mr. Tweakle had time to expostulate, she was gone.

As soon as Tweakle was alone, he rose from his chair, breathing very hard, and gazed about him in a half-pleased, half-scared manner, like a bad boy at the moment when he drops into a forbidden orchard. To carry out the resemblance, he stooped down, placed his hands on his thighs, and, sliding up to the window stealthily, listened. The outer door closed with a bang, on which the beadle started upright, as if he had been straightened by the blow, winked one eye at the other, and muttered— "Tweakle, she *is* gone for your 'bacca!"

What there was in that to alarm Mr. Tweakle is not clear, on the face of it, but it must have struck him as an extraordinary proceeding, for he turned quite pale, and fell to unbuttoning his waistcoat. Then he buttoned himself up again, put on his hat, and was about to quit the house apparently, when the rattle of a key in the outer door threw him into a hot perspiration, and he bounced into his chair, trying to look undisturbed.

It was not Mrs. Bell who entered. She was delayed by the Pippin; who, approaching her unperceived, touched her arm and whispered—

"Can I do anything for you, mum?"

"Why do you ask?" replied she, looking at him keenly. She had forgotten him.

"I thought Woppits might be in trouble!"

"Do you know that he is?"

"I pooty well guess, mum."

"Do you know *where* he is?"

"Oh, then they raally have sloped it! I say, who's that pleeceman cove up at your place? He ain't arter him, is he? I'm the one as used to be called Pippin, you know."

Mrs. Bell had now no difficulty in explaining that there was no policeman at her place, but only a friend of Woppits.

"A *reg'lar* friend?"

"The best he's got in this world."

"Show him to me, mum! Let me have a talk to him! I think I can put him up to another sort of friend!"

And without waiting for a reply, the Pippin hurried before her to the house.

CHAPTER XXXI.

DIGNITY AND IMPUDENCE.

MR. TWEAKLE was thrown into another hot perspiration as he heard Mrs. Bell ascending the stairs; and he heard her so distinctly that the Pippin's footsteps went for nothing. However, he seemed greatly relieved, as well as surprised, when he saw a third party standing in the doorway as Mrs. Bell entered. The third party tripped off his hat, pulled up his shirt-collar, and took the seat nearest the door, as the ragged man does who attends your church.

"This young man," said Mrs. Bell, addressing Tweakle, "Mr. ——"

"Wigget!" ejaculated the Pippin, with a glance at the constable's staff, which still lay on the table.

"Mr. Wigget—has something to say to you about our friend. This gentleman's name is Tweakle," she added, turning to the Pippin.

"Tweak, is it? Heard on you afore, Mr. Tweak."

"Dessay you have; which if so be you have, young man, you ought to know better; you ought to know that familiarities breed contempt!"

Mrs. Bell interposed. "Mr. Wigget," said she, "you're mistaken the name; it's Tweakle, not Tweak."

"I beg the genelman's pardon, 'm sure! 'Ow are yer, sir?"

"Granted to *you*, sir," rejoined Tweakle, with majestic condescension. "And how are you?"

"Toll-loll!" said the Pippin.

"Oh!" said the beadle. "Anything catching?"

"Wot d'yer mean?" asked the Pippin, sharply. He was used to double meanings, was the Pippin, and their several professions made him rather suspicious of the company into which he had fallen.

Tweakle turned to appeal to Mrs. Bell.

"He means that he's pretty well!" said she.

"Oh, does he? Very good!" and Tweakle filled his pipe.

"And now what have you got to tell us?"

Thereupon the Pippin advanced his chair to the table, as Mrs. Bell had done, and recounted his interview with Mr. Hatcher, faithfully as to the general facts, but rather wide of the truth in respect to particulars.

"Humph!" ejaculated the beadle. Mrs. Bell, who had listened to the Pippin's story with parted lips and 'bated breath, was about to speak, when Tweakle, waving his pipe at her in a dignified manner, threw himself back in the chair à la Gorelam, and remarked, "Leave him to me, ma'am—leave him to me, if you please!" And while he prepared himself with a loud "ahem!" Wigget, *alias* the Pippin, involuntarily assumed his Old Bailey demeanour, and looked innocently at the ceiling.

"Now, Mr. Wigget, describe the appearance of this extraordinary person! What was he like?"

"Oh, all a swell!" responded the Pippin.

"All as well, eh? Ah! Go on, my man," said Tweakle, in a weaker voice.

"Fluted dickey and a blue benjamin with brass buttons."

Tweakle's dignity departed: it was heard to crepitate in his hair like an expiring flame, as he turned helplessly to Mrs. Bell. Said she—

"The gentleman does not mean how was this person dressed, but what sort of man was he. His features, you know!"

"Features? Oh! Features you said! Well, he wasn't a beauty, mum. He was a mouser!" And while the Pippin delivered these words, he delivered his chin at Mr. Tweakle, elongated his jaws, sharpened his nose, cocked his ears, and attacked the aforesaid beadle with a gaze so purblind and fishy, that he threw up his elbow in a pugilistic manner to ward it off.

"That's him!" added the Pippin, quietly restoring his countenance to its accustomed expression of affected stupidity.

"Him?" exclaimed Tweakle, starting from his chair at the same moment. "Don't say another word, Mr. Wigget! Not a word, ma'am! I apprehend that man in the name of the law. Where is he?" And Tweakle brandished his staff in the active and intelligent manner of his profession.

"He's to meet me at Yallops's—where I lodge—at ten o'clock," said the Pippin. "If you want to take him—which such sneakin' warmin ought to be took—you'd better be there a little afore. It's time we started now."

"Come on, then! Keep your spirits up, ma'am! we'll have the mate of the *Black Bull* right enough in a werry short time ; and when I've lodged him secure, ma'am—if you've no objection—I'll—I'll come back and smoke my pipe out."

And Mr. Tweakle and the Pippin departed together ; the former leading the way, the latter following ; the latter rather dejected, the former very magnificent and important indeed.

The silence that may be felt accompanied the expedition. Tweakle no less than his companion was very dumb and very thoughtful during a considerable portion of the journey. The former was revolving in his mind what course to pursue with regard to Hatcher ; for the pretence upon which he was to be arrested, the crime with which he was to be charged, was a difficulty of which no solution readily presented itself. However, he ultimately resolved to leave that question to be disposed of by the inspiration of the moment ; and thereupon reposed his thoughts upon an imaginary picture of himself, smoking tobacco in Mrs. Bell's room, and framed in the walls thereof.

As for the Pippin, he was in a quandary too. It had occurred to him that it was not friendly to Woppits to take his respectable friend Mr. Tweakle to Yallops's, whose every inmate was a thief or a beggar. He knew Woppits's scruples ; that he would rather forget Yallops, upon the whole, and keep his friends in ignorance of his ever having moved in the society of the ex-prizefighter's kitchen. The Pippin accordingly cudgelled his brains for an expedient to keep Mr. Tweakle in ignorance of the character of the place and the people to whom he was about to be introduced ; but his brains were dull, or the cudgels were sapless, for he had arrived at no conclusion when Mr. Tweakle inquired—

"Where *is* Yallops's ?"

"Oh, up here," replied the Pippin, describing a circle with his head, while his elbows took an uncertain north-easterly direction.

"What sort of a place is it? What do you do there, Wigget ?"

"Sort of a place? Haven't I told you? Oh—it's a kind of a night refuge for idiots. I'm helper there!" replied the Pippin, blurting out the expedient upon which he happened to be engaged at the moment, and blaming himself very much for having done so afterwards.

"Oh, indeed!" remarked Mr. Tweakle, faltering slightly in his gait.

"Yes ; and the worst of it is (Wigget was obliged to go through with the expedient now, and resolved to make the most of it)—the worst of it is, I promised to meet that party in the kitchen, all amongst 'em!"

"That was very indiscreet of you, Wigget, wasn't it ?"

"Think so, sir ?"

"Yes, I do, Wigget! I call that one of the most indiscreetest things I ever heard of!" replied Mr. Tweakle, stopping to wag his head at the indiscretion, and showing no disposition to move on again.

"Oh, come on, sir! They're werry mild about these parts ; there ain't a wiolent one among 'em! Besides, the rawinest case as ever was gives in if you know how to treat it."

"Oh, I ain't afraid, Wigget!" replied Mr. Tweakle, reassured ; and they walked on. "How *do* you treat 'em?" continued the beadle, after a little silence.

"Well, we generally manages them through their appytite! We find that a juicy steak's not a bad antidoke for the worst of symptoms."

"They're particular fond of steaks, then, Mr. Wigget ?"

"We find their fancy runs on 'em a good deal, sir."

"We couldn't do better than take a pound or two in with us, could we ?"

"Well, we'll wait till we gets in ; it ain't certain how many of 'em's been sent to bed by this time. Here it is, sir," added the Pippin, suddenly darting into a doorway. "Oh, ah! I forgot to mention that you'll have to give twopence to a party sittin' in that box there, and he'll give you a ticket. It's a kind of stranger's fee !"

The Pippin now led the way, closely followed by Mr. Tweakle, in a confusion of spirit that was not allayed when William, taking the good man's money, favoured him with as large a stare as his eyes could possibly hold. In fact, they didn't seem capable of holding it, for it flowed over ; and Mr. Tweakle felt it projected into his hat, running down his back, and finally trickling into his boots. Focussing his eyes on William in return, he said to the Pippin, in an awful whisper—

"He's one of 'em, ain't he ?"

"*Him !* Bless your 'art, he's a long way off o' that! He's doorkeeper."

Mr. Tweakle wondered what sort of people he should meet inside in that case ; but he had no time to say as much ere he found himself in the kitchen.

"Sit here a minnit," said the Pippin, showing the beadle to a seat, "while I go and speak to the governor."

The surprise that had at first been depicted upon the faces of the company upon Tweakle's entrance—very various, but with something very uncommon upon the whole—subsided, and gave place to pleasant observations, to knowing winks and grins, all which were interpreted by Mr. Tweakle according to his instructions, as the gibes and gibberings of lunacy in the earlier stages. Under these circumstances, he kept his eyes pretty much on the Pippin ; saw him approach the big man with the white apron—saw the big man look stern and shake his head at first—saw him gradually relax into a metallic smile, and saw him turn away from the Pippin with a toss of the head, which might mean anything the spectator chose to imagine.

"It's all right," said the thief, wandering back to the beadle, with the air of a man who has many things to take into consideration ; "I s'pose you meant what you said about the steaks ?"

"Certingly," Mr. Tweakle replied.

"Then," said the leary one—to express in thieves' language all that was, or perhaps could be said about the Pippin, "I'll jest tell 'em all about it ; you watch 'em while I do." Then the speaker established himself on a chair.

"Attention !" he cried. "Every one of yer fix your heye on me."

As a natural consequence, this order was obeyed.

"I've brought a genelman among you," continued the Pippin, "as is werry sorry for your afflictions ; and bein' werry sorry, offers to stand a steak for as many on yer as would like one. Give the gentleman three cheers!"

The effect of this speech is included among the category of things more easy to be conceived than transcribed. The Pippin maintained his gravity, and made no sign that anything in the nature of a joke was intended ; nevertheless, there seemed to be some doubt in the bosoms of the company assembled. Some cheered in hope ; some cheered in derision of hope, some laughed ; some met the announcement with an eloquent stare, and some with an equally eloquent whiff of tobacco. Upon the whole, the announcement fell dead ; there followed a silence so solemn, so melancholy, that it appeared as if it (the announcement) had been buried also, and as if the whole party had assisted at the funeral.

"Very extraordinary, upon my word," said Mr. Tweakle, in a whisper that was perfectly audible in the remotest corner of the kitchen. "Poor creatures! They don't seem quite to understand you, Mr. Wigget."

Replied Wigget, "Well, some on 'em *is* duller than others. They'll understand it sharp enough when they hears the beef friezlin' over the fire. S'pose we sends for the stuff at once?"

85

The beadle handed him some money under the table, in an artful manner, supposed to be Greek or a Grecian proceeding to the idiots in question. Then the Pippin called a very young idiot to him.

"Benjamin," said he, "you go into the Borough, and fetch seven pound of juicy steak, at ninepence-halfpenny a pound. And, do you hear? be sure you finds your way back, or else it may be orkard for you. You understand, don't you?"

The young idiot rather confusedly answered that he did, and departed on his errand.

"Dear me! You can trust 'em to go and buy things, then, can you?" remarked Mr. Tweakle.

"Well, hardly. I don't think this one is touched as bad as some on 'em," responded the Pippin.

The departure of the little idiot with six shillings in his hand (it only needed a glance at the idiot's knuckles to assure one half of the company of the exact sum enclosed within his palm) had a visible effect upon the idiots generally. The freemasonry of winking was observed to pass between several of the company, while the less initiate of the asylum betook themselves to nudging each other in the most patent manner; in short, the refugees behaved entirely to Mr. Wigget's satisfaction. The return of the little one with the beefsteaks increased these demonstrations to an almost alarming extent; and when they (the steaks, not the demonstrations) were skewered upon fourteen skewers, and the happy murmuring of broiled beef hushed the kitchen, it was with some difficulty that the Refuge restrained its various emotions.

Touched by this display, and anxious, perhaps, for the appearance of Mr. Hatcher, Mr. Tweakle desisted from burying his face in a handkerchief under pretence of taking snuff, and turned to address his friend Wigget. Judge of the good man's alarm when, on looking up, he beheld every idiot in the room scowling at him. He was seized with a sudden apprehension that Wigget's specific had failed on this occasion. He remembered having read that when tigers once taste blood they refuse all other sustenance whatever. If tigers, why not idiots? If blood, why not a beadle's blood? The conclusion was not logical—that must be admitted; but Tweakle's was a position in which it will not do to chop straw with schoolmen, and his alarm was commensurate. Nor was it at all abated when he saw the imbeciles grouped about his Staff, which was passed from one to another of them like the burning brand which assembles the Highlanders together whenever there's a Royal Charlie about, seeking his own again. However, Tweakle was somewhat reassured when he saw Mr. Wigget plunge into the hostile throng, box one idiot's ear, strike another under the fifth rib, and otherwise behave like a man that is a man. He wrested the staff from a big idiot in a fur cap; he addressed words of warning to a little old party in military costume; he threatened the idiots generally; and finally restored the official insignium to Mr. Tweakle with an adequate air of indignation.

"That's the wust o' them hidjots," said he in Tweakle's ear. "So werry playful and full o' fun they are. They ain't took anythink else of yours, have they, sir?"

"Well, 'pon my word," replied Mr. Tweakle, who began to feel as if his head were a large ball of worsted hopelessly tangled, "I did have my spectacles about me. Yes," said he, patting himself solicitously, and not to outrage anybody's feelings, "yes, and I'm almost sure that I had a pocket-handkerchief; but really I do not feel 'em now!"

Thereupon exclaimed Mr. Wigget, "I'll break old Barker's blessed neck!" and plunging into the crowd like a shark among little fishes, he seized the small man in military costume by his brocaded collar, and seemed to shake out of him Mr. Tweakle's property. The shake, however, was so rapid, that it more properly might be called a twinkling; for in about the time it takes a twinkling to twinkle, Wigget returned to Mr. Tweakle with the missing articles.

"I say," said he, when he had restored them to his pockets, "it's eleven o'clock, Mr. Wigget. That person won't be here to-night, I should think. S'pose we go, eh?"

The Pippin was nothing loath. The latter conduct of the idiots had been more than equivocal, and he saw that Mr. Tweakle began to speculate upon the peculiar form of imbecility exhibited by the refugees around him.

Piloted by the Pippin, Tweakle returned to Bulger's Gardens, where Mrs. Bell anxiously awaited him. A few words explained that the party unknown had not made his appearance; a fact which he, Mr. Tweakle, all the more regretted because his present leave of absence expired on the morrow. For Mrs. Bell, however, that day had already proved fruitful enough, and on the whole it was a relief to her that no new event occurred to divide her thoughts. There was a painful joy in her heart which filled it full, so that it seemed to her that if she moved it would overflow, and put out the light there—a wide deep calm, as still, as solitary, as profound, as melancholy as those lakes that lie high in the bosom of the mountains, faithfully reflecting the serene heavens, and they alone. It was well that it should not be disturbed for that night, and Mr. Tweakle's journey to town had not been so bootless as he imagined.

He was, indeed, in a very dejected frame of mind, smoking his pipe in slow and lingering whiffs, as was his manner after an inquest. However, he was very glad, he said, that he knew the facts of the case; he was happy at having convicted that mysterious party of connoguing against Woppits, as was shown by the invention of that romance about the voyage to foreign parts; but though he, Mr. Tweakle, could not shut his eyes to the connoguing, he couldn't at all divine its object; and was at the same time assured that Woppits's own conduct had not provoked the persecution. It must be all on account of the little girl, whose history according to Woppits he firmly believed. "Unless, ma'am," added he, "this party is one of his unnatural parents. Don't you think it might be his father?"

Mrs. Bell shook her head, and therewith that heart-full of hers shook too; and some little drops trickling over, the vital spark trembled. You might have seen it flickering in her eyes.

"You don't think so? Well, ma'am, it ain't easy, as you say, to 'magine our young friend's parent answer to the descriptions of Mr. Wigget. There's nothing of the mouser, ma'am, in our young friend's face that I can see: but I tell you what I do think, ma'am," added he, confidentially.

"Yes?"

"I think he's a gentleman's son!" and Mr. Tweakle stabbed her in the bosom with his tobacco-pipe. The suggestion, also, seemed to strike her, and to draw blood; but she made no remark, leaving Mr. Tweakle the satisfaction of having made a hit, and of approving himself a shrewd fellow.

However, the blood continued to flow internally. It faded from her cheeks, it ebbed from her lips; and after the lapse of a few minutes she was constrained to say, rising—

"I think—I think, Mr. Tweakle, I must bid you good night. If you can manage to sleep in Woppits's room once more, you may have a chance of seeing him before you go away."

"Mrs. Bell, ma'am, I'm very much obleeged to you!" Tweakle rose also, and bowed.

"No; I to you. You don't know how much! You don't know," cried she—and back came the crimson into her face—"how much reason I have to love you—how I do love you!" And seizing Tweakle's hand, which was limp with astonishment, she kissed it a dozen times.

"Raly, ma'am," he stammered, looking along his fingers when they were released, as if he saw those kisses shining there like so many gay gold rings, "I ain't at all—at all used to——"

"To be thanked for precious services in such a cold way? Well, then," she exclaimed, with a sudden smile upon her lips and a sudden flood in her eyes, which together made a glorious bow to shine about her, "this must do!" and deliberately kissed Mr. Tweakle over the first gray whisker that presented itself. Then "God bless you!" added she, and was gone.

"Now what did I say when she went for the 'bacca!" And having made this remark; and having shook his head at it; and having gazed for several minutes upon his jewelled hand, Mr. Tweakle took his candle, and was gone too.

CHAPTER XXXII.

MOTHER'S LOVE.

BIDDLES'S ark had one thing in common with the olden ark: it had a wonderful capacity—a capacity undreamed of when viewed from the outside. The exterior, however, did prepare you, like many other show-vans, for a degree of neatness, of cleanliness and comfort, almost equal to that which distinguish the Dutch school of housewifery. Behold how fresh and bright the paint is! what hospitable warmth glows in the brass knocker on the door there! what beautiful white curtains hang in the little windows, themselves so bright that they reflect every wag of the donkey's tail! For there is a private apartment in Mr. Biddles's van carpeted; it has little cane-bottomed chairs in it; and a looking-glass; and a cat; and a lamp which may have been Aladdin's, so often is it scoured; and a pictorial tea-tray; and a pot of mignionette; and a bullfinch miraculously piping; and portraits of Mrs. Siddons, Mr. T. P. Cooke, and the infant Roscius. A big tool-chest serves as a table, and looks very like one to the inexperienced eye, covered as it with a cloth of brilliant tartan, on which Mr. Biddles and the late lamented crocodile used to play draughts on "off" evenings. The locker itself is a wonder of capacity. There is a compartment for wearing apparel, a compartment for crockery, a drawer for tools, a compartment or a drawer for a dozen other purposes. Bright cooking utensils hang upon the walls, and from the ceiling is slung a hammock, which ingeniously furls itself away in day-time, showing like a white cloud in the arky firmament. This apartment is called the Bower.

The Bower occupies about one-third of the whole length of the ark; the rest is devoted to the public. But the public are not confined to this space. Mr. Biddles has an ingenious contrivance for extending it on show days, by letting down the further wall of the van, in the manner of the "tail-board" of a cart; then a light sliding panel (more tarpaulin than timber) is thrown out on either side, and from the roof. Curtains are thrown across the entrance, and the public are at liberty to walk up. At night another hammock is slung in this compartment also: here the crocodile reposes. His rightful habitation, however, is supposed to be in a boat-like structure (designed by Biddles as best suited to the amphibious nature of the animal) hanging from the rear of the van, between the wheels. The public are deluded in this matter. The monster does indeed shed his skin into the boat-like structure, after the fatigues of business, but it is for the most part occupied by a nose-bag, some hay, a reserve of corn, and half a sack of potatoes. I have nothing to add to this description of the economy of Biddles's caravan, save that little Ruth is delicately lodged in the Bower, while a third hammock is rigged up in the show-room on Mr. Biddles's behalf.

Two whole days have passed since Woppits fell in with the showman, and the evening has come again. (What *would* the days do if the evenings didn't come again? How the monsters would stare at each other, with their great hot unfringed eyes! Like Lord Mayors going out and Lord Mayors coming in!) The caravan is disposed for the night in an eligible and unfrequented lane, and the large white donkey browses at large. There is very good grass in the lane, but Jacob is not partaking of it; he only nibbles a blade or two for pastime, or to soothe his con-templations. Naturally a gloomy animal, and inclined to view the world rather below than above the "blinkers," he is remark-ably cheerful to-night. But what are the facts? Twice has the corn-measure been filled for him to-day, and a carrot was sliced into it on both occasions. Biddles is seated at his door (the knocker of which employed Ruth half the morning to burnish) smoking mild "returns," like a philosopher and a gentleman. His placidity, too, is delightful; the evening itself is not more placid, more happy, more confident of a fine day to-morrow—for receipts. The new crocodile is an unprecedented success, and the treasury at this moment contains four shillings and sevenpence more than ever before was taken in that caravan in one day. The ark had been followed by an enraptured public, even to its present resting-place; and it was not until Mr. Biddles announced that the crocodile positively refused to appear again that night—that importunity only aggravated him, and that if he was once roused, he (Mr. Biddles) would not answer for the consequences—that the mob dispersed.

While the showman's imagination, brooding over the success of the day, laid numberless golden eggs, and finally carried him into the lesseeship of Drury Lane Theatre, Woppits was busy with hammer and nails within, and Ruth tinkled among the tea-cups, for the evening meal was over. What Woppits was so busy about I do not know; but it seemed to engage all his

attention, and to have a cheerful effect upon his naturally cheer-ful mind. Ruth, however, appeared dull: she tinkled among the tea-cups absently, and had that air about her which woman wears when she wishes you to understand that she has something on her mind, and which she would like to talk to you about if you wouldn't be cross. At length, summoning resolution, Ruth remarked—

"I wonder how mother is, Woppits!"

"Do you, my dear?" replied he, coming pensively forward, and stroking her hair. "Well, so do I. I've been wondering the same thing all the afternoon, and I rather think that last hornpipe wasn't quite up to the mark, in consekence!"

"*I* don't want to see you do it any more."

"What! not the hornpipe the sailors of H.M.S. *Blunderbore* learned me?"

"No!" replied she, with tears in her eyes; "I don't like to see you crawling and jumping about like an animal! I like to see you stand upright best!"

"Oh! come, come, Ruthy; you mustn't go on like that!" said Woppits, rather startled at this view of the matter, and blushing at himself. "There's wuss crawling than mine going on in the world—you may take your davit o' that, my dear. You know I'm *not* a animal, and that ought to be a comfort to you when you see me tryin' to look like one. Besides, if you're going into particulars, ain't it something to amuse people, and teach 'em the power of kindness at the same time?"

Ruth shook her pretty golden head, and, returning to the point whence the conversation started, said that for all that she couldn't help wondering how mother was.

Woppits was perplexed. Hitherto the child had seemed so contented that he was not prepared for this little scene; and looking at her grave, tearful face, it now occurred to him for the first time that it might soon be necessary to explain to her the actual state of affairs, and her own relation thereto.

Drawing her towards him, he said—"I can't tell you all the why and the wherefore of our being here, my pet, for you're only a little thing, you know, and wouldn't understand it rightly. Of course it's very natural for you to want to see mother, and much more pleasant to be with her than with Mr. Biddles and me."

"Woppits, dear! I didn't say that."

"Oh yes, you did! You're such a little thing you don't know what you said; for words ain't everything, Ruth; and I dare say you 'magine me very unkind not to take you back to mother. But the fact is, I can't; at least not for a little while, which is all for your sake too. So you be a good gal, and don't you cry, and I'll go bymeby and see mother, and bring you back word how she is, my dear."

This harangue pacified the child.

At the very moment when Mr. Biddles had terminated an unprecedented season of success as lessee of Drury Lane, and at the climax of a little speech to an uproarious audience, announc-ing that the state of the treasury was such, that he had not only paid his rent, but had a thousand pounds to reopen the campaign with after the holidays, Woppits appeared at the door with his hat on his head and a stick under his arm, and requested him (Biddles) to get out of the way; for he was seated on the door-steps. He looked round and the applause of his audience died away; they faded mistily; the treasury was empty; Drury Lane itself sank into the bowels of the earth.

"Mr. Woppits, sir!" cried Biddles, in faltering tones, "where—where are you going, sir?"

"To town, Mr. Biddles, if you please!"

"You're not going to cut the business, I hope, my dear young man? You won't desert the business after you've revived its hopes? You haven't the heart to smash such a brilliant suc-cess as we've seen the beginning of to-day?" He nervously dived into the pockets of his little green coat, and almost produced the powder-flask again, so painfully did the mere imagination of such a catastrophe work upon his feelings.

"Cert'in'y not! I'm just goin' to see after my private affairs, and 'll be back by ten o'clock, faithful!"

"'Pon your wordanonor?"

"I said faithful, didn't I?"

"Oh, all right, then; and you'll leave your sister along of me?"

"Which you'd better take care of her!" responded Woppits rather loftily, and went his way.

The re-assured Biddles wagged his head at the young man's retreating figure, and therewith rolled his eyes about, as if preparatory to slinging them after the young man, as he muttered knowingly, "I will, my friend. As much care of her I'll take as if she were a pledge of affection, instead of being in pawn for my two pound!" and so he resumed his seat and his pipe. In five minutes Drury Lane was entirely rebuilt by Mr. Biddles, with new scenery and decorations.

Tooting is not more than six or seven miles from Kennington; and, as Woppits obtained a chance seat on a mail-coach, he speedily arrived in Bulger's Gardens. He called all his knowledge of the locality into play as he approached the house, and kept so watchful a look-out, favoured by the darkness as he was, that he entered the Gardens unobserved. Also, he opened the door, with a little private key, unheard—as the Pippin had done; and, like the Pippin, he crept up-stairs softly as a shadow, and peeped through the keyhole of Mrs. Bell's sitting-room. He saw her by the fireside, with a wonderful pale light beaming in, not on, her countenance; with a big book on her knees, and her hands folded upon it.

There was something in that pale face that affected Woppits very much. It seemed to flow through the keyhole into his own heart, and to get up a kind of "fantocini" there, in which all sorts of shadows came and went. There was the shadow of little Woppits lying broad awake in the dormitory of Latherwell workhouse, looking out at the moonshine, and softly crying. There was the shadow of Hunger, the shadow of Loneliness, the shadow of that great, vague, wandering Love that kept little Woppits awake looking at the moonshine—that approached him nearest, that sometimes seemed to stand at his very side as he dropped to sleep, that started away, and hovered bigger and more indistinct out in the air when he opened his eyes again, and vanished when he gazed too eagerly. And when at that moment, more by sympathy than design, he gazed just as eagerly at Mrs. Bell and her big book and her folded hands, *she* faded away into a shapeless distance!

When it came to that, Woppits drew himself up breathless, and stood staring at the door in the dark, as if he saw through it. Had he done so, he would have witnessed a phenomenon ill calculated to restore his self-possession. Now, be it said, that he had all this while made no sound louder than the rustling of a leaf. Yet, suddenly, mother within turned her eyes to the door, seeming to listen as well as to look with them. The wonderful pale light grew paler and brighter. She unfolded her hands, and passed one of them in a sad distraught way across her lips, and rose, and stole to the door as swiftly, as noiselessly, as much unlike a flesh-and-blood woman, as a ghost is unlike such an one. She opened the door; and, finding him there whom she expected to find, screamed a small stifled scream, and seized his two hands in a passion of love.

"Why, mother!" cried Woppits. But then he always called her by that name.

"My dear son!" cried she; and Mrs. Bell always called him that same. But the words came so hoarsely over *his* lips, and so sweetly over hers, that they had an unusual sound on this occasion.

If they themselves observed this, they said nothing about it. Not by word of mouth, that is; but I am aware from certain experiences, obtained when I went courting, that people's fingers are capable of talking together; and the hands of Woppits and Mrs. Bell were not disengaged for at least a minute after they entered the room. So we are not in a position to judge authoritatively of what did pass between them.

Considering how many things they had to say to each other, the silence in which they sat for some time after Woppits entered was very remarkable; especially as there was no embarrassment in the silence, though it was peculiar enough. Woppits's first remark was that it had been a lovely day; to which Mrs. Bell answered that she had never known a more beautiful day in her life, or a longer one. There was a considerable pause after this—during which they never once looked at each other; and when Mrs. Bell presently rose to place a white cloth and a white loaf on the table, she moved with a strange, stealthy air, as if Woppits had been a dead man; while, in fact, he was never so much

alive, his life had never stirred so strongly in him, as at that moment. Longer as the silence lasted, a grave, almost solemn thoughtfulness gathered in his eyes; and for the first time Woppits—foundling, pauper, waif, crocodile as he had been—discovered that he was a Man also.

There was one peculiarity in the room, I must remark, which both Woppits and Mrs. Bell noticed and almost dreaded: a mad thing, which forced itself on them in the midst of their reflections. This was, that the atmosphere grew lighter and warmer; and that the vague space was full of something that lived, moving hither and thither with swift, liquid, electric motion—very busy. Sometimes it seemed to tremble through them; and now and then came a sort of paroxysm, in which they seem drowned, washed out into some wide dark sea of unconsciousness. Very curious, that.

At length Woppits spoke.

"How did you know I was at the door, Mrs. Bell? You couldn't have heard me."

Said she, "I heard the beating of your heart, I suppose."

"Or perhaps you was thinking of me?"

"I think I was."

"I *know* you was! Very strange! In fact, Mrs. Bell," continued Woppits, looking about him for the first time, "it all seems strange to-night! You haven't been bewitching me, have you, ma'am—saying the Lord's Prayer back'ards?" and with an odd smile he pointed to the book which had lain on the woman's knees.

Mrs. Bell laughed outright. It was better to laugh than to cry, and there was no other alternative. "Why, you silly boy," said she, "don't you see that I'm bewitched too?"

"Well, if you put it to me in that way," replied Woppits, looking very gravely *toward* her, and *at* the figure he had seen by the fireside, "I must say—I think—you are!"

"Look wild about the eyes, I suppose?" and she laughed again, drew her chair opposite him, and tapped his arm that rested on the table.

"Not wild—yes!—I'll tell you what you look like, ma'am. Like one of those evenings when a red light comes down into the streets, as if somebody had breathed red breath into them; and everything's still as death, wondering—houses and all—whether the heavens are not goin' to open, and the world come to an end!"

"Yes!" murmured Mrs. Bell, grave enough now, and amazed, as well she might be, to hear Woppits talk in that manner. "Yes!"

"And, as if you was goin' to change to somebody else," continued Woppits. "And as if I should not be sorry if you did!"

Now Woppits laughed. Mrs. Bell didn't; but gazed at him as if he were miles away, and still tapped his arm.

"Why don't you laugh at that, then?" cried Woppits, himself stopping short, in considerable confusion.

"I can't, my dear," she said. "And who should I change to?"

"I know well enough!"

"Tell me!"

"If I do, I shall tell you how *I'm* bewitched."

"Well?"

"Well," repeated Woppits, in that strange new manner of his, "when I said that you looked as if you were goin' to change into somebody else, I thought of a ghost I used to know when I was a little boy. For you know, ma'am——'

"Say mother, Woppits."

"For you know, mother, I was a very lonely little boy, because I didn't belong to anybody, and nobody belonged to me. There was two other boys like as I was, and a deaf and dumb boy; and we four was natural companions. We understood the deaf and dumb one, somehow, better than anybody else; and he—he seemed to understand us. He seemed to make it out that we was deaf and dumb too; and so we was, so far as our 'fections went, which never heard anythink, and never was taught to speak. Very curious we used to look at each other sometimes—round the fire, wonderin' what we'd done not to be like other people, and what the difference was. Now, lonely little boys think strange things! Nobody knows but themselves what comes into their heads, and comes and comes again, till it's as true as a book and real as flesh and blood! Don't you believe, ma'am,

MR. HATCHER IS AGAIN FOILED.

because little boys have got no father nor mother, nor sisters nor brothers, and p'rhaps not even a kind old gentleman that's a beadle as I had, that Gord leaves their hearts be empty! You should have heard young Hampton talk about his white bird to *us*—to us and the deaf and dumb one! He'd always got something new to tell about that bird; which I'm sure I don't know what he'd done without it, for he was a deliket boy, and soon died. The deaf and dumb one told me of that, when it happened. He laughed and put out his hands, fluttering them like wings. *I* knew what he meant!"

Woppits's voice had been sinking lower and lower, and at this point died away—fluttered away, like the bird.

"And what did the white bird mean?" asked Mrs. Bell. Her voice seemed to have some difficulty in breaking a way through the charm that was woven about her.

"Mean? We—we never asked that. We never dared think what it might mean. I took it for granted it was like my ghost, and I don't quite know what that meant. Sometimes I asked myself, but before the other Me could answer, I ran away!"

Again Mrs. Bell laughed; but there was a good deal of the above-mentioned alternative in the laugh. Its wings were drugged with tears, and it seemed not to rise from her lips, but to fall over and expire straightway, poor bird! Then ——

"Ah, you foolish, soft heart!" she murmured.

"And only to think that it should all come back to-night, along of you saying the Lord's Prayer back'ards!" continued Woppits, smiling, but still with his eyes turned to the floor. "Here I am, one o' them little lonely boys again! And here I lay in my workhouse crib, cryin'; very soft I'm cryin', because the

other boys 'll laugh if they hear me. (The back of Woppits's hand goes across his face; which, humble face as it is, is more and more illumined, as with inspiration.) "And here's that other hunger comin' on me, that isn't want of wittles. I can't make out what that other hunger is; but I feel there's something about me that could satisfy it, if it would only come into my heart. But that something's uncommon shy; and won't so much as be thought of, hardly. So I says to my heart, 'You be quite still. You pretend to go to sleep. You know that what's-its-name won't come near while you're staring at it, and straining arter it; but if you shut your eyes, maybe it'll try to creep in unbeknown.' So I make my heart a sort of trap for it; and steals off, and shuts my eyes; and sure enough here it comes! Here comes my ghost! It's like a cloud! It holds out its arms to me, and looks at me with its eyes. If I wake a little, and look at it, it melts away; if I go more to sleep, it comes nearer to me. In the mornin' when I looks into my trap, I find it gone; but I feel the warm place where it's been layin' all night long!"

Mrs. Bell has nothing to remark at present. Indeed, I should say she wasn't capable of making any rational remark, at present; judging by that bloodless, cold, stony look of hers. It would seem as if her tears were of the nature of certain Derbyshire waters; and, instead of refreshing, had petrified her. Woppits has risen from his chair, and is pacing up and down the room. His agitation increases every minute; and more and more he wonders why.

At length he stands before Mrs. Bell, looking at her. Instantly she falls a-trembling; tries to return his gaze, but her regards glance off to the right, to the left; and then return upon her, like the dove to the ark, with no olive branch whatever. Then she says :—

"And is that the somebody else you fancied I might change to?"

"—That I fancied you *did* change to—just now!"

"What do you call it, my dear?"

"Shall I let the other Me answer, at last—right out! bold!"

"Yes," she rejoined, taking his hand as if to prevent his running away this time.

"Mother's love!"

"Mine!" cried she aloud. And, without more ado, fell on the young man's neck in a passion of tears.

No further explanation was needed. At any rate, there *was* no further explanation.

Half an hour afterwards these two spirits were as calm as if nothing had happened. Those great emotions that come in with a flood often tide out as rapidly; and as for the heart they have covered, "they leave it firm, they leave it bright, they leave it clad in unearthly light"—and all is well. But for this arrangement, the heart, the mind, or whatever we agree to call it, would drown outright; as, indeed, it sometimes does. Woppits and Mrs. Bell were rescued from that fate, and there they were, rather sparkling than otherwise in the drops the deluge had left upon them.

"Ah!" said Woppits, "If *this* is being bewitched—! See here; I'm—I'm taller!"

"So you are, my son. And handsomer—ten times handsomer!"

"Well, I think I am; inside and out! But dear me, how late it is! I must be back at once!" So saying, Woppits took up his hat, and prepared to return to Ruth, the caravan, and his crocodile existence; it did not occur to him that he had fulfilled no purpose of his errand. Mrs. Bell had to remind him of that. Said she—

"But you haven't told me where you are staying, nor what you propose to do, nor even what you are here for to-night, I verily believe!"

"No more I have!" replied he.

And so they came to business. Woppits rather avoided going into details about Mr. Biddles and the crocodile—he was afraid that if it gave Ruth pain to see him adopt the habits of an alligator, Mrs. Bell would hardly be pleased at it. He had come to report himself well, to hear if that person had turned up again, and to ask her to change her lodgings. He would then bring Ruth back to be taken great care of, while he remained absent for a few months. He had fallen in with a very friendly showman, to whom he could be useful, and who very conveniently travelled from town to town. He, Woppits, *had* been thinking of going to the police, and by telling them all Ruth's story, and setting them on the reverend Mr. Bellows's track, settle all the difficulty; but who knew then into whose hands the child would fall, by right, or course of law? And how did he know whether she would thank him for his pains?

Then rose up Mrs. Bell, and related what had happened in Woppits's absence. But she, too, had something to conceal—the fainting part of her interview with Tweakle. But she blundered so much, hurrying over this little episode, that Woppits had his suspicions, and said, "Bless that old beadle! He's always doin' good of some sort!"

But the best part of the narrative was that in which Mr. Bellows was discomfited. Here was a revelation which set Woppits quite at his ease as regarded himself, though his experience of that reverend gentleman proved him capable of any cunning or desperate scheme to get Ruth into his hands. But it was a great discovery that he, Woppits, had no reason to fear Mr. Bellows in any legal sense; that Bellows was himself to be bearded, bullied—even assaulted, perhaps—and threatened with the police. Woppits longed to meet him at that moment (he was not far off), and he rather regretted that his engagements with Mr. Biddles would delay the pleasure of an interview.

The clouds were opening, then! Not only had that red light broken through, giving Mrs. Bell somebody else's appearance, but now the tables might be turned upon Woppits's persecutor. There was nothing to be done save to keep a watchful eye on

Ruth, lest the reverend Bellows should steal her, and, if possible, seize *him*, and shake out of him a little information.

All this was talked over and agreed upon, and Ruth's transmission to the new lodgings arranged for, in half an hour; and then Woppits had to hurry off. He seemed very much bewitched again as he prepared to depart; and so did Mrs. Bell, for that matter. Both were greatly altered. She looked littler, and younger, and less grave, of all things; he looked bigger, handsomer, and by at least three years more of a man. Nevertheless, he was the foolishest of the two, as they stood there, saying good-bye. As for her, the delight she took in seeing him so childish—blushing, nervous, and all abroad—maintained her in a certain state of superiority; however, it was a giddy elevation, to make the best of it; and once or twice she suffered such a determination of blood to the heart, that only with great difficulty did she manage to keep her feet.

However, the leave-taking was very simple, after all. The end of Woppits's foolishness was, that he presently gave a short nod, muttered, "Well, good-bye, ma'am !" and walked downstairs forthwith! When Mrs. Bell heard the door close behind him, she stamped her little foot at herself, in quite an angry, showery storm! To think that she should let him go like THAT !

A gentleman, casually passing, saw Woppits turn out of Bulger's Gardens. The gentleman followed him. Woppits was too much engaged with his new reflections to observe this, and it was pitchy dark. He hurried on (it was now near twelve o'clock) with his head downward, thinking his thoughts out; the other party faithfully following, though he seemed to have some difficulty in maintaining the pace, for now and then he broke into a little soft trot. What troubled the stranger more than Woppits's speed, however, was a trick he had of stopping short, at intervals, to gnaw at some little mental knot, as it were. But every time he thus paused, the stranger imagined he had been discovered; and made sudden and painful dodges under a wall, or behind a tree. At length, Woppits came to a very hard knot indeed, it would seem; he was then near a small patch of scrub, not far from Tooting, and into this he sauntered to argue the matter out, or, perhaps, to have his fill of reflection before it was extinguished in the caravan. The stranger did not observe this movement, in consequence of having dodged into a ditch one moment too soon; and trotted on past the patch of scrub, and past Woppits. Fifty yards farther he came to a cross road; and felt that the chase had ended. However, losing not a moment in purposeless reflection, he chose the road to the right, and scudded softly along.

Two or three hundreds yards further in some discouragement, and the stranger's tread was startled by a shrill cry, not uttered by the wind, though that piped fresh and chill enough. He craned his neck in the direction whence the sound proceeded, and beheld something white hurrying towards him, fluttering as it came, and crying. The gentleman was seized with a superstitious fear. He stopped, walked slowly backwards, when suddenly a little child flew into his arms.

"Why, what's the matter, my little dear," he muttered, crossing himself slily. "What are you crying about?"

"Oh, I'm lost! I've lost my way looking for them. Mr. Biddles went to look for brother, and left me alone in the yellow house. And oh! I wish I could find him !" How the little creature sobbed and cried !

"Who's Mr. Biddles? who's your brother?"

"Oh, you know them! Mr. Biddles keeps the yellow showhouse, and my brother's his crocodile."

If this answer did not appeal to the stranger's heart, it seemed to affect his knees; for down he went upon them, put his face close to the child's, and gazing through the dark at her beautiful eyes and her hair streaming down the little bare shoulders, thought of gnomes and fairies treacherous, in spite of himself.

"And what do you call your brother?" said he.

"Woppits, sir."

"Who?" shouted Mr. Hatcher.

"Woppits, if you please !" the child answered, more frightened than ever.

"Then," cried he, clutching at her hand, "you come along of me !"

She knew him, and with another cry, she broke from him,

bounded over a neighbouring style, and away over the fields like a hare. But alas for poor puss! Hatcher was upon her like a hound, and overtook her as she neared the opposite edge. He was upon her like an hound in more meanings than one; for he pinned her by the throat—she dumb with terror—and going on his knees again, tore away the kerchief that hid the mark upon it.

He didn't know that Richard Biddles had heard the child's cry, and had seen her chased across the field by the lean hound. He did not observe the little green man stealing towards him in the shadow of the hedge, nor was he otherwise aware of Mr. Biddles's proximity, till he felt a smart application behind from Richard's boot, which rolled him over, and beheld the little man flourishing a large stick over his head in a manner which for expression was never surpassed on any stage whatever.

CHAPTER XXXIII.

THE FOX TRAPPED.

OF all the professions, whose children are so fond and faithful as the Drama's? and of all mothers, who more foolish or more fond than she? She is not a provident mother, and though undoubtedly domestic in her proclivities, has the loosest ideas of housekeeping. No; she is rather a gossiping, thriftless, soft-hearted one, with handsome eyes much given to weeping. She adores her children, who are devotedly attached to her, readily making any sacrifices on her behalf; and nothing is more delightful than to see them grouped about her, in appropriate attitudes, so genteel, so simple, so good-natured, so strangely attired, so profoundly self-satisfied, so sadly and ludicrously engrossed in the pot which mother cannot always keep boiling, though she pawn her gown in the attempt. When this happens, she will sit for hours and hours with her feet on the fender, and her high noble nose in the chimney, waiting for something to turn up; and devising for her offspring the magnificent fortunes to which they are naturally prone; meanwhile, she laces their pinafores, and forgets to darn them. A sad, slipshod, thriftless mother, the Drama; but with something about her that compensates for all her shortcomings, and makes her children happy, spite of Fate, her natural enemy. Behold her in her rouge, and her melancholy old flowers and ribbons, cutting thick bread and butter for the darlings; you perceive that a certain air of cold chicken pervades her, giving gentility to the operation and adding savour to the meal. How it tickles the darlings' palates! For the savour is not only of cold chicken, or any mere modern and fleshly dish. It is a savour of the *profession*, combining subtle hints of all that is delicate or comforting in the world, and some things that are departed out of it, as sack, hippocras, metheg in, hum, ambergris, and other delicacies of the period. And so the good creature's influence is ever at work. It animates all situations, gives a strange zest to misfortune, and colours all events, the most wretched and the most happy, with the scene-painter's brush. If Jack Thespis loses himself as the "Prisoner of Chillon," he loses himself with almost equal facility in the Queen's Bench; and Walter Harcourt is a sybarite on twelve pounds a week. The "situation" is the thing, whether in the hour of danger, or in the crowning moment of felicity; and as for the rest, all the world's a stage.

These remarks are not inapplicable to Mr. Biddles.

"Here's a tablow!" said he, standing over the prostrate Hatcher, in an attitude as rigid, as motionless as stone—after the manner of the man who does the Grecian statues, including the well-known one of Cain slaying Abel. In striking this attitude, Biddles had projected his hat over his right eye, which was the more inconvenient, because the other was an enfeebled or game eye. However, the die was cast; and Biddles no more thought of disturbing his pose to adjust a mere hat, than of slaughtering Mr. Hatcher in order to complete the effect. Nor was that necessary at the moment; for he lay still as death—a heap of confusion, fast fermenting into a state of spontaneous combustion.

At length, while Biddles's stony eye (was it not rather like a glass eye?) was still fixed on Hatcher's prostrate form, the flames began to leap over that person's countenance. Bending his

backbone like a bow, he suddenly released it, and, projecting himself at Mr. Biddles's legs, snapped his jaws at them, howling. All that was statuesque departed the showman. "Ha, viper! would you?" cried he, and, hopping now on one leg, now on the other, as they were alternately threatened, he poked Hatcher vigorously with his stick, in order to keep him down. But such was the ferocity of the attack that Biddles's manœuvres were soon thrown into confusion. The enemy grasped one of his legs, his teeth penetrated the gaiters, and he sprang upright. This being the case, the courageous little showman felt obliged to deliver a sharp blow on the enemy's head, purely as a measure of self-defence. The enemy was now brought to a stand; finding it necessary to recall his senses, which had taken flight in a brilliant discharge of fireworks.

"Now, then!" cried Biddles, assuming a favourite attitude of the late Mr. Widdicomb, "who are you?"

"How—how dare you assault and batter a gentleman in this way?" demanded the other in return.

"*You're* no gentleman—it is ridiculous to try *that* on! Come, are you going to tell me who you are, and what your game is, chasing after this young woman?"

"She's my daughter!" responded Hatcher, boldly; "stolen from me. And I advise you to go about your business peaceable, and leave me to mine, or you'll get into trouble, sir, I assure you."

The moon struggled through the clouds to have a peep at this ingenious gentleman, and enabled Biddles to take a glance at him also.

"Don't believe him!" cried Ruth, clinging to the little green coat. "He's a bad man! He's been bad to us before—somewhere—before!" She was half wild with bewilderment and terror.

"Oh, she's yours, is she? (Be quiet, little 'un, be quiet! Nobody shall hurt you while Richard Biddles is about!) Oh! Does that other one belong to you, then?"

"What other one?"

"Her brother—Mr. Woppits?"

"Oh, of course he does! He's my son, the undutiful blackguard!"

"Dear me! You must have been a father very young!" and the little man, closing one of his eyes, seemed literally to screw the other into Mr. Hatcher, so pointed were its glances. "Well," continued he, assuming the other favourite attitude of Mr. Widdicomb, "that clinches it. I don't feel it my duty to part with you just yet. Old Woppits, follow me!" And the showman, motioning Hatcher to move on, prepared to follow *him*.

"Where to? What am I to go with you for?" said Hatcher, in some trepidation.

"Why, to clear up the mystery! To yonder caravan, where you will find your wonderful son!"

"Anybody else?"

"Ain't he enough? How many more relations have you got about? Come on, sir. He'll be very glad to see you, I dessay, if he's come back."

Hatcher felt so confident of a triumph over Woppits, and that one fair engagement with him in a fair field would finally dispose of the business, that he offered no objection to this arrangement; indeed, he hurried forward with an alacrity which awoke some misgiving in the showman's mind.

Meanwhile, Woppits had brought his cogitations to a close, or rather he folded his thoughts away for another Sabbath of reflection, and prepared to enter the caravan in a loose, easy ready frame of mind. He found the Bower empty. A bright fire burned in the little stove, a cloth was laid for supper, Biddles's tobacco-pipe rested in the fender, and near it, reposing on a dish, and protected by a basin, was a pudding—the first that had appeared in the Bower for five years. Ruth had made it, to the delight of Mr. Biddles. Long after Woppits had departed on his errand to town, did the showman remain lost in thought on the ladder. Night fell, and still he sat there, to Ruth's anxiety, immersed up to his neck in reflection, a character in which he reminds one of a bather squatted on the steps of a bathing-machine. At length Ruth felt it her duty to speak to him, and ask him what was the matter.

"My dear," said he, "I'm troubled in my mind about what we're to have for supper. This day ought to be celebrated by something festive and uncommon; but the resources of my establishment ain't equal to its production. There's a leg of mutton and trimmings, you'll say; or stewed lamb and peas; or a little spare-rib of pork and apple sarce; or I wouldn't mind goin' the length of poultry; but where's the quizzeen to come from? No, we'll have to fall back on eggs and bacon, my dear."

"Don't you think I could make a pudding of something, sir?"

"You! a pudding! Are you equal to it?"

"I've seen mother make them, and I'll try."

"You wait a bit, then?"

Biddles sallied into the village, and speedily returned with eggs, flour, and two fat pigeons prepared to hand. "Now," said he, "you make a pudding out of that, and let me see you do it!"

The brightest, tiniest, busiest little housekeeper that ever was seen, surrounded herself with knives and plates and basins, pepper-castors, salt-cellars, and other rightful implements, and fell to. Biddles lit another pipe, and sat down to view the operation; and a curious eye he viewed it with. The Bower was a comfortable bower, at all times, and Biddles was happy in it; but now, when Ruth went busily to and fro, on that simple business of pudding-making, and rolled the paste, and peppered the pigeons, and adjusted all so neatly and carefully, there was a touch of beauty about the very walls which affected Mr. Biddles. Some secret intelligence seemed to pass between the child and the plates she touched, the spoon she handled, the lamp that shone on her—the everything, in fact. The whole Bower had its eyes on her, watched her, caught new rays of cheerfulness from every movement of her little white arms, until the place was full of the glow, the soft glory of home.

It was as much as Biddles could do to stand it. The hardware *was* too much for him; for, as he gazed upon a row of three effulgent saucepan lids, tears came into his eyes. Ruth herself was beatified; she was in a rapture of cookery (we have seen grown women enraptured with less worthy objects); and it was impossible to look *her* in the face. Biddles was driven to taking casual glances at the back of her head; the curls dancing and bobbing there were significant enough for him in his present disposition of mind.

At last—much too soon—the pudding was made. The showman could have wished the business three hours long; but Ruth was not to be tampered with; there was no help for it, and in due course the pudding disappeared into a saucepan. Then Ruth cleared away, and stood before the fire, folding her hands over her apron strings, and watching the pot boil.

Whether a sense of responsibility gave a new air to her face, or from some other reason unknown, Biddles was now struck by the discovery that Ruth was very like her brother; and no sooner had the resemblance occurred to him, than he flew off at a tangent to certain reminiscences, long-forgotten. They were not uninteresting, nor without connection with this story, as the reader would have admitted, had not the showman been interrupted, just as he was about to relate them to Ruth, by the boiling over of that pudding. Darting at the saucepan, all mere reminiscences were scattered into oblivion again, and henceforth the showman's whole soul was in the pudding cloth. So is mine, sometimes; so there's nothing remarkable in that.

"I say," he remarked, with some consternation, "Tempus is fugiting it pretty stiff! I hope your brother'll be back in pudding time! How long will it be before it's done, my dear?"

"It's nearly done now, I think."

"Good heavens! I wouldn't have that pudding spoilt for a golden guinea. My nice little commemoration supper, that we was going to have so cosy, with rum punch afterwards, *mustn't* be spoilt, my dear! Wonder what's become of him! But then he doesn't know that we've killed the fatted pigeon for him!"

Still no Woppits appeared, and more serious considerations came in to disquiet Mr. Biddles. His anxiety, however, was as nothing compared with Ruth's; and at length, partly to soothe her, and partly for his own satisfaction, the showman sallied out in search of the young man. There was a chance that he had mistaken his way at the cross roads. What happened to little Ruth when she found herself alone in the ark, needs no explanation. Her anxiety grew into terror. Looking in the fire, she saw Woppits waylaid and murdered; she saw him perishing in a snowdrift under a hedge, in company of two young lambs; she imagined herself entombed in the caravan (Woppits thought it *was* a mausoleum at first) and ultimately dug up through the roof. More than all was the dead stillness of the night, the dead unfathomable dark, that closed up to the very windows, as the sea closes over the sunken ships, and swallowed up her hand when she ventured to thrust it out at the door. "Thud!" came some stupid night-beetle against the window pane. Swoop came a gust of wind, caught up the knocker, and rapped two faint and ghostly raps, and then the stillness was dead as ever. No little Ruth, with fine-strung nerves and vivid fancy, could endure that state of things long: and at last she hurried out to seek her friends too, and flew into the arms of Mr. Hatcher, as we have seen.

Now the dear reader knows all about it. He sees how it came to pass that Woppits found the Bower unusually bright and deserted.

Surprised and alarmed in his turn, Woppits descended into the open air, and began to busy himself with conjecture, when he was somewhat relieved by the approaching sound of voices. That was the voice of Biddles, clearly. There! there was no mistaking Ruth's voice! But what third one was that? The young man deemed it prudent to assure himself on that head before he joined the company, and accordingly dived under the caravan, crouching there quietly. From this position he heard the remnant of a conversation, apparently of a friendly and confidential nature.

"So you see—"

("Bellows, by all that's good!" exclaimed Woppits, in a whisper.)

"—I was right; and yet, as you say, I was wrong, when I said he was my son. He's my son by law, and he ain't by nature."

"How's his mother?"

"As wicious as ever when I saw her last; but that, thank goodness! is years ago! Drink! My eye, you should see her drink!"

Woppits trembled to that degree—not with fear—that he shook the whole caravan, and was audible in the crockery chest. But neither Biddles, nor Ruth, nor the stranger noticed it, for they were then entering the ark. Then Woppits came forth, and so disposed himself that he could hear all that passed within.

"Ah, he's not come home!" remarked the showman. "Take a chair, sir; and make yourself happy!"

"Happy I can never be! No, of course he's not come back. I know him better than you do, my poor friend. He's got your two pound, he knows I'm on his track, and now he's off for good and all. Ah! I've known him before to-day, and he's robbed *me* through thick and thin!"

"And yet he burdens himself with this little one, that can be nothing but expense to him. Such is life!" said Biddles.

"Burden,—expense! nothing of the sort, sir! It's all self-interest and swindling. He knows I dote on my daughter; he takes my daughter away in her infancy; and he writes me 'arrowing letters, saying she's ill—that she's dying—that he hasn't food to give her, and she's starved to a skelinton; and of course he gets money out of me. Has it left in holler trees!"

Ruth's little heart was aching with indignation; but she had been privily enjoined by Mr. Biddles to say not a word, and so she restrained herself. Besides, the showman held her hand, and he gave it a kindly squeeze whenever he felt its pulse beating faster than was good.

"Oh, that's his character, is it? Well, you see, two pound ain't a trifle to a poor man like me," said Biddles, reflectively. "Besides"—here he gave Ruth's hand a particularly kind squeeze—"it isn't like as if I'd known him long, and I don't know whether I mightn't be inclined—if—" The showman looked significantly at Mr. Hatcher, and left the sentence to be completed in that person's imagination.

"It *isn't* a trifle!" responded he. "But don't suppose you are going to lose your money: no, sir! He's a minor; and I'm responsible for his debts, which while I've a shillin' I'll pay honourable. Here's the two sovereigns you so kindly and unsuspiciously advanced; and thank you, my dear sir—thank you!

AN UNEXPECTED RECONTRE.

Anybody that does a good turn for a member of my family—whoever may be that member—does it for me. And now I don't think I'll wait any longer. All I could say to my son-in-law would do him no good; and as I've found my daughter—"

Herewith Hatcher addressed a furtive glance at Ruth, so full of a cruel, threatening meaning, that it had almost had the effect he intended it should have—of paralysing any objection she might take to being carried off. But Biddles, whose head was turned aside at the moment, caught this glance reflected in a shaving-glass; and it settled whatever doubt he might have had as to the stranger's honesty.

"Oh, don't hurry yourself, pray!" said the little man. "We've a lovely pigeon pudding here, sir, that'll pay you for waiting, take my word for it. Besides, he won't be long now; you stop and tackle him. Dear me! I should like to see you and him stand up together on that bit of grass out there—upon my word I should, sir! I'd see fair!"

"Well, I should like it myself, much!" returned Hatcher, with a shallow grin; "but I couldn't disgrace myself so far. His wretched mother—"

A rap was heard at the door—an impatient rap. It was delivered by Woppits—not because he had any delicacy about entering unannounced, but because the showman had quietly bolted the door, to make sure of his prisoner.

"That's him," cried Biddles.

"Well, let him come on!" said the other, with a grim, odd smile. Ruth clasped her little hands in terror.

"Wait a bit," remarked the showman, seized with a professional idea. "You hide behind the screen. Go in there! You'll hear everything. Mark well! and appear at the first good point that turns up."

So saying, he thrust Mr. Hatcher, who was delighted with the idea, into an extremely dark corner of the show department.

Now the door was opened and Woppits beheld the showman on the threshold, with his finger to his nose, and his eyes twinkling with wonderful intelligence. The young man at once understood the cause of the delay in opening the door, and acted upon the warning so mysteriously conveyed.

"You're late, young man!" said Biddles aloud, and with some asperity.

Woppits tenderly kissed little Ruth, and then replied, "Well, I am, sir! I've been kept by important business."

"So's this nice pigeon pudding, that your sister made. Ruth, my dear, let's have it up comfortably, and then we'll hear what the business is."

While these remarks were passing, Mr. Biddles was deeply engaged asking invisible questions, by writing them out on the table with his forefinger. His hand was very bold and firm, so that Woppits had no difficulty in making it out. The first question was, "Know a lean man—carroty?" Woppits nodded. "Father-in-law?" Woppits shook his head violently. "Shall we smoke him?" The young man smiled: he was willing.

Having received so much information, Mr. Biddles proceeded to impart some, in pantomime. He spread his arms abroad to denote space, or the open air; then rushing a tip-toe at Ruth, he caught her by the throat, knelt down before the child as Hatcher had done, and made a feint of stripping her. That Woppits also understood, and burned with wrath. However, Biddles damped the fires with a nod and a wink, and supper by this time being laid, the little party fell to.

Dismal in the ears of Hatcher was the clinking of plates and glasses; and Biddles made a tremendous clatter, partly on professional grounds, and partly because he was in high spirits. He ate very fast—as is the custom on the stage—making a succession of headlong dives into his plate, and meeting himself half-way with his fork; which played into his mouth with a rapidity that gave you the notion that he was conjuring, and would presently proceed to swallow the knives.

The exertion thus occasioned was relieved by intervals of graceful languor; during which he threw one arm over the back of his chair, threw back his head, and made some observation.

"So your business, Mr. Woppits, was important, was it? eh? Pretty woman in the case?"

"Ye-es; rather."

"Rather pretty, eh? Sly dog! Now, who may she be?" And if Mr. Biddles had been his own crocodile, and had suddenly caught sight of a trout sporting in the gravy, he could hardly have dived into his plate with greater avidity. "Secret, eh? Never mind me, you know!"

"Oh, no secret; we call her mother—don't we, Ruth?"

"And she's a dear mother; isn't she, Woppits?" returned the child.

"Come, come, don't beguile the young and innocent, Mr. Woppits. I know all about it. I've had a little conversation with your father-in-law, to-night."

"Indeed! What sort of a person is he?"

"Don't pretend ignorance of your father-in-law, young man! Because the mystery that a ribald proverb wraps fathers in doesn't apply. Your step-parent is a very good-looking gentleman, with a noble forehead, a speakin' eye, and a fine head of hair."

This remark rather unsettled Mr. Hatcher, who, while the conversation was going on, had been flitting up and down the partition that divided the Bower from the business-room, in search of a chink or hole, like a mouse at the wires of a trap. As for Ruth, Mr. Biddles's description tickled her to such a degree that she would have laughed outright had he not pinched her leg under the table.

"Don't recognize the portrait," said Woppits. "There is a party that takes an interest in me, but he's not good-looking nor a gentleman. He hasn't got a forehead at all—leastways, none worth mentioning: his eyes are sheep's eyes, with a dash of the cat in 'em; and as for his hair, it's of a bricky colour, and there isn't half a head of that."

Mr. Hatcher was not irritated by these remarks, though they failed to allay a certain apprehension at the course the conversation was now taking.

"Well!" said Biddles, "looks is a matter of opinion; and now I consider it, your description does come nearer the mark, perhaps. But that's not to the purpose, young man. He is your father-in-law, you know; and as such, it is very wrong of you to go running about the country with his dear and only child, and write letters to him, threatening that you will send him back her skeleton if he don't leave money for you in hollow trees."

Woppits looked up in silent amazement.

"Ah, but you do, you know!" continued the showman, interpreting and answering Woppits's stare—"he told me so himself. Oh, Mr. Woppits, hadn't that poor man got enough trouble with your wretched mother—so dreadfully given to drink as she was, the creature! Don't contradict—your father-in-law said so; the very words he used were, 'My eyes, you should see her drink!' Now, when a man talks like that, there must be something in it. That's my opinion."

"I'll tell you what's in it in a minute," cried Woppits, who could not enter into the fun of the thing so completely as the showman. "That man threw this child here into a lime-kiln, having first tried to strangle her. Here are the marks! Here are the prints of his fingers! I fished her out of the kiln; he discovered that; and ever since he has been trying by bribes, and threats, and scheming, and telling more crammers than would fill this caravan, if none of 'em was bigger than a mustard seed, to get her back, and murder her outright. Send him her skelinton! The prettiest present his 'art could wish for, that would be it!"

Now it was Biddles's turn to stare. Woppits's manner was

something more than histrionic; so were his tones; so were his flashing eyes, and the tremor of his limbs, trembling in their anxiety to be employed in re Hatcher. The little farce was taking a tragic turn. "Why didn't you tell me all that before?" said the showman.

"Because I didn't quite know the rights of it myself before this evening. And if you're a friend to my father-in-law, advise him to keep out of my way, when you see him again."

There was naturally a pause after this declaration, which was as new and as marvellous to Ruth as it could have been to Biddles, or to any showman whatever. In the silence was heard a small uneasy shuffling in the adjoining apartment. This sound restored Biddles to his jocose equanimity, the professional spirit returned upon him, and suddenly banging the table with his open palm, he exclaimed,

"Mr. Woppits, sir! I don't believe a word of it. I saw the mark of care upon your father's face! I saw the tear of grief within that father's eye! That father handed me two pound in gold—honourable—that I mightn't be loser by his bad son's goings on, which, I need not add, that father was not called upon to do! What's my inference? That he's a melancholy and injured man! That, if I may so express it, he's naturally of a soft-reed nature, free of his money, and liable to be imposed upon. But innocence shall not be triumphed over in my van! On the contrary, innocence shall be vindicated in my van. You shall meet your accuser face to face!" and throwing back the door of the Bower, Biddles continued in a solemn voice, "Come forth, old Mr. Woppits; come forth, sir, and confound your unnatural child."

The showman, striking an attitude, cast his eyes to the ceiling, and awaited the entrance of the injured party. The injured party, however, did not respond to the invitation with such alacrity as might have been expected of him. Indeed, he declined to come forth altogether; and when, after some moments of suspense, the little party entered the cage, the bird was nowhere visible. An ungenerous suspicion momentarily flitted through Woppits's mind; as for the mind of Mr. Biddles, it seemed to have oozed out into the vacant space around him. It was reserved for little Ruth to divine the mystery. Bounding towards a trap door that opened upon the crocodile's den, she tugged courageously at the ring by which it was lifted. Her strength was not equal to her courage; but Biddles, as well as Woppits, was only too ready to relieve her of the labour.

Six eager eyes, gazing into the den, beheld a curious spectacle, by the light that streamed through the open door. They beheld two lively human legs waving from the jaws of the crocodile; the human body to which they appertained making insane endeavours to get devoured. Obviously, this was Mr. Hatcher, who, alarmed (as well he might be) by the conversation between Woppits and the showman, sought a means of escape. Groping on hands and knees in this endeavour, he had alighted on the ring in the floor, and hopefully lifted the trap, expecting to drop through it to the earth. In this expectation he was disappointed; but thrusting his arm into an apparently interminable vacancy, he plunged into it at the words, "Come forth!" hoping to get happily out at the other end. Mr. Hatcher had lost his wits by this time.

"Why, old Mr. Woppits!" cried the showman; "what are you doing? This way, sir, this way! Here he is!"

The legs replied with a spasmodic quiver, which propelled Mr. Hatcher several inches farther into the bowels of the beast.

"Oh, come, come!" said Biddles, soothingly patting Mr. Hatcher's calves. "Be calm!"

However Mr. Hatcher might have taken this advice had he been permitted time to consider it, Woppits could restrain himself no longer. He seized Hatcher's legs, and by a prodigious effort landed him, still wedged in the scaly hide. There he lay, panting. You could see him moving within, in a slow and rather revolting manner; reminding you of that story of the goat that was swallowed by the boa-constrictor, and whose horns were seen making a slow voyage inward, day by day.

"Come out, old Mr. Woppits!" the showman exclaimed, gently jerking Hatcher by the shoe-string.

A faint voice from the interior answered, "Never!"

"Well, now, that will be very inconvenient for me, you

know! Can't you manage it? Here, young man, why don't you assist your poor father-in-law!" cried Biddles, winking at his lieutenant, and pointing to the slit in the crocodile's side. "Just touch him on the nose! Wait a bit—I'll give the word of command."

Woppits's services were quite at Mr. Hatcher's disposal. Deftly inserting his arm into the crocodile's side, he placed his foot on the tail, and waited till the showman had obtained a firm hold of Hatcher's ancles.

"Now!" cried Biddles; and at the same moment he tugged at Hatcher's legs, while a gentle but sufficient tap was administered to his nose.

The effect was all that could be desired. One jerk freed Hatcher from restraint, and then he backed out of the monster's jaws. Light from the Bower played full on Hatcher's head, as it slowly emerged from the recesses of the brute: it also played full on the crocodile's jaws; revealing the profoundest amazement in the one animal, and a quaint and ferocious equanimity in the other. They lay prone in a right line, their extremes dying off in the dark on either side, their noses within an inch of each other. It was as if light had first pierced the antediluvian darkness, revealing those creatures to each other, so astonished seemed they at the interview.

Hatcher all but fainted. He was drawn up like a drowned man, and propped in a chair, where Biddles and Woppits gave him time to recover, while they discussed the question, how to dispose of him. Biddles's idea was that Woppits was bound to call him out, for the insult to his (Woppits's) mother; and producing two property rapiers, he suggested that as such affairs were better arranged quietly, the combatants should have it out at once over the table.

Hatcher, pale as a ghost already, groaned at this proposition, but made no further objection. It was Woppits who rejected it, declaring his determination that Hatcher should not only be punished, but made to reveal his designs. "There's nothing else to be done," said he. "I'll go and charge him with attempting to murder little Ruth. That'll bring him out!"

Manacles and his mother rose before Joel's imagination, and filled the measure of his despair. "It's all over," he groaned. Then rising out of his chair, with sudden calmness and courage, he thus addressed the company—

"Listen to me. My game's not so bad as you think; but it's up now. I'm tired of it. Do as you like, but let me tell you this: there's things I needn't tell a magistrate, and things I never will tell a magistrate, which I'll give you the particulars of, if you treat me well. Besides, by lugging out before the world what I can quietly let you into, you'd do more harm to this little 'un than you've the least idea of. Now then!"

Woppits looked perplexed. Biddles exclaimed:—

"But let us know what part you're cast for in the business. Are you first robber, or second robber, or what?"

"Well," replied Joel, with desperate frankness, "I'm neither one nor the other. I'm third robber. The other two are more than robbers."

"You're a hanger-on, then? Bought?"

"My silence is bought. Now, I'll sell it to you again, if you'll give me a week."

"What! let you go?" shouted Woppits. "No, fox; that hole's closed."

"Well, keep me here! Give me six days to arrange my affairs in, by letter, as well as I can, and then I'll tell you my secret, on condition that you let me off forty-eight hours before you act on the information!"

"What do you think of it, Mr. Biddles?" Woppits asked.

"Seems reasonable enough," replied the showman; "only I don't see how we're to keep him idling about here. After all, I think you'd better clap him under lock and key."

"I'll do anything to make myself useful, gentlemen," Mr. Hatcher said, humbly. "Perhaps a little music on the flute would enliven your entertainment."

"A little of your grandmother! No soft moosic here!" rejoined the showman. "Do you know the drum? Can you play the pandeens?"

"I'm sure I'll try; it'll only be tempory."

"Get 'em out, Woppits—their performance does interfere with my speaking—and let's see what he can do."

The drum and the reed organ were produced, and rigged on Mr. Hatcher in the orthodox manner.

"All right?" cried Biddles.

"All right, sir," sighed Joel.

"Then do 'The Last Rose of Summer,' after which the Kershooker. Off we go!"

Now Hatcher had had some practice on the reed-organ while a boy, and, urged by the occasion, acquitted himself in a manner not wholly unsatisfactory to the showman.

"There, that'll do; the public'll stand a week of it, I dare say. What's your name?"

"Baker, sir."

"Then consider yourself engaged, Baker, till you've settled your affairs, and satisfied my friend and crocodile, Mr. Woppits. Salary, you won't get any. As regards your board, that'll be paid for out of the £2 you were good enough to give me, and Mr. Woppits will indulge you with the loan of a hammock. Baker, you may go to bed now. Hi! wait a bit! Just slip your boots off, will you? And now I think of it, I'll come in and take the rest of your clothes presently. They'll be safer locked up; and you can have them again in the morning, you know!"

CHAPTER XXXIV.

OLD ACQUAINTANCE.

As it were to assist her reflections, after Woppits's unceremonious farewell, Mrs. Bell took Hatcher's money-bag from the drawer in which she had bestowed it, placed it on the table, and looked at it. Presently she untied the mouth of the bag, and in the same abstracted manner tossed the coins backward and forward in her lap, and counted them. First, there were eleven, then twenty-three; now the whole amounted to seventeen pounds, three shillings, and fivepence; now, to twenty years ago. Detecting herself in that absurd error, she was about to restore the money to the money-bag, when she observed some writing upon it.

Mrs. Bell had never detected that inscription before, for two sufficient reasons. In the first place, Mrs. Hatcher's hand (in which the scrawl was written) was so eccentric as to be scarcely recognizable as a hand at all; and, secondly, the bag had been toned by too much use and too little washing into the colour of Mrs. Hatcher's ink. However, less eager eyes than Mrs. Bell's might have deciphered the legend—"J. Hatcher, Sleaford." That is how it ran, or rather staggered; for Mrs. Hatcher's hand seemed given to drink—now bolting forward almost on its nose, now brought up suddenly by an upstroke like a lamp-post, and meandering from side to side in a helpless way at all times.

But to Mrs. Bell the inscription was as luminous, as mysterious, as startling, as that writing on the wall which dismayed Babylon. Sleaford! That towny village she knew well enough—who better? But Hatcher?—

After some reflection, Mrs. Bell thought of a rabbit-hutch, which immediately reminded her of an old woman named Hatcher, who kept a little broker's shop at the extremity of the town. She was a widow, with a sickly-looking boy who kept guinea-pigs, with which Lucy Howlet used to fancy he shared a strong family likeness. Was that little boy and the owner of the money-bag one and the same person? Mrs. Bell instantly imagined a guinea-pig, took it into her bosom, and compared it with the portrait of himself which Hatcher had already lodged there. Yes! There was still a striking ensemble of resemblance.

The acute reader, who sees at once that Lucy Howlet and Mrs. Bell are one, and who remembers where she was born (and Woppits too, for that matter), will not be surprised to learn that she was thrown by this discovery into new confusion. It was odd, to say the least of it, that this man, who had shown so constant and so mysterious an interest in her boy, should live in the place so memorable to her, and where a certain nameless one lived, or used to live. That J. Hatcher should have a still greater interest in Ruth was more strange. If the one might be accounted for—[here a spasm inserted itself into Mrs. Bell's reflections]—how should the other interest be explained?

But I shall not attempt to follow her through all her reflections, her suspicions, and still less her dreams, which were wildest. Results are what we care for; and the result in this case was, that Mrs. Bell determined to beard the guinea-pig in his hutch. Assured that he was playing a part in an intrigue which seriously affected her dear ones, she felt that to master him would be to master it; and who knew what the mystery might conceal?

Prompt was Mrs. Bell's action. It was not very far to Old Sleaford, even in coaching times; and, with an army of memories storming her heart, which certainly would have been breached and taken but for the fortitude which garrisoned it, she was set down in Sleaford High Street. She hardly knew the place, it had grown so much. 'Twas quite a town now. It had an hôtel in it, in stucco; and was become so well-to-do, that it would not recognize her. However, she forgave Sleaford; she was glad to walk unobserved from under that plaster portico into the shadow of Sleaford's greatness, which accompanied her till down the street. At the further end thereof, she noticed a "furniture emporium," which (she thought) must have distanced even Sleaford itself, if it had grown out of Mrs. Hatcher's little shop; and hers certainly was the name painted over the door. Mrs. Bell observed a man in the shop—Simmonds; and through a glass door beyond, a bonnet—Joel's mother.

Joel's mother had not "gone home" yet then. She still wore the bonnet; the "rheumatiz" still had possession of her back; there was no change in the old woman, save that her features and her avarice had sharpened with increasing years, and that she idolized Joly more than ever.

At present she sits over the fire, mumbling the cud of conjectures between her poor old jaws. What had become of Joly? What screw was that that was loose in the K. business? Had the K. business brought him into trouble? Ah! had he lost his money? had he been robbed in that wicked London, so fatal to youth?

If anything could have warmed the old woman's blood, that conjecture would have done it. She did begin to feel some heat when Simmonds entered, circled his mouth with his hands, and bawled the announcement—

"A lady, ma'am!"

Mrs. Hatcher lost half her infirmities at the news. Assisted by a crutched stick, she walked almost nimbly into the shop.

"What article can we show you, ma'am?" said she.

"I beg pardon for troubling you, but I wish to see a Mr. J. Hatcher. Does he live here?"

"He's my son!" said the old woman, proudly. "He ain't at home just now, but any business you may have with him you can do with me, ma'am? It's all one; we're mother and son—and partners too."

"Do you expect your son home this evening?"

"Expect him? I've been expecting him two or three evenings. He's gone to London. What might be your business with him, ma'am?" added the old woman sharply, as a suspicion flashed into her mind—

(If I were asked what the old woman's mind was like, I should say one of the old-fashioned, angular, tight-waisted fire-stoves, of the dice-box pattern.)

—that Joel had been courting in secret, with a view to bringing a wife home.

"I am not sure that it is your son I want to see, and must defer opening my business till I'm assured of that."

"Oh, well. There's my Joel behind you. Now you can tell whether it's him or no."

Mrs. Bell turned with a start, as the old woman pointed to a portrait hanging on the wall of her sitting-room.

"That's the man!" And without waiting for an invitation, Mrs. Bell walked into the room, closer to examine the picture; Mrs. Hatcher tottered after, and closing the door.

The old woman watched the eager, half-frightened eyes of Mrs. Bell as she scanned the portrait; and when she turned from it, very pale, the old Bonnet asked shrilly—

"Well, now what about him? Do you want to sell anything, or buy anything, or what? If it's business, you'll do better with me than him, for he's a hard nail to drive sometimes."

"Do you know on what errand your son's gone to London?"

"A sale. To buy furniture. That's what he told me."

"Had he no other business?"

"None that I know of," replied the old woman, nervously. "What a lot of questions you ask? Nothing have happened to him, have it?"

"I can't say—at present," rejoined the other, looking stedfastly into Mrs. Hatcher's eyes. "But I'm afraid something will happen to him if he's not careful. A few days ago he came to my house inquiring for a little girl whom I've adopted."

"Then I don't know anything about it!" the old woman cried in a high voice, shutting her eyes, and shaking her head emphatically. "I don't know a bit about my son's affairs. He's as close as a post, he is."

"A little girl who has a peculiar mark on her throat."

"'Tain't here, I tell you! 'Tain't here!" returned the old woman fiercely, snapping these denials at Mrs. Bell like pistol shots. "You've come to the wrong place. There's plenty of Hatchers about—must be, I'm sure. Where was you directed to?"

"If that's your son's portrait, your son it was who came to my house. He pretended, among other things, that he was a constable. I don't know what his reasons were for adopting such a character, or what his opportunities for studying it may have been."

"'Tain't here! 'tain't here!" repeated the old woman, shutting her eyes again in a tremor of apprehension. "There's another Sleaford in Yorkshire, I daresay, or somewhere down in those parts."

"Well, do you know this?" Mrs. Bell produced the money-bag, and, what was more to the purpose, the money in it.

The widow opened her eyes widely enough when she heard that delightful chinking. Know that bag? Didn't she give twopence halfpenny for it at Mrs. Okey's? Did she not tie it up when Joly went away, and place it in his pocket with her own hands? Mumbling unintelligibly, she took the proffered treasure with trembling eagerness, and caressed the sweet pieces through the canvas. Ah! why are not all coins called "angels?"

Never had Mrs. Hatcher experienced so sore a trial as that she was now exposed to; never had her love for Joly or her submission to his will been so severely exercised. The money was undoubtedly his—hers; and she dare not claim it! Agony of agonies, she had to hand it back to that stranger-woman, whom plainly it did not belong to.

Her crazy fingers played faster and faster about the money-bag—fondly too, as once they played among the infant Joel's locks—as she restored it to Mrs. Bell; or rather as she placed it on a table near Mrs. Bell, a compromise which appeared to soothe the widow much.

"Know it?" she said—"that bag o' money? No, I don't. It ain't ours, and we'll have nothing to do with it. I couldn't help taking it in my hands, you see; for 'tisn't often poor people get the chance of handling such a lot of money. All in gold too! No, I never set eyes on it before, ma'am."

"How do you know it's all in gold, then?"

"There she is! there she is!—down on me again!" groaned the old woman, addressing herself to the fire-place. "I do wish Mr. Hatcher was at home, I do. He'd tackle her!"

"I see," said Mrs. Bell, "that you will give me no information. Very well, I must try what can be done with the nearest magistrate."

Now the nearest magistrate was Mr. Keppel.

"Heart alive, woman, what information do you want? Oh, lor! oh, dear! what do you come worriting an old woman like me for? Sit down, sit down, and tell me what you want to know about my Joel."

"This, then: every particular concerning the child he threw into a limekiln!"

"What!" screamed the old woman, "do they say he did that? Where are they? Where is he? Take me to him—I'll soon prove his innocence! Let 'em give me my son, and take back their m—— Who are you?"

The old woman had crept close to the young one during this passionate harangue, and it was when their faces most nearly approached that Mrs. Hatcher suddenly paused, and then burst into that exclamation, "Who are you?"

"My name's Bell!" replied she whom we have also known as Lucy Howlet. Lucy Howlet was abashed.

DURING MR. BIDDLES'S EXHIBITION, HATCHER RECEIVES AN IMPORTANT COMMUNICATION.

"Oh my! oh dear!" chuckled the widow, childishly. "Here's the last day, and judgment coming, sure-ly! The dead coming to life, and the live going to death! Oh lor! it's wonderful!"

Mrs. Bell turned deadly pale, at any rate. She saw that despite the changeful influence of twenty years, the old woman recognised her. The widow noted the alteration in her demeanour, and eagerly followed up the advantage.

"So you're married—eh, Lucy? You didn't find all your sweethearts so fickle, then, as your first love, my dear? Is he as handsome as that one was?"

Mrs. Bell could make no reply to that, nor could she withdraw her burning eyes from Widow Hatcher's, twinkling with malicious fascination.

"Ah!" continued the old woman, "you didn't play your cards well, my lass. But then you had no chance, had you? playing hearts while that other one, Miss Butler, played diamonds?"

For the life of her, Mrs. Bell could not help repeating in an inquiring tone, "Butler? Miss Butler?"

"Ay, ay! you remember, surely, child! Mr. Butler bought the Keppel estate, didn't he?—and Mr. Horace married Butler's daughter. She wasn't such a beauty as you was, my dear. Ah, you ain't such a beauty now as you were then. It would be no use angling for a fine gentleman now. But no matter, your fortune's made, and Mr. Bell's none the worse because you couldn't marry Mr. Keppel—is he, my dear? He! he! Oh, the days when we was young!"

How the old woman mowed at the young one! How the young one crimsoned—how shameful she looked, yet how steady!

"Has Mr. Keppel any children?"

Widow Hatcher was still more delighted when she heard this question. Then this other one did not know to whom belonged the child she had adopted! What a joke that was!

"Never had but one child, and that he lost!"

Now the old woman used this word in its deadly sense; in which it is generally understood in reference to children. But Mrs. Bell's mind was full of a child who was strangely found; and the word struck her with a double meaning.

"Lost?" she rejoined. "How lost?"

"Died!" cried the other boldly.

But Mrs. Bell did not hear the reply. Her own question had thrown her into such wonder, that she heard and saw nothing. Emerging out of it as breathless as if it had been a big wave, she repeated impatiently—

"Well, how lost?"

"Died! I told you so before!" and the old woman fumbled at her apron strings.

"You are not telling me the truth, Mrs. Hatcher!"

"Oh dear! I am a liar now, am I? Lucy Howlet, I shan't answer you another word! Oh, lor! oh, lor!—I ought never to have answered you a word at all!"

The old woman was in despair again. She drew her chair up to the fire and swayed to and fro, to and fro, groaning painfully. Mrs. Bell made no attempt to re-engage her attention—that, she saw, was useless—and wherefore should she? Had she not already learned enough?—too much, perhaps?

Without another word, Mrs. Bell softly voided the parlour, passed through the emporium, and gained the street. Now, to be confirmed! half the town could answer the question—"How lost?" And what might not the answer signify—for Ruth, for herself, for Hatcher, for——

Suppose we do not ask the question, then? And yet what harm could be done by *her* knowledge on the matter? She had borne painful secrets heretofore, and one more secret added to the burden could make little difference, especially if borne for others' sake. Far less endurable was uncertainty.

But how shall she ask the question, and of whom? Mrs. Hatcher had rent the disguise in which she believed herself hidden, and now, as she walked rapidly through the town, it seemed as if every one she met looked askance at her. She quitted the streets, turned off into a lane, and wandered on till by and by she saw the dark walls of Keppel Lodge glooming among the trees.

At this sight Mrs. Bell neither fainted nor trembled, nor felt any pang. The feeling she did have was rather of calm surprise, or curiosity. Had she seen the old house in a vision long ago, or if in some pre-existence she had been born in such a house, dreaming, suffering, and dying in it, she might have experienced just such an emotion. She was carried away out of herself, and viewed all those scenes with a wide, wise, spiritual eye—sad, of course, as silence is sad—but without a ripple of emotion; and, as for her appearance, there was nothing in that to strike a casual person or the vulgar—for the only differences were, that her gray eyes were of a paler colour than usual and her lips were parted.

So much was she separate from herself, in this dreamy spiritual way, that she was quite unconscious of the manner in which she sometimes hurried along, and sometimes loitered, or where she loitered, or why she loitered, or whither she went. Of course we know. We know she visited a hundred familiar spots; but I, for one, refuse to sort them over. Let any one who has read this story from the beginning, imagine what they were and must have been; that will be enough for him.

But for the very story's sake, one exception must be made. The reader may remember Springfield Lane. It was in Springfield Lane where Horace Keppel and Lucy Howlet met when he essayed to teach her the names of the stars, and where he first kissed her. Now the stars were out again by this time, though the evening was yet young and beautifully clear. Without intention, without consciousness, with that pale unvarying judicial light in her eyes, Mrs. Bell entered Springfield Lane once more. In no respect was the scene changed, neither as to the earth beneath nor the heavens above. Even the wind that so kindly kissed away her blushes on that evening of stellar memory, seemed to have returned; and if Mrs. Bell had been disposed to break down, now was the time and this the scene. But it was not so. She was observant enough, for that matter. She saw those same stars, heard that same familiar voice, felt that sweet wind rippling over her forehead, and was still as calm, as judicial, as essential, as somebody else's angel.

When she had advanced half down the lane, she saw a slow, melancholy figure advancing from the other end. A slow, large figure, uncertain of gait, with rounded shoulders, and head declining. The figure stopped where the leafy avenue was broken by some low wooden pales. Against these the figure leaned, and took off its hat, and looked about it in a purposeless manner. It would be absurd to pretend that the woman at one end of the lane did not immediately recognise the man at the other. Even *that* failed to disturb her: only she ceased to breathe for a while, that was all. She walked up the avenue without hesitation; and in passing the stranger, gazing upwards, as once before, to "Calliope" and Mars, and the rest of them, looked into his face steadily. *He* knew her not—she was sure he would not; but, dark as it was, she scanned and recognised every line in his countenance. It was altered since she beheld it last; it is altered since we beheld it last—so much the better for him. Pale, sullen, and spiritless it was; with that poor, wandering, helpless look upon it which one often sees, and would entirely pity, if there was not something awful in it too; as if some mightier fingers than the finger of time or care had passed over it, quenching the light of the flesh.

Observing that, something like an emotion did pass through Mrs. Bell's mind for the first time. Judge how evanescent it must have been, when *another* observation, still more striking and to the purpose, also sank into her mind, and was lost, a moment after it had been made. It was this. She plainly saw Ruth's face, while she slept, in the stranger's face, dully looking up to Mars and the rest. Was not this a revelation?

After that, it is scarcely worth while to accompany Mrs. Bell further. Who cares that she might have been seen by and by near a cottage before mentioned? Or after that again, when the stellar world had been lifted out of sight, and Mr. Keppel sat at home, drumming his fingers on the table, that she appeared in a church-yard, and what is called made a fool of herself over her mother's grave?

This was reprehensible in Mrs. Bell. What business had she there? What did she mean by breaking down in *that* sacred place? We, who are notoriously respectable—persons of whom society cannot say that black is the white of our eyes, must really disapprove of this. Statistics—which in these few years have settled the business of human life, tabulated its passions, buckled its virtues in lots, pigeon-holed its vices, discovered the square-root of Christianity, and defined the apostles—prove that that sort of thing is all humbug; and so is everything else—but statistics.

CHAPTER XXXV.

MUSIC AND THE DRUMMER.

MRS. BELL's visit, and its ominous purport, combined with Joly's long absence and mysterious letter, had a disastrous effect on Mrs. Hatcher. The sands of her life [that's neat and new, isn't it?] had nearly run out already; and this shock precipitated an undue number of grains into the glass. Rheumatism, in the back or elsewhere, is not a light subject. As I gaze at the poor old woman on the morrow made memorable by Mrs. Bell, I recall any indecent reference I may hitherto have made to the racking malady, in connection with Joel's mother. Poor old girl! it is hard to say, though, where her "rheumatiz" is seated this morning, or rather where is its capital seat; for there are symptoms of its having made a settlement in her heart, to say nothing of its head. Both ache, at any rate, and as violently as ever her back did or does. To use a phrase very favourite in the City from its force and humour, I should like to insure her life this morning; and would stand something handsome if with her life I could profit by her love, for surely, sordid as she is, cruel as she is sometimes, and not too honest, she does love her Joly dearly. She is in a fever about Joly—and the money. A real spasmodic thrill reinforces the pains of "rheumatiz" as she associates the one with a prison and the other with restitution. She is very ill indeed.

And not only is Mrs. Hatcher sick, in body and mind, but she has no friends. Simmonds can hardly be called a friend; and as for Simmonds's wife (the only other person with whom she is intimate, in the neighbourly or kindred sense of the word), she only comes to char, not to perform the offices of friendship, which is quite another thing. Friendship is a flower to whose growth the clay of which Mrs. Hatcher is composed (a damp, cold clay—witness the "rheumatiz") has ever been unfavourable; and that Joly is so completely clay of her clay has something to do with her great love for him, perhaps. That hardy plant, Mr. Skinner, has succeeded more than any one else in "striking" into that same soil, owing to a certain admixture in it of religious apprehension; and for him she resolves to send in this emergency.

Far be it from me to misrepresent Mr. Skinner; it was his misfortune that he mistook his vocation, which was worldly, as his appearance was. That affair of the "Fat of Sinners Food for Fire" was awkward, though I believe he wrote the little work, and that the Bosjesmen (to whom it was supplied gratis, by subscription) read it in considerable numbers. The quarterly reports of its distribution and workings are before me, with a statement of moneys subscribed, the cost of printing, freight, etc. Also a copy of verses composed by a young Bosjesman who had derived much benefit from "Fat of Sinners," and in which the line "Tank you, O my white-faced brudder" occurs with touching frequency. Besides, the leather-seller who protested against the "Fat of Sinners," and endeavoured to show that not a hundred copies of the pamphlet had ever been printed, failed to make out his case, and only succeeded in bringing scandal and controversy into the town. At the same time, it is certain that Mr. Skinner is not improved as a man nor as a shepherd. The enthusiasm which led him to the care of souls, and made him useful in a rough, rude sort of way, has abated. It is a thing, that enthusiasm, which will subside, leaving the shore upon which it rolled with such force and majesty very muddy—dull, flat, unwholesome, despised. Those who pass that way lift their hands in wonder. Oh, what a falling off! Who *would* have thought it? But the result is very natural indeed, and quite to be accounted for.

Mr. Skinner received the summons with satisfaction. Nothing pleased him more than a summons to a sick-bed, the more hopeless the better; as some old women delight in performing the "last offices" to the dead. He had visions as he picked his way towards Mrs. Hatcher's abode—visions which, for fear of offending just susceptibilities, I must refer to no further than to observe that there was stationery in them—pens, ink, paper, a piece of green ferret, and a pounce-box. These visions came out in bolder lines, in brighter lines, when on entering Mrs. Hatcher's room he beheld a writing-desk open at a table near her bedside. Looking upon the fair paper and the new-nibbed pen for a moment, the gravity which oppressed Mr. Skinner took a richer, softer quality; acquiring a tone, a savour, a bouquet as grateful as if it had been twenty years in bottle. Bellworthy, the fashionable undertaker, who furnishes for the nobility, and who appears to take death into custody with that grand judicial manner of his, seldom drew off his gloves with a more appropriate air than did Mr. Skinner on this occasion. He drew off his gloves, placed them on the crown of his hat, and smoothing Mrs. Hatcher's pillow, said : "I am here obedient to your wishes—the servant of the meanest of my flock in life or death. What shall I do for you?"

Mrs. Hatcher replied that she did not know what could be done for her, hardly. She was going home—she knew that, and it would be a blessing and a release for all parties. The "rheumatiz" she'd had enough of, and there was very little comfort in the world to make up for it. She was ready to leave the world, and if any poor woman deserved that epitaph, "Afflictions sore long time I bore," it was she. Only there was something on her mind. Oh, Mr. Skinner, you have never been a mother, and you don't know her anxiety about that boy! If she could put him on his guard; if she could only ascertain what had befallen him in that wicked London, she should be happy.

This was all very well, but it was hardly the sort of feeling which pleased Mr. Skinner. He adjured her to take no more thought of worldly affairs, save to set them in order. To set them in order once for all, and then wait for release. The old woman groaned a good deal during his remarks, sometimes with a touch of impatience. When he had done, she said—

"Will you write for me, Mr. Skinner?"

"I will, Mrs. Hatcher!" and he drew up to the table. "Now," continued he, dipping a pen into the ink, "what is it to be? Be calm, be calm, and remember the solemn nature of the pass to which you are brought !"

"Oh lor'! oh dear! Are you ready?"

"Proceed, at your leisure. Shall I call our friend Simmonds in ?"

"What good'll he do?" returned the old woman, sharply.

"As a witness, ma'am ; a witness is—"

"Witness! Simmonds a witness!" she gasped, starting up in her bed.

"Why not, Mrs. Hatcher? He's a respectable, though a misguided person. His testimony is as good as anybody's, in the eye of the law."

"It's false! He knows nothing about it! His testimony's a lie, and so I'll tell him before all the lawyers in Cristendom. Oh lor'! that woman's been a tampering with him! Oh dear, what a world it is! I wish I was out of it !"

And the old woman grew so hysterical, that Mrs. Simmonds's appearance was quite opportune. However, it did not please Mrs. Hatcher. She turned wrathfully upon her, as soon as her cap appeared within the bed-curtains, demanded to be informed what she wanted there, and dismissing her to her stairs with an injunction to take care of the soap, for she would get no more. Nor did the charwoman's entrance please Mr. Skinner, He followed the already crest-fallen woman out of the room (if the term crest may be applied to her cap, which was easily dejected), and said he, snapping at her with his finger and thumb, "Woman, you have been listening ! You have been

prying at the keyhole ! Be warned. Go to your stairs, remember what your suffering mistress said about the soap, and pry no more !"

Mrs. Simmonds went to her stairs crushed—so impressive was Mr. Skinner's manner. She said it was like Daniel and the den of lions. As for Skinner himself, he returned to Mrs. Hatcher's bedside with a more judicial appearance about him than ever, and something medical too. Her sudden exclamation startled him ; and he hardly knew whether he was about to listen to a death-bed confession or to the ravings of fever.

He had reason to be annoyed at Mrs. Simmonds's intrusion. The explosion of which she was the victim seemed to tranquillise the old woman at a very critical moment. She was still greatly excited, it is true : and sought her pastor's eye with tenfold dread and doubt. But she had recovered her self-possession, or that principle called cunning, which does duty for so many qualities, and is known sometimes to constitute the whole mental and moral machinery of a man. Her meaning look inclined Mr. Skinner to the belief that she was *pro tem* insane ; but that made no difference as to his course of action. He seated himself again took up the pen, and said—

"Now, my dear Mrs. Hatcher, we will resume the melancholy but necessary business which the intrusion of that person interrupted. Simmonds shall not be called, if you object."

"What does he know about it ?"

"Nothing, I *presume*," replied Skinner, blandly.

"Then please write—'My dear Joly.'"

"My dear Joly," repeated Mr. Skinner, committing the words to paper with a bad grace. "Yes, I've got 'My dear Joly.'"

"—This leaves me in a sinkin' state, which I hope you're well at present. What did that young woman want, that come here yesterday about the K business? and——"

"Wait a bit, wait a bit ! Kay business—how do you spell it ?" asked Mr. Skinner, who began to feel interested.

"Never mind, write K business—letter K."

"My dear madam," Mr. Skinner exclaimed, throwing down his pen, "he'll never understand that, you may depend on it. K? K may mean king, K may mean carrots, or anything. Give it in full, ma'am ; give it in full, and don't mind me. K don't stand for conspiracy, I dare say."

"Conspiracy? Oh dear no, Mr. Skinner. (Oh, lor! *he's* down on me now !) We leave that to the world, sir, and our dealin's is respectable ; but we've our little family secrets, you know, sir ; and you'll oblige me very much if you write K business."

"Oh, very good, Mrs. Hatcher. *I'm* not a papish priest, nor am I a beast of Babylon in the confessional. Proceed."

"— Come here yesterday about the K business, and bullied your poor mother worse than a pickpocket. She said she had adopted a certain little party, and she come and offered me your bag of money, which she tried to try me with, and I had to give it back to her, though I knew as well as the nose on my face that it belonged to us. My dear Joly, I have the 'rheumatiz' worse than ever, and my heart aches for you, my child ; for she have sowed suspicions in it of your being took to—"

"Of your bein' took to—Yes, ma'am ; I've got 'took to.'"

"Took ! I said 'in trouble,' 'being in trouble,' Mr. Skinner."

"Oh, did you ? Very well. Go on—'in trouble.'"

"——all along of this K business, which you said yourself there was a screw loose, and I'm all on thorns. Return immediate. She said if I wouldn't give information about that business, she'd go to the—nearest—"

"Yes, ma'am."

"Say 'the nearest M which you know it's a K?' He'll understand it sir," said Mrs. Hatcher, coaxingly.

"I can't do it, ma'am—I must really give it up ! How do I know that this is not a snare—that in the hands of my enemies this mysterious and hieroglyphical writing may not be used to my downfall? The K business ! the nearest M which you know is a K! No, I really can't do it," and Mr. Skinner rose and brushed his hat with his gloves, as if about to depart.

"Oh, don't sir, I beg of you. It's only a little innocent matter—about a Christmas party—it ain't indeed, sir. Go on!"

"Ah, but what's to compensate me for the risk, my dear Mrs. Hatcher? especially as at your age nobody knows how soon one may be called away where flesh is grass, and money is dross, and the goods of this world are no more, and when you may not be here to explain the mysterious writing!"

"What you say is true, sir. Money *is* dross, and I shall soon have to leave my few pounds behind me," whined the old woman, keeping her eye on the reverend Mr. Skinner, "and if a half-sovereign would be of any use toward your little new chapel, sir, I'm sure you're welcome to it beforehand."

"I shall say nothing against that, for the true use of wealth is good works, and if you show yourself thus disinterested, why should not I? Yes, I will proceed with the writing;" and Skinner resumed his seat with as much resolution as if he had been going to the stake. "All right—'go to the nearest M which you know it's a K.'"

"My dear Joly, that put me in such a flutter you can't think; but I found her out, and I brazened her out; but who do you think she is? Oh, my son! I think the judgment's coming, for she is signs and wonders more than heart can tell! Be wise as serpents; and come and see your old mother before she dies, please heaven. Come or send a letter; and if so be as you're in any trouble, let the business—the business——"

"The K business?" suggested Mr. Skinner.

"Yes, the K business. Let it——"

"Well, ma'am, what's the word?"

"Bust!" replied Mrs. Hatcher; and fell back on her pillow as if she herself had exploded. "Oh, lor'! why wasn't I taught readin, ritin, and 'rithmetic?"

"And now, my dear Mrs. Hatcher, what are you going to do with this letter?" Mr. Skinner asked, when he had folded it in the approved manner.

"Have you give him my love?"

"I have said: 'So no more at present from your affectionate parent unto death.'"

"Then address to his uncle, please, sir. His direction is, Mr. B. Mawley, 222, Smartin's Lane. Send it by post; and thankee for your trouble, I'm sure."

Here the "rheumatiz" seized the old woman so savagely, that the reverend Mr. Skinner was fain to leave the house.

"Poor old woman," said he to himself; "her anxiety and her innocence are wonderfully and beautifully made! Why this mystery? Why, carnal that I am! do I find myself associating it with the Hatchers' prosperity? But what then, I ask? Am I to turn my back on an afflicted sister, because of my unjust suspicions? No. Rather turn the other cheek! Rather do more than less than she requests. Post the letter! Post a missive upon which so much may depend! Perish the thought! Take it yourself, Eb. Skinner, for the mortification of flesh; you've nothing else to do; your reward is sure; and this half-sovereign may be lawfully considered as so much in advance on the expense."

The coach was just about to start from the Keppel Hotel, when Mr. Skinner arrived at the door. The inside places were all taken, to the manifest disappointment of a person who had much of the lady in her appearance, though she was rather poorly dressed. Half an hour before, this person had bidden farewell to a stout, white-haired old woman—eighty years old if a day—who had accompanied her from beyond the village, till the Sleaford houses came fairly into view. The stout old woman was Mrs. Joliffe; the disappointed woman was Mrs. Bell; and Mr. Skinner was at once interested in her. He wondered whether this was the mysterious woman who had come about the K business, who had adopted a certain party, and who threatened to go to the nearest M that was a K? He put his head on one side, and having viewed her in that manner, came to the conclusion that her appearance rather favoured the supposition.

Accordingly, when Mrs. Bell had taken her seat on the coach, Mr. Skinner ascended and placed himself immediately opposite her. At the same moment he put on his gloves and his thoughtful, suffering air; but it was apparent that even he could not help taking an interest—melancholy though it might be—in the bustle of the scene. He stood up as the coach rattled from the town, drew out his handkerchief, and waved a heart-rending farewell over Mrs. Bell's head to some person or persons invisible; though they evidently returned the salute, for he smiled so tenderly that his white teeth threatened to shed themselves in a shower of love and sadness. He took it much to heart when the town disappeared; and kept his eyes fixed on the distance that engulphed it—*i. e.*, in a right line past Mrs. Bell's left ear. Thus she had a fine opportunity of studying the play of emotion in a simple, unsophisticated, pastorly man. But she seemed to derive little pleasure from the study, whatever the advantage may have been.

Mr. Skinner gave her several variations on himself, too. A large, soft boy, like a baby seen through a strong magnifying glass, came piping after the coach, halting at intervals to bite at a huge piece of bread-and-butter. The guard, observing this, stopped the coach, got down, ran to meet the tardy boy; and taking him from behind, like a big ball, bowled him along at a much accelerated pace. Mr. Skinner immediately came out of his abstraction, and gazed at the youth with a deep paternal and philosophical interest, as he painfully made the ascent of the coach.

"Ah!" remarked the reverend gentleman, smiling and looking Mrs. Bell fairly in the face for the first time—"such is life. Youth, fresh and buoyant, leaps from his mother's arms, eager to enter the arena of existence, eager for the strife. Scarce has he thrown aside his rattle—" (Here the youth made a ferocious face at Mr. Skinner behind his back)—"than he longs to try his strength with men."

("No he don't," growled the youth; "or else he'd jolly soon try it with you.")

"Here's our young friend—he listens for the bugle-horn that shall announce that the coach is wending its way to London. His mind full of golden visions, he bounds forth, cheerfully takes his place, and hooray! he is on his way to make his fortune. Isn't that the case, my young friend?" added Mr. Skinner, as he turned to the large soft boy.

"You dunno what you're talking of, you don't! You've been having too much. I'm a goin' to fetch home four pigs, if you wants to know what I'm got on this coach for!"

Mr. Skinner was not at all abashed by this answer. Again addressing Mrs. Bell, he continued:—

"Innocent youth! But we, ma'am, who've seen the downfall of young ambition, and have fought with the cares and disappointments of life, we have found out its illusions. H'm?"

"Oh, yes!" replied Mrs. Bell.

"We have little romance left in us, though mysteries crowd many a seeming happy household, and embitter the cup that's drained by many an apparently contented heart. H'm?"

"Ah, indeed!"

"A skeleton in every house, you know! Anxious travail and journeyings to and fro—this is our lot. Eh?"

"Is it *your* lot?"

"Ah, indeed and indeed! What do you suppose I am on my way to town for? Travail and anxious journeying! I seek the son of a dying mother; a son whom you may know if you have any friends in Sleaford. H'm?"

"I have not," replied Mrs. Bell, who began to feel uneasy.

"Well, well! The case is the same. The mother is dying; the son's absence is unexplained and prolonged. The pastor is sent for. The case is laid before him; and he, who has only one object in life, to right the wrong, to remedy the evil, to clear away the clouds that obscure innocence, or conceal guilt, is on his way to find that son." And Skinner concluded with a smile at once humble and benevolent.

Mrs. Bell made no reply to this odd address. Not that she had much doubt as to what the man was aiming at, but she deliberated whether she should maintain an appearance of indifference to his observations or whether she should boldly respond to them.

She had resolved on this latter course, and was just about to address a question point-blank at Mr. Skinner, when the coach suddenly swept round an angle of the road, and she beheld an object which brought a cry to her lips. Mr. Skinner followed her eyes, and uttered an ejaculation of surprise too, ordered the coachman to stop, and slipped off into a crowd of people assembled about a show-van.

Mr. Biddles was standing at the door, haranguing the populace on the merits of his crocodile, of which he exhibited a small portion, to satisfy the sceptical. This—the showman, not the crocodile—was the object which had startled Mrs. Bell.

It was a much more curious object, however, which Mr. Skinner's vision lighted on. At a little distance from the door of the caravan stood Mr. Hatcher. A white hat was on his head, misery was in his eye, a big drum was slung about his neck, and a set of pandean-pipes was lashed into his cravat. Banging the drum, jerking his head along these pipes, he was making the "Lass of Richmond Hill" hideous on those instruments; and the more he played the more dejected he appeared.

Hatcher was in captivity : he was buckled to the big drum; the pipes kept his head at such an elevation that he could see no mortal creature within four feet of him; and his elbows were ingeniously connected behind, which accounted for the eccentric style in which he performed on the drum—like a chicken flapping its wings.

To this condition had he been brought by those conspirators, Messrs. Woppits and Biddles. Deprived of his clothes by night, harnessed to the drum by day, flight was out of the question, and yet how should his affairs be settled by proxy? All he could do was to write to his uncle, the sheriff's officer, giving him urgent instructions to sell the broker's business and stock privately, for cash only, and within five days. (This letter was read by Woppits, he undertaking, on his honour, to [post it without looking at the direction.) For the rest, he could only trust that the property might be sold; and then, at the expiration of the six days, he would faithfully perform his part of the contract, sweep his money together, sweep up the old woman, and be off to commence life anew in foreign parts.

He had just recommenced the "Lass of Richmond Hill," and, for the hundredth time, a review of his melancholy situation, when he felt a hand laid gently on his arm. He turned about, and, with a shriek in C, recognised Mr. Skinner. Not by his countenance, however—Joel's pipes were pitched too high in his cravat to admit of his looking so low; he knew Mr. Skinner by the singular disposition of his ears.

The squeak in C nearly frightened to death a little boy who at that moment was feeling the crocodile's tail. The showman, however, did not notice it, much to Hatcher's relief; for it was impossible to guess what might not be the result of his being seen in conversation with so sleek and mysterious a person as Mr. Skinner. So he banged away at the drum harder than ever, to drown any blundering exclamation that his friend might indulge in, at the same time jerking the word "Whoosh!" at that gentleman, as one addresses a strange cat.

"You know me, I believe, Mr. Hatcher?" said the other, in a low voice. "My name's Skinner!"

"Be off!" returned the other, suddenly, taking advantage of a long dodge from the upper to the lower reeds of his mouth-organ. "Whoosh!"

"I've a message from your mother." And shuffling into position just behind Hatcher, the reverend gentleman poured the contents of the letter into his ear softly.

Now Hatcher's consternation was complete. However, by a superhuman effort, he continued his performance, bemused as he was. At length he nudged Mr. Skinner, and addressed him in little bits of speech, thrust between the bars of the music.

"Follow the caravan—till it puts—up for the night. Get a suit of clothes—to fit me—anything'll do.—Wait till we're asleep—one o'clock.—Then wait—few yards off.—Be careful—my only chance.—Explain afterwards."

More than convinced by Hatcher's manner that he was deeply in earnest, Mr. Skinner inquired no further, but sidled out of the throng.

The performances were over; they had again been most successful; the yellow house was pitched on a dreary piece of waste ground for the night, and Biddles smoked his pipe in peace, with Hatcher's boots under his chair for surety. Also, he drank grog, of which he administered small quantities from time to time to Mr. Hatcher, in a teacup. "Mr. Baker," says he, on every such occasion, "your health, sir."

"Thank you," replies Baker, "same to you, I'm sure," and they nod to each other over the liquor, and drink; one as if he enjoyed it very much, and the other as if he did not. Woppits is seated in grave contemplation, looking from time to time at Joel's long harlequin figure, and wondering what change the

world will take when touched by that secret of his. At length, carefully locking up the house, and pocketing the key, he retires.

"Now, Baker!" cries the showman, "here's just a spoonful more for you, and I trust you're satisfied with the way that you've walked into the rum to-night. I hope you consider, sir, that you've had your whack of it. All I can say is, that the bottle you were good enough to stand is out; and it's too late now for you to send for another."

"Well, there's another day to-morrow," replied Hatcher, waving his teacup in a bacchanal manner. "We'll have another bowl—several bowls—before we part."

"Oh, I'm agreeable! Why don't you go to roost, Baker?"

"I didn't know——"

"Oh yes, you did; I've been waiting this three minutes. Come, give us your coat! Now your waistcoat! Very good! I'll fetch your braces presently."

On which Hatcher also retired, gladly. The punch he had drunk only seemed to inspire him; and he knew that Biddles had imbibed enough to make him sleep like a dead man, almost. So much the better; for he usually slept like a living cat. Woppits's slumbers were always deep.

The lights were out, and all was still. A distant church chimed eleven—twelve; and then Hatcher, lying awake with his ears at full cock, heard the softest rustle of a footstep amongst the weeds. Then he thrust an arm from his hammock (which was slung near the side of the van), and with a penknife worked round a screw with which the smallest window in the world had been fastened up, in consequence of a defective hinge. In a few moments he had the screw out; back swung the window on its rotten hinge; and with the merest twist possible, off it came. Luckily, the window was to leeward of the ark; or the wind, blowing on Biddle's face, might have awakened him.

Any one looking at the aperture left by the window would have said that Hatcher had greatly miscalculated his chance of escape through it. He had no doubt about the matter. He had tested the thing by squeezing his shoulders between the door and the door-post, measuring the distance between these, and comparing it with the height of the window. No sooner had he got the sash out, therefore, than he placed it in the hammock, placed his hands on the window-sill, drew out one foot, and planted it on a rib of the ark, and in two minutes fell headlong among the weeds.

His knees were much bruised; but leaping up instantly, he vanished like a sheeted ghost into a recess in the hedge, where he had espied Mr. Skinner standing.

"Out with 'em!" said Hatcher, in a whisper, which fell from his mouth in little flakes, like chaff from a chaff-cutting machine, he shivered so much. "Out with the clothes!"

Skinner drew a pin from a bundle at his feet, and produced a complete suit of sailor's slops, which he had selected, he said, because they would be sure to fit; but he had also another motive. They were very cheap, and he had little money.

Hatcher, leaping into one garment, and hauling on another, finally crowned himself with a round straw hat, saying to himself, "Now, old woman, I'm with you in a twinkling; and I'll make a sailor of you, too, before the week's out."

CHAPTER XXXVI.

A VERY VARIOUS CHAPTER.

BIDDLES was the first to rise, the morning after Hatcher's escape. When, a few minutes after, Woppits turned out, he found his colleague lost in contemplation, and plunged into the recesses of his breeches-pockets. Hatcher's boots, his hat, all mentionable garments that to him belonged, and some that are unmentionable, were displayed upon the ground; and there stood the showman gazing at them. "Gone!" he muttered to himself. "Dissolved into a jew!" And waving his hand as Woppits approached, to bespeak the young man's gravest demeanour, renewed his contemplations.

"Woppits!" he said, as they at length raised their astonished eyes, "what do you think of your father-in-law now? Vanished up the flue! Strained through the ventilator! Off without his clothes in a populous and civilised country!"

Woppits had no explanation to offer, but vexed his lips with his teeth, as Hatcher's disappearance vexed his mind.

"It's enough to make a man think your father-in-law doesn't want clothes at all—except when he's occasion to visit this sublernary spear, seeking whom he may devour. But I don't (sniff)—smell—(sniff) anything sulphurous either!" continued the showman, elevating Hatcher's waistcoat to a level with his nose.

They looked about for further intelligence, and spied the open window. Mr. Biddles's theory of the flue and the ventilator instantly collapsed, giving place to a more satisfactory explanation. However, the showman, like many learned men in similar case, distinctly preferred the theory, looking upon the solution as vulgar and commonplace. And I almost think Woppits would have preferred it too; for it would have relieved him of much matter-of-fact vexation.

Indeed, this event threw him into a despairing mood. He felt more and more that he was engaged in an affair of greater magnitude than he could compass—of the proportions of which he was entirely ignorant : that he was fighting in the dark, and for no definite object, against expert swordsmen. However, this was the day on which he was to restore Ruth to Mrs. Bell's care. They were to meet on the road leading to Kennington, and he should have the satisfaction of telling the strange story, and of hearing her opinion of the matter.

Mr. Biddles was very sorry to part with Ruth, and his leave-taking was marked with much wholesome emotion. "Good-bye," said he, when he had accompanied her a few paces from his black and yellow house, "I s'pose I shall never see *you* again, my little woilet; and I expect I shall think of you a precious deal oftener than you will of me. I never eat such victuals as she cooks!" he continued, turning to Woppits, "nor had such toast, nor drank such tea. The way she makes the latter article draw, beats me hollow."

"Don't make fun of me," cried Ruth, blushing with satisfaction at these encomiums. "Good-bye, Uncle Biddles! I'll come and see you again."

"Will you, my dear? Then you'll be as welcome as flowers in May. Good-bye *what*, did you say?"

"Uncle Biddles!"

"Uncle Biddles!" repeated the showman to himself, contemptuously, as he turned away. "Ain't you ashamed of yourself, Dick, to be called uncle by a little angel like that?" And all the way back to the van, and all the way up the steps and into the Bower, he taunted himself with "Uncle Biddles!"—groaning at himself, yah-ing at himself, goosing himself in the character of Uncle Biddles, as he never was goosed on the stage in his life, which is saying a great deal. It took three pipes of tobacco to soothe him.

Mrs. Bell listened to Woppits's story, when they met, with less surprise than he had expected. He did not know that she had herself seen Mr. Hatcher harnessed to the showman's drum, and had guessed that he had fallen into the hands of Woppits. Moreover, her own discoveries or suspicions went deeper than all that Hatcher had revealed, though they were much strengthened by it.

"Why, mother," said he, when he had concluded, "you don't seem to take much interest in what I've told you."

She looked from Woppits to Ruth, and from Ruth to Woppits, in a manner so peculiar and so full of meaning, that it was as if she said the whole interest of her life, past and present, was bound in it.

"I mean," added the young man, "you don't seem much surprised."

"I'm not, my dear," said she.

"What has happened since I saw you last, then?"

"I think I've made a strange discovery,—I hope not a tragical one, my dear, for then it would be terrible, not only for our darling (here Mrs. Bell glanced at the little silk neckerchief which Ruth wore about her throat), but for you and for me. However, it is better that I made the discovery at all events, rather than any one else in the world; and you—you *last* of all!"

"Why?" asked Woppits, solicitously.

"That is the thing I can never tell you," replied the mother, trembling. The young man trembled too, slightly.

"But who," said he, "is concerned in all this, besides us, then? If you know——"

"Ask no questions now, my dear boy," mother said, looking very pale meanwhile; "and pray observe these things. Take no step—do not move, do not say a word—in reference to Ruth or that man Hatcher; and——"

"Oh, Hatcher!" muttered Woppits. "Is that the name of the man who escaped last night? Or which?"

Mother's heart was torn to pieces, it seemed to her. After a while, she answered, "That is the name of your stranger. I found it out by its being written on the money-bag he left me."

Woppits gave a great sigh, in which the words "Thank Heaven for that!" were suffocated at the birth. "Well, mother, what else?"

"That's all. Trust to me; and if I have some secrets from you now, my dear (and I may have others), do not love me any the less; for I bear them for your sake, as well as my own. Let us be content awhile. The time will come! The time will come, my dear; and perhaps, in a week even, I may answer all you desire to ask."

The young man looked at her with bashful eyes, full of tears and kindliness, and said, "Well, never mind! It's only the name that I'd ask about; and as for little Ruth, do as you please about her. You shall do what you like, and tell me as much as you can. And now we'll drop the subject."

"Our part of it. But I have something to say yet about—— My dear boy, I want your friend Tweakle to do something for me that I dare not ask you to do. Now, you're not to ask questions, you know; but you don't feel hurt at that, do you?"

"Not a bit! You'll explain it, some day!"

"Now, I could write to him by post; but this is so grave a matter, that I cannot trust that means of communication. Couldn't you manage to go and see the dear old fellow yourself, and take my letter with you?"

At first, Woppits's countenance brightened at the suggestion; he had had that visit in contemplation any time for five years past. But purple clouds of confusion came down to obscure the brightness. He blushed all over; and, after two or three attempts at articulation, which mother observed with some anxiety, he faltered out—

"You—you ain't going to marry old Tweak, are you?"

Mother burst into laughter and two tears simultaneously; the first at the oddity of the notion, the other with joy at her boy's fear of losing her.

"No!" she cried, loudly.

Then Woppits laughed, and, taking his mother's hand, said sheepishly, "Ain't I a young stupid, eh?" and laughed again.

"God bless your foolishness," she replied, "and send more of it into the world. Well, then, you'll go. At once?"

"Well, you see, mother" (very gravely), "I'm under a sort of engagement, and my friend's behaved out and out well. More than that, money's tight. You haven't got a shilling in your purse—only two fourpennies. I saw 'em when you took it out with your handkerchief."

"You sly rogue, you know better! Who left a sovereign in a teacup the last time he was at home, and nearly choked his poor mother with gold?"

Woppits grinned, delighted. "You've spent it! You know you have! Not but what I'm pretty well stocked," said he, drawing some money from his pockets. "Five days' performance gives me eighteen shillings, and everything found; and a pound over is one pound eighteen. Besides what I took away. Here, where's that teacup?" and taking mother's hand again, he slipped two pieces of yellow coin into her glove. She buttoned up the glove, and with it all her sentiments on this part of the young man's conduct. The gloves buttoned pretty easily; the sentiments did not.

"Now, I'll tell you what I can do," he continued. "I can try and persuade my friend to take a round towards Latherwell, and that'll be combining two bits of business and one pleasure. Will that do, mother?"

"Very well, my dear."

"Then I'll say good-bye. Here's the toll-gate; you haven't half-an-hour's walk before you now, Ruth; good-bye!"

The child, who had all this while been wandering at her own sweet will, from this side of the path to the other, now ahead, now lagging behind, came bounding towards him. He kissed her. He kissed mother, right out in the open daylight; and bidding her write to him under cover to Tweakle, and promising to keep her well informed of his whereabouts, he turned back. Mother was glad that he would be well out of the way for a week or two, and went home almost light of heart again.

Happy also was the showman when he beheld his crocodile returning, and when that animal expressed his determination to stick to business for the future. Now a fair was to be held at Dartford within a few days, and as soon as Biddles had heard the crocodile out, he proposed that they should move in the direction of that town at once, in order to secure their ground.

Accordingly they got on the road, and jogged along in quiet talk. "I shall stay at Dartford three days, you know," said the showman, "and then I think we'll take Gravesend, Strood, and Rochester for it."

"Couldn't you take Latherwell for it too?" insinuated Woppits; "That's a likely place, I think. Do you know it?"

"I do, by some token! Latherwell!" repeated the showman, looking at Woppits, just as reflectively as he had looked on Ruth, as she stood by the fire when the pudding was boiling. "I was thinking the other night, when your sister—for that's what she is, I can tell by the likeness!——"

Woppits stared.

"I was wondering to myself where I had seen her before. When I went to roost—just in the very act of slipping in—I thought of Latherwell. 'No,' says I, 'couldn't be there, for I cannot have been in the place since she was born.' 'Then,' says I, 'it must be the brother I saw there.' 'No,' says I, 'that won't do either, Richard, because——"

"Why, I was born in Latherwell!" cried Woppits, interrupting the little man; "leastways, I was found there!" he added, rather ashamed.

"*Found* there?"

"Yes, at the side of a pond, when I was a baby in long clothes, I believe."

"And pray how old are you now?" asked Biddles, forgetting to shut the door of his speech after that last word.

"Well, I don't know to a trifle; but it was in the warm weather, in the year——"

"Hold hard! Whoa! whoa!" cried the little man; and stopping the van, he darted into the Bower at a pace which his coat tails could not keep up with, and presently flew out again like a large green swallow, with an old playbill in his hand.

"Now, my noble crocodile!" he said in a voice bass with importance and excitement, "I think I can a tale unfold that will make your hat stand on end, like the fretful porcupine's."

Then he read from the playbill, accentuating the lines according to the size of the type:—

"Biddles's Royal Dramatic Troupe. On Monday evening next will be performed, by the above matchless and celebrated company, an entirely new tragedy, entitled The Brigand of the Heath; or, the Corpse of the Dismal Copse! Sir Harold Hawkbeak—a Villain Rich and Reckless—Mr. W. Hammer. Fanny Faithful—afterwards the Dismal Corpse—Miss Louisa Coventry, of the Theatres Royal Drury Lane and Covent Garden. Daft David—Fanny's father, and the Maniac of the Heath—Mr. Algernon Blater Higg."

"I don't feel my hair rising yet!" said Woppits, smiling in spite of himself.

"Oh, you don't Very well, then we'll come to the bottom, which reads as follows—'Don't forget August the tenth, 1807!' you were born a few weeks before that day, or I'm very much mistaken."

"How do you know? you never saw my mother, did you?" returned poor Woppits, with a face in which half-a-dozen emotions contended.

"I beg your pardon! and I believe that no one would have seen her alive after me, if I had been near her one minute later on the 10th of August, 1807. What do you think of that?"

"I—I don't know what to think! It's more than I can understand!"

"Mind you, I don't know that I can account for you, but here's the story." And setting the yellow house in motion again, the little green man started off with the relation.

"That time o' day, you must know, I warn't in the line I am at this present speaking. I've seen better days, Mr. Woppits. My good lady was alive, then, and so was old Baxter, her father, who gave me over his theatrical business as soon as I married his Polly, and did old men in the troupe till he died. We travelled, as many a good troupe has done before now. Well, on the very day after that mentioned in the bill I read to you just now, I was due at Rochester—in fact, our posters had gone on before, and billed the town. Somehow, I was all behind with my screed in the Brigand, and when we stopped for a rest at Latherwell, in the evening, I strolled away and got down into a hollow near a clump of trees, and went on with my part. Just as I got to the place where I hurl defiance in the teeth of Sir Harold Hawkbeak—whoo! I heard a scream close by, such as I never heard before, and don't want to hear again. What do I do? I get off the ground where I was laying, finding that attitude good for study, and looks about me, Nobody visible. Then there comes another cry, fainter; and looking through the trees, I see a person in the water. I rush forward! I see a woman gently floating off with her face towards the skies. I plunge in, and I fetch her out, insensible. Insensible, sir, as anything. Here was a pretty fix! It was time to start again; we were already in motion, of which my good lady came to apprise me. Says I, 'Polly, what's to be done with this poor woman that has tried to drown herself, and who your husband has rescued from a watery grave?' Says she, 'Rochester's playcarded, Richard, and is waiting for you. We can't wait, and we can't leave her here—no woman with a heart could do it. Let us lift her along. I'll bring her to, and then she can go back to her friends, and they needn't know what a fool she's made of herself!' My missis had as good a head and as good a heart as any woman in England; and played Roxana better. Well, we lifted her along. She didn't recover till next morning, and then the best half of her was absent: her intellects. She wandered. She cried. She talked a rare lot of stuff about her baby, which considering that we'd only buried our little Dick a fortnight before, was rather hard on us at the time, I remember. For the same reason, my good lady couldn't bear to hear about her being left in an infirmary—and sometimes when I looked in on 'em unexpected, I used to overhear them two a talking about their children, when I didn't know which was the queerest in the head, Mrs. Biddles or the other one. However, all of a sudden she was off. We never clapped eyes on her again, and that's all, my boy."

"That's all!" muttered Woppits. "And am I like her?" he asked, a few paces further.

"Very like her. Like the little one too, mind you!"

The young man walked steadily on a few paces more. Then he began to feel giddy, and generally to give in.

"Go on, Biddles," said he, in the faintest voice. "I'm going in for a minute."

"Good, my noble crocodile," replied the showman, and as Woppits clambered into the Bower, Mr. Biddles hooked his arm in the bridle reins, thrust his hands in his pockets, and remarked, "Come on, Jacob; he'll be all right presently." And began to whistle softly, so that nobody might hear him.

More than an hour elapsed, and still Woppits did not reappear. Then the showman became anxious, and what is more, hungry; for the yellow house had jogged some distance into the afternoon, and had left the dinner hour at least two miles behind. So Biddles called a halt, and crept quietly into the Bower to get some bread and cheese, and to see what had happened to Woppits. He was asleep. There he sat by the little table, his arms folded on it, and his head reclining on them, fast as a church, as Biddles expressed it. A slate, on which the showman made his calculations and pencilled out his routes, had been left on the table; and glancing at it, he saw it written all over with strange names and bits of sentences, a dozen times repeated. There was Lath—and Lather—and Latherwell; Tweak, old Tweak, and Mr. Tweakle; Bell, and Bellows; Mother, fifty times at least, sometimes with a little weak "my" before it. The bits of sentences were bits of the showman's sentences; he recognized them as he read, "lifted her along," "lot of stuff about her baby," "she was off," and so on.

"Poor cove!" said the little man to himself, trying to get a peep at the lad's face. "I do think he have been crying, and taking on so jolly bad that he's tired himself out. Very well, old fellow, have your sleep through. It's the best medicine going, and the only good thing in this world that poor people get their fair whack of."

And having refreshed himself, he took out the powder-flask, placed it under the sleeper's right hand, and jogged on again. "A little drop of that when he wakes will be welcome as flowers in May," said he.

Another mile was accomplished, and Woppits emerged from the Bower bright and cheerful, his face fresh washed and his hair new combed.

"Biddles," said he, shaking the showman by the hand, "God bless you!"

"Let's hope so," replied the other. And it was understood that the conversation on that head was concluded.

Woppits now threw a bright glance over the country, to see where he had emerged out of the waters of oblivion. He thought he knew the place. Yes! "Why, good heavens, Mr. Biddles, this is Latherwell!"

"Right you are, my son. Thought it would please you. It won't make much difference to us, you know; we can cut across to Dartford."

"Bless my heart!" cried Woppits, standing on the door of the yellow house, and shading his eyes with his hand, "there's the jolly old pump, and the church, and—here, I say, Biddles, you see that wall! That's the workhouse wall, and I dropped it! How precious low it looks to what it did!"

"No, no. You were low in those days. It isn't in the nature of bricks and mortar to grow up like people!" remarked Biddles, profoundly. "Now, is there anybody in the place you want to see?"

"Of course there is—Mr. Tweakle, the beadle. But it's too early to call on him yet, I'm afraid. Suppose we work the town for a few hours. Any time after dark will do for me."

"As you like. Well, that seems a tidy pitch, yonder; you get in, and make ready."

The pitch in question was at the entrance to the town, just beyond a big square house with a great deal of glass in it, two large lions at the little portico, and round about it a garden; chiefly red, on account of the quantity of drive and path that consumed it. New rich gravel had been thrown down; and as the black and yellow house passed by, its inhabitants beheld a small pauper-man sitting on a big iron roller in the drive, and wiping his forehead with the stray ends of his neckerchief. Under the portico stood a stout magnificent gentleman, with an iron-gray head, on the back of which his hat rested, in an easy, indifferent manner. The eye of the magnificent man rested on the mean one with disapprobation—large, fine disapprobation; and as if he was really vexed with the laziness of mankind. He walked softly down the drive, and suddenly, with folded arms, revealed his awful presence to the pauper-man, regarding him more in sorrow than in anger.

"It's werry heavy, sir," whimpered the roller-man. "I've been at it since six, sir."

The grand gentleman did not reply. With a wave of that white fat hand of his, he motioned little bald head off the roller, took up the handle, and drew the machine full six yards.

"There, Scragg! That's how heavy it is!" said the grand gentleman, politely giving up the handle of the roller. "Now let me see what you can do, my man. Off with you."

Poor little bald-head bent his back, and away he went with as much liveliness as he could muster. The grand gentleman watched him for a moment with a smile, and then swept the horizon for the approval of the gods.

Olympus, however, was beyond his ken: not so the caravan. He spied it "pitched" just past the house; and darting out at a side-gate, he suddenly knocked at the door of the Bower. Biddles immediately appeared with a teapot in his hand.

"Well!" shouted the grand gentleman, "what are you doing here?"

"I'm making a cup of tea, if you don't mind, sir!" replied Biddles, making a bow, in which the teapot, answering for itself, took the greater part.

"So I perceive!" rejoined the big gentleman. "Bacon, too, upon my word! And yet," he continued, tapping the showman's rasher with the ferule end of his walking-stick, "and yet trade's bad, and the poor man can't get bread! I suppose, now, you find it dreadful hard to make both ends meet, eh?"

"Thankee, sir, no I don't! I'm pretty comfortable."

"Oh, you are, are you?" cried the other, irritated at this information. "And pray what's your business in Latherwell? You're a strolling peep-show man, or I'm very much mistaken?"

"Begging your pardon, sir, but you are mistaken!"

"Don't contradict me, sir; I'm not accustomed to it! What have you got in there?" said the grand gentleman, tapping at a door that opened into the show-room.

"The famous crocodile of the Nail, jist arrived from the river Egypt, on the Ganges; who, whale in his natif woods, thinks no maw——"

"Tut! tut! I'm not deaf, nor blind, nor an idiot! If you think me either one or the other, you'll soon find your mistake! You say you have a crocodile; bring it out."

"Lor, sir," replied Biddles, in a wheedling tone, having strong doubts as to whether the imposture would pass with an observer of this kind, "it ain't a sight for a learned and scientific gentleman like you, who, I'll be bound, has seen hundreds of crocodiles in your travels. Mine's just an ordinary animal."

The grand gentleman was mollified. "Yes, yes," said he, "I quite understand you, my good man. I do, as you say, take a great interest in these things; and I've studied the crocodile in Buffon's 'Natural History,' which I've got at home. Is this one of yours tame?"

"As tame and as harmless as one of our own specie!" replied the showman.

"Then suppose you draw your waggon into my grounds; we'll have the animal out on the lawn."

So saying, and indicating the gate at which the caravan was to enter, the grand gentleman swung his cane round, and departed.

In great trepidation, Biddles hurried into his colleague. "My eye," said he, "here's a go! Here's an old swell that has got all Buffer's 'Natural History' at his fingers' ends, and heaven knows what beside, wants you for a private view!"

"I heard him," murmured the crocodile; "and I know him too! He's the one who persecuted and prosecuted me while I was in the House here. He's the top man in the parish; and I think we had better be off!"

"Can't be off!" returned Biddles, "Jacob's too tired. I think we must chance it!"

"Oh, very well, I'm agreeable."

The show-house was backed on to Mr. Gorelam's lawn, whereupon Mr. Gorelam, with his wife, his children, his man-servant, and his maid-servants, presently appeared. Gorelam headed the throng, with his thumbs in the armholes of his waistcoat, and his hat thrown still further from his forehead, to allow free play to his intellectual bumps, now on the point of expanding. Behind him came a boy in a striped jacket, bearing several books. In the background stood another conspicuous person, Mr. Tweakle, who happened to have waited on Mr. Gorelam on some parochial business.

"Do you give the signal, sir?" asked Mr. Biddles, coming forward with his hat in his hand, when all was ready.

Mr. Gorelam took out one of his thumbs, and waving it, said: "I do. Now, my dear, now girls, attention!"

Biddles blew a little whistle without producing any result (and without expecting any, as far as the arrangements of the show were concerned), and then turning a winch, down came the tail-board of the waggon, and the crocodile slid upon the lawn. For a moment he lay perfectly calm, an accidental wag of the tail only indicating that he existed. Then turning about to view his audience, the animal suddenly encountered the gaze of Mr. Tweakle! A torrent of emotion swelled in the crocodile's bosom; and, carried away by his feelings, he made a rush at the beadle, carrying all before him.

Mr. Gorelam turned pale. His wife threw herself on his neck, and his children took refuge in his legs; his maid-servants gathered up their garments, and scudded away like sea-birds, screaming; while Mr. Tweakle, who was too fat to run, and too old to take refuge in Mr. Gorelam's embraces, summoned heart of grace, and smote the monster's snout.

"I—I thought you said the creature was quite tame!" Gorelam shouted, alarmed but blustering.

"As a chicken, sir!" replied the showman, who was utterly at a loss to account for Woppits's rash behaviour. "Perhaps it was the gentleman's red smalls that done it; which you know red serves bullocks the same way, sir. And then, again, perhaps

THE RULING PASSION STRONG IN DEATH.

it was only his playfulness. We'll soon see! The wagging of his tail is the proof of his temper. Attention!" continued Biddles, facing round towards the crocodile. "Allicom, are you pleased, or are you angry, with the gentleman in the red smalls?"

The tail wagged till it creaked again.

"Pleased it is!" cried the showman, triumphantly. "You'd never forgive yourself if you hurt a hair of that gentleman's head, would you, Allicom?"

Another expressive wag.

"And you invite him to stroke the place where he hit you, as a proof that you owe no malice?"

The docile and intelligent creature crept humbly to Mr. Tweakle's knees, and submitted its nose to his hand, amidst the applause of the spectators. "Lor, now! Look at that!" said the upper housemaid, putting the corner of her apron into her eye.

But Mr. Gorelam did not applaud. He was not pleased that Tweakle should have all the glory to himself; he intended to show his domestics how indifferent to all sorts of monsters is a superior man, a landed proprietor, a magistrate, and a student of natural history.

"Tweakle," he shouted, "you're a fool! Don't you know that hypocrisy is the nature of the beast? Haven't you heard of crocodile's tears? [Mrs. Gorelam had. She heard of them every time Mr. Gorelam bullied her, and she began to cry.] Haven't you read of their weeping like a baby, in order to circumvent innocent young black women into their den? It's a mercy it didn't bite your hand off!"

"Lor bless you, sir! he ain't a animal of that sort," the show-man interposed. "Whatever may have been his natural vicious ness in his natif woods, I've made a perfect cure of him. When he gives a friendly wag, he means it!"

"Don't tell me, sir! He wags his tail whenever you speak to him. Come, now, ask him if he's pleased with me!"

"Allicom! Are you pleased, or are you not, with the stout gentleman in the black sating waistcoat?"

Pleased! The animal was in a frenzy of delight. Detaching Mr. Gorelam from his family by a dexterous flank movement, the crocodile bounded at him and about him with all the playfulness of a lapdog, and something more. It burst in at his legs; it made playful demonstrations from behind; it ran at him from all points of the compass; while Mr. Gorelam, pale and ridiculous, dodged hither and thither, crying "Stop him!" and aiming futile blows at the animal with his walking-stick. At length he bethought himself that the crocodile has so intractable a back-bone, that he finds it very difficult to turn on his own axis; and, consequently, if once you can take him in the rear, you may easily maintain that position, and laugh the devourer to scorn.

"Wait a bit!" cried Mr. Gorelam, when this reflection occurred to him. "Keep off, showman; I'll manage him!"

At the same time he leapt aside with elephantine agility, made a feint to the right, a dodge to the left, and with another bound, stood calm and triumphant at the extremity of the animal's tail.

"There, my man!" said he, folding his arms and moving at the crocodile's extremity as the pole-star does not follow the variations of the needle; "there, my dear Eliza, that's the way to overcome the Nile crocodile. You observe I am proof against his cunning, my dear!"

Now, it was true of this crocodile, if of no other, that he could not easily turn; and Mr. Gorelam's taunt irritated him. He tried several times to veer round upon his ancient enemy, but the enemy cried, "Ha! ha!" wagged his head, dodging successfully aside! The crocodile considered a moment, then, struck with a sudden inspiration, he ran at Mr. Gorelam backwards, and delivered his tail right across that gentleman's stomach. The blow doubled up the gentleman, and jerked his hat off; which the animal no sooner perceived than he danced on it.

Mr. Gorelam was not much hurt, but he was dreadfully excited. "Tweakle!" he roared, "take 'em into custody—man, van, beast, and all! Off with 'em to the pound and the lock-up! I see through this business. It's a done thing—it's a Tike conspiracy! Take 'em away! I'll inquire into your case to-morrow, my little man!" And casting a furious glance at the showman, he disappeared through the portico.

A constable appeared on the spot immediately, and led Biddles away; while Tweakle, encouraged by the crocodile's docile demeanour, so far as he was concerned, cast a rope round its jaws, and solemnly took it in tow. The pound was situate at no great distance from Gorelam's Paradise Lodge, but short as was the journey thither, it was attended by a considerable company of idlers and audacious boys. Luckily, a strong stable was attached to the pound, and in this the animal was bestowed, apart from vulgar curiosity, and the persecutions of the boys, who would have stoned him. Woppits himself enjoyed the fun of the situation, and offered no opposition when he was secured to a staple in the vicinity of a new truss of straw, and locked up. There would be no difficulty in getting away at any moment, with his skin under his arm.

Mr. Tweakle was in a quandary. To animals of various kinds—horses, asses, geese, oxen, swine—he had often been jailer, but to a crocodile never! According to statute law, every animal impounded was to be provided with a sufficient supply of food and water; now, what food ought to be supplied to a crocodile? He went down town big with this question, and put it to such jurymen as happened to be standing at their shop doors. The dentist said that if Mr. Tweakle would hold open the animal's jaws, he would tell him how far it was herbivorous or carnivorous; at which Tweakle said, "Thankee," and went a little further. The butcher had heard of an animal which fed on other animals, alive, bolting them whole; but he rather thought that was a dromedary. The tailor was sure that the crocodile's favourite food was a young child; and, being a Tikeite, he grimly suggested that Mr. Gorelam would readily give an order on the workhouse for two or three babies: those that had measles would do, the tailor thought. Tweakle swore his advisers to secrecy, for fear of raising the town; but he rejected their suggestions, and finally made application to Mr. Biddles. That person, however, after a long consultation with the powder-flask, declined all correspondence with his captors.

Evening found Tweakle as doubtful as ever. Acting to the best of his knowledge, however, he placed in the stable a pail of water, several skewers of dog's-meat, two tame rabbits, a bundle of cabbage-plants, and an armful of hay.

Apparently, the crocodile slept soundly in the straw during these preparations for his sustenance. The beadle observed that he made strange noises in his sleep, a sort of gurgling or chuckle, which Tweakle attributed to dreams; and being curious to know how the animal's tastes might incline, and also being filled with a sense of responsibility, he next provided himself with some tobacco, lit a lantern, and took a seat on a pail near the door.

Obesity, at its third pipe, is somnolent. Mr. Tweakle, however, had a conviction that he was wide awake, when his name was murmured through the keyhole. Putting forth his hand, he opened the door and looked out; there was nobody in sight save a pale, lean boy, who had established himself on the furthermost rails of the pound, evidently with some idea of being devoured by the crocodile. However, he bolted as soon as Mr. Tweakle's head appeared, and was no more seen.

"That boy!" murmured the beadle, relighting his pipe at the lantern.

"I say, old fellow!"

Now Mr. Tweakle had his eye on the crocodile this time, and could have no doubt that from it proceeded these words. The portals of his speech swung ajar. "Wh-hat!" he ejaculated.

"You haven't forgot me, have you, Mr. Tweakle?" pursued the animal, in friendly though hollow tones.

"Oh no," replied Tweakle, backing to the door in utterest consternation. "I ain't forgot you. You'll find several nice little things against the wall!"

The crocodile walked leisurely out of the stall, and, as far as his tether would allow, approached the door. "Don't make fun of a fellow!" said he. "You're all alone, ain't you?"

"No!" roared Tweakle, remembering what Mr. Gorelam had said about the artfulness and hypocrisy of the beast. "I'm not. There's about forty people waiting outside; and if I holler——"

"Don't holler, there's a dear old man, but come and cut this confounded string at my side. I've got it into a knot."

Was this the craft of the animal? Tweakle rushed at the door, calculating that, at the worst, the brute could only snap a piece out of his leg, for the rope was stretched taut, and still the brute's nose fell short of the doorway.

"Don't go!" roared the beast. "Don't go! Don't you know me? I'm Woppits! Confound this string! There! Now do you see who I am?"

And Woppits, having at length burst the string that looped up the mummy at the side, thrust out his head for the beadle's inspection.

* * * * *

The effect of the apparition and the scene that followed are beyond description. Nothing was said for several minutes; and then the first remark (by Tweakle) was as follows:—

"Bless the boy! He's as tall as a granideer."

The second remark worth mentioning was also Mr. Tweakle's. He blushed, and said—

"And how's your mother?"

"All right. I say, do you know, I fancy she's got her eye on you."

Tweakle had his eye on Woppits instantly. "Get out!" he said—and quitted the stable without another word.

In a few minutes he returned with a hat, of which Woppits was destitute. "Now, you be off to my place!" said the beadle. "You know it. I'll lock up and be with you in ten minutes. We must have a talk over this!"

It was done. The night was all spent in reminiscence and the interchange of story. There were passages at which both men—the young man and the old one—laughed as if they meant to have cried, and cried as if they meant to have laughed; and, upon the whole, Woppits's history was voted a regular romance.

At the conclusion, Woppits handed his mother's note to Mr. Tweakle.

"And you're not to tell me anything that's in it," the young man said.

Tweakle became scarlet as his own smalls at this, took out his spectacles with some trepidation, and painfully read the letter. "Painfully" is the word; or if not that, most gravely. Once or twice during the perusal, he glanced anxiously at Woppits, to the latter's distress; and when at last the old man folded the letter away, he seemed to have more intelligence than he could possibly hold. He swelled with it, like an over-full cask. Woppits almost fancied that the old man's ribs creaked with the strain; and once, when their eyes met, he was so plainly going to burst, that the young man rose and cried—

"No, Mr. Tweakle! No! Not a word! It's best not, as my mother wouldn't wish it.'

"Very well," faltered Tweakle: "then all I can say is, Good night! I'll let her know, faithful." And off he went to bed, audibly locking himself in his room.

Of Woppits, at this point, I have no more to say, save that he passed the rest of the night in the late Henrietta's easy-chair. Next morning, the true nature of the crocodile of the Nile was privately reported to Mr. Gorelam, who, in consideration of the affair being kept secret from the Tike party, and, indeed, from everybody, allowed the black and yellow house, the proprietary and effects, to depart free of fine or distress. Tweakle made no objection to Woppits's immediate departure (which Mr. Gorelam insisted on), and they bade farewell, the beadle with much gravity.

His proceedings after he locked himself up, the previous

evening, are worth recording. He sat himself down upon the edge of his four-poster, and muttered—

"Sleaford? Any gentleman at Old Sleaford who lost an only child—little daughter—five or six years ago? Or was stole? Or died? Stole? I needn't go there, ma'am, to inquire after that!"

And, taking an old dusty pocket-book from a shelf, he drew out from its pockets a copy of those bills that were posted at Keppel's gates.

"Here's the information you want, Mrs. Bell—in print big enough to put your eyes out! Big enough to make you cry your eyes out, and me mine too, if it's possible that that little Woppits was the one who stole—— But, no. I'm a poor beadle, but I ain't such a fool as not to read human natur' better than that; and human natur' ain't such a cheat as to go putting on such villainous disguises, so as to make a hass of a hold man like me!

"However, you shall have this playcard, Mrs. Bell, by to-morrow's post!"

CHAPTER XXXVII.
SLANTING AWAY.

WE now behold Messieurs Hatcher and Skinner (how well their names would have read over a shop window!) bowling homeward in a hired chaise; for, though the first-named person had quitted the yellow house in a very unfledged condition as regards the habiliments of man, he took care to be well provided with that which covereth a multitude of sins—money (See the "Bible of the Counting-house," p. 497). They had bowled half-way home in dead quiet, when Skinner's silence began to move. It is a stupid way to express my meaning, but Skinner seemed to smoke previous to bursting into a flame of conversation. The other was conscious of it, and coughed a great deal. At length the fire appeared, not, however, in a flame, but in a sulphurous flicker. Said Skinner in a smoky voice—

"This is a strange affair, sir."

"Very," replied Hatcher, curling up like a hedgehog, mentally speaking. "Very."

"What do you mean to do when you get home?"

"Get into a comfortable suit of clothes."

"As a preliminary measure, of course. Are you cold, sir?"

"Yes, I am. How are you, sir?"

"*I'm* warm—warm in my anxiety about the K business. What about that?"

"Well, what about it?" The mental hedgehog opened its little keen ears—invisible to the naked eye of Mr. Skinner.

"Oh, come—come!" said he, with much less smoke and a great deal more fire; "if I'm to be of any use to you, don't let us have any affectation of reserve. Be as frank with me as your mother was. You won't compromise yourself, Mr. Hatcher, I assure you. I know all about it—about the bag and its contents, and the person that brought it (a female), and the whole turn-out. And I say it's a bad job, a very bad job; but we must make the best of it. You're not like a man without means, that's one thing in our favour, Mr. Joel."

Probably Mr. Joel would not have allowed his friend to proceed to the conclusion of this little speech, if he had not been lost in cogitation over one part of it—that relating to his mother's confidences. He had his confidences too, and in nobody had more confidence than in the Old Woman; and having during his reflections found no sudden reason to alter his opinion of her, he replied to Mr. Skinner with considerable caution.

"Mother told you all about it, did she?" said he.

"Everything."

"Then what do you advise me to do?"

Mr. Skinner seemed to have discovered a "raw" in the horse's hide, and to have tickled it; for the animal shot forward at this question, to which no answer was returned for several minutes. Not before the pace had moderated did he reply—

"I think I should go into hiding for a while."

"What for?"

"Till it blows over!"

"Ah; but it's a long time now since the burglary was committed," said the fox.

Mr. Skinner's eyes twinkled, visibly. "So it is," he said.

"And then again Kingston's many miles from here."

"So it is!" (He really trembled with excitement, that Skinner did). "And if it was not for the existence of the bag——"

"That I left part of the plunder in, in the garden?"

"That's the one."

"Ha, ha! You've got it, Mr. Skinner! Keep it! It's your fair share," chuckled Mr. Hatcher. "Now, if you please, I'll get down and walk the rest of the way. I wouldn't have a gentleman of your cloth get into trouble on my account for the world; and we'd better not be seen together, for your sake."

"I'll tell you what!" cried the other rather, crestfallen, "if you don't behave more reasonably, I'll——"

"Wait a bit. You shall have reason enough to send you home like a lamb. Did I ever tell you that I am executor at Wainfleet, the printer of your beautiful tract, the 'Fat of Sinners?' and that I have his accounts and papers in my possession, including some letters of yours in reference to the 'Fat?' No! Well, good day, sir; we'll talk that little matter over another time. Meanwhile, just have the goodness to lend me your hat and coat. You can take mine, you know; and you'll look as if you'd just come home from a voyage to the Bosjesmen, in them!"

Mr. Skinner was beaten, and tacitly acknowledged his defeat. He offered no resistance when Hatcher, blandly laying hands on the reins, stopped the horse, and descended; while as for the interchange of apparel, of course that could only be regarded as a joke. However, it was a joke which Mr. Skinner thought it well to humour, though the result was certainly to convert him into a guy and a scoffing.

Joyful was the heart of the broker, yet not with an unmixed joy, when he stood at his own door again. Conscious of a certain degree of security, he seasoned it with imaginary dangers, pungent enough to throw him into a high state of perspiration though they *were* imaginary. "Suppose now!" said he, as he approached within a few yards of the emporium, "that footstep behind me belonged to Mr. Townsend, the celebrated runner? Suppose he's just turning round the corner? He will spy me in five seconds, at my own door, if I don't find the key in the first pocket I put my hand into, or if I miss the keyhole at the first poke!" The footstep grew more audible; the key was *not* in the pocket first searched by Mr. Hatcher, nor in the second pocket; and it was not till the imaginary Townsend had projected the brim of his hat round the corner, that Hatcher slipped across his threshold and breathed again. And then came that blessed sense of "It's only a dream," which is as life to us when we wake after burning our grandmothers, officiating at a brain-feast, or suffering from premature interment.

All was quiet in the "emporium," and Hatcher went straight to his mother's room. The old woman had been shifted nearer to the grave by several degrees since her interview with Mr. Skinner; and she was sensible of the change. So not to be shifted along too fast, she got out of bed and established herself in a big easy-chair, the arms of which she held unwearied, day and night. As for sleep, that overcame her only by resorting to stratagem. When her Joly entered she was sitting with her eyes so fiercely wakeful that it must have been a bold slumber that approached within a yard of her.

She had an additional reason for desiring to remain alive and wide awake till her son returned. That very day a person had come down with Mr. Mawley, the avuncular sheriff's officer, and between them they had actually concluded a bargain for the lease, the stock-in-trade, good-will, fixtures, domestic furniture, and all that appertained to Hatcher's "emporium," without consulting her, or betraying the least concern at her wrathful protestations or her many tears. When the business was concluded, the purchaser intimated that he should find it convenient to sleep on the premises until Mrs. Hatcher had cleared out; Mr. Mawley bade his sister "Ta ta!" and the thing was done. Only that the old woman would not hear of the stranger's sleeping on the premises—on the counter, nor under the counter, nor in the cellars beneath. She vowed she would set the chimney a-fire if he dared attempt any such thing; so that being, as he said, a feasible man, behaving in these matters as affable as circumstances allowed, he contented himself with taking an inventory (in which he included the bonnet), and then took himself away.

The old woman's eyes dilated more and more, and firmer was her grip upon the elbows of her chair, when she heard the sound of footsteps on the stairs. She knew to whom they belonged; and she watched for the intrusion of Joel's ferrety head as anxiously as she might have watched for the angel of life.

"Oh, here he is!" she cried, when she did appear; "that's Joly. Come on! come and kiss me. I'm so outrageous glad you've come back! Oh, lor! Oh, heaven's goodness! and that wretch selling us up this very day, and my prodigal son—here he is! Oh, lor to massy, Joly, that ever your poor mother should live to see this day!"

After which exclamation came a burst of tears, as you need not be told.

"Hullo! what's the matter now, mother?" cries the son, flinging Mr. Skinner's hat on to the bed.

"What's the matter! what's the matter, he says! And he's got sailor's trousers on, as I'm alive to see 'em, which I'm sure I never expected to do, much as I held on to these elbers. Slantin' away as I was, on the perpendickler, before I took to 'em. Look here! I'm holdin' on now, like grim Thingumbob —Heaven forgive me, for calling it by sich blaspheming names! But what can be expected of a poor old woman whose son comes back after all, though he do come back with the bed sold from under him, and in sailor's breeches, like the 'poor little cabin boy, that crossed the watery main!'" The old woman chirped out this line to music—such as it was—and then she laughed a small laugh, or something in that way.

"I say!" remonstrated Joel, "don't kick up that row, mother! What have you been taking?"

Mrs. Hatcher loosened her hold on the chair now, put up her hands, and whimpered, "Ah, that's him, all over! He never will laugh with me, nor cry with me! After all my trainin' of him up in the way he should go, when he gets old he do depart from it, and from me too."

"Well, of course I was going to kiss you, and that," rejoined the son in a penitential voice. "Here you are!" and he kissed her.

"Here I are, indeed! With the very chair I'm holdin' on to to keep life in me, down in a hinwentory! Do you know that? Oh, Joly! who done it? and what's it for? If you want to get rid of me, say so! I'm happy and willin' to go into the House to-morrow, and lay my rheumatiz on straw if so be such is your desires, and you can bring in any chit of a thing who chooses to rob a mother of her son's affection, like a shameful baggage as she is, that'll ruin you before a year's out; but why give up business? Why a hinwentory?"

"I'll tell you, mother, in a minute, if you can be still long enough, with your holdin' on. The sale's all right; it was done on my account, clever and ready, and the money's safe. For the game's up; and though you ain't requested to lay your rheumatiz on straw, as yet, you'll have to take it out of this house in a very short time. Ah, old girl, it's no use looking so blank! We've not done amiss after all; and we must make the best of a bad bargain."

The old woman offered no interruption now, and so her son proceeded to narrate his adventures in London.

"Ah!" sighed she, calm and business-like once more. "And what you intend to do is——"

"Pack up what money I can get together, and be off."

"Put the screw on tighter up at the Lodge, and be off altogether; eh?"

"Eh!" echoed the son.

"Why, of course you'll have a last pull, Joly!"

"Now to think that that should have struck you before me!" said Joly, gazing at his mother with admiring eyes. "You are a woman! Have a last pull, you said. I believe you! I will!"

"Do, my dear. Go and have it before your hands are anyways tied, dear. And now, Joly, now I know all, and seen you safe, I think I'll ventur on the perpendicklars again. If it's come to runnin', I don't know as I can be of any use to you; so there's no use holdin' on any more. If I've got to take my rheumatiz out of this house, where it was bred and born, and in the house before it, I may as well take it where it won't be no illconvenience to you. So you get me into bed; and go and do

that bit of business at the Lodge (do it fair, Joly, do it fair a you can), and as for your old mother, she'll just slant off into the tomb!"

"Just slant up into a vehicle, you mean! and go and live by the seaside along of me, with every comfort to make you happy. There you are! Now good night! Don't you talk no more nonsense about tombs; and if you're took queer, hammer at the wall, that's all!" And Mr. Hatcher retired to an adjoining apartment.

Now the old woman was taken queer in the night. She lay half-awake and half-thoughtful, when a sudden excitement seized her, and she hammered at the wall with a will. According to promise, her son speedily made his appearance.

"Hullo!" he cried, "what is it? Wuss?"

"Ah, my dear," said she, "give me your hand! I've had such a beautiful thought! Do you know what you'll do when you've settled this little affair?"

Now it happened that Joly had been lying awake too, asking himself this very question, and finding it very troublesome to answer. In his anxiety to answer it, or to ease his heaving chest, heaving with the weight of the question, he had risen upon his elbow, and was thrown out of all human calculation by a vision of his cat, Phil, which sat on the foot of the bed, staring at him.

"What I shall do, mother!" he repeated, trembling.

"Why don't you know? Oh, Joly, you'll Retire! To think that you, which your poor mother scarce could get bread for, should Retire! To think of you, who started, when a boy, with breeding white mice and selling 'em ninepence a dozen, Retiring!"

"You go to sleep!" gasped Jolly. And neither of them slept another wink that night.

However, the morning brought sleep to the eyes of the widow, and courage to the heart of her son. When, on his way to Keppel Lodge for the last time, he heard "the small birdes sing," he sang too; or, he hummed. And if he did not hum for joy, as the small birds sang, but rather to lighten the load of his labouring thought, why then he was no more to be blamed than the bees—perhaps.

Keppel Lodge is altered little during these years. Without the house and about the house nothing betokens the dreariness within. Even there, a degree of order still prevails; and if its servants are fewer, they are neither worse fed nor worse paid; and with food and fee who shall not be content? But where the master is, there is change, and—no, not discontent; for beyond that there is something more, as there is death beyond disease. Thus we have always upon this earth a company of the dead, and they are divided. There are those who belong to Death the Avenger, and those who belong to Death the Deliverer; and here they remain above ground for a warning and an example to you and me. Dear reader, you know who they are. You have already classed amongst them those wise, those cunning criminals, who, after years and years of successful warfare against the world, suddenly become asses, whom any child can lead to the halter: and whose madness in providing for the discovery of their guilt is more surprising than any sin can possibly be. They are dead men, my dear reader; you know they are. The power to do harm is mercifully taken away, and nothing is left for them but to stink, that all men's attention may be called to their offence, and cart them away; with as much pity as may be, but also warned! This is Death the Avenger.

Not among these examples is to be ranked a certain French king, long regarded as the most politic monarch in Europe. Cunning? No royal cunning was more profound than his. Very crafty he was (in politics), dexterous in the use of men and the distribution of money. But what say I? His name was Modern Ulysses. Now Modern Ulysses died two years six months and three days before it was at all necessary to inter him, or before he was any less lively, any less intelligent, any more indifferent to his morning paper or a little music in the evening, than nine-tenths of all the old gentlemen extant. But it is nevertheless true that he died in an English boat, crossing from France to Dover; and his ghost (which assumed the name of Smith), talked to an hotel-keeper there in a way which has been regarded as supernatural ever since.

And I'm willing to wager my life against any Frenchman's

freedom, (and I suppose *that* odds will be considered heavy enough), that we shall soon have as fine an example of this sort of death as ever was recorded. I know an Emperor—(the name and address I shall keep secret at present), who is the artfullest Emperor — the most profound, the most mighty, the most secret volcano of an Emperor that ever lived, perhaps. He is so great and wise that his nation needs no other statesman, councillor, journalist, magistrate, lawyer, lord mayor, beadle, burgess, or hangman whatever. It has got no other; and it says—all the millions of that nation say—that they want no other. And I believe them! But if that potentate do not write himself down Ass at last, trust me no more. Why, I can see his ears already. I distinctly heard him bray a little while ago, by means of a broadsheet (the "Muffler" I think it is called); which having rolled into the shape of an ear-trumpet, I addressed its mouth (the mouth of the trumpet, not of the journal—it hasn't got any; only a hole whence puffs of smoke sometimes issue) toward the limbo of old tyrannies. When this potentate dies his moral and mental death, it will probably be on a pyre, for which he is now preparing a large quantity of material; but whether he will have any conversation with an hotel-keeper afterwards—as Mr. Smith or what not—is more than one can say. But of course he'll be very welcome, if the hotel-keeper doesn't mind.

But let us return to our muttons; and we shall find that not only the black sheep, but the lambs and tender ones also, are subject to death in life. There is that spinning maiden, for instance, to whose memory the Germans have erected a cross and written a ballad. Her lover was made captive among the Paynim, and was only to be released for a heavy ransom; which when Gretchen heard, she took her distaff and sat by the wayside, spinning, spinning, spinning, day by day, and selling her wool fabrics to wayfarers. Her little hoard lay near her, on a stone; and day by day she brooded over it, watching its slow increase with anxious eyes and an anxious heart, but spinning still. At length, after a long time, when the little hoard had become almost a great one, news came that the prisoner was dead; and 'twas of no use spinning any more. It never was of any use spinning at all. Ah! there was news for the faithful, hopeful little Gretchen! But with the news came the Deliverer, and touched her on the forehead, and—still the distaff trundled busily. Gretchen had passed through the Valley of the Shadow of Death, though there she sat still—the beauty of the other world shining on her face—spinning, spinning, spinning; and all to ransom her lover. I wish I had seen her! I wish I had been one of those who pitifully added a coin to the store on the stone, and beheld how the grave, ghostly face smiled! One of these days I certainly will go and see the cross they have erected (with her treasure) on the spot where she used to sit. But who is this whose husband was buried last summer, and now is so wonderfully gentle and odd in her manner? She is of the Deliverer's company, likewise; and so are many others, male and female. Gretchen and the widow are only two of a thousand.

By a mercy, which, as fellow-sinners, we must say he scarcely deserves, Horace Keppel is in similar case. I have already said that he has changed, and this is the sort of change. The passions that once agitated that carcase of his have departed: he has scarcely a desire to call his own. Five years of remorse, of terror, of dread, of too much wine, of solitary contemplation under the eye of the jailer his valet, have worn him out; he has passed through the fires, raging and swearing, rebellious, and whining, and drunken; and has come out ashen gray and ashen cold. His man may take away his wine now, at any time; he may deny him his dinner, or his fire; reduce him to an allowance of pocket-money, or beat his dog; and Keppel will not complain. He goes to bed at night, and he rises in the morning, with the same pale, outwearied face; he wanders about with it all day, or looks into the fire, or gazes through the window-panes, and there is never a smile the more upon it, nor a shadow the less. There is no more life in him, or for him. He is like an abandoned ship (which, I suppose, is as dead as anything can be), out of which all intelligence, good and bad, all virtue, all wickedness, has departed; which drives before every breeze that blows, and whether it burn or whether it drown, whether it split upon the rocks, or float in sunshine and soft winds for ever, is equally unconcerned. Mr. Horace Keppel has been very prettily punished; but the punishment is over, for this life. He is like

an eye that once flashed with love and anger, and the light of a thousand thoughts; and is now blind. He is a poor, vague, opaque mortal, harmless, insensible to harm—deceased, to all intents and purposes.

As such, he is such a punishment to Mark Howlet as can scarcely be conceived. The valet had always to bear about with him the guilt of that Plan, by which he betrayed his master into the murder of his child; but hitherto there was the solace of having a chief accomplice in her death; the excitement of bullying that accomplice; the satisfaction of making him avow every day that he (Keppel) *was* the murderer; and a sense of being all this while the avenger of his sister's injuries and his own dishonour. But now the case is altered. It is as if he had to bear about with him the corpse of his accomplice; and not only his corpse, but his share of the sin. As if the whole responsibility of Ruth's death had now devolved on him—valet as he was—with the guilt of having betrayed and ruined his master into the bargain. It is not Mr. Keppel, but Mr. Howlet, who now trembles at the sound of Ruth's name. Indeed, the poor gentleman is often heard repeating it to himself, as he wanders about the house and grounds, and has read a novel in which the name frequently occurs, at least four or five times through, in these later days. At this very moment he is doing—what do you think? Drawing, upon a blank leaf in that book, little Ruth herself, as she lay on the floor that eventful evening. There she lies in the fantastic shadows, dead enough to all appearance; and the candle burning in the corner, the door half-opened, the gloom lurking in the draperies of the bed, are all as faithfully indicated as if the sketch had been made on the spot by our own artist. How tenderly the pencil goes over the lines of that little face, working over it and about it, and amongst the fair tresses, so caressingly! And as one looks on the poor gentleman, one can but think of a blind or idiot mother passing her fingers over her baby's face, doubtfully and awfully.

Yes, Mr. Horace Keppel has paid dearly enough, and now he is—but here comes Mr. Hatcher.

CHAPTER XXXVIII.

BOOTY OF THE THIRD ROBBER.

MR. KEPPEL did not hear Hatcher announced, nor observe his entrance. He went on with his pencilling, at any rate; his back to the door, his eye wandering over the lines of the drawing, as if they had lost their way without knowing it. Hatcher, seeing a man deeply engaged with his pencil and a book, took it for granted that he must be making up his accounts; and as this was a matter which particularly interested him at the moment, he stepped softly up and looked over Mr. Keppel's shoulder.

How the broker's eyes wandered over the lines of the drawing! Rather, how they leapt over it—snatching up a little bit here and a little bit there, like a greedy boy in a scramble! In a twinkling he pocketed every detail; drew a long, long breath, and then muttered in Keppel's ear—

"God bless my soul! That's how you did it, eh? Why, it's like the babes in the wood!"

Keppel clapped-to the book, starting in great confusion. "What are you doing here, sir?" he asked.

"Oh, this unfortunate business, Mr. Keppel, which I see you're always worriting about, as well you may!"

"Would you like to buy the sketch, Hatcher?" said Keppel, smiling an unearthly smile, and tapping the book. "Sketch of the scene, by the murderer's own hand."

"Great heaven, sir, how free you talk! Like to buy it," repeated Joel, after a little consideration. "No, Mr. Keppel! I would not have it at a gift. As it is, I cannot sleep at night, and I'm resolved to get out of the business altogether."

"Very well; if that will assist your plans, take it and welcome!" Here Keppel tore out the leaf containing his sketch, and placed it quietly on the table. "Can I do anything more for you? Say the word, and you shall have the murderer wrapping the poor little body in his cloak. You shall have him toiling along in the dark, or stopping to listen, like a hunted beast, if you please. Or standing by the lime-pit; or flying headlong over the fields; and I'll draw you the wind howling at him, the leaves hissing at him, the weeds grasping at his feet. You shall see how his own limbs were strange to him; and as for the face, it shall be a speaking likeness, Hatcher, speaking of—speaking——"

Here the poor gentleman's voice dwindled away.

"My dear sir!" exclaimed Hatcher in great alarm, who saw that his errand would be profitless, if Mr. Keppel continued in this detestable frame of mind, "you are not well, are you?"

"My dear broker," returned the other, "those who do ill can never be well. You'll find it out, too, one of these days. Have patience."

Hatcher was confounded.

"Well, what do you say to my proposition?"

"About the drawings, sir? What use could they be to *me?* I don't want to do you a injury!"

"Thank you. But your forbearance is unkind!"

"On the contrary. At the same time if you go on talking like this, the cat'll soon be out!"

"Let it go, Hatcher! Open the bag! It is playing the deuce with your entrails; and if ever you see your friend my servant, you know how desperately *his* heart is torn. No, gnawed; that's the word. As for me!" added Keppel, striking his breast, but still speaking in the softest and most unmoved voice, "I have no heart left. It's gone, Hatcher! I'm empty. The worm has eaten the kernel clean out, and there's neither sense nor use in the shell. It'll burn, however, and that's all. So pray do not take me into consideration, with respect to the cat. Let it out, Hatcher, if it suits your purpose."

Here there was a long silence, in which Hatcher contemplated the utter impracticability of "putting the screw" upon such yielding material as Keppel had become. Threatening was clearly of no avail now; and threats were his only weapons.

"I am going abroad!" ejaculated Mr. Hatcher at last.

"Well, that will do for an accessory after the fact."

"Only, you see, sir, I'm so poor; and I shall have to give up a good business, and taking women across the seas is expensive, especially if they're old and got the rheumatiz. I was thinking that as I shouldn't trouble you any more, you might be good enough to draw me a handsome cheque."

"Couldn't you make that drawing do?" remarked Keppel, pointing to the sketch which still lay on the table. There's a reward, I suppose, or some sort of information money, to be had?"

"I don't know about that, sir. I only know that pencil pictures are no good to me. I want some money."

"Then don't ask it of me, pray; because I've got none."

"Well—I'll take jewels," said Hatcher with a little grin.

"Half of them are pawned; and the rest must remain mine."

"Oh, Mr. Keppel, that's all nonsense, you know."

"You shall be permitted to make whatever remarks you please to-day."

"Mr. Keppel, understand me!" began Hatcher with assumed severity.

"Stop! wouldn't it be as well for you to understand me? Now listen." And, for the first time, Keppel evinced some liveliness of glance and tone. "I shouldn't care to give you money, if I had it; I would not, in fact. But I have none to give. My own recklessness, and the demands which you and Mr. Howlet are pleased to make, have thoroughly impoverished me, sir. Indeed, I have on several occasions had to borrow a hundred pounds or so from my valet.'

"Do what?" Hatcher was a new man, to look at.

"Borrow money of my man. Degrading, isn't it, Hatcher?"

"And he has been making demands, too, has he? Mr. Keppel, you've been robbed, sir! Swindled and fleeced for years, sir! You pay *him!* That's good too! Now, does he keep the money in the house?"

No answer deigned.

"Because it's trust money, that is, Mr. Keppel."

"Oh!" said the other, nodding carelessly.

"Yes, sir, he holds it in trust for me. Now I want it! Now I'm going to have it!"

"Indeed! You never appeared ——"

"Where was the use, while I thought him a lean beast, and not worth the killing? How he must have been fattening! Why, he's worth a thousand pounds, perhaps!"

"Oh, yes!"

"Lor! lor! To think so much money has been saving up for me, and I not know it!" And Joel wrung his hands, he was so pleased.

"And when he has given up this money, he is to try and bleed my property anew. I see. Well, the blood won't flow, and he'll be disappointed. But it will be rather a nuisance to me, I suppose."

"What for? Look here, Mr. Keppel: I never loved your man; he has snubbed and insulted me a hundred times; now I'll square it off with him. Suppose I tell you something that will enable you to kick him out of the house whenever he shows himself disagreeable. Look here!"

Hatcher leered forward, and was just about to open those thin lips of his again, when the door opened, and Mr. Howlet appeared, with some precipitation.

"Oh, here you are, sir! We were just talking about you!"

"I know you were," replied Mark, very pale and determined. "Now what have you to say?"

"Well, something about your little savings, Mark. I want them!"

"And do you suppose, you fool, that you'll get a penny of me?"

"I suppose, Mr. Mark, that I shall get every penny you're possessed of."

He went to the fireside, laid his hand on the bell-rope, and continued: "Now keep off, and don't attempt to leave the room, or I'll ring the bell down, call up all the servants, and tell them the little secret I was just going to impart to your master."

Mark's face underwent a terrible change. Turning his back on his enemy, he opened a cabinet, and drew open a drawer.

"Don't be alarmed, Mr. Hatcher!" Keppel remarked, resting his elbow on the mantel-piece. "They're not loaded."

And Mark turned about with a double-barrelled pistol in his hand.

But Hatcher saw the shining of the steel, and heard the click of the lock before Keppel's observation had reached his ears.

"What!" he cried in a high suppressed voice, "would you shoot me, you strangler? Here then!"

His hand had fallen from the bell-rope in his terror. He was about to clutch it again, when Howlet threw down the pistol, again startling his enemy.

"Stop! stop, fool!" he almost shouted. Now, in two words, what do you want?"

"The thieves are falling out!" said Keppel, quietly.

"I want to leave this den of murderers!"

"Leave it, then!"

"Not without your money, Mark Howlet, or I'll hang you! Not without every shilling of it!"

"In a black box, I believe," again interposed Mr. Keppel, with that strange quiet manner of his.

Howlet threw a glance at his impracticable master, and another at his trembling enemy, full of the direst wrath and hate. And then he dropped into a chair, and trembled too.

"You're going abroad. Take half my savings."

"Half! What do you mean? Bring down the black box —I'll have it all! I'll not leave you a pound! Shoot me, will you? Now, then, I ring before you can count five, if you don't choose how it's to be!"

The valet rose. "I'll fetch the box," said he, in a hoarse voice.

"Oh, don't trouble yourself" (here the bell rang). "Suppose you send some one to fetch it for you; some accident might happen to it."

Mark's chance was gone. "Take these keys," he said to the man who entered, "and bring a small japanned box from a drawer in my dressing-table."

In a few minutes the box was produced.

"Dear, dear, it's a very little box!" said Hatcher. "How much is there in it?"

"Not so much as you think," the other replied, trembling with excitement. He had tried speculation, and had lost his investments, naturally. "About £900, in notes and gold. Let me open it; let us see how much there is. Besides there are some little documents—I O U's, and so on—that would be of no use to you, and might set me up again."

Hatcher shook the box, and heard the sound of coin.

"Don't trouble yourself," he said, with a great flash of satisfaction in his eyes; "it will be handier to carry altogether. Anything I don't happen to want, you shall have back to-morrow."

Spreading his handkerchief over the box, he tucked it under his arm, and backed towards the door with the least possible delay.

"I wish you good day, gentlemen. Mr. Keppel, your obedient servant, sir. Mr. Mark, I hope when next we meet it will be in a more friendly spirit than we part."

CHAPTER XXXIX.

THE WIDOW GETS WARNING, AND GOES HOME.

MR. HATCHER's journey from Keppel Lodge to the emporium was one of the most remarkable he had ever experienced. He seemed to see himself, rather than be himself, scudding along home, with that black box under his arm, and a great trembling in his bosom. His success was so great, he could hardly believe in it; but then there was the feeling of having set his feet in a path from which there was now no retreat, and any obstacle in which would be ruin. "I have done it now!" he repeated to himself fifty times. "I must be off—off at once!" Then he began to run, or rather to trot; and had to check himself, and endeavour to compose his mind. But came some quick footstep behind him, and discomposed it again immediately. If that were Mark! No; a woman with garden-stuff. Then came an odd-looking man towards him, evidently with some intentions. The strange man suddenly stops and searches his pockets, crying—

"I say, mister!"

"Not my name, my good man. My name's B—Baker!" quaked Joel.

"No matter for the name, mister. I only wanted a light for my pipe, if you've got such a thing about you."

"Is that all? No, I haven't. I don't smoke. Good-bye, my friend, good-bye!" and, having shook the stranger warmly by the hand, Hatcher set off again at a rejoicing trot.

As he crossed his threshold, Hatcher felt for the first time that his mother was a difficulty. He had never before been called upon to think of her as a distinct individual. He was she, and she was he; and together they made up "Hatcher." That was all very well in quiet plodding times, but now it was most necessary for "Hatcher" to look alive, to bustle up, to catch railway-trains and fast-sailing ships, to face the stormy deep, and brave all sorts of fatigues and dangers. True, one party was lively enough, but the other moiety was old, sick, and threatened to die. To ask her to bustle up and face the stormy deep, seemed almost out of the question—she who had never travelled fifty miles in her life; and yet what was to be done? But perhaps she was better now.

"How's mother, Simmonds?" asked Joel anxiously, as he passed that person, who was beguiling time by "teasing" horse-hair in a corner of the shop.

"Very curious, Mr. Joel; very curious. My wife says she's blowed if she can make her out. She's been crying like winkin'. Got up for a little while, and then went to bed again."

A strange and dreadful feeling passed into Hatcher's mind, whether he would or no. A sensation which, if I may so express it, was partly a tickling and partly a pain. A feeling of awe and grief, with a wild wilful tingling of satisfaction in it. To do him justice, Hatcher was ashamed of this feeling; but it would turn up, now and then, while he locked the black box in a cupboard, and while he put on his slippers, and went up-stairs to see the widow.

The old woman was a-bed sure enough. Her clothes were folded and carefully placed on a chair by the bedside, as usual; and Joel's eyes mechanically wandered to a certain peg, where, for the first time in the young man's recollection, the bonnet was *not*. From this circumstance he drew the worst conclusions.

"Is that you, Joly?" said the widow, raising her poor weeping puckered old face from the pillow.

"Yes, it's me. How are you? Where's that mother Simmonds been and put your bonnet?"

"I've give it away! I've give it to her. Ah, Joly, I shall never want no bonnet again!"

"Why won't you want it again? I suppose she's been stuffing you with that idea, just to get it out of you."

"Oh no, no—nobody's been stuffing me, Jolly. I heard it with my own ears. Be still, and you will hear it too. Hark!"

The old woman's terror-stricken face rose still higher in the bed, and she held up her forefinger, intensely listening. Her son was constrained to listen too, and that with apprehension, so terribly in earnest was his mother's manner. One, two, three—fifty seconds were counted off, and still there was dead silence. Fifty, sixty, and seventy seconds poured through the glass, and there sat those two listening with all their might, and staring at each other with looks full of fear and expectancy. Seventy, eighty, ninety seconds—

Tick! tick! tick! tick! There it was, distinct enough.

The old woman uttered a little weak cry, and cowered down into the bed, her hands pressed to her ears.

"That's it! That's the token! When your poor father died, Joly, and when my brother Micah died, we all heard it. Oh, don't let us be wicked any more, my son. Let us turn over a new leaf, and do the right thing by everybody."

"I—I don't believe in death-watches," ejaculated Joel, who was to the full as superstitious as his mother. "It's only a beetle that rubs its legs against its wings or something. At least—I don't know!" continued he, in an apologetic tone (for who knew but that the death-watch might be listening?)—"that's what I've heard."

"Oh, don't try to deceive me, Joly—I know better. These things is given to us——"

Tick! tick! tick!

"Ah, there it is again! It will soon be over. I shall not be a burden to you much longer, Joly!"

Much longer! These words reminded Mr. Hatcher that Time was still flying, and that he was not safe now for an instant. He was afraid of Mark Howlet; afraid that Mrs. Bell had taken measures, the consequences of which might come upon him at any moment; afraid that the showman would raise a hue and cry; afraid, too, of Keppel, who appeared as indifferent to disclosure now as once he had been anxious to avoid it. Every hour exposed the broker to risks, which he felt the more acutely on account of that new and great acquisition, the black box.

The widow bemoaned herself, and her son brooded over the situation.

"How long—I say, how long is he supposed to keep up that ticking, mother, before—before——"

Joel stammered and blushed. Yes, blushed! so you may pretty nearly guess how he felt.

The old woman replied in an awful whisper—

"Oh, he'll keep on till he has ticked off as many years as I am old. Sixty-three the 9th of December—only sixty-three!—and then he'll stop. And then, oh, Joly, Joly! I shall stop too. Oh, if I had my time over again! Come here, my son; let us repent. Get down the Bible, Joel, and read me something. There's a part about the penitent thief—get it down and read it."

But Joel was an impenitent thief. He took no heed of his mother's exhortations, for his mind was wandering other where. He paced wearily across and across the room, softly opened the window, and looked up the street and down the street, closed the window, and began pacing the room again. The time was flying.

"How many do you think it has told off already? how many ticks, I mean?"

"That's where it is, Joly," the old woman whimpered; "perhaps I heard him the first tick, and perhaps he was half done before then."

"Well, I wish he'd never begun, 'or—or something. It's precious awkward, just now. I don't know what to do, I'm sure."

"Find that part I was speaking on, dear," said the widow, in a coaxing tone; "and sit down and read it to me quietly."

"Oh, what jolly nonsense!" Hatcher exclaimed, stamping impatiently. "At least—there, don't cry, mother. I don't say the part's nonsense, but how can I sit down quietly, while I expect a rap at the door every minute? Besides, suppose that ticking thing should be wrong after all?"

"I tell you no!" replied she, almost fiercely. There! It's answering you itself."

The ticking was repeated five or six times as Widow Hatcher ceased speaking.

"Confound the thing!" ejaculated Hatcher, half audibly, and going once more to the window; "it's all humbug and superstition. I wonder how long this is going to last? I wonder how many that last lot made?"

The mother did not hear, or did not reply to this remark, but lay terribly wakeful, her attention strained in the direction whence proceeded the innocent sound that alarmed her. She was still as death. Joel himself was breathless with a thousand apprehensions; and so the minutes passed, as he paced up and down, up and down. The ticking had ceased; and the poor old woman began evidently to fear that all the sixty-three years of her existence had been told off. Then it was that Joel, whether from mere thoughtlessness, or with a desire to show that *he* had a contempt for death-watches and their bodings, and so to encourage his mother, cried "Tick! tick!" as a man chirps to a canary bird.

As though the sound had severed a cord that bound her to the bed, Mrs. Hatcher sprang up, and shot a glance burning with grief and anger at her son. He staggered before it, and his very ears tingled.

"Call him again, Joel, call him again!" she screamed. "Oh, what a son! To call death to fetch his mother!"

Hatcher covered his face with his hands. If he loved anything in the world more than money, it was this old woman; and he couldn't withstand such a reproach from her. He ran to her, and threw his arms round her neck.

"I don't want you to die, mother! Why should I? Haven't you been the only one that ever I cared for, or that ever cared for me? Haven't you been my right hand in everything? But you don't know our danger. We are not safe one hour over another. Any moment they may come and haul me off to prison, and you, too, perhaps; or if not, what but the workhouse is for you, if they take me?"

"Then go without me," said the old woman, softened by this display of affection. "They won't find me alive—never fear. I shall be ticked clean off before they can get at me, my son. You go. Get away at once, and leave me here in quiet to count off the rest of 'em. It won't take very long—something tells me that, that's told me true many a time before."

"Oh, if you *could* rouse yourself! If you could only manage to pull yourself together a bit, and let us get away together! I say, you never asked me how I got on up yonder. Brought away £900, good money! Howlet seems to have kept his cash pretty well within arm's reach, like me. What have we got, now, at home?"

Hatcher was endeavouring to lead his mother off the subject of death-watches, and on to one more strengthening.

"I don't know," replied she, apathetically. "It's all there! I ain't bought so much as a bit of ribbon for myself this six months. Take it all with you—I shan't want any of it. Only leave me five pound—no, three pound ten will do. Plain elm, you know, Joly, without any flimsy kivering. They cheat awful in that way. Kiver up any rubbish, they do. No, let it be elm and black nails.

Hatcher's perplexity increased a hundredfold. Still time was flying, and still his mother persisted in declaring that she would die, in anything but a dying voice. She had resumed her recumbent position, and again lay listening.

Suddenly, Hatcher started and looked hopeful. He had bethought himself of something that should inspire his mother, if all else failed. Going down-stairs softly, he presently returned with the black box. Placing it on a table at his mother's bedside, and almost wholly concealed from her view by the hangings, he opened the box, and examined its contents. There were some loose coins, about a dozen rouleaus of gold, each containing five-and-twenty pieces, and a sheaf of bank notes. He spread the dear, delightful crisp sheets all over the table, took out the rouleaus, and then prepared to fire them off into the iron box and against the citadel of superstition. Standing with a pocket-knife in one hand, and a rouleau in the other, he suddenly ripped it

up; and clang fell the gold into the black box. Then another with better effect still: the clangour of gold upon gold! The citadel trembled visibly. Clang! bang! clang! The citadel was stirred to its foundations! Bang! clang! clang! Flags of truce; the old woman's arms are thrown up. No quarter! Clang! Down fall the gates, and out sallies the crazy enemy, taking the artilleryman considerably by surprise, and capturing his remaining guns.

In other words, when the first clinking was heard, the old woman turned in her bed, and tried to see *what* gold that was, through the thin and well-worn hangings. As the firing proceeded, she became more and more excited, sat up, listened with a new and a more dreadful expression, thrust aside the curtains, fed her eyes for an instant upon the heaped gold and the richly-scattered notes, and then fell forward upon the table, sweeping the treasure toward her. Alas! her time had come. That famine-like look in her poor old eyes was not *all* lit by avarice—there was a flash of madness in it, and the dull glow of departing life.

"Be off!" she cried, waving her son away. "Who are you, bruising my beautiful gold—stealing my beautiful gold?"

"Good heavens, mother! Why, this is worse than ever!" said Hatcher aghast. "Pray, compose yourself!"

"Don't talk to me of composing, you villain. If you don't compose yourself out of this house in a minute," said she, seizing Joel's pocket knife, "I'll cut your head off."

"Lay down, mother, that's a dear soul, and I'll read you the Penitent Thief, or anything you like."

Their eyes met, and they gazed fixedly at each other—Hatcher in grief and terror, the old woman with that fierce famine-look. Presently, however, her eyes began to assume another expression; softer—softer—the most human and tender that ever was seen in them these twenty years. "Joly," she cried, extending her arms toward him, "My son!" and fell forward on the table. The bank notes were scattered, the black box fell to the floor with a crash, and Mrs. Hatcher was a dead woman.

CHAPTER XL.

IN WHICH ANOTHER ONE IS TICKED OFF.

So eloquent was the manner of Mrs. Hatcher's death that her son needed no second glance to assure him of it. But for the space of a minute he gazed upon the poor old body with eyes as fixed and unspeculative as her own; he kept them on her as he sidled out of the room, which he locked, and then backed, shuffled, crept, flitted—anything but walked, out into the street.

Not with any purpose. On the contrary, he went "mooning" about the town with a greater itch to inquire into things of no earthly interest to him than ever he had experienced in his life before. He stopped at the farrier's, and, lounging over the wicket, lingered there long enough to see a brown horse fitted with a pair of hind shoes. Then on he went again, wondering why the major number of horses were brown; nor was the question permitted to escape till he came to the post-office, where he became deeply interested in a placard informing the public that on and after a certain date letters to Sweden should be prepaid.

Not that he was at all forgetful of his position. Every time the farrier's hammer clinked on the anvil, Joel heard the clinking of gold upon gold. When the farrier drove nails into the horse's hoof—tick-tack, tick-tack—there was that foolish death-watch again; and down came the black box with an awful clamour when he threw aside his hammer on a pile of iron bars. So at the post-office. That placard about the Swedish mail had lines in it, legible to Hatcher alone, about a hundred pounds reward; and the sailing of the fast ship *Lightning* for America; and funerals conducted with secrecy and despatch. A vague and fog-bound state of mind this, and very common, like all the other mercies of heaven. For it is as much a mercy as sleep is; it is like sleep, exactly as that state of mind which belonged to Keppel and the Spinning Maiden is like death; and but for it, coming suddenly upon us after some great mental shock or exertion, half the world would be mad by this time.

The sudden ignition of a lamp by the road-side awoke Hatcher

LAST APPEARANCE OF MR. JOEL HATCHER.

from slumber, and he stopped and shivered, he felt so cold. Why, it was almost night! All the good daylight wasted, and not a farthing secured, no step taken out of the maze that was growing up about him! Moreover, that room must be entered once more, and he must enter it alone; for all the money was there. So Mr. Hatcher shivered home again, his hands in his pockets, and wondering to find that he could retrace in less than an hour all the wanderings of the afternoon.

Mrs. Simmonds had been obliged to devote that afternoon to the cultivation of her children; it was Simmonds's business never to leave the shop; and thus the day had gone down on the undiscovered body of Mrs. Hatcher. The lamps over the way were the first to know anything of her decease, after Mr. Joel and the day. They might have been seen looking in at the window in a surprised, scared manner, and holding uneasy converse with those mutes of shadows crowding within the four bed-posts, and under the chimney, and in all the corners. Beside these, the room was full of all sorts of ghosts or genii—voiceless, but full of eyes, which watched the poor corpse in the absence of human creatures. What could they have been, congregated there thick as bees, flitting by now and then in a slightly luminous way? All the old woman's passions, perhaps, her greater hopes and affections, scourged out of her by death, but unwilling to depart. So there they lingered, crowded together, watching her eagerly with all their eyes; as might the dead hunter's hound that hunted for him, the hawk that soared for him, the fawn that ate from his hand, the dove that lay in his bosom.

Whether any of these ghosts came down-stairs and appeared to Simmonds (say that Passion for "nagging," and throwing brooms at his head, with which the shopman had long been familiar), I do not know; but his master found him very pale, and with a dread consciousness upon him that there was something wrong up-stairs. Hatcher turned a shade paler too, when Simmonds apprised him of this mysterious boding, and hastily asked whether he had heard anything moving above stairs? To which the fair-haired young man replied that he had not, and that was just it! Hatcher, however, seemed to be relieved by the intelligence, rather than otherwise.

After a few minutes of deep reflection, he sent Simmonds home, saying that to-morrow he must leave for London, early; that he, Simmonds, had better take the keys; and that certain instructions would be left for him on the parlour mantelpiece. Simmonds departed, shaking his head.

The banging-to of the outer door gave Hatcher a mighty shock, at the wrong moment; for he felt that now he must nerve himself. Was not that room to be entered? Brandy is good for the nerves; he swallowed two glasses of it, threw them down his throat one after the other with the rapidity of an experienced dram-drinker, but more, perhaps, taking his appearance altogether, like a *del. trem.* patient, who, leaping at the forbidden bottle when his nurse's back is turned, makes the most of his opportunity. But Hatcher allowed no sufficient time for the working of the potent water; and when, a minute after swallowing it, he lighted a candle and went up to his mother's room, his heels smote twice on the stairs at every footfall. Arrived at the door, he hesitated; he placed the candlestick on the floor, and wiped his forehead with his coat-tails; he gave a great gulp, as if he had hitherto retained the brandy in his mouth; he extended his hands further through his sleeves, as a porter does when about to exhibit his strength, and took up the candle, and entered the room.

It was not seeing those shadows leap aside that first shocked Mr. Hatcher, but he heard them rustling audibly, like scared wolves in a wood; and there they lay watching like wolves, threatening him from under the bed, and over the bed, and from the corners. They watched his motions and followed them stealthily; so that at length, for very dread, he stood quite still. Then the lamps over the way would steal their scared glances into the room, spite of Hatcher's candle, which was a feeble thing. Then those great uncurtained windows, staring like two cold gray eyes that had seen all and knew all about it—he dare not look at them at all.

But the greatest shock had yet to come. Hitherto he had averted his eyes from his mother's body; though, indeed, he had been thereto invited more than once by the winking of some gold piece that had rolled from the heap scattered beneath her. At length he lifted the candle above his head, turned a slow, unwilling glance upon her, and gasped again when he saw that she had not moved a jot since he beheld her last. Nothing, of course, was more natural or more certain to have happened; but to see his own mother huddled there exactly as she had fallen four hours ago—half upon the bed half upon the table, her gray hair escaped from her cap, her forehead resting on her left arm, and her right hand full of money—it seemed to Hatcher the most supernatural sight that ever was conceived. And to make it more impressive, a draught from the open door took up a rag of ribbon and a lock of gray hair, and they fluttered on the poor old woman's head, toying together.

But Hatcher's sensations were of a nature which inspired him to action too, when the first chill of astonishment had passed through him. Pulling the blind over those staring windows, he took his mother in his arms tenderly and replaced her in her bed, where she lay calmly enough now. Then he drew the curtains about her, hesitated, put his hand within them, kissed the old girl, and came out with a sort of tear in his eyes. "'Tis no use, mother," said he, softly: "I must go. If it would do you any good to stop, why I'd do it; but it wouldn't. You said that yourself before——" He had not courage to complete the sentence; so he went on his knees, and picked the money up. He was still engaged in this occupation, and had crawled under the bed in search of any coin that might have strayed there, when there came a little timid knock at the outer door. Hatcher started as suddenly as if he had been shot, and he did sustain a serious blow on the back of his head, which he involuntarily struck against one of the timbers of the bedstead. A knock at the door! Who could that be? He crept from under the bed, crept to a window on all fours, and raising it at the rate of an inch a minute, looked out. Almost at the same minute he drew his head in again, and cursed Mrs. Simmonds. What did she want? Why, Sim had come home in *such* a way about Mrs. Hatcher, that she could not rest till she had run in, and she would sit up all night with her. Well, she need not trouble herself, Mr. Joel said, blandly. Mother was gone off in a beautiful sleep—fast asleep she was. He was going to sit up all night himself, having matters of business to arrange, and would call Mrs. Simmonds, if need be.

Hatcher did not withdraw his head this time till he had fairly watched Mrs. Simmonds out of sight; but he failed to descry a patient-looking man who overheard the above conversation, and who followed the charwoman, and engaged with her in friendly talk.

This little episode rather brightened Mr. Hatcher up. It brought his every-day weapons into use again, and inspired him once more with the necessity of getting to business. No more hesitations after this. The bank-notes were gathered together, and restored to the black box with the rest of Howlet's money. Then it appeared that Hatcher also had a black box, wonderfully like the other. It contained *his* private resources, which he too had taken care should be cast in the form of hard cash, or paper everywhere convertible into cash. This treasure was all placed in a leathern bag, together with a single change of clothes; and, when midnight was fairly passed, when one o'clock had been told off, Joel put on a great-coat, caught up the bag, and sallied out.

Now the old woman was alone with the genii again. How-ever, Joel had left the candle burning for company's sake, and it shone upon some eight or ten sovereigns. What could they have been left for? The old woman said three pound ten would be enough to bury her with!

Mr. Hatcher had a walk of seven miles before him, and three hours to do it in. It was about that distance to Rochester, where (and not at Sleaford) he proposed to take coach; and this vehicle started at four o'clock A.M., as he was well advised. Therefore, Mr. Joel was at liberty to choose his own roads, which he did with preference for the roundabout and the solitary. But those cowardly members, the legs, which are the first to betray the weakness of mankind, whether at the " booze " or on the battle-field, hurried him along willy-nilly; and he found himself stretching along at the rate of six miles an hour immediately after he had resolved to abate his speed to three. So he was compelled, towards the close of the journey, to make an occasional pause, during which he once or twice imagined that he heard the sound of footsteps behind him. However, he knew what tricks imagination can play in the dark, and comforted himself.

It was the season when the sun rises late; it had two hours longer to lie when Mr. Hatcher appeared in the coach-office. The inside places were engaged, which he took to heart; but two outside places remained unoccupied, and one of these he secured. The other was taken by a grazier, obviously; by his drab great-coat, his drab gaiters, his slouching felt hat, his leathern gloves, his noble black whiskers, his stiff knee, and his ashen staff. As for the rest of the company, there was the jolly woman, and the cross one with the boxes; the heavy friend of the coachman's; the legal-like passenger; the jolly one's husband; an old man and a young woman; a soldier and a young woman; and the raw long-boned youth without a young woman, and rather afraid of such.

The coach rattled to the door, and the passengers took their places. The soldier took leave of the young woman with tears in his manly eyes, and then scaling the coach as desperately as if it were a breach and he a forlorn hope, seated himself by Hatcher's side; that is to say, behind the coachman. The grazier accompanied the guard; the other people distributed themselves generally. Hatcher's precious bag was cuddled on his knees.

In an astonishing short time the soldier recovered his spirits and entertained Hatcher with some lively remarks about the young person he, the man of war, had just parted from. He said if she wasn't as fine a gal as any in England, he'd be dee'd, which I have no doubt he was eventually. But she wasn't his sort, for all that. And then he told Mr. Hatcher (who grinned like an old roué of course) what his sort was, illustrating his remarks with anecdotes, and enforcing them by digs and blows in Mr. Hatcher's side. At length this became wearying, and Joel shifted his leathern bag round so as to protect his ribs. When, therefore, the soldier next came to a funny place in his conversation, he delivered his elbow against the black box, and that so sharply that a jingling ensued. Then the soldier rubbed his elbow, and was wroth. He wanted to know what on earth the other meant by that? Why the dickens didn't he put his luggage out of peoples' way—carrying a heavenly cash-box about with him, as if everybody was thieves? How the soldier did bawl out these words, "cash-box and thieves," to be sure! They made Hatcher tremble in every limb; for everyone must have heard them—from the coachman in front to the grazier behind.

"Lor, soldier, how you talk !" said Joel, tittering. "Cash-box ! He he ! I only wish it was, my friend. It's locks ! I'm a locksmith !"

"Well, pitch them up behind, then. Give 'em to the guard, can't you ?"

"Ay, give your luggage to me, sir, I'll take care on it."

"Oh, of course, of course !"

And not to bring any further suspicion of cash-boxes on his luggage, Hatcher handed it over to the guard. Oh, how desolate the young man felt now ! How nervous, how anxious ! for there was still so much darkness about that it quite swallowed up the bag, and its guardian too.

The grazier's hat was blown off, or an overhanging bough took it off, or something. Be that as it may, the grazier, suddenly clapping his hands to his head, found it uncovered, and shouted to the coachman to stop. Then he grumbled something to the guard about his stiff knee, upon which the obliging fellow answered, "Here, hold this bag, sir! I'll find it for you!" as in duty bound.

Now that was not an honest grazier. No sooner had the guard descended than he (the grazier) turned his back on the other passengers, as though peering after his hat, whipped a knife out of his pocket, and drew it sharply along Hatcher's bag, just under the mouth; or rather he would have done so, but the blade caught in the lock-plate almost at starting, and snapped short off. The grazier cursed the knife—which had no interest in the matter either way—and threw it to the ground. A passionate idea prompted him to throw the bag after it; but by this time the guard was seen returning, a lamp in one hand and the hat in the other. So he thanked the guard, in his gruff grazier-like voice, and Mr. Hatcher's treasure was restored to safer keeping.

Daylight came, and the grazier buried his big whiskers in his coat-collar, and dozed. Noon came, and the coach arrived at its destination in Bishopsgate Street. Joel recovered his treasure—it was safe. He entered the coffee-room; so did the insides, the old gentleman and his daughter, the legal passenger, the jolly woman, the jolly woman's husband, and the grazier. The latter ordered coffee, folded his arms on the table, laid his face on them, and dozed again. Hatcher ordered half-a-pint of sherry and the morning papers; which having obtained, he perused the shipping advertisements with much interest. After a while he made a note or two in his pocket-book, caught up the leather-bag, and departed; the door closing after him with so rude a jar that it roused the grazier, who got on his legs, shook himself, and went out too.

Hatcher had not proceeded far before he espied a saddler's shop, at which he was pleased; and entering, he bought a wide woollen band, such as is used to confine a horse's stable-cloth at nights. Much satisfied with this purchase, he next looked about him for a nice quiet lodging: no hotels, no taverns for him. What better than that coffee-house—decent, teetotal, and retired—with "good beds," so neatly inscribed on the door?

There was no difficulty about it—he could be accommodated, though only one room remained disengaged; a double-bedded room. Very well. Could he see the room? Could he be obliged with a needle and some thread? The chambermaid reciprocated the confusion with which he preferred this request; she giggled, blushed, and produced the required articles. No sooner had the maid retired than Hatcher locked the door, stuffed a piece of sponge which he found on the dressing-table into the keyhole, and proceeded to convert the horse-girth into a money-belt. He was not handy at his needle, and his work was dreadfully cobbled, though it cost him an hour's labour. However, it was secure; and when he buckled it about him, stuffed with all his store of gold and paper of price, he experienced an infinite relief. Better a weight about the loins than a weight on the heart; and so slippery a friend as money should be close hugged. Now Mr. Hatcher feared no such mischance as had occurred on the coach. Briskly he walked down-stairs, chirpingly he ordered tea and chops at seven, and like a sparrow he hopped off the premises—without the leathern bag.

A farmer or grazier entered almost at the same moment.

"Beds?" said he to the waiter.

"No sir, last one engaged, sir, this very minnit."

"Oh, dang it, doantee turn a mun out again. I'm a stranger. Any place'll do for me. I'll pay for un."

"Jane, did that last gentleman engage the whole of No. 3 room?"

"No—he said nothing about it," replied the chambermaid to the waiter.

"Then, I think, sir, you can have part of a double-bedded room, sir."

"That'll do. Show un to me."

The farmer or grazier was prepared to be satisfied with the room, but when he saw a black leathern bag on a chair there, his eyes positively flashed with pleasure. This was accommodation indeed.

"Well, lass, take this shillun' and go out with ye. I'm goin' to have a freshner." By which he meant that he was going to wash himself. The maid giggled again, and retired accordingly.

The grazier now approached the leathern bag with a reverential greed, a trembling avarice, as the bridegroom approacheth his bride. For a moment he allowed his eyes to dwell upon it, with such feelings as sometimes come over you on receiving a letter from a dear familiar hand, hesitating to break the seal. You break the seal; the dear one says that you can have your ugly portrait back whenever you like, and she hates herself for ever having bestowed a thought on such a creature. The grazier lifted the bag—there was nothing in it! "Sewed it up in his clothes!" he exclaimed, catching sight of the needle and thread; "and it's ten to one he'll never return! Done, by—" How that grazier swore! After which he took his "freshner"—not to excite suspicion in the chambermaid's bosom—and going down into the coffee-room, ate chops and read the newspapers in a corner all alone. Whenever the door opened, his eyes were on it instantly.

'Twas late that evening when Hatcher returned, looking very haggard and careworn, but with every reason to be satisfied, as he assured himself a hundred times. That was the worst of it. He had to assure himself of his good fortune so often, and after all believed in it so little. But what were the facts? He had been successful at the shipping office. A vessel had that very morning left the London Dock for Boston, U.S., but she was to make a two days' stay at Gravesend to take in certain necessaries. A cabin berth was vacant; it was his in five minutes. There was an outfitter's within a hundred yards of the dock gates; and the outfitter had engaged to get a well-found sea-chest on board the Cormorant by the next evening; for the tide made at midnight, and then the ship would sail. Now what could be better than that? And yet Mr. Hatcher was as melancholy as an owl!

As bed-time drew on, he became worse and worse, till he was cold through with misery, overdone with foreboding. No doubt the evil glances which the grazier shot towards him now and then had some influence over the fugitive, though he was unaware of them; but, in my opinion, that second four-poster in his bedroom up-stairs had more to do with it. He could not help thinking of a similiar four-poster at home, and he dreaded to be left alone with it. Above all things he wished for sleep, to set the gulf of a long oblivious night between himself—the watching, scheming, anxious Hatcher—and the scenes of the last twenty-four hours. Moreover, he was very weary; but hour after hour passed away, midnight once more approached, and still he hesitated to order his candlestick, and retire to the company of that other four-poster and his own reflections. It was not altogether to his annoyance, therefore, when at length he did move bedward, to find that the second bed was occupied. Of course he was surprised at first, and alarmed; but the waiter declared it was a most respectable party—farmer or country gentleman; he (Hatcher) dreaded to be left quite alone, and it was better to have the other bed occupied by a living farmer than the ghost of a poor old dead mother, whose body he had abandoned.

How the farmer snored—a hearty, honest, British snore—from amidst those closely-drawn curtains. He was asleep, he was: and when he was asleep he snored; and if you didn't like it, you had only to do the other thing—leave it alone. Hatcher liked the tone of that snore; but he was very cautious, nevertheless. He locked the door, and hid the key in his pillow-case. He examined the chimney. He took from his pocket a bran-new pistol, and placed it on a chair by his bed-side, farthest from the farmer. These little arrangements concluded, Hatcher extinguished the candle, and undressed in the dark. But as for the belt, he kept that on. It was necessary to shift it, indeed, for it had chafed him sorely; and though he unbuckled it with the utmost care, it was impossible to stifle a certain clinking, which had never been disagreeable to Mr. Hatcher till now. However, the farmer snored heartily as ever, and Mr. Joel regirded his loins and got into bed.

But the farmer had been snoring with his eyes open. Previous to Hatcher's appearance, he had torn a little hole in the bed-curtains, and applying his eyes thereto, he had watched every movement of that gentleman. Also the farmer slept with his ears open, and had heard the jingle that emanated from what, though he could not distinctly make it out, he knew to be something that Mr. Hatcher wore about his body. "That's it, then—as I guessed!" said he to himself, accompanied by the most placid of snores. "He has got it all buckled round his carcass! Hang him! I wonder what sort of a pistol that is! Stay till he's asleep!"

So with his eye to the hole in the curtain, he continued to feign sleep with all his patience; and he needed it. For when after an hour-long performance, he ceased to breathe and took to listening, Mr. Hatcher's breath stopped too, significantly; and the farmer had to begin over again. Another hour, and then he gently moved in his bed, to see what effect that might produce. A very decided effect. Hatcher's head was lifted slowly from his pillow, and his hand appeared above the bed-clothes, ready to take up the pistol, evidently. Then the farmer was more wroth than ever. But at last the one grew tired of performing and the other of lying awake to listen, and both rogues fell asleep, wearied out.

The bad angel of one of them—the farmer, to wit—talked with him all the night, it seemed; for when he woke, and found Mr. Joel already dressed and about to leave the room, his heart filled with malignity. Another time foiled, his best chance gone, farmer Howlet ground his teeth with rage and hate, and then settled gradually into a pale dread resolution, not to be described in words; which never took the form of words on farmer Howlet's own lips, nor the form of an idea in his mind. But it was a firm resolution, nevertheless; and what it signified was, that Joel Hatcher had had it all his own way long enough, and that he should never leave England with that money, whoever might profit by it or he hanged for it. Had not the farmer been robbed? And was he to stand by and see the cunning thief sail away triumphant? No. To bear the burden of a guilty mind, year after year, and then to be stripped of the little gains which salved the sore was not to be endured. The guilty mind could only be a little more guilty, at the worst, and what a satisfaction it would be to spoil the triumphant rogue, after all!

The soft autumn expired that day. It came in with the morning for the last time, bright and fair, and ineffably sad—reminding one of an Eastern widow, walking to the funeral pyre in her whitest robes and her costliest jewels, and with a cold and fainting heart. Her jewels are stripped from her, her fair garments are rent, she mounts the pile, and there's an end of her. So at noon of this day, wind-clouds and snow-clouds came down from the north, and overtook the faltering autumn. She trembled and turned pale—that is to say, her sunshine flickered away, and died out suddenly. Then the wind smote her to the ground: and the snow-clouds came up overhead, and buried her. After which they had it all to themselves. The sky was leaden, the air was chill, the wind piped an overture to a score of storms, in which the roaring of the seas, and the crushing of the ships, and the shrieking of their strained and tortured ropes, and the cry of their drowning men—was all imitated in a marvellous and a fearful manner. The night came in a good hour earlier, and winter hailed it joyfully. It blowed more, it snored more; and to prove itself the faithful colleague it had ever been, the night looked its blackest: it was dark as pitch.

Such a day must have made all men miserable, surely; but, I hope, none so sad as Mr. Joel Hatcher. The exultation he experienced on rising, to find himself unmurdered and unrobbed, and nearer to safe harbour on a distant shore, did not last over breakfast-time. The melancholy sunshine came flooding into the room, and with it a dozen recollections that had lain in his heart asleep for twenty years. Surely this was the same sunshine that used to gild up the walls of the church at home, twenty years ago; when he—a lean, hungry little boy—used to sit there with his mother on Sunday afternoons, dozing, drowsing, dreaming, with an eye on pretty little Betsy Brown, and designs to win her heart with the present of a halfpenny—when he should get one. The gentle air that blew in at the window, it wafted him back to the buttercup and daisy days; to fishing with a crooked pin under the little old bridge; to solitary rambles after school-time, when nobody would play with him. It brought back the scent of the wallflowers that grew in mother's garden (and they smelled like no other wallflowers in the world); and once more he stood picking scarlet beans into a big yellow dish; and it was

a sunny Sunday morning, and the bells began to ring. And how that old mother of his would come into these retrospections! Standing at the door again, in that mighty bonnet with the bow a-top—glorious in a red and yellow cotton gown that had been worn to tatters years and years ago; cutting bread and butter by the light of a winter fire; singing her droning old song of Lord Bateman to him as he sat there in a night-cap and the scarlet fever; stealing up to his bed at night to give him a kiss; or to place a surprising pair of new boots on his pillow, to greet him when he awoke. These, and fifty other homely scenes, returned to him, softened by the far distance of twenty years; and so plainly did they show in the autumn sunshine, so distinctly did the old life move in them again, inspired by the breath of that soft wind, that the most trifling details became clear, and he was aware of every sound. He heard the rushing of the river over its stony bed as distinctly as if he were actually fishing there again with his crooked pins; he saw the kingfisher come down and perch on a branch which floated with the stream; he heard farmer White's cows lowing in the meadow beyond, and the reeds rustled and waved, and dipped their flags lazily into the water. Hum! hum! That was the droning of the school-room; and there was Johnny Wigget asleep again, with his head on the long inky desk, and the sun kindling his red hair into a flame.

But no more. These reminiscences were new to Mr. Hatcher, and they oppressed him with their strangeness and their force. He began to wish that he had never grown to be a man; and when, by and by, the sky became overcast, and the wind rose and the snow fell, he went on to wish that he had never been born. Then the events of a later time returned to him. From the picture of his mother singing her "Lord Bateman" by the fireside, he turned to another where she lay dead and alone in a deserted house. He looked upon the child, Joel, munching apples in church, his conscience threatening him with the doom of Ananias and Sapphira for that same; and, raising his head, he beheld in a looking-glass the face of the man Joel, conspirator and thief, dreading only the penalties of human law. The sight was not a pleasant one. The man, Joel, in the looking-glass had a ghastly, anxious face furrowed and lean; the mouth twitched, like a coward's; the eyes were also full of dread; and beads of perspiration dotted lip and forehead. He was afraid of himself. He was alarmed at his own reflections—those reminiscences of his, so faithful and so strong. There was a spell upon him, he said; and the sudden change in the weather, he did not like that—it seemed ominous too.

In fretting and foreboding the day sped fast, and at length it was time to start for Gravesend, if he was to sail that night. Then came the great struggle. *Should* he go? or should he return to Sleaford, restore his ill-gotten gains, make amends to Keppel by lifting the weight of murder from his conscience, bury the old woman decently, and begin the world anew? Truth to tell, the struggle was brief. What! After all the risks he had run, the anxiety he had groaned under, give up now—now, when the game was played out, and the stakes snug in his possession? And suppose he was to be quietly arrested in Sleaford before he could manifest his virtuous intentions? No—let us have the bill; having gone so far, we must proceed on the easy path that goes down devilward. It would be sad work to carry all that money back again.

Once on the road, Mr. Hatcher's scruples abated; and he was chiefly anxious to retrieve the time he had lost in chicken-hearted speculations. But the night was dark and the weather was foul, and over and over again he found himself very far from jolly.

As for farmer Howlet, he would seem to have discovered that Hatcher was bound to Gravesend that afternoon; for, after a brief visit to the Bishopsgate Street Inn, where his portmanteau had been left, he reappeared in the character of a travelling gentleman—in a wide cloak, a big muffler, and a double eye-glass; also, he had a heavy walking-stick.

Thus equipped, he accompanied Mr. Hatcher every step of the road, never losing sight of him for an instant, though always keeping aloof. That was because no good opportunity offered for closer intercourse; which is as much as to say that Hatcher was never alone, never beyond hail of help, during all the journey! At which Mr. Howlet chafed more and more, more eagerly watched and waited, grew paler and colder, and more confirmed in that unspeakable resolve.

So we alight at Gravesend, and it is eleven o'clock. Therefore Gravesend is for the most part asleep, and dark as Gehenna. Hatcher hurries into a tavern by the waterside, and asks whether the *Cormorant* has come up. He is told that she came up yesterday, and lies over against Tilbury. Thereupon he swallows a glass of brandy and water, and hurries away to the waterside, resolved to lose not an instant in getting aboard.

In five minutes he finds himself bewildered on the strand, it is so dark.

"Boat!" he cries.

"This way, sir!" answers a gruff voice at his elbow; and the boatman who had a cloak on one minute ago, leads him down to the water's edge.

But the boatman had no expectation of finding a boat there. He intends to help his fare over the Styx, not the Thames; and as soon as we come to the water's edge, he will face round upon him, fell him to the ground, rip that auriferous belt off if possible, or, if not, murder him outright, and roll his body towards the rising tide. So down they go to the water's edge together.

Now it happens that there *is* a boat on the strand. It is attached by a long rope to the shore, and the river is just about to lift it on its bosom. Hatcher looking eagerly to the left of him (the boatman is in advance, on the right) first spies the boat.

"Here it is!" cries he; and without more ado skips into it and takes his seat at the after end.

The boatman hesitates. This proceeding does not accord with his plans; which Mr. Hatcher has interfered with on several occasions previously.

"You must come out, sir!" says he, in his gruff voice, having evidently caught cold, "or else I can't push off."

"Oh yes, you can; the boat's afloat now nearly." Which it was.

Then the boatman grinned unhandsomely. The resolution before mentioned surged up to the surface without disguise, taking a rather jocular turn. He pushed the boat further into the water, leapt in, took the oars, and rowed out without a word.

"To the *Cormorant*, lying over against Tilbury. Those her lights?"

"Ay, ay, sir."

The boatman is not expert; but he manages to pull out into the middle of the river before any accident occurs, and then he clumsily—or shall we say dexterously?—unships an oar, so as to bring it into the boat. He stoops to take it up, and takes up the plug in the bottom of the boat also; which done, he makes a pretence of rowing again.

But when the plug's out of a boat, she soon fills. The water rises momently, but the boatman rows on; while, as for Mr. Hatcher, he begins to remark that it is very cold on the water: his feet are like ice—his legs also. That the boat is sinking, or that it makes no way, he does not perceive. But now he raises his feet to stamp some warmth into them, and the fact flashes into his mind. His feet are leaden; and when he moves them there is a dreadful plashing, while the disturbed water shimmers dimly.

Such a cry as that—such a cry as he gave just now, is not often heard; and nobody heard that one save you and I, and the boatman. For a great gust of wind came by at the moment, and caught it up, and tossed it hither and thither till nobody could tell where it had got to. Ah, how he cries! How his knees knock together! How like a drunken man he rises—with some idea, evidently, of throwing himself into the boatman's arms for help. That is hopeless. The boatman rises too—steadily and silently; he stands up in the sinking boat, with an oar grasped in both hands, and extended before him. "Keep off!" shouts he, in a voice which is no longer a farmer's or a boatman's, but unmistakeably Mark Howlet's. The other rogue is stricken dumb; and before he can recover his speech—Sough! —down goes the boat, and down goes Mr. Hatcher, like a stone. That belt did it.

As for Howlet, if he is an inexpert boatman he is an excellent swimmer; and he has an oar to support him, remember. He arranges it under him in a scientific manner, and strikes boldly out for the opposite shore. But his veins are full of fire, and the water is cold as death.

CHAPTER XLI.

REVELATION.

A HOUSE of mourning is a house of mourning, whether it be a thing of brick and stone, permanently situate in a fashionable square, or whether it be a thing of timber, painted yellow and drawn upon wheels. I'll answer for it that Mr. Biddles had that within that passeth show, while as for the weeds and trappings of woe, he had done his best in that regard also; for he had pulled the blinds down over the windows, and had tied up the knocker in a white kid glove. Weeds of woe? He smoked twelve tearful pipes a-day.

I hope the reader does not imagine, though, that this was on the late Joel Hatcher's account. That misguided person was alive when the yellow house went into mourning—for a broken leg; for Woppits's broken leg. Enthusiastic crocodile as he was, he essayed a new and astonishing *pas* in a certain village, hoping that the fame thereof would precede the exhibition into Gravesend: failed, and broke his leg.

Nobody was aware of the accident save poor Woppits himself, until the performance was over. He was too much a hero and an actor to make an outcry in the face of the public; conduct which Biddles no sooner became acquainted with, than he positively wept for pride and pity. What could be done for a friend and a crocodile capable of such behaviour? Alas, only one thing could be done for him, and that not the most graceful —to take him to an hospital. The first hospital that occurred to Biddles's mind was Greenwich Hospital; but although the crocodile is an amphibious animal, and a warlike animal, and though Woppits had suffered in the interest of his Majesty's subjects—Biddles doubted whether he was a fit object for the charity, after all. But surely there was an infirmary at Gravesend, which was only two or three miles distant; and thither Biddles resolved to proceed at once.

On this journey there was something about the yellow van much less vanny than usual. It looked—I don't know why— almost hearse-like, as it toiled slowly down the dusty road. Perhaps it was on account of Jacob, who hung his conscious ears, and went with a solemn pace which many an undertaker's horse might have imitated to profit, or to the edification of decency at any rate. Biddles himself walked in black; black, he vowed, should be his only wear, till his friend was fairly started on his legs again. He *did* think, at one time, of retrieving from that insatiable box of his a crape hat-band worn at Mrs. Biddles's decease; mounting it, not as a sign of sorrow, but as one means of letting off his grief, which otherwise threatened to blow up, and shatter his carcase into fifty fragments. However, it appeared to the showman, upon reflection, that his sentiments might be mistaken; so he abandoned the idea. But real sorrow needs no hat-band; and those who beheld the procession wending its slow length along, had some inkling, I am convinced, of some poor creature lying a-sick bed within; only Woppits's hammock was worth all the beds in the world, in his present case. In due time the yellow house drew up before the infirmary, and Woppits was slung in at its hospitable doors.

Of course, Mrs. Bell had to be apprised of the accident, which was done by a letter so touching in some parts, and so jocose in others, that I dare not print it. Between laughing and crying there is pain; and shall I pain the dear reader? Never.

A few hours after Woppits had been made snug, another patient was introduced into the hospital, and he became the young man's neighbour. This man, they said, had been found stranded on the other side of the water, exhausted, insensible, clinging desperately to an oar. When he was brought-to, his benefactors found themselves unable to bring back his reason also. He had fallen into fever and delirium, and there he lay, raving at doctor and nurses, till it was thought expedient to shave his head, and to confine him in a strait-jacket. When his head was shaven, he looked madder than ever; his skull seemed to bristle with insanity; but, upon the whole, he was more composed. A weight was off his head, if not off his mind; from which no one is to argue that he must have been more light-headed, because he was not; and he justified the doctors. After raving came sullenness. The madman refused even to move his head; but that did not prevent him from watching the matron, who had superintended the shaving, and at whom he made terrible eyes.

At last, as she passed close to his bed, he called her to him.

"Ain't this thing fastened on with buckles?" said he.

"What, the waistcoat? Yes, dear, with six nice little buckles," replied the matron in a coaxing voice.

"Ah, I thought so. Stoop down here. I know all about a gold mine."

"Oh, lor, that's capital!" replied the nurse, adjusting the pillow more comfortably under his head. "Where might it be?"

"Undo the buckles" (this in the most mysterious of whispers); "it is underneath. I heard it chink just now."

"Sure you ain't making a mistake, now?"

"Mistake! Do you think I don't know the chink of my own money?" he asked, with sudden ferocity. "Didn't I see it, dark as it was, spangling his body, like the spots on a snake? Undo the buckles, quick! He's gone a long way; he won't be back for a long time. In fact," continued he, in a low voice, and with a quiet, inquisitive magpie look, "he's gone a-fishing! Please—please undo the buckles before he comes up again."

"Ah, we'll see all about it," rejoined the matron, manfully tucking him in. He was not the first mad man she had had dealings with by many a one.

Having got the crotchet into his head that the buckles of the strait-waistcoat kept him out of his property, he failed not to importune every one that passed to come to his assistance. Just one buckle, he implored, that they might be satisfied that his body really was solid gold. One half his treasure was the reward he offered to any person or persons who would perform this little service for him. Indeed, he offered a third to the house-surgeon, whose interest in the case was interpreted by the madman as a disposition to come to terms.

These paroxysms considerably disturbed our friend Woppits, though at first they made him forget his own agony; and when the madman grew tiresome, and Woppits's aching body throbbed anew, as in one great pain, he thanked heaven that he had only a broken leg after all. It *was* tiring, however, to be kept awake the whole night through by a "heap of clotted nonsense" about impossible gold-mines, and by a shattered limb into the bargain; and Woppits did not fail to complain of it to mother, when she brought her aching heart and little Ruth's weeping eyes to his bedside. Of course, the lunatic overheard all that was said, and, struck with a new idea, he loudly accused Woppits of stealing under his waistcoat, and robbing him of his treasure. Mrs. Bell had enough sympathy to spare to give one pitying glance at the poor creature moaning and crying there; but, after all, the boy's broken leg was of more consequence to her than all the witless heads in the three kingdoms. And after this one glance, she turned her tender eyes to Woppits's pillow, and busied herself about him in a hundred nameless ways. But it was to be observed that she often looked again towards the madman's bed, and every time she withdrew her eyes, they seemed to fill more full of a vague twilight, as it were, of compassion, and also of wonder. Perhaps there was a little perplexity in them too; for she began to consider where she had seen a mad patient before. As for little Ruth, she stood with more of awe than terror, her hands folded before her, watching him, and wondering whether she herself should ever look so odd or behave so strangely. Presently his eyes met hers; and though they were cunning enough heretofore, they were tenfold more cunning now. Awaiting the moment when Mrs. Bell was most solicitously engaged by Woppits's bedside, he beckoned the child towards him, and either of her own fearless will, or fascinated by the magnetism of his gaze, she unhesitatingly obeyed the gesture.

"Unfasten this buckle, my dear little child. It is hurting me," he whispered.

"This one, sir?" asked Ruth.

"Yes, be quick. Oh, how it pains me."

The child's nimble fingers were immediately busied with the buckle, and the madman, feeling his shoulder at liberty, chuckled almost aloud, trembling with excitement.

"You do it beautiful!" said he. "Now another, my darling. Now another!"

This time, however, his voice was hoarse and too eager. The

child was terrified at it; and starting back, the little shawl she wore fell from her shoulder, leaving those livid finger-marks visible. Immediately a wonderful change passed over the mad patient's countenance. The madness seemed to leave it, and to leave it blank. Then came the light of reason, and following that, but mingling with it, a look of conscious terror. He uttered a great cry, and fainted outright.

In a moment, Mrs. Bell, the matron, and a half-dozen nurses, crowded round his bed, where he lay like a dead man. However, death had not yet arrived; this was only a profound swoon, out of which he presently emerged, as it were, a reasonable creature, but dreadfully shattered.

"Who was that by my bedside just now?" he asked.

"Why, me, to be sure," replied the matron.

"No, no! A little girl; a little girl with yellow hair. Did no one see her? Has she gone?"

As these words were uttered, the twilight in Mrs. Bell's eyes deepened more and more, and again she asked herself where she had seen a mad patient before. It would seem, from the current of her ideas, in a cottage, or in a school, or in a garden where there were currant-bushes. Meanwhile, however, she answered his inquiry by taking Ruth by the hand, and leading her, terrified enough, to the bedside.

"Nearer," said he. "Loose my arms, nurse—I am sane enough now. Let me feel this little one's hand."

It was done. But not only did he take the child by the hand, but he lifted her on to his bed, looked at her fixedly for a moment, and then muttered—

"There can be no doubt about it. She is alive! This is Ruth Keppel!"

Two days ago, this would have been news to Mrs. Bell; but she had received Tweakle's communication since then, with the copy of the placard, and knew all about it. But who was this mad patient who had so strangely recovered his reason? Suddenly the twilight of doubt passed away, and the dawn of certainty appeared.

"Mark!" she whispered, the word lingering on her pale lips.

The mad patient shaded his eyes with his hands, and steadily addressed his gaze towards her. After a moment the hands fell, and were clasped together. "Lucy!" answered he; and the recognition was complete.

The nurses turned their backs upon a scene which ceased to interest them, now that their help was no longer needed. Ruth was glad to creep back to Woppits's bedside, and talk with him about the strange man whom mother was bending over; while, as for these two, they were engaged a long, long hour in earnest converse, which, though not a word of it was heard beyond the confines of the curtains, seemed to hush all the ward.

The long hour was brief enough to them. In it, Mark Howlet told all he knew of Ruth's history, as we have written it here.

CHAPTER XLII.

CONCLUSION.

WE want a good dictionary of the emotions—a handy volume, fairly classifying them under appropriate headings, and with some information as to their roots and generic qualities. At present, our knowledge of them is very confused; we cannot distinguish one from another ofttimes; and are puzzled by the appearance of most surprising sorts in spots where very different ones were expected. You see a man sowing wrath-seed in his wife's bosom: coming again when the crop should be ripe, behold, it is all love. Here should be gratitude, here sorrow, here gladness, here content. Alas! your friend burns with injurious hate, and would consume you in the burning; the widow smiles across her husband's grave to some tawdry new future; the bride wakes with a moan sometimes, and silently cries herself to sleep again. But that is not the most mysterious part of it. Why, when my loss is irreparable, am I cheerful and benevolent? Why do I laugh when my heart is ready to break? Why do I chaff my love, in my elegant-satanic manner, when I know I ought to beg her pardon, and am dying to kiss the soft reproach from her eyes? This is the happiest day of my life; aunt has discharged all my debts, and Matilda is mine—bright, beautiful, and worth twelve thousand pounds. Her father, Eliot of the Treasury, is smiling at my board, and only five minutes ago he whispered me as follows: "Hyacinth, my boy, that little appointment is yours." But if any gentleman will be good enough to lead me into some convenient solitude, where I may meditate on the miseries of my kind, and, if necessary, blow my brains out, I shall be obliged to him.

Now, if I cannot explain the operations of my own mind, it is not to be supposed that I can expound Mrs. Bell's. It would have been much easier for me, if, while she listened to the dreadful story related by her brother, a pang had shot through her heart; or she had trembled violently; or been overwhelmed in a rush of agonising memories; or (better still) fell fainting to the ground. A pang is a pang; a thing which everybody who is troubled with spasms is familiar with. Trembling, again, may be forcibly described in several ways, and with more similes than we know what to do with—poetical ones, too. A rush of memories—the reader must understand what that is, after so many descriptions of it; while as for a faint, it is the most compendious form you can cast emotion into. It answers every purpose, and saves a world of trouble both to the reader and the writer. It requires no reflection in the one, no discrimination in the other.

But Mrs. Bell, *née* Lucy Howlet, denies me these advantages. She did not faint; she did not fall senseless to the ground; no pang shot through her heart; but she listened to her brother's story immoveable, with a face pale and fixed as marble. It seemed almost as if she had heard it before, in a dream; as if it were an old, old story that once was terrible and true, but was so now no more.

This demeanour, which was not the product of reason, or calculation, or even of experience, but clearly a gift of the gods, accompanied her through some other trying scenes which yet remained. When her brother died of the fever, which it was certain he would do from the time he was found exhausted on the shore, she followed him to the grave, gravely; and burying him, also buried whatever of blame she had cast on him, and that shame which might have lasted had he lived. There was another scene, however, more trying still: her first interview with Horace Keppel. This story is told; but there were certain touches in that interview which we would not dwell upon, even if we were not anxious to hurry to the end. Besides, how shall we describe—and you, dear reader, how should you understand—the feelings of Lucy Howlet when she stood at the gate of Keppel Lodge once more, with the fair-haired little beauty Ruth at her side? Suppose we were to tell you that ere they had proceeded half-way up the path they were met by a grave melancholy gentleman, sauntering aimlessly along, and puffing a cigar? There was neither humour in it to amuse, nor pathos to awaken the sweet pain of sympathy, unless you could dwell for a moment in the heart of the woman, and behold how the dull light of his over-wearied mind kindled in his face again. Without saying a word—almost with a frightened air, he turned about, and led the way into the house. He did not look back to see whether the strangers followed him or no, but his attention was wholly cast back to them, and perhaps beyond them into some past time, that seemed a hundred years old. Not that he had any definite notion as to who the strangers were—on the contrary, he appeared nervously anxious *not* to come to a conclusion at present. In his distraught and childish manner, he would have liked to have scanned them in detail—in a series of shifty little glances, unobserved, before he did come to any conclusion, though all the while he knew in his heart that there could be only one. But he had no convenient resources for carrying out this plan; and had to content himself by imagining how they looked as they followed him into the house. He held open the door of his sitting-room, while the woman and the child entered. Then as carefully he closed the door; and as for the rest, I saw nothing of it; I heard not a word of it; however, we can all guess pretty nearly how the scene went on. But I did peep in at the window, and will tell you accurately what I saw.

The woman seated at a centre table, her arms thrown over it, her face resting on her arms—very still. Keppel sunk in an easy-chair, with Ruth between his knees; and as with one hand he hid that sad stain, the other caressed her hair. I saw in his tearful eyes, and on his otherwise pale and stolid face, a blush that was the dawning of a new love, a light that was the earnest of a long-desired, belated peace. Who shall say how profoundly grateful was the sense of relief from that old terror and remorse of his? Who shall say how at heart he was stirred at the sight of that little living child, gazing at him with her dreamy eyes, or what a new and comfortable life glowed in his veins, and gathered in his bosom, at the touch of that tiny, warm, white hand! The last time he saw it, it looked too white, he thought, with the moonbeams streaming on it.

But the new peace, and the new love, and even that comfortable new life—they arrived a little too late, perhaps; though that may be only our view of the case, to whom all things are not revealed—who dwell under a cloud, that hides many of the mercies as well as the mysteries of heaven. He was not jubilant—not a whit elated; and if he had a desire, it was that he might sleep a long deep sleep.

What Mrs. Bell thought and felt at that moment is easier of comprehension. To her it was a moment of completest satisfaction. It was something to reflect that she had been instrumental in restoring peace to him who had so ruthlessly destroyed her own. There was a touch of sweet revenge in it, too; the revenge which alone *is* sweet, and which the gods haste to pardon. But especially she rejoiced in the knowledge that her boy—her boy, disgraced and abandoned, should, by sheer goodness of heart, have saved and preserved that precious little life, on which so much depended.

There is this to add. Lucy Howlet never left Keppel Lodge again, except to return to it as to her own home. After a few weeks had passed, and the first surprise and satisfaction was over, she became Keppel's wife. Woppits, meanwhile, was slowly recovering—in hospital too; for though he was not unaware of what had passed at Keppel Lodge, and of his real relations to the occupants thereof, he declined to take any advantage from them, and insisted upon getting well in his own way. He was not present at his mother's marriage, of course; indeed, he was wholly in ignorance of it, till she came one day and told him the secret, not without symptoms of grief as well as of satisfaction. Mr. Tweakle, however, was present—not as a beadle, but as a man; though it must be acknowledged that his conduct on the occasion was less manly and candid than might have been expected of him. When first discovered, he was lurking in the rear of the church (which belonged neither to Sleaford nor to Latherwell), contemplating an ungraven slab, upon which he had chalked the lady's name; and thinking in his heart how much pleasanter it looked there than it could look in the marriage-register. And when he had chalked his own name underneath, finishing off with a skull and cross-bones tied up in a true lover's knot, he retired a step or two, eyeing the production with a grim and tearful satisfaction.

Tweakle's meditations were at this point interrupted by the arrival of a single close carriage. Instantly he pocketed the chalk, effaced the impromptu inscription with the sleeve of his coat, and was next seen ducking in a pew immediately opposite the marriage-altar. The beadle could not refrain from repeating "Amen!" aloud whenever that word occurred in the marriage-service; but the man gnashed his teeth at the beadle, as an ass, after every such exclamation. The man was so angry with the beadle—his feelings were so lacerated and confused, that when at length he heard the woman's voice respond "I will," he sallied out of the church. He had arrived at that state of mind in which any diversion is providential. Mr. Tweakle's mind was diverted. As he passed down the aisle, he espied the head of a boy who had clambered up the church wall, and was viewing the ceremony through a window with rapt attention. Tweakle hurried out, and sidling along the church wall, took off one of his boots, and fell suddenly upon the youth with the leg thereof. At first, the boy was panic-striken; but his courage revived when he had got away to a little distance, when he cried, "Yah!" and derided Mr. Tweakle. He didn't care for that. He pulled his boot on again, and hurried off along a quiet road that wound up a hill. From this position, he beheld the carriage drive away; and then, like the soldier in the song, he wiped away a tear. He did more. First assuring himself that he was unobserved, he drew from a breast-pocket his brass tobacco-box, and, with a wild flourish, cast its contents to the wind.

"There, William Tweakle," said he, addressing himself in

pathetic tones. "There it goes! There goes the 'bacca she bought you, and which you would have no more thought of smoking than you would of chewing the box. Not, mind you, that ever she gave you the inch of which you took the ell. But love is blind, and love is presumptuous; and, perhaps, after all, you are only a hold fool doing as many another hold fool has done before. At any rate, it's all over, William; think no more about it."

Fortified by such reflections, Mr. Tweakle soon recovered his equanimity, and survived his love-sickness several jolly years.

Keppel, too, after his marriage, had many a bright and cheerful hour; but, upon the whole, for him the cloud never passed away. He was a grave, sad man to the last; touching in his feebleness, touching in his penitence and a constant sense of gratitude. I suppose there was as much love in his quiet household, now, as in any house in the land. Ruth was scarcely permitted to quit his side: and when he grew older and feebler, he seemed to live through her, speaking by her voice and thinking with her thought. Between Keppel and his wife an affection existed scarcely less strong, but chastened, reserved—almost ceremonial. They buried the past silently between them, but they never forgot that their hearth was built upon its grave.

As for Woppits, we leave him as we found him—original and alone. Many schemes were proposed to make a gentleman of him—sometimes by his mother, sometimes by Keppel himself, who often brooded over the subject, in his slow, painful way, unknown to any one. He made his proposals (there was always a tutor and travelling in them) through his solicitors, Messrs. Bedford, Row, and Bedfords; but whether entreated by his mother, or reasoned with by the astonished Row, he turned a deaf ear to all their charming. Biddles, whom Woppits consulted on the subject, combated the idea with great warmth. "No, sir," said he, "you're a born comedian; and a born comedian ought not to throw himself away in the enervatin' atmosphere of gilded saloons. Comedy is declined; comedy is on her last legs, Mr.

Woppits. Yours is the mission—set her up again. I am convinced, sir, that if you and me had about a couple of hundred pounds—towards which I have two tenners, a fiver, and what the van would fetch—if, Mr. Woppits, you and me had about a couple of hundred pounds ——!"

Biddles never finished the sentence, but his looks were big with undelivered prophecy. So once upon a time, on a day after Mrs. Keppel had again entreated him to be made a gentleman of, a cheque for the above-named sum was left at Woppits's lodgings, and he accepted it: it was charged against Ruth's estate. And what was the result? At this very moment, Mr. Biddles is one of the most successful managers, and our old friend Woppits one of the most popular comedians, alive. You may not recognize the names, but that is not my affair. And at the close of every season, the manager slaps the comedian on the back, and cries, "I say, old boy, what did I tell you? The words I used were, 'Mr. Woppits, you're a born comedian, sir; and if we had only two hundred pounds ——' Do you remember?" Then the comedian slaps the manager on the back, and replies, "I do! and I tell you what, sir; you shall dine with me on Saturday; and my sister Ruth shall come to town, and make you another pudding!"

For although Woppits elected to pursue his own path, the idea of estrangement from his mother and dear little Ruth was the last and the most terrible that entered his head. I believe he remains a bachelor purely on that account. The state of single misery in which he feigned to live, obliged the ladies to come to town pretty often to see how he fared; and what white days were those! What beautiful snug little dinners did the jovial, innocent-hearted actor entertain them at, in his lodgings at Rochester Street, Strand! Have I not been present at them myself? Have I not with these very eyes seen?——But really there must be an end to this. These eyes aforesaid are tired: they long to look upon the word CONCLUSION.

THE END.

www.ingramcontent.com/pod-product-compliance
Lightning Source LLC
Chambersburg PA
CBHW081155170626
46813CB00009B/3205